MW00329852

THE AFTER

SAVE THE NEW UNION

THE AFTER

CHIP SCHORR

REBELLION BOOKS

Published by Rebellion Books, LLC.

ISBN: 978-1-7323868-2-2

Editor: Marcus Trower (via Reedsy.com)

Cover design, illustration & interior formatting:
Mark Thomas / Coverness.com (via Reedsy.com)

For Burwell, the love of my life

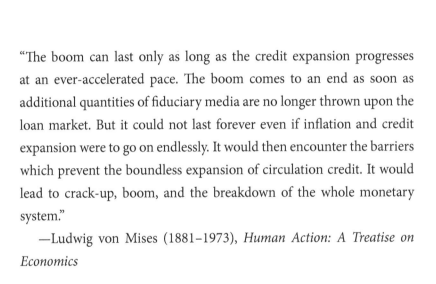

"The boom can last only as long as the credit expansion progresses at an ever-accelerated pace. The boom comes to an end as soon as additional quantities of fiduciary media are no longer thrown upon the loan market. But it could not last forever even if inflation and credit expansion were to go on endlessly. It would then encounter the barriers which prevent the boundless expansion of circulation credit. It would lead to crack-up, boom, and the breakdown of the whole monetary system."

—Ludwig von Mises (1881–1973), *Human Action: A Treatise on Economics*

PROLOGUE

Lagos, Nigeria

February 4, 2014, 11:48 p.m. West African Time

Jack gunned the throttle and shifted as he accelerated the black Ducati Monster out of the alley and onto the crowded thoroughfare. Danny raced past Jack on a matching bike and weaved into the oncoming lanes in order to pass a slow-moving bus.

"One second everything is going by the book, and the next a sniper is shooting at our guys," said Danny over the secure radio. "There is no way that happens without a leak. Someone sold us out, and Justin almost took a round."

Jack accelerated to close up the distance with Danny and almost ran into a guy on a scooter. "This traffic is a little sporty," said Jack as he swerved to narrowly avoid a car. "Let's just count our blessings that you spotted the laser sight on Justin's shoulder before the shooter could fire. Now we need to salvage this mess and get the hell out of here."

"Lion, this is Rover, we need support now! We have some local regulars closing in on our six!" Justin yelled over the secure comms. "We are on Bale, passing Toku, heading for Mobil. This is fubar."

"En route to intercept. Make for Mobil and Apapa. We will have you in two mikes," replied Danny, the roar of his motorcycle engine clearly transmitted over the channel.

"Danny," said Jack over a different frequency. "We were totally blown. I have used Phillips's frequency twenty times, as well as the emergency channel for him. The man is in the wind. I think we now know the source of the problems, but that is for later. Now we have to give Justin and the team some breathing room. We need to create a diversion so that they can get lost in the city."

"Now, Lion!" yelled Justin again.

"One mike," answered Danny, his voice calm and neutral, as he weaved the wrong way through traffic down a connecting road to intercept their teammates. Car horns blared and drivers screamed at the two black-clad motorcyclists roaring by.

Jack and Danny turned a hard right onto Mobil just before Apapa, and Jack said, "Rover, we have you in sight and are closing. We will engage your tail. You break off left, turn up ahead, and disappear. We will meet you at point Z at zero two hundred hours for extraction. Point Z only. Assume everything is compromised."

"Copy that, Lion," replied Justin.

Jack looked up ahead and could see a soldier trying to stand in the back of a speeding jeep-type vehicle and fire a rifle. "Gun!" said Jack.

Danny pulled a Glock and put two shots directly between the seats of the vehicle. One passed through the plastic sheeting that served as the back glass and shattered the windshield, the other embedded in the console. He had purposely aimed to avoid personnel damage. The open-topped truck slowed noticeably and turned hard right. The soldier who had been preparing to fire nearly fell out of the vehicle due to the maneuver. He quickly regained his balance and turned to fire a blast at the closest bike.

Jack raised his Glock and put a shot through the soldier's forearm. The rifle went flying, and the soldier disappeared to the floor of the vehicle. Jack saw Danny flip a flash bang into the truck's cab as he passed the army vehicle. Jack put six more shots into the two back tires—three each—and then gunned the throttle, chasing Danny's bike down the road and away from the now-disabled military vehicle. The flash bang went off right after the bike cleared the vehicle's front bumper.

As the two riders executed a series of dizzying turns down the streets of Lagos, Jack keyed his mic one last time and said, "I am going to hunt you down, Phillips, and kill you personally." The anger in his voice was palpable.

Standing in the living room of the safe house, Listir felt the hairs on the back of his neck stand up. He turned off the radio. He did not want to hear any more. It was time to go. He keyed a secure text message on his BlackBerry to his CIA handler: *Op blown. Executing exfil plan.* The message was part of his ass-covering plan. He knew no one would ever be able to prove he had blown it.

·

CHAPTER ONE

21 February 1850 – United States Capitol, Washington, DC

February 21, 1850, 1:15 a.m. Eastern

Sam Houston watched the smoke from the end of his cigar drift toward the ceiling. He tried to avoid eye contact with the other five senators for a little bit longer. Texas badly needed the deal, and everyone in the room knew it, but he still played his last hand of political poker.

The logs blazing in the fireplace popped and hissed. Sam appeared to study them intently, as if the answers to all of life's questions could be found in the fire in the large marble hearth. He looked at the eagle carved into the mantel and was surprised to see that the artisan who carved it had left one wing slightly shorter than the other. He wondered if that occurred in nature. Houston watched the other senators as he pulled on his cigar. Clay sat in a large leather chair in the center of the room with his back to a half-moon window. Webster and Douglas sat to his right on a leather couch, while William Seward sat to his left on a bench. Dickinson sat in a low chair beside Seward.

"Gentlemen, I just don't know. You're demanding such a terrible price. Terrible!" Houston shook his head while he spoke. He hoped his voice sounded as calm as he did not feel.

Daniel Webster peered at him over a tall glass of bourbon. "Sam, you are a wonderful politician, which makes you a good liar, but not that good. Texas needs this deal. We all know this is a wonderful arrangement for Texas."

"Daniel is correct," added Stephen Douglas, the diminutive senator from Illinois. "Sam, we are offering to take Texas's debt and make it the country's debt. You recognize that this is a huge benefit to Texas. Frankly, I think it is we who are paying too high a price."

"I sympathize with your arguments, gentlemen, surely do," replied Houston with a dismissive wave of his cigar. "However, let's remember that y'all are getting something equally bountiful. The Compromise would have us agree to release our land claims to the territories outside our current boundaries, lands that equal almost the entirety of the current nation in size. Lands that rightly belong to Texas." Houston paused, pulled a wood match from the box, struck it, and relit his cigar. He took his time slowly nursing the cigar back to light. "Personally, I'm surely pleased that slavery will be limited in the states that develop in those lands. In terms of taking over Texas's debts, we think that it's a fair price that the country is paying to, shall we say, *acquire* these lands from the Great State of Texas? Why you need this other arrangement is well beyond this simple man's understanding." Houston worked his cigar some more.

"I think that this other simple clause that we are asking for in the context of all that the federal government and the state of Texas are offering to do for each other in the spirit of partnership is more than warranted," offered Henry Clay, his rich voice resonating off the walls of the office in which they crowded.

Daniel Dickinson made an approving noise, about the most anyone ever heard out of him these days.

"I know what y'all are asking, but how would it appear to the rest of the nation? To God-fearing Texans?" questioned Houston. He paused to take a deep swallow of his drink. "What you propose weakens our rights and in the cold light of day makes us appear without principle. Heck, what's left to distinguish us from Judas clutching thirty pieces of silver in his grubby hands?"

No one said anything, but Clay seemed to be conducting a mental straw poll of his four other companions before turning back. "All right, Sam, suppose we do not include this part of the arrangements in the actual Compromise." As he spoke, Houston shifted forward in his seat. "We will make the Compromise about the absorption of Texas's debt, release of Texas's land claims, defining where slavery will and will not be allowed, and the non-slave states legally agreeing to return runaway slaves."

Houston appeared to like what he was hearing; he sat up a bit straighter. He might end up with more than he had promised his colleagues in Austin. Winning at poker was nearly always about patience.

"However, Texas signs a secret compact." Clay spoke with great solemnity. "Personally, I just cannot continue to endorse the Compromise without you agreeing to this final provision. If for the pride of Texas it needs to stay in the shadows to accomplish these greater goals, so be it."

Seward nodded aggressively. Houston knew that Seward opposed the Compromise for not going far enough in its demands. But he also knew Seward wanted the land claims settled. Houston suspected that Seward architected this new request in the first place. If he had not, he certainly grabbed an instrument and jumped on the bandwagon. Houston stared up at the ceiling and looked at the fog of tobacco smoke hanging against the pale-blue paint. The room had a smell of cigar, the wood smoke from the fireplace, and too many men in a small space.

Houston wasted more time with his cigar while all five men watched him. He would have to agree. He had been authorized by the governor to agree to this issue in the Compromise itself or any other document that his Senate colleagues so desired, so already he had exceeded expectations. It would not be in the law. It would not be in public view. It was a clear victory.

"I don't like it. I don't like you placing restrictions on Texas's rights." Houston played his bad hand for all it was worth. He paused for effect and worked his cigar back to light. "I will agree to it, but only on the following conditions."

Seward scowled at him. Damn, Seward.

"First of all, the compact remains secret; only the people in this room should ever know about it. Second, only two copies are made. One will go back to a special holding area of the Texas Archives, the other should be kept by one of you very, very securely."

Clay looked to his right and left. And though Seward looked like he had sucked on a lemon, Houston saw him make an almost imperceptible nod at Clay.

"Gentlemen, I believe we can say that we have ourselves an agreement." Clay smiled and extended his hand. Houston tried not to let his relief show as he grasped the outstretched hand. *Full house!* He had just won a huge hand of high-stakes Texas Hold'em.

PART I:
THE END

CHAPTER TWO

Paris, France

January 5, 2014, 11:36 a.m. Central European Time

Jackson Dodge IV, known as Jack, walked along the Fontaine Stravinsky in the fourth arrondissement pretending to study the Niki de Saint Phalle sculptures placed throughout the fountain. In reality, Jack's eyes, hidden behind black Ray-Ban sunglasses, looked everywhere but at the water, scanning for threats.

He stopped at the edge of the fountain and removed a guidebook from a pocket inside the brown suede Loro Piana jacket he wore. He removed one of his black calfskin gloves and pretended to study the book for a minute, a minute he used to check again and see if anyone was tailing him. He had stopped suddenly on purpose and used the book ruse as a means to quickly turn his body the way he had come. However, no one behind him seemed to be dashing for doorways or caught awkwardly trying to reverse direction. Additionally, none of the faces looked familiar, and Jack constantly studied and committed faces to memory.

He took his time pretending to study the book to give him a chance to survey the entire area yet again. His destination, the Centre Pompidou, loomed just in front. The brightly colored exposed external pipes stood out against the gray metal building and dull winter sky. He checked his watch and found he still had nearly ten minutes before his rendezvous with a contact he knew only as John Phillips.

A young woman stopped at Jack's side; she had long, beautiful chestnut hair and large gray eyes. She gave Jack a sly smile and asked if he needed assistance in beautifully accented English. At six foot four with wavy sandy-brown hair, a very athletic build, and chiseled jaw, Jack often attracted attention. His high school football teammates called him Marlboro, not because he smoked but because he resembled the Marlboro Man, even more so today with a couple of days' growth of beard.

He lowered his glasses and looked at her directly with his piercing gray-green eyes. He smiled back at the beautiful girl and replied in French, "*Non, merci.*" She smiled one more time, shrugged, and walked off with a hair flip. Women were always attracted to Jack Dodge, but he did not play the field; he was taken.

Jack walked up to the Pompidou and pushed into the lobby, which was crowded primarily with women. Given the exhibition, *Femmes!*, of women artists in the National Museum collection, the patrons' gender made sense, but Jack would have preferred more men with which to blend.

He approached one of the kiosks and picked up a floor plan for the museum, though he intended to see very little of the exhibit. Instead he used the time provided looking at the various pamphlets available to ensure again that no one was tailing him. Satisfied, he headed off to his prearranged meeting in the lobby men's room.

Jack entered the men's room, checked the stalls, and found the room completely empty. About thirty seconds later, a man entered. Jack stood at the farthest sink, washing his hands, as per the instructions. Jack studied the new man in the long mirror that covered the wall above the rows of sinks. He appeared to be around fifty-five, with thinning gray hair flecked with some lingering black patches. His skin had a gray pallor, as if he spent too much time indoors or eschewed sunlight for night. He was neither thin nor stocky but of average build and height. The man was eminently forgettable, perfect for a CIA agent.

Satisfied they were alone, the man walked up to the sink next to Jack and began to wash his hands. Neither man looked directly at the other.

Finally, Jack's contact spoke.

"Have you seen the bronze sculpture on the second floor?"

"No, I have been looking at the library on the third," replied Jack.

Both men had confirmation that that they had found the person they sought.

"Do you have something for me?" asked Jack.

The man reached into the inside pocket of his jacket and removed a thick five-by-seven-inch manila envelope. He placed the envelope on the edge of the sink between him and Jack.

Jack quickly picked up the envelope and slipped it in the pocket with his guidebook.

"It's all there. Everything you need to take down the target in Lagos. I will be your liaison. When you return to your hotel, you will find three burner phones in your room and multiple SIM cards. I have also left a small card that gives the order for the phones and cards, and the numbers and corresponding dates for my phones. Commit it to memory. We should not meet in person again until this is over, as I am too close to the target."

Jack nodded and walked away. Something about the man, code name John Phillips, bothered him. Jack had always had a sixth sense about people that instantly allowed him to separate the good from the bad, truth tellers from liars. Jack's radar told him John Phillips was firmly in the bad pile.

He felt a shiver run down his spine as he ascended to the second floor and joined the throngs of women exploring the exhibit. He had a bad feeling about Nigeria.

In the bathroom, Peter Listir, aka John Phillips, watched the door swing closed. He would take several minutes to dry his hands before he followed Jack Dodge back out into the museum. That would be enough time so that he and Dodge would never be in the same place together. Listir would exit the museum and head directly for the RER station in Les Halles and back to Charles de Gaulle Airport. He knew Dodge's instructions required him to spend twenty minutes in the museum before leaving for his hotel. Listir read Dodge's file before coming to the meeting. The man would follow his orders. He was a tremendously decorated operative and a Boy Scout; Listir hated Boy Scouts.

CHAPTER THREE

Georgetown, Washington, DC

February 2, 2021, 9:47 p.m. Eastern

"We need a plan to end all the programs," said the woman sitting in the large leather wingback chair facing her mentor across the low George III table.

"Luckily, that is no longer my responsibility," replied the older man before taking another sip of his scotch. He focused on his glass when he next spoke. "It was never expected to go on this long, or this extensively. There is simply no precedent. It was just supposed to be a temporary kick start, but now here we are with a balance sheet that has grown by nearly three-point-five trillion dollars, government debt approaching twenty trillion, and interest rates at five-hundred-year lows."

"You understand my concerns?" she said quietly. "I was always one hundred percent supportive of you, and I appreciate the faith you showed in giving me this incredible opportunity. However, I do feel like the last person at a party, who gets to clean up and turn out the lights. The air is already beginning to smell foul."

He paused and took a drink. "I will continue to support you both publicly and privately," he replied, staring her in the eye. "I architected this strategy and kept increasing our investments in the various programs. I pulled the lever on the printing press and created trillions of dollars of new money out of thin air, money that is worth less than the paper it is printed on. You will always have my support and counsel and my best thoughts on how to end it without another massive recession or hyperinflation. However, you should know that neither I nor any experts with whom I have consulted have any ideas how to safely land the plane. We have created Frankenstein, and our only hope is that no one notices."

"We have at least achieved a recovery," offered the lady half-heartedly. "Unemployment is down, housing prices recovered, and the equity markets soaring. Maybe Frankenstein is not so bad."

"Yes, we have managed to create several new bubbles and push the prices of high-risk assets to new highs. We have encouraged widows and orphans to invest their meager savings in the riskiest of assets at unsustainable prices and historically low yields. Made the one percent even richer. If anything, we have lit the fuse on a time bomb. The only difference is that this time there is nothing left in the tool kit to extend the timer. Inflation will soar, credit will dry up, the stock market will swoon, and soup kitchens will line the streets. The bomb will soon explode and kill us all. Maybe that is a blessing; there will be no one left to record the disaster."

They sat quietly in the small study. Every once in a while a hiss or crack emerged from the radiator, or ice bumped the side of one of their glasses, but otherwise there was silence.

CHAPTER FOUR

Fort Meade, Maryland

April 9, 2021, 6:15 p.m. Eastern

Jack Dodge heard the leather of the chair creaking as he shifted his frame forward. He saw Danny Winters do the exact same thing, seemingly bringing their heads closer together, but actually it was only an illusion. The Applied Minds–designed holographic videoconferencing system provided a realistic appearance of sharing a room. Danny's chair sat tucked away four thousand miles from Maryland in a nondescript, very secure facility in the town of Sankt Augustin, near Bonn, Germany. The German eagle symbol hung on the wall behind Danny's head, surrounded by wings of gold, the badge of the Grenzschutzgruppe 9, better known as GSG 9, the antiterrorism arm of the German Federal Police.

On another screen, both Danny and Jack could see an overhead view of an apartment building in Hamburg. Jack watched as over twenty green figures converged on the building from both ends of the front street, the rear courtyard, and the roofs of both adjacent buildings. The drone kept circling, giving the whole scene the appearance of turning counterclockwise. Jack bored into the image with his eyes. His strong, square jaw was firmly set. He twisted the Naval Academy ring on his right hand again. Danny was doing the same with his ring.

Jack and Danny met at the Naval Academy and bonded quickly, with their shared Texas roots. Following graduation and early service, both went on to SEAL training and missions from Afghanistan to the Philippines and various spots in West Africa. When Jack was seconded to the NSA to help coordinate the clandestine agencies' activities with the various US Special Forces, Danny stayed active in the SEALs, and the two continued to work together on multiple missions.

"Halt!" came a voice from the men on the ground in Hamburg over the secure comms link.

Jack watched all the green figures stop in place. He looked at the man seated next to Danny. He sat ramrod straight and took a piece of paper from a file in front of him, glanced at it, and then in rapid-fire German provided some last-minute instructions. Almost before he finished speaking, the men on the screen began to move again.

No one in the conference rooms in Fort Meade or Sankt Augustin spoke. They just sat watching the overhead shot and listening to the field communications. Though neither Danny nor Jack could understand the language, the tones spoke volumes. Calm, professional, and brief, just as one would expect from well-trained soldiers.

Jack ran a hand through his hair, the tension rising each time one of the green figures disappeared inside the building. Jack trained his eyes on the darkened third-floor windows. They had watched the lights go out just after 10 p.m. as Farhad Gul turned in from a long day of travel. Gul had flown from Tehran to Istanbul to Brno and then driven to Hamburg. They tracked Gul every step of the way, and though the man was well trained, they had the resources to ensure he never fell out of sight.

A slight man of thirty-four, Gul studied engineering but somehow ended up as the paymaster of Hezbollah in Europe. It had taken the NSA nearly two years to unravel the threads and find Gul, but they had, and tonight they and the Germans had the chance to destroy Hezbollah in Europe and its potential threat to US interests and airlines. The NSA called the operation Penny Pincher—choke off the pennies, arrest the paymasters, and kill the network.

Jack looked back at Danny and saw the tension etched in his face. Danny sat with his jaw clinched and his brow furrowed. He had personally helped orchestrate this mission with the GSG 9 and had been back and forth to Bonn more times than anyone could count. Jack gave his longtime friend and colleague a smile and nodded at him, but he could not get the usually jovial African American to smile in return. Danny simply had too much invested in the success of the mission. Jack watched as Danny repeatedly ran his hands over his closely cut hair, not realizing he was doing it over and over. Meanwhile, the German next to Danny appeared to never move.

All of a sudden the communications from the team in Hamburg spiked. Splintering wood, the sound of flash bangs exploding, and shouted commands reverberated from the speakers in both conference rooms. As rapidly as the noise escalated came a deafening silence.

"They have Mr. Gul in custody," said the middle-aged German sitting next to Danny with the same level of excitement he might have used to order a beer and a pretzel. "There were no casualties, and Mr. Gul will shortly be placed on a helicopter on his way here for questioning. Congratulations, Mr. Winters, on a very successful operation." The German patted Danny on the shoulder.

"Thank you," Danny said. "Congratulations to you and your men on a perfectly executed mission. Any news about his computer?"

Jack could see the tension drain out of his friend's massive body. Danny Winters was built like a refrigerator, a solid mass of muscle.

"I understand that his belongings are all being secured and will be brought here as well." A series of rapid German exchanges took place.

"The computers appeared to have suffered no obvious damage," stated the German. "Mr. Gul did not make it out of his bed before our forces had him secured."

Jack let out an audible exhale and rose out of his chair. He stretched and extended his arms toward the ceiling.

"Great work, Danny," he said to his friend. "And Commandant Stauffenberg, I commend you and your men on running a flawless operation this evening. Y'all never cease to amaze us with your professionalism. It's a pleasure for all of us at the NSA and Homeland Security to work with you, sir."

"Thank you for your kind words. It is always a pleasure to collaborate with you, Jack, and of course Herr Winters," said the commandant, bowing ever so slightly in his chair. "We appreciate your assistance and look forward to jointly analyzing all of the intelligence in Mr. Gul's possession."

Jack felt his phone vibrate in his pocket and looked at the clock. Nearly 2:00 a.m. Central European time. It would be a very long evening for his friend as he began to chip away at Mr. Gul. He reached for his phone as the lighting in the room brightened dramatically with the termination of the videoconference.

THE AFTER

*

George Washington Carver Middle School, The Bronx, New York City

April 9, 2021, 7:26 p.m. Eastern

The click of her heels echoed off the tiled walls and lockers in the deserted corridor. She checked the time on her iPhone. It was considerably later than she liked to leave the school, especially since the economy had gone into free fall. There was more crime in the city every day, with inflation beginning to rise and layoffs rolling through nearly every industry again. She stopped just inside the double doors to the school and tapped out a text.

Lvg school. 2 needed xtra help. Will call when home. Love M.

She hit send and pushed through the doors while tucking the phone inside the backpack she carried to school. She heard the familiar ding of an incoming text, which she knew would be the response from Jack, but she did not dare check it on the street. She knew he would be worried, but she would deal with that later. Phones had become a dangerous item to take out on the street. The *New York Post* carried story after story about muggings occurring over the devices. Crime in general continued to soar as the economy worsened, and the police had lost control of the city.

She walked quickly up the street, keeping her eyes moving, watching for any sign of trouble. The subway stop was four blocks from school, and though the streets were generally well traveled, crime overwhelmed the New York City police. Criminals were emboldened by their city's political leaders letting protests run amuck, and had taken control of the city from the police. Twenty-five years of declining crime came to a sudden end. She would never admit it to Jack, but she was nervous and looking forward to the end of the semester and leaving New York.

She thought of their fight the previous weekend when he visited from DC.

"Marissa, this place is falling apart. The whole country is falling apart. It's just not safe for you here," Jack had pleaded. "You need to leave New York, and let's both go back to Texas. Now."

"Jack Dodge, I will not be ordered around by you." She knew he was right, but they were getting married in four months, and she was not going to be his "little woman", she would be her own person. "My students need me, frankly now more than ever. I am going to finish this school year, and then we can move back to Austin."

They stared at each other across the tiny table in the small kitchen of Marissa's Upper East Side rental. The sun streamed in through the south-facing window, and her bright-green eyes flamed in the light. Jack looked away and bit his lip. He needed to change tactics; all he had done was seem to make her angrier and more determined to resist his request.

"I am not saying the kids don't need you. And I am not trying to imply that what you do is not important. It is. All I am saying is that it is not safe here anymore. Things are going from bad to worse, and I am worried." He spoke softly, and she could see the concern in his face. "I can leave the service and the NSA now. We can go home. You can teach in Austin. I guarantee you that there are children who need you there too."

"I will leave when the school year ends, and that is final." She knew he was right, but she did not feel like backing down. Her mother always said that she was more stubborn than a mule.

Truth be told, she was worried as well. In a blink of an eye, New York City had gone from the halcyon days of the Bloomberg administration, when one could walk home across the park at night, to a city where Marissa's neighbor had been mugged in broad daylight at the corner of Seventy-First and Third.

He bowed his head and stared into his mug of black coffee and said, "Please promise me you will be careful."

His words were ringing in her ears as she neared the subway station. The lateness of the hour coupled with the heavy overcast made it nearly dark, and the streets were not well lit. A broken streetlamp stood at the corner. People lurked in doorways in small groups and singles, and she felt eyes on her as she walked.

She reached the entrance to the station and started down the stairs. The stairwell smelled of urine. Trash and old newspapers lay on the steps. She had to be careful not to slip. She rounded the tiled corner and headed for the turnstile.

She slipped her MetroCard into the slot and pushed through. She looked left and right on the platform, but there were very few people. She settled in to wait near the turnstiles, feeling a bit safer in the light and with more space around her. The electronic board showed it would be nine minutes until the next train arrived.

She felt him behind her before she heard him. She started to turn, "Do not turn around!" The voice was heavily accented and very firm. "Give me the backpack and your watch now."

She slipped the backpack off her shoulder and felt it pulled away from her. She fumbled with the clasp on the Cartier watch on her left wrist. "Hurry up," said the voice, and she got a shove in the back. She heard herself make a small noise, mainly from the surprise of being shoved.

"Shut the fuck up! Make another sound and I will kill you."

She fumbled with the watch again. Her hands shook uncontrollably. She could not believe there was no one around to help her. She wanted to cry. Finally getting the clasp open, she felt the watch ripped away.

"You are very pretty."

She felt his hand grab her ponytail and breath on her left ear. Her head was spinning. A hand roughly grabbed her left breast over the silk of her blouse. How could this be happening on a subway platform in New York City at seven thirty in the evening? Reflexively, she kicked back with her right foot and brought her heel down heavily on her attacker's foot.

"Bitch!"

The grip loosed and she tried to pull away, and that was when she felt the searing pain in her back. She couldn't catch her breath. She tried to yell for help, but nothing came out but a gurgling noise.

*

Columbia Presbyterian Hospital, New York, New York

April 10, 2021, 1:36 a.m. Eastern

Dodge held his E-ZPass tag high up on the windshield as he sped through the toll plaza for the George Washington Bridge. Rain beat down and wind buffeted the car as he navigated the bridge. The wind blew so hard that the truck next to him kept encroaching on his lane.

He pushed down harder on the accelerator and slipped past the truck. He followed the signs for the Henry Hudson. He gripped the wheel hard at the first stoplight. Finally, he pulled up at the Columbia Presbyterian Hospital Emergency Room entrance, leaving the car in an open space that was clearly marked "No Standing," and ran across the slick pavement and into hospital.

The waiting room was full of people. Parents held children wrapped in blankets. People sat in wheelchairs. He felt like he was underwater, trying to swim back to the surface. *Marissa!* his mind kept screaming.

Jack ran up to the glass window, but the attendant was facing away, talking on a cell phone. He rapped on the thick glass with his Naval Academy ring. The sharp sound echoed like breaking glass, and the attendant flipped around in his chair.

"I will be with you in a minute," the attendant said, glaring.

Just then the doors to the treatment area swung open, so Jack disregarded the attendant and sprinted into the Emergency Room. He heard the attendant yelling after him that he could not enter, but he did not care.

The treatment area was chaos. Patients lay on gurneys in curtained bays and in the walkways. Doctors, nurses, and other hospital personnel huddled over patients, many of them groaning. Bells and beeps came from every corner of the room. Somewhere a voice yelled "Clear!" and a thump and beep sounded.

Jack grabbed the first nurse he could find. "I am looking for Marissa Callahan. She was brought in in critical condition several hours ago." He noticed the attendant pointing him out to a security guard, but he concentrated on the nurse, staring at the woman. "Please help me," he pleaded.

The guard approached. "You need to come with me. You cannot be here."

Jack ignored the man, who reached out for his arm. He shook the man off.

"I need to find my fiancée," said Jack to the nurse, who nodded at Jack and waved the guard off.

Jack followed the nurse to a central station and waited while she checked the log.

His worst fears were confirmed by her body language. She had not even looked up from the log, but her whole body slumped, and in that instant Jack knew Marissa was dead. He felt the room begin to spin. He held on to the counter.

The nurse stopped a doctor, whispered something to him, and then stepped back.

The doctor looked at Jack and then said quietly, "Sir, would you mind following me?"

Jack nodded dumbly and followed the man. Everything seemed to be happening in slow motion.

Ten minutes later, Jackson Dodge IV, scion of one of America's richest and most powerful families, a decorated Navy SEAL, a leader of America's counterterrorism field efforts, lay down on a gurney next to his dead fiancée and hugged her lifeless body while he sobbed. He could not stop holding her and crying no matter how many times someone from the hospital came to try to convince him to come away. The sun had come up by the time Dodge was persuaded to go make arrangements to transfer Marissa's body back to Texas.

CHAPTER FIVE

East Ninety-Fifth and Second Avenue, New York, New York

July 9, 2021, 9:37 p.m. Eastern

The heat wave was in its tenth day. The temperature in Central Park topped 108 degrees in the middle of the afternoon, with a humidity level barely reached outside the tropics.

Sergeant Worley leaned back up against the driver's door while his partner, Officer Lippstreu, stood opposite, smoking a cigarette. The two could not be physically more dissimilar, with Worley fifty pounds overweight, and Lippstreu tall and lean. Cops rarely sat in stationary cars anymore, not with the increasing violence against the police. They listened to the police radio traffic. Ten minutes had passed since they had pulled over to try and let their overheating Chevrolet cool down.

"I don't know how the fuck you can smoke when it's so damn hot." Worley was sweating profusely.

His partner just shrugged in response and took another drag

on his cigarette.

"You know, I drive to Jersey to buy these things. Between the taxes and the inflation, I can't afford to smoke New York cigarettes," offered Lippstreu.

"Maybe God is trying to tell you to stop smoking and use what little money you have for food or something," replied Worley. "Hell, with the way the economy has started going, you are going to need that fucking money to buy food."

Worley looked up the pavement at a couple of young men crossing in the pool of a streetlamp. They appeared harmless, but he watched them until they turned the corner. He turned back toward his partner when the light from the streetlamp disappeared. In fact, they were suddenly plunged into darkness. Lippstreu threw his cigarette and both men unholstered their service weapons.

Worley opened the car door and picked up the radio. "Central, six Adam David."

"Go ahead, six Adam David."

"We are at ninety-five and two, repeat ninety-five and two, and every light in every direction is out."

"Copy that, six Adam David. Multiple similar reports of complete blackout. Advise that you all drive around with your lights flashing as a show of presence. This is liable to be a very long night."

"Copy that, Central. Six Adam David out."

"Fucking great," said Lippstreu as he headed for the passenger side of the car. "A hundred fucking degrees and now no air-conditioning in this overheating piece of shit. You know what is going to happen? This place will go up in smoke tonight. I guess we are now going to be the new Baltimore!"

"Yeah, and we are supposed to drive around with our lights on! What a fucking joke!" said Worley as he turned on the cruiser and flipped on the lights. "Let's head up Third Avenue. I have a feeling there are probably a few shopkeepers who may be in need of our—what did they call it? Oh yeah, presence."

As the cruiser approached 103rd and Third, the officers could see groups on every corner and around every store on the west side of the street. People defiantly crossed the avenue without looking or just stopped in the middle of the street carrying on conversations, leaving traffic unable to pass.

Worley hit the siren a few times to try and move them along, but they just turned and looked at the squad car with hostility. The animosity to the police had been building since the incidents in Ferguson, Missouri, and in Baltimore, and was made worse by the blustering activist mayor of New York. Worley hit the siren again, and a large group of men stepped off the curb and walked toward the car.

"What the fuck is your problem, pig?" asked a very large man in a T-shirt with a picture of Malcolm X.

Christ, thought Lippstreu, this was going to quickly become like Baltimore. They needed to get control of the situation quickly.

"My problem is that you and your friends are blocking a street and causing serious traffic congestion," said Lippstreu. "That is my fucking problem, and now yours."

Lippstreu got out of the car in spite of Worley warning to let it go. He quickly walked around the car and started yelling at the men to disperse and for Malcolm X to put his hands on the hood.

Worley heard glass break behind him and turned to see the window of a bodega on the previous block shatter. A crowd surged forward into the store and started grabbing things off the shelves. He leaned out the driver's window to yell at Lippstreu when the distinctive pop of a gunshot sounded and Lippstreu fell to the pavement.

Worley grabbed for his weapon and the radio at the same time.

"Shots fired…"

His transmission stopped as hands dragged him through the driver's window and into the mob.

As the two officers lay bleeding in the street, someone tossed a Molotov cocktail into the bodega. Cheers and the sound of another store's windows smashing quickly followed the whoosh of the fire erupting.

The scene repeated across all five boroughs of New York, and other cities of the Northeast.

CHAPTER SIX

Fort Meade, Maryland

August 15, 2021, 8:10 a.m. Eastern

Jack sat in the anteroom of Rear Admiral Brand's office. He wore his full dress captain's uniform, his left breast covered with a range of service ribbons. He sat with his cap on his knees, waiting for his 8:15 a.m. meeting. He looked like a naval recruiting poster in his perfectly tailored uniform. Marissa had always said he looked his best in full dress, good enough to eat.

At precisely 8:15 a.m., Jack walked into Brand's office. He stood at attention and saluted, and Brand returned the salute, said "At ease," and motioned to a chair.

"What's on your mind, Jack?" said Admiral Brand.

Jack sat and began, "Admiral, I appreciate you making time for me today. I am truly sorry to say that I have decided to resign my commission and return home to Texas."

Admiral Brand stood up from behind his desk and walked around to sit in the other leather guest chair. "Jack, I am so sorry to hear you say that, but are you sure? Would you like to take some more time and retain the option to return in, say, another month? I am sure I can extend your bereavement leave. We need your service."

"Admiral," continued Jack. He had rehearsed the conversation in his mind before the meeting because he knew what he needed to do and did not want to lose his nerve with the admiral. "You, the navy, and the NSA have all been incredibly generous already. Unfortunately, time is not helping. I am not sure what will ever help this, but I know that I am no longer effective in my post, and returning to Texas is probably the best course of action. Maybe the only course."

Admiral Brand stared at Jack for several minutes, and Jack held his gaze. Finally, the admiral stood and extended his hand.

"Jack, it has been a sincere pleasure. You have served your country with honor and distinction. I personally am extremely sorry to see you go, especially just as things both here and abroad are becoming increasingly unstable."

Jack shook the man's hand, saluted, and left his naval career behind. He walked down the hall, through the lobby, and out into bright morning sun. He took one last look at NSA headquarters and got in his Ford Explorer for the drive back to Austin.

CHAPTER SEVEN

Chevy Chase, Maryland

January 23, 2022, 2:34 a.m. Eastern

Peter Listir crouched next to Greg Brown at the edge of the manicured yard, the Chevy Chase Club just behind them. They had made their way through the darkened golf course to ensure their vehicle was seen nowhere near the house, even though the plates had been stolen from another car in a Walmart parking lot.

Listir took another look around through his night-vision goggles. Absolutely nothing moved and the house stood completely dark. They had disconnected the alarm via remote access before setting off across the golf course, and Listir could see the steady green light of the disarmed console from next to the patio door. Nothing like the trend toward people using home automation systems making it easier to break into houses.

In the last two months, Listir had used the threat of force to acquire control over a fuel storage tank company, an auto body repair facility, and a food distribution warehouse. He was nothing if not adaptable and creative, and now was the time for maximum creativity. Creativity was what had led him to a backyard in Chevy Chase, where he would be making his next acquisition.

Just when he thought he would be retiring to a life of bone fishing off some little island in the Bahamas, he had found himself worried about the future. He had spent his thirty-year CIA career focused solely on his number one job, making sure that he took care of himself, but overnight a few months earlier, all his plans failed. The bank in Vaduz, Liechtenstein, in which he had deposited all his illicitly obtained cash failed. With that went his $2.1 million in euros, dollars, and gold coins. Financial panics and sell-offs were rolling across every market, and banks were failing at alarming rates.

Listir tapped Brown's shoulder and pointed at the rear of the house. Both men set off in a crouched run for the residence, but with the heavy tree line around the property, they were well hidden. Listir unlocked the door, and the two slipped inside and headed for the second floor.

Listir slowly moved up one side of the king-size bed, while Brown moved around to the far side of the room. Neither of the figures in the bed moved, and the only sound was loud snoring coming from the figure closest to Listir.

Listir turned on his flashlight and trained the intensely bright light directly into the face of the snoring sixty-five-year-old man.

"What's going on?" said the man, coming awake.

Listir struck him in the face. The man's wife was now wide awake and clinging to a pillow, her mouth hanging open.

"Shut up!" commanded Listir. "This is going to be very simple. You are going to remain quiet, and you are going to sign over your liquor distribution business to a company we represent."

"What are you talking about? Why would I do that?" sputtered the man indignantly.

Brown smiled, while Listir laughed. He reached out and pistol-whipped the man with his Heckler & Koch VP9. Blood poured from a gash in his forehead, and his wife screamed.

"I am sorry, but maybe I was not clear enough," said Listir calmly. "You are going to do what I am saying, or I am going to let my friend over there torture the two of you to death. Starting with your wife."

Listir shined the light at Brown, who stared back at the couple with cold, dead eyes. Brown had run several of the blackest of the black prisons that the CIA had operated in the post-9/11 era. The man was an absolutely confirmed psychopath, who had been drummed out of the CIA for what were termed "overly egregious" human rights violations in a period when human rights violations were tolerated.

Listir retrained the light on the homeowner's face, which had lost all its color.

"But it will never hold up," said the man.

"You let me worry about that," replied Listir. "You just sign. I have already wired a hundred thousand dollars to your account. I had the documents prenotarized and witnessed, and all they require is your firm signature."

"No one will ever believe I sold my business for a hundred thousand dollars. It's worth one thousand times that much," said the old man, not sounding as bold as before as he pressed his hand against his head.

Listir knew the man could feel his fingers becoming sticky with blood, which would terrify him. The truth was that head wounds bleed profusely because of all the blood vessels, but there was something more frightening to the average person about blood coming out of their head versus a leg. The blood loss might be the same, but the fear was orders of magnitude higher.

"Maybe so, but you will say you wanted and agreed to this deal. You will say it earnestly, and you will believe it. Here is why," said Listir, enjoying seeing the uncertainty in the man's eyes. Listir held out a cell phone and hit play. The room instantly filled with the sound of giggling children. The man and woman leaned in closely, and the woman let out another scream, covering her mouth with her hand. "Your grandchildren are lovely, happy little children. I am sure you would like to keep them that way."

Listir held out a pen. "Are you ready to sign?"

The man nodded, grabbed the pen, and signed the documents.

"Pleasure doing business with you," said Listir.

Brown walked toward the bedroom door, while Listir just stood shining the light in the man's face.

Listir cocked his head to one side and studied the cowering man. "Two more things before we go. First, do not even think about causing a problem. We know where you live, where you go, everything about you. You and your wife would not survive. Second, we will kill your grandchildren before we kill you if you cause us any problems."

The woman whimpered, and the man reached over to comfort her, but Listir brought the gun crashing down on the back of his head. The man crumpled like a sack of flour. The woman screamed, while Brown stood laughing out in the hallway.

*

Federal Reserve headquarters, Eccles Building, Washington, DC

February 28, 2022, 12:24 a.m. Eastern

The three figures sat across from each other with the marble fireplace between them. No one had bothered to lay a fire, since everyone was supposed to be in the conference in the boardroom. They retreated to the office upon realizing they were utterly defeated. The emergency meeting of the world's central bankers had collapsed.

"I think Hideki was right." The chairwoman of the Fed referred to her Japanese colleague. "There is nothing that can be done to stop the panic."

The former chairman of the Fed nodded his agreement.

The Chancellor of the Exchequer stared back at her, his face a mask of fear. Finally, he found some words.

"The system will collapse. China's economy has collapsed. Equity and bond markets around the globe have wiped out investors, pensions, you name it. Credit is frozen. There is no way to halt the panic. Prices will continue to skyrocket. Paper money will become more worthless than it already is. We played God, but we were clearly not. I feel utterly powerless."

All three sat staring into space.

The Chancellor broke the silence. "I feel weak saying this, but honestly, I am worried about my own family. No one is immune from this thing. We are going to make late-twenties Germany look like a period of great financial stability. Europe is already in chaos after Greece, France, Italy and Portugal left the euro."

"I cannot believe it." The former Fed chairman rubbed his gray beard while speaking. "I spent my whole career trying to learn from the sins of the Depression and ensure it never happened again, and now it is clear I presided over an experiment that will make the Depression look like a boom time." Neither of his colleagues tried to change his mind. They were all guilty. "I always thought we would figure a way to return to normal."

"We all thought that eventually there would be enough stability in the economy to stop all the programs, to stop the bubbles," the

Chancellor finally offered up. "But you could not know that the Chinese were faking all their numbers. No one did."

"We all knew the Chinese were not being straightforward. We should have planned for it," the Fed chairwoman countered. "It just never occurred to me that their real-estate market would collapse so quickly and their banks held so much bad paper. It never dawned on anyone that the gigantic profits they were earning from trade with the rest of the world would be dwarfed by their own internal losses supporting unproductive assets. Who could have conceived that their banking system would collapse so quickly, and that the problems would be so widespread? All our models failed. We failed."

The former Fed chairman looked down at his hands before speaking. "Around ad 15, Caesar Augustus minted the silver denarius coin, decreeing that it be made entirely of silver. It took Roman emperors until ad 280 to have debased the currency so far that the denarius was ninety-eight-percent copper. We managed to debase the US dollar over ninety-nine percent from the founding of the Fed just over one hundred years ago, basically a percentage point per year."

The Chancellor stared at the chandelier in silence. The chandeliers in the Eccles Building were designed to be replicas of those in Napoleon's retreat at Malmaison. It was odd that America, for all its democratic virtues, had built a city based on Roman and French imperial designs and themes. Everything in Washington was designed to strike the viewer as worthy of imperial glory.

"If only our end would be as gracious as Napoleon's exile to Elba," whispered the Chancellor. "My don at Cambridge once said something that has never seemed more appropriate: All empires die horrible, tortured deaths." The former chair had just put the comparison of empires in perfect juxtaposition.

"There is just no stopping interest rates from soaring with the

Chinese dumping all the debt and investments they own to raise cash to try to recapitalize their banks. But the rates are really irrelevant; there is no credit to be lent. Meanwhile, people everywhere are in a panic and all their investments are being wiped out by the market implosion." The chairwoman's tone was subdued, almost melancholy. "The Chinese are facing widespread protests and riots, which only cause their government to panic even more. Paris is on fire. Poland, Ukraine, and most of Eastern Europe have no heat. Russia will not provide gas on credit, only for gold. Our debt prices are plummeting, investor accounts globally are being decimated, and the Fed's own balance sheet has been destroyed."

"I know. We are having the same problem. I have already told the prime minister that the Bank of England will need more capital." The Chancellor stood and walked to the sideboard, then poured himself three more fingers of Glenfiddich. "All that debt we bought in order to provide liquidity to the markets is now going to suck the liquidity out of those same markets in order to try and save the Bank of England."

"I gave the president almost the same report last week, and he literally threw up in the trash bin beside his desk," the chairwoman said. "I almost laughed, because I had done the same before going to the White House. I told him that on a mark-to-market basis the Federal Reserve was bankrupt and would require roughly two-point-five trillion dollars to start, preferably in gold credits. I also informed him that the US dollar was, for all intents and purposes, worthless. The man literally lost all composure."

The three sat in silence for a minute. All had bloodshot eyes and, compared to any pictures that could have been found from a year prior, had aged seemingly ten years. The former chairman's famous salt-and-pepper beard had gone completely white. They each slumped in their chairs with the posture of the truly defeated.

They continued to talk late into the evening, but all the potential solutions had long ago been exhausted, and no one had any fresh ideas. Every line of discussion led back to the same place: the modern global financial system was collapsing, and their countries were bankrupt.

Finally, more than a little drunk, the Chancellor took his leave. The chairwoman soon followed him out, with the former chairman asking to sit a little longer.

The former chairman sat in the large ornate office finishing the last of the bottle of single malt. He opened the satchel next to his couch and removed the files he had taken to the conference, files that outlined plans for coordinated actions by all the global players that would never be implemented. They were probably pointless plans, but at least it was a last attempt. No one had the will; fear had broken their backs. Underneath the papers, at the bottom, lay the Colt 45 he had added just that morning.

He had not fired the Colt in years, but he had cleaned and oiled it regularly. He took one last drink and put the gun up to his temple. He moved like a determined man with no hesitation. Out loud to the empty room, he announced, "I am very sorry. Please forgive me!"

Outside the heavy wooden door, the chairwoman's executive aide started up from his chair. The federal officer who guarded the chairwoman's office did the same. The old clock had just sounded 1:00 a.m. Monday morning. The bang clearly sounded like a gunshot.

The uniformed officer reached the door first and came through it with his weapon drawn. Both he and the aide stood looking at the former chairman of the Federal Reserve sprawled across the couch, blood pouring from his head and a pistol still gripped in his hand. The smell of gunpowder hung in the air.

"Holy shit!"

The aide finally moved and felt for a pulse. He could hear the officer on the radio.

"Call 911. We need an ambulance immediately! We have a man down! GSW to the head!"

The aide could not find a pulse. He pulled the chairman off the sofa onto the floor and began CPR. The officer came over to help him, and they worked in tandem, compressing and breathing, but could not get a pulse. As the minutes ticked by, more security personnel arrived, and finally the ambulance crew came through the door and began work on the chairman. But even after repeated shocks there was no pulse.

At 1:38 a.m., Bloomberg terminals around the globe carried the headline "Unconfirmed: Ambulance called to Fed HQ. Man reportedly shot in Chairwoman's office."

Several minutes later, Tokyo, Hong Kong, and Singapore suspended trading following severe imbalances on the sell side. The dollar showed no bids on the buy side.

At 2:14 a.m., Bloomberg updated its story.

"Confirmed: Hospital sources confirm former Fed Chairman dead of self-inflicted gunshot to head."

"Rory, come look at this, now!"

The head trader at GMP, a global macro fund, stood up at his desk, screaming across the floor of London's largest hedge fund and pointing at the charts on his screen. Everyone on the floor stared at his or her screens, panic written on each face. GMP's CEO came running across the floor in time to see already-bad charts go off the scales.

European futures immediately moved deeply red, showing that if the markets opened, London, Paris, and Frankfurt would each record their largest single trading losses ever.

Kohala Coast, Big Island, Hawaii

March 5, 2022, 2:36 p.m. Hawaii-Aleutian Time

All he could hear was his ragged breathing and the metallic swish of the chain swiftly moving through the derailleur. His eyes remained fixed on the top of the hill ahead of him. His legs moved up and down like pistons. He glanced at his RPM indicator and saw 89, a fast pace up a hill, but he pushed himself and saw it tick up to 92. His quads screamed, but he did not back off.

He reached the crest of the hill and was hit in the chest by a hot gust of wind coming across the endless black lava fields. He risked another look at the digital pad mounted on his handlebars; he was running just over a four-hour pace on the 112-mile course with only four miles to go. He ticked up the pace again. His legs threatened to seize up, but his brain just kept pushing. A car went past him, the driver shouting encouragement. It was clear from the speed and the set of Jack's jaw that he was not a casual biker.

A few minutes later, he crossed the finish line of what would have been the bike stage of the Ironman World Championship in Kona. At 4:21, his time would have been one of the fastest bike stages on record.

He unclipped and flipped one leg over the saddle while gently braking to a stop. He dismounted and tried walking his bike, but it was difficult. Nearly four hours in the saddle left his hips locked up. He grabbed his water bottle and sucked down what was left of the electrolyte-infused water while trying to get his legs to move normally.

He had been in Hawaii for nearly five weeks, pushing himself to total exhaustion nearly every day between long swims, bike rides, and marathon-distance runs up the side of the volcanoes. His already-fit body was becoming a finely chiseled example of perfection, but still the pain of loss was there. He had come to Hawaii because he was not finding any peace at home in Texas. Everywhere he went reminded him of Marissa, and everyone he ran into wanted to help but only succeeded in keeping the memories front and center.

He walked the bike toward his rental car and put it in the rack on the back. He reached into the back seat and grabbed another bottle of electrolyte water that had been chilling in a small collapsible cooler. Leaning against the side of the car, standing in the shade of several palm trees, he gulped the water in between sucking in lungfuls of air. He heard his phone ringing and debated ignoring it. He pulled it out and looked at the screen to see the word "Dad" on the screen.

"Hi," said Jack.

"You sound exhausted," replied his father. "What ya playin' at now?"

"Nothing much. Just took a bike ride," offered Jack before drinking some more water.

"Your idea of a bike ride is most folks' idea of a death march," said Jackson Dodge III. "I hope you've enjoyed yourself, though it hasn't sounded very relaxing to me. If you asked me, you should've gone hunting at the ranch. Killing things always helps me relax."

"Dad," said Jack, "do you have a purpose? Or are you just bored and want to give me a hard time?"

"Have you been watching the news, checking stock prices, or following anything going on in the real world?"

"No. I have just been trying to get my head straight, work out, and read all the books I have not read over the last many years. Why? What's up?"

"The world has officially gone to hell in a handbasket, and your vacation's over. I need to see you back in Austin right quick," said the elder Dodge. "The Gulfstream's on its way to Kona. Go pack your things and get back here. Texas needs you. I need you. I will tell you about it when you get back to the ranch. I love you, but it is time to stop feeling sorry for yourself and get back to work."

Jackson Dodge hung up, leaving Jack staring at his phone. His father's phone call could mean only one thing.

*

Greenwich, Connecticut

March 6, 2022, 1:36 a.m. Eastern

He rubbed his ear. The Plantronics CS70N wireless headset had been on Alastair McKenzie's ear as he sat in his home office for over six hours. He rubbed his bald head, and then rubbed his eyes extensively. He could barely focus on the three screens in front of him containing ever-changing prices from the Asian markets. The breakdown of the talks in Washington, the death of the Fed chairman, and the continuing economic meltdown in China brought increased havoc to the global markets. Every security on McKenzie's screen glowed red.

McKenzie guided the largest asset-management firm in the world. His rise was featured in the *Wall Street Journal* and every business magazine year after year. On the bookshelf to the left of his desk stood a beautiful Tiffany picture frame with the *Forbes* cover anointing him "The Current King of Wall Street," usually a warning sign of an imminent stumble, but in his case bestowed before his biggest year ever. Eventually, his firm, started only twenty-five years before, was deemed too big to fail by the US government. He was the expert's expert, and he was lost. The firm bled billions every minute. Its long positions were not working, nor were the shorts, nor hedges.

McKenzie had spoken with the secretary of the treasury, the Fed chairwoman, and the head of the IMF earlier in the day and received the same basic message. The boat is sinking; there are no lifeboats, so you better learn to swim on your own. *Too big to fail, my ass*, McKenzie thought.

His eyes flicked to CNBC. The screen showed a massive apartment building on fire. The shot clearly came from a helicopter, and the camera now panned to a street near the apartment building. McKenzie hit the mute button on his Cisco VoIP phone and turned up the volume on CNBC. The anchor, nearly breathless, announced, "You can see the cars piled up in the street, some of them in flames. On the left side of the screen are Parisian firefighters, unable to get through the barricades. On the right are barricades manned by a group calling itself al-Qaeda de France. The group claims complete control of the eighteenth arrondissement of Paris, where the burning buildings sit. The firefighters have reportedly taken fire from automatic weapons. Just in: reports of at least two dead firefighters..."

Someone kept saying his name, but he felt like he was swimming underwater. Finally, he focused.

"Alastair, what do we do?" The voice was that of Rich Steains, his head of capital markets for Asia.

"Dump it, dump it all," McKenzie responded. His voice sounded distant even to his own ear.

"Are you fucking serious, mate? We hold over seventy billion dollars of equity and debt securities in Asia alone. Seventy billion is going to rock the markets!" With panic evident in Steains's voice, the laid-back Australian was now scared.

"No, our clients had seventy billion at market's open today, down from ninety billion a couple of weeks ago. By my calculation, we have lost nearly twelve billion so far today with no end in sight. If you think that this is going to stop, you are sadly mistaken. We are not going to rock the market. The market is rocking us, and everyone else. Governments around the globe are tapped out and powerless. Japanese, European, and American money printing has finally been exposed as a foolish plan, and China is imploding. I am literally watching Paris burn, something the Nazis could not accomplish. We sell. I am not sure why, because there is nowhere safe to put the money. Money itself is worth less than the paper and ink used to make it. There is really no point to selling, but it is what we are going to do because it is all we can do. Now." McKenzie never raised his voice, the tone never modulated. "And if I was you, I would take your lovely wife and beautiful children and get on a Qantas flight to Melbourne before it's too late. At least you can grow food on your farm."

The silence on the conference call was deafening. The smartest man on Wall Street had just told his overpaid, brilliant subordinates that it was ad 852.

As he finished talking, a flash caught his eye. He stood and looked out the french doors of his home office toward the pool house. It flashed again. A very concentrated beam of light played across one of the pool house windows. Someone on the phone screamed something in full panic, but he had lost interest.

McKenzie walked out of the office and down the hall to the kitchen door. He was wearing a sweatshirt and jeans already, but he slipped his feet into a pair of L.L. Bean boots that sat under the bench by the back door. He grabbed a flashlight from the shelf above the coats and keyed off the alarm. Letting himself out the door, he was immediately struck by a blast of cold air blowing off Long Island Sound across his lawn. Beyond the pool house, the gray water of the sound was whipped up by the wind, the white caps shining in the moonlit clear winter sky.

He closed the door behind him, checking to make sure he disengaged the lock so that he could get back into the house. The ground crunched under his feet, the remnants of last week's ice storm still on the surface of the snow. The light flashed again. He opened the gate and walked around the covered pool toward the pool house doors. He had not turned on his flashlight and now hesitated. He stood close enough now to see at least two figures in the pool house, one with the light fixed on a spot on the floor, the other moving around behind the kneeling first man.

"Fuck," McKenzie swore under his breath.

The men in the pool house stood over the spot where McKenzie installed a floor safe a couple of years before. A very large floor safe that contained nearly sixty thousand one-quarter-ounce gold coins. McKenzie called it his Armageddon Wallet. His wife thought it ridiculous, but he believed if the end came, gold coins might still have value.

McKenzie moved closer to the pool house glass doors. He was close enough now to see the men clearly. Four men were inside. One of them was his caretaker!

McKenzie ripped open the pool house door. "What the fuck are you doing?"

The shotgun blast ripped a hole in his sweatshirt where it used to say "Yale." Alastair McKenzie looked at his chest and fell to the floor, dead.

"We're taking your fucking gold, you piece of shit!" yelled his former caretaker.

Bethesda, Maryland

March 9, 2022, 9:43 p.m. Eastern

Listir sat in the small warehouse office overlooking racks of liquor, cigarettes, canned goods, and stolen or abandoned vehicles. He shook out a cigarette and lit it with a gold Cartier lighter. He leaned back in his desk chair and watched the smoke drift toward the ceiling. After the shock of losing everything with the collapse of the Liechtenstein bank, and with his government pension appearing as if it would go up in smoke with the US collapse, he was well on his way to building a large black-market enterprise.

"May I have one of those?"

The voice belonged to a beautiful blond Russian girl standing next to him wearing nothing but black stilettos. He loved the fact that she did not have the slightest embarrassment.

He handed her a cigarette and struck a flame on the lighter. She took a drag and went back to lie down on the sofa. Life on the dark side had its definite advantages. He felt more like James Bond than he ever did working for the Agency. He had the money, the cars, the girls, and the power that come from controlling things.

His phone vibrated on the desk. He looked at the screen and answered it. He listened closely and then said, "This is very simple. Explain to them that they have twenty-four hours to pay their bills, after which time we will eliminate them."

He hung up. Business was good and growing, but it did have its challenges. He smiled to himself. Who would have ever thought that Peter Listir, longtime CIA field spook, actually had an even better head for business than he did for clandestine operations?

CHAPTER EIGHT

Joint Base McGuire-Dix-Lakehurst, Burlington County, New Jersey

May 7, 2022, 8:46 a.m. Eastern

"Ten-Hut!"

The assembled officers snapped to attention as Brigadier General James Rogers walked into the staff room. The sound of thirty-two highly polished combat boots hitting the floor reflected off of the cinder-block walls.

"Thank you, Master Sergeant. At ease, ladies and gentlemen," said Rogers, nodding to his right-hand man. The master sergeant stood at parade rest. Only five foot ten and nearly sixty years old, he had not one of his gray hairs out of place, and the master sergeant's uniform looked like it had been ironed on his athletic body.

Rogers stood in the front of the room, his compact frame perfect for a fighter pilot, which is how he had started his air force career. He distinguished himself in the First Gulf War and had been targeted for leadership responsibilities. Eventually, he had found himself commanding ever-growing air groups in Iraq and Afghanistan. After over twenty-five years in the US Air Force, Rogers found himself in command of Fort Dix, in New Jersey, a command that included navy and army units. The posting came with his first star.

He nodded to the master sergeant, who closed the door, and then he looked at the officers assembled in front of him. Many of the people in the room had served with Rogers in previous commands, and he handpicked them to join him at the Fort, a process he sped up as the US retreated from its overseas commitments due to America's faltering finances.

Rogers continued to stand and look from person to person, his dark eyes, nearly black thanks to his mother's Mexican heritage, falling on each soldier. His hair, which had been dark and curly, had thinned considerably and gone almost completely white. He still retained his lean, athletic build, helped by a crushing daily fitness routine. Finally, he began to speak.

"As you all know, the situation in the country is deteriorating, as it is globally. Every day our mobility units are being deployed to bring back troops or refuel other aircraft that are returning troops from foreign postings. Massive cuts have and are being made across the entire military, and from what I hear they will only intensify. With Texas threatening to leave the United States, there is considerable talk that other states may follow." Rogers paused and looked at the map of the United States affixed to the bulletin board. He studied the map for a few minutes and then turned to face the group. "I picked every single person in this room for this posting. Like me, all of you are from the Northeast and have ties to this region. It is my expectation that the circumstances in the country are going to continue to worsen and that the US will splinter." A murmur rose from the assembled officers, and

Rogers had to raise his usually quiet voice a bit to regain control. "It is not my hope, but I believe that this is a likely scenario."

The master sergeant moved forward and handed the general a large folder. Rogers opened it, studied the top page, and continued. "I have been doing some contingency planning for this scenario, with the help of the master sergeant. We have made some assumptions based on the premise that the base becomes an island, cut off from access to land for a period of five years. Currently, the base has three thousand six hundred seventy-three military personnel, and another two thousand three hundred forty-five contractors. We have assumed a multiplier of three and one half times and made plans for twenty-one thousand sixty-three to accommodate dependents. Obviously, in a complete breakdown, some of those people will take advantage of the opportunity to move to Texas or other more stable regions of the country, where they may have ties, so we believe that we have created a buffer in our numbers. Master Sergeant."

"Thank you, General." Master Sergeant Stanley Baptiste came forward holding his own copy of the checklist. "For the past year, we have been stockpiling medicine, meals ready to eat, ammunition, maintenance supplies, fuel, batteries, every conceivable item we can think of to cover the roughly twenty-one thousand personnel for a five-year period of time."

"Excuse me, General," a young major who first served with Rogers at Bagram interjected. Rogers nodded his assent and the major continued. "Why did you settle on five years?"

"There is no science behind the number, but we looked at previous periods of complete social upheaval around the globe throughout history. Whether it was the Russian Revolution, the Depression, the fall of the Ming dynasty, or the end of the Shogunate and the Meiji Restoration—obviously, there is no perfect parallel—it appears that some form of regional or national order emerged within a four-year time frame. Providing for five years seemed to offer us a buffer."

"Sir?" Captain Sarah Carpenter waited to be acknowledged and then continued. "Are you saying this is complete?"

Master Sergeant Baptiste jumped in. "We are close, and it is becoming increasingly hard for us to hide our activities. You will note that we moved a number of functions to our smaller facility at New Hanover under the guise of maintenance. Most of the maintenance actually consisted of construction and excavation to accommodate the storage of these supplies. However, we still have a considerable amount to do to get ready, including fortifying the perimeter and bringing in additional fuel and alternative energy sources, such as more solar panels, waste-to-energy units, and the like. We also have nearly completed the new command and control facilities."

The general continued. "Ladies and gentlemen, we are bringing you under the tent now because it is our view that the end is near, and we need to use any remaining time to efficiently gather anything we missed and turn our base into an impregnable, self-sufficient island. Additionally, we need to prepare to become the command authority in this region. Barring any objections or declines, which are your right, I will be meeting with each of you individually to give you primary responsibility for tasks from power to medical, ammunition to perimeter defense."

Rogers waited, watching the room carefully, and saw not a single objection or even remotely disapproving gesture or bit of body language. He turned and walked out of the room, with the master sergeant belting out "Dismissed!" and the sound of boots banging the floor ringing in the hallway.

Eight Bar Ranch, outside San Angelo, Texas

May 9, 2022, 5:46 p.m. Central

The Gulfstream 650ER touched down smoothly on the baking-hot asphalt and immediately deployed its thrust reversers. A driver sat in a red Ford Explorer watching the silver-and-blue plane slow to a complete stop and then execute a 180-degree turn to taxi back toward the midpoint of the runway and the lone taxiway that led to a large ramp. The ramp was already crowded with Gulfstreams, Falcons, and a couple of Citation Xs. Two men emerged from the side door of the lone hangar, carrying chocks, and headed toward one of the few open spots left to direct the aircraft.

As soon as the driver saw the two red wands cross, signaling a full stop of the aircraft, he slipped the Explorer into gear and drove toward the bottom of the swiftly deploying airstairs. The SUV stopped, and the driver jumped out and opened the back door of the vehicle as three men in nearly matching attire of khaki trousers, white button-downs, and navy-blue blazers came down the stairs carrying briefcases and overnight bags. The driver took the overnight bags and headed for the tailgate, while two of the men got in the back seat and one got in the front passenger seat. The driver returned to the driver's seat, waved goodbye to the ground crew, and drove toward the exit gate by the tarmac.

"Welcome to Eight Bar Ranch, gents," said the driver. "If it's all right with you, Mr. Dodge asked me to bring you directly to the main house, as the others have already gathered there for cocktails and dinner." He received a nod from the man next to him, so he continued. "I'll put y'all's bags in the River Cabin, where y'all be stayin'. After dinner, any of the staff can show you to the cabin. I hope y'all enjoy your stay."

"Thank you," replied the older man in the passenger seat.

The three passengers said nothing else until the vehicle pulled into the forecourt of the large ranch house and another thank-you was offered as they left the vehicle.

The large bronze door opened as the men walked toward the house, and Jackson Dodge emerged from the house dressed in a pair of brown leather cowboy boots, faded jeans, and a white dress shirt. He wore a heavy silver belt buckle with a large piece of turquoise embedded in the center.

"A big welcome to the boys from Kansas. We've been expectin' y'all," offered Dodge as he gave each man a full Jackson, a bear hug. A half Jackson was a handshake with his free arm grabbing the recipient's shoulder.

Jackson Dodge III was a bear of a man, every bit as tall as his son, but sixty pounds heavier. Not fat, just big all around and strong as a bull. In Texas politics, Jackson loomed larger than life.

The three visitors exchanged pleasantries with their host and then followed him as he escorted them into the great room of the ranch. The room was enormous, with a soaring ceiling, and yet tastefully done. There were multiple seating areas of soft leather furniture, low glass tables, and sterling silver family photographs. The highly polished mahogany floor shimmered in the late-afternoon sunlight. A white-coated waiter approached the three men and uniformly was told "sparkling water."

Jackson Dodge picked his beer up off the table and said, "Let's make the rounds so that everyone knows everyone."

The small group of mainly men, only a couple of women thrown into the mix, introduced themselves and exchanged handshakes with the new arrivals. Most had met before at various meetings of governors, political conventions, or business meetings. The three recent arrivals from Kansas were introduced to the delegations from Oklahoma, Nebraska, both Dakotas, New Mexico, Colorado, Wyoming, Montana, Utah, Idaho, Arizona, Nevada, Louisiana, Arkansas, Kentucky, Tennessee, Mississippi, and Alabama.

Dodge moved quietly toward the back of the great room after making the introductions and appraised the group. Some states sent just political leaders, such as South Dakota, whose current governor, beloved former governor, and sitting US senator were clustered together with their counterparts from Louisiana. The group made easy conversation that comes from years and years of working the chicken-dinner circuit. Meanwhile, Kansas's representatives included their sitting governor and the Meader brothers, two of the wealthiest men in the world. The Meaders stood off to one side of the room, studying the scene like clinicians.

The Dodges and Meaders were well acquainted. Over the years, the Dodge family energy interests and pipeline companies had been in numerous business deals with the Meaders' holdings. They were highly political, but rarely spoke publicly or even expressed their views in small groups. All of their political influence came one-on-one behind very firmly closed doors. Dodge told Nelson Lufkin that it showed the extraordinary level of importance of the meeting that the Meaders were attending in person.

The more Jackson studied the group, the more he saw patterns. The representatives of the mountain states gravitated toward each other, while the plains states people moved over by the fireplace, and the Southerners stood by the windows. Jackson smiled; the future alignments were already visible. No one could read a room like Jackson Dodge.

He caught Nelson's eye and nodded.

"Ladies and gentlemen, please take a seat," said Jackson over the din of conversation.

His booming voice carried quite clearly across the big room. The conversation quickly died down, and everyone sought a place. No one had come for the cocktails and dinner; they were here to discuss the future.

"We appreciate the effort that y'all made to come on down here on short notice. There is a Texas-size amount to cover tonight and tomorrow." Jackson paused, smiled, and looked at the faces all staring back at him expectantly. "I don't think there is any question about why y'all are here, or what we plan. We're going to hand out some binders, and Nelson's going to walk y'all through our thoughts. We hope that y'all will speak your minds, and that this will be a completely open discussion. Tonight is our presentation, and then we will have a fantastic dinner of the best steaks in the world from right here on my ranch. Tomorrow will be a series of working sessions."

Jackson reached behind a large leather captain's chair and removed a banker's box. He opened the top and began passing out red file folders with the seal of the State of Texas on the front. While all the files were being distributed, he picked up a remote control, and floor-to-ceiling shades descended to cover the windows. The shade in the center of the glass wall doubled as a screen for a projection display.

Nelson Hobby Lufkin stood up to open the meeting. He had rehearsed this speech multiple times over the last few days with multiple parties. It had become the most rehearsed speech his staff could remember in his long political life. The room was small enough that he and Jackson had decided he should stand without a podium, which meant heavy rehearsal to memorize all the points and master the delivery.

At sixty-one years old, Lufkin had become one of the most politically powerful men on the North American continent. He came from an old Texas family but had been educated at Yale. He could play the good ol' boy in public and the economist that he was in private. Lufkin was tall and athletic, with a natural ruddy complexion that made it appear he had been out working in the sun. He had only just begun to show a little gray in his thick hair, which gave his already telegenic presence a more distinguished look.

This was the biggest speech of Lufkin's life, and Dodge could tell he was a little nervous. He swallowed deeply. Even though the audience was receptive, advocating revolution was a big step. He looked over at Jackson Dodge, who gave him a big, broad smile and a nod, so he began; clearly the economist part was going to lead this discussion.

"Ladies and gentlemen, we appreciate you traveling here today. As you know, Texas is exercising its God-given and legal rights to leave the United States of America. We have invited y'all here today to discuss our detailed plans, and to present your states with an opportunity to join us in the Republic of Texas."

Lufkin noticed that no one blinked when he said Republic of Texas. Dodge had been correct; everyone wanted out of the failing United States so urgently that Texas would be able to drive a tough bargain. Just last night over drinks by the fire pit, Dodge had said, "If you have the only lifeboat, you can dictate who comes on board and how." Jackson Dodge knew people and he knew how to make deals. Lufkin relaxed a bit.

On the screen behind Lufkin, a series of maps of the United States appeared, and then they were overlaid with the detail of the original land claims of the Republic of Texas, stretching across portions of Texas, Oklahoma, Arkansas, Louisiana, Kansas, Colorado, Wyoming, Arizona, and New Mexico.

"Behind me, you will note the historic land claims of Texas. As we leave the current country, it is our position that this entire territory constitutes the core of Texas, and thus it's unquestionable in our opinion that these lands have the inalienable right to secede with us should they choose to do so."

He flipped to a new slide, which showed the former territory of Mexico and Spanish claims in the US up until Napoleon took the territory back from Spain in 1800 and then sold it to the United States in the Louisiana Purchase. Lufkin turned from the map and flipped through several more, showing geological formations, and said, "We believe that every state represented in this room, and several others, all can draw on history and geology to link its territory with that of Texas, and our historians and legal teams have drafted the necessary arguments and indexed the supporting documentation, which is now being placed in each of your cabins. These documents will show our position on the historical ties between these lands, including aquifers, mineral seams, native populations, Spanish and French land claims, and other such positions."

Lufkin paused and looked around the room before continuing. "We believe our people and your people will welcome uniting under the Republic of Texas, and that the United States will be powerless to stop us all from going. Furthermore, we think that Washington and Oregon moving to join Canada, and Hawaii Japan, only further strengthens our position." Lufkin could see that nearly every head was nodding in assent. "Before I go deeper, move on to timeline, actions required, and the structure of the Republic of Texas's government, does anyone here believe their state would be unlikely to want to join the Republic of Texas? Because if so, we would like to know now and continue the dialogue with you in a separate forum."

Lufkin stared around the room at each and every participant.

Dodge was conducting his own straw poll of eyes, and he took note of the fact that all participants had their heads up and were making eye contact. *Exactly as predicted*, thought Dodge. *No one wants to be left behind after the rodeo leaves town.*

"All right, allow me to move on to some of the details. The proposed Republic of Texas Constitution is included in your packets; we believe we have corrected many of the flaws in the United States Constitution. Specifically, the Republic of Texas will not be able to run a budget deficit except in time of declared war. We will allow no political parties. Unions are outlawed, as are concepts such as teacher tenure. People will have a right to work, and workers will be expected to perform. We will have absolute equality under the law. We will have no income tax, just property tax, value-added tax, import duties, and sales tax. Our children will learn to read. We will be fiscally sound. And the business of Texas will be business."

Jackson Dodge counted noses again as Lufkin continued to detail the structure, and the number of heads bobbing up and down in unison continued to demonstrate that he had been right. He actually thought he saw the Meaders smile for a brief second. They all wanted in, and the terms could be of Texas's choosing.

*

Eight Bar Ranch, outside San Angelo, Texas

May 10, 2022, 7:03 p.m. Central Time

Jack Dodge walked along the wood-chip path toward one of the cabins along the river. He could smell the wood smoke from the barbeque and hear the river water rushing by. The trees became thicker and the air cooler. He stepped onto the porch and looked at the two men sitting in large outdoor chairs. They appeared relaxed.

One of the boards popped as Jack walked across the porch, and both men looked in his direction.

"Jack!" came the booming voice of his father, who jumped up to deliver a full Jackson. It was followed by a warm handshake from the governor of Texas. "Sit down, Jack."

Jack dropped down in another of the oversize chairs. One of the ranch hands working the grill walked over and slipped a bottle of cold Coors into Jack's hand.

Jack looked at the two men while taking a sip of his beer and then said, "I take it the meeting went well. The Meaders left happy?"

Lufkin said, "Happier than pigs in shit. It went better than your daddy expected. Hell, it was a turkey shoot. They're all in on our terms. Maybe we should have driven a harder bargain, Jackson." Jack raised an eyebrow and shifted slightly in his chair.

"Jack, my boy, ya still uncomfortable?" asked his father, staring at his son over the rim of a heavy glass tumbler.

Jack watched the river for a second, looked from his father to the governor, and then replied, "Y'all know I took an oath."

Lufkin raised a hand to silence Jackson Dodge, who was about to jump in, and leaned toward Jack. "Jack, my boy, we all took oaths. I swore an oath when I joined up with the guard. Your daddy took an oath when he went in the Senate. Nobody likes it, and if they say they do they're a liar. However, it's happening, and we can either go down with the ship or live to fight another day. I see it as our first duty to save as many people as we can. We start with Texas and Texans, because this is our home. Then we try and save as many of the rest." Lufkin stared Jack directly in the eyes.

"Yes, sir," said Jack, holding the man's gaze. "I appreciate what you say and know that intellectually you're right. My heart wants to fight on, but it just isn't practical. I'm on board."

Jackson Dodge relaxed and leaned back in his chair, took another swig of his whiskey, and eyed his son carefully. Jack looked relaxed and confident, but still carried a sad look that he had never had in the past. Marissa's death, and now the breakdown of the country for which Jack had given his professional life and lost so many fellow soldiers, aged him.

"Governor," said Jack, "we worked up a plan for creating the intelligence operations you wanted. Earlier today I left a secure copy with your chief of staff." Jack reached into his pocket and pulled out two thumb drives. "Here are two more copies for each of you; the password is Longhorn. I apologize for the length of the document, but this is a complex operation. I included a budget and a complete action plan, detailing people, capabilities, and timeline."

"What's the bottom line, son?" asked Jackson.

Jack stared at the river. "It depends on whether or not my assumptions are correct. For instance, is Utah in?"

"Damn straight those little Mormon bastards are in," said Lufkin.

"Well, that gives us the NSA data center complex in Utah, which means we have our own copy of PRISM," replied Jack. "In a nutshell, we can have a bare-bones intelligence operation up and running within three months of joining with Utah, a clandestine operation within six months, and a fully functioning intelligence service in fifteen months."

"Make it twelve months," said Lufkin. "By the way, Jack, congratulations."

"Sorry, sir?" said Jack.

Lufkin smiled broadly, as did Jackson Dodge. "Congratulations on being named the first head of the covert intelligence operations of the Republic of Texas."

Austin, Texas, USA/Republic of Texas

July 12, 2022, 11:04 a.m. Central

Nelson Hobby Lufkin walked out onto the steps of the Texas Capitol. He looked ahead at the podium and teleprompters. A folder with his remarks already lay on the podium in case he needed to refer to paper. He could hear the shutter clicks of the cameras from the hundreds of photographers who crouched on the steps. The plaza below the steps overflowed with people. Behind Lufkin marched the governors of Oklahoma, Kansas, Arkansas, Georgia, Alabama, Mississippi, South Carolina, North Carolina, Virginia, Tennessee, Kentucky, West Virginia, South Dakota, North Dakota, Nebraska, New Mexico, Colorado, Wyoming, Utah, Idaho, Montana, Arizona, and Nevada. Trailing the state representatives were some of the leading military figures from across these same states, including the head of STRATCOM and other leading generals.

In Washington, DC, the president of the United States of America sat in the Oval Office on a sofa with his chief of staff and other senior staff members looking at a television that had been placed in the room for this purpose. He had become president just eight weeks before when the president resigned and the vice president refused to take the job, calling it a fool's errand. The former president immediately left the US and sought asylum in Namibia—no extradition treaty. The speaker of the house had taken the job because he "felt a sense of duty" and, after sixteen terms, he "could not hide from the responsibility." In addition, he was "too damned old to go anywhere else."

They all watched Lufkin, a man they had known for years, walk up to the podium and begin his speech. Lufkin turned slightly toward the assembled group of dignitaries behind him, smiled, nodded, and then turned back and opened a leather-bound folder in front of him.

Lufkin gestured to people assembled behind him. "Ladies and gentlemen, it is my honor and privilege to welcome you here today to Austin. However, it is not just to you as friends that I extend my welcome, and that on behalf of the people of the Republic of Texas. I extend my country's hand and invite your lands to join our new nation as we build a bright, prosperous, and free future…"

"The governor of California holding," said the note slipped to the president by his executive assistant. He nodded and picked up the phone.

"Good afternoon, Governor," said the president.

"Are you fucking kidding me? What is good about it? Are you watching this fucking guy? He just declared war on the United States," the governor of California sputtered, and the president could feel his rage and fear coming down the phone line. The president closed his eyes and pictured the now-aged governor in his long-ago hippie days. "It is one thing for Texas to form its own country. Total bullshit! Now these fucking guys are trying to take everybody with them! Texas would have the bulk of the oil and gas, minerals, agriculture, water, you name it. They have come as a thief in the night!"

"No, Governor, it is broad daylight, and there is nothing we can do to stop them," replied the president. He sensed all his aides staring at him, so he swiveled in the chair and looked out the bulletproof bay window into the Rose Garden. It amazed him how some things seemed so normal in spite of nothing being normal. The garden looked lovely, just like when Jackie Kennedy first unveiled it. Very surreal.

"What do you mean, there is nothing we can do to stop him? Send in the military and occupy these fucking states!" the governor fumed. "We are in deep shit, and my state is on the verge of collapse. We cannot lose the economic support of all that territory. I do not even want to think about what will happen if they stop sending us Colorado River water. Christ, the people who don't die of thirst will die in riots."

"Governor, I met with the joint chiefs last night, and they informed me that they are not with us in this fight. In fact, they told me to expect the entire South to petition to join the Republic of Texas, which from the television looks to have already happened. I also see on my screen that most every military leader I care about is standing behind Lufkin. You should also know that the chiefs told me where their allegiances lie by kindly giving me a geography lesson and informing me that the Pentagon sits in Virginia. I have reports of naval vessels breaking out the flag of the Republic of Texas, and aircraft leaving bases in places like Ohio and reappearing in Kansas.

"I think that as of this moment you should consider that the United States of America consists of California, Illinois, Indiana, Ohio, Michigan, Pennsylvania, Maryland, New York, Vermont, New Hampshire, Maine, Massachusetts, Rhode Island, Connecticut, New Jersey, and Delaware. Florida will leave, with the only question being to join Texas or as a Latin American–oriented independent state. Oregon, Washington, and Hawaii are gone."

"You must be joking. This has to be some sick joke." The governor sounded deflated. "Do something, man!"

The president finally found something to smile about: the governor was still a hippie at heart.

"No, it's no joke. And unfortunately, I think it is only going to get worse, and there is nothing that you or I can do. I understand that Maine has reached out to the Eastern Canadians about joining with them. Vermont is contemplating becoming its own republic with New Hampshire, which is ironic since just after the War of Independence,

Vermont was briefly a republic. I had not known that about Vermont until one of the smart guys around here told me. The governor of Hawaii is currently in Japan, finalizing the terms of Hawaii's federation with Japan. I was told that they might even revive the Hawaiian royal family."

"I am glad that you find this so interesting on a historical and political level, Mr. President, but we are dying out here. The combination of our massive debts, drought, and failing economic base has us on our knees."

"I am sorry that I gave you the wrong impression. I do not find it interesting at all. I find it tragic," replied the president, his voice sounding strained. "For years, I and all my colleagues in government spent and spent with abandon, did not listen to the advice of anyone who told us to be practical, and now we are all going down with the ship. For sixty years, we were told that the ship was going to run into the rocks and we ignored it. I ignored it. We used to talk about the fact that these were problems for the future. Well, guess what: the future has arrived with a bang. Crime is the order of the day. The reports from most of the Rust Belt and the Northeast are about gangs taking control neighborhood by neighborhood. In many places, these gangs are actually the former police forces switching sides and deciding to run their own game. We are done, and I am here to turn out the lights.

"Governor, I am very sorry that there is nothing I can do to stop this, to help you, or to frankly do anything at all. The suffering is going to get worse, and we have no one to blame but ourselves. May God bless you and forgive all of us for what we did and failed to do."

A few hours later, while watching a speech by the governor of Florida, the president received another note. The governor, backed by the commanding officers of Pensacola, Eglin, and many of the other Florida bases, announced that the Florida Assembly unanimously approved a law, which the governor signed on camera, authorizing the attorney general of Florida to negotiate admittance to the Republic of Texas. The president unfolded the note to read, "The Governor of California found dead in his office, an apparent suicide. His note said simply, *Better to die quickly*."

PART II: THE AFTER

CHAPTER NINE

Fort Meade, Maryland, former USA

February 26, 2025, 9:56 p.m. Eastern

Dr. Vincent Mulvaney sat in his office staring at the data displayed on his computer. He removed his glasses and rubbed his eyes again. At nearly sixty-five years old, Mulvaney found the endless computer time hard on his vision. Data still continued to pour into the NSA from around the globe and across the former United States care of PRISM and other systems, but unlike in the first decades of the century, there was very little for the NSA to do with the information. The resources were not there, the legions of analysts gone, the agency a shell.

He leaned back in his chair and studied the picture of his wife. Though it was late, he really had nowhere else to go. His wife had died five years earlier, and he never had much relationship with his only daughter, mainly because the agency had always been his child. His daughter attended the University of Georgia, married a man from Atlanta, and now literally lived in a different country.

Mulvaney spent most of his adult life perfecting the policies and systems that allowed the United States to collect and dissect the world's communications and hunt down its enemies. He helped to design and direct many of the agency's most successful programs for analyzing data and searching for patterns and then responding to the patterns with countermeasures, usually cyber-countermeasures but sometimes human. He had jointly managed strike teams with the CIA and the Pentagon that had dealt with America's enemies everywhere. At one time, Dr. Mulvaney had controlled dozens of hacker teams actively disrupting foreign governments and terrorist organizations, and his department had functioned around the clock. His people also kept an eye on nearly everyone in America, making sure they ferreted out domestic terrorists and terrorist sympathizers. Now there was almost no one in the cube field sitting below his raised office. The only people that remained were either working on some project of their own, usually nefarious, or trying to find a way out of the collapsing northeast.

He swiveled around in his chair and took a bottle of Old Grand-Dad out of the lower drawer of the large wooden credenza. The drawer stuck a little and he had to yank it. "Crap," he muttered. The place was slowly falling apart. He was pissed; he valued order and discipline, and there was only chaos. He grabbed his coffee cup and poured the remnants into the pot of a fern that had seen better days, then refilled the cup with a generous measure of cheap liquor. He winced when he took a sip, but liquor had become scarcer, and even Old Grand-Dad commanded high cash prices. Single malts were unavailable and hard cash—Texas cash—a precious commodity in the dead zone.

He rubbed his hand over his closely cropped hair. He had kept it tight since his days in the service. His posture was still ramrod straight, and he came to the office every morning even though no one had paid him in years. Almost no one was left. Many nights he just slept on his office couch. Inside the fort was safer than anywhere else. Not like he had anywhere else to be.

He felt his phone vibrating in his pant pocket and looked at the screen, where he saw a familiar name, "Spook."

"Are you still sitting in your office, trying to find a kernel of hope?" asked the voice on the other end of the phone.

Mulvaney glared at the phone. After devoting his entire life to service of his country, all he wanted was to see that country back together.

"What if I am?" Mulvaney answered with more anger than he intended.

"Whoa, partner, you and I are still on the same team," responded the former CIA field officer, who Mulvaney long ago christened Spook because he hid everything from everyone. "I am just giving you a hard time."

Taking a deep breath and another sip of his whiskey, Mulvaney responded, "I know. I am sorry. I am just sitting here in the birdcage, looking out over rows of empty cubes and watching data streams and flagged messages go unread. Our country fell apart and we were left holding the trash bag, while the Texans just waltz away into the future. It is killing me."

Spook's voice softened. "Vince, honestly, that ship has sailed, and those of us who missed the boat need to figure out what we can do to make the port habitable. The Texans moved very quickly; the borders are tightly sealed and controlled, something they always wanted. They have deported millions of people from our zone back to us, people we cannot feed. Meanwhile, social order on our side is gone. I understand your anger, but we need to focus on what we can control, or at least try to control, and that is the function of our small immediate area."

Mulvaney rubbed his eyes again and then ran his hand back and forth across the stubble on his face. It was not lost on him that Spook seemed to be thriving in the new chaos, living better than everyone else, always with access to whatever anyone needed. He had to proceed with care. Spook pretended to be his friend, but Mulvaney knew Listir's only friend was himself. But at a minimum, Mulvaney needed a friend in high places in the new environment.

"I have a tough time accepting that, Listir, and have retasked some still-functioning assets to keep an eye on the Texans," Mulvaney stated. "It is not easy, because our operational efficiency declines every day, while Herring makes great strides increasing his organization's capabilities. I have to say that Herring always impressed me, but he just gets better and better. Then there is Jack Dodge. He could have done nothing with his life but enjoy all that money; instead he chose to serve." Vince paused by taking another deep pull on his drink.

Listir paused before replying, the mention of Dodge causing his anger to flare. "Vince, I did not call to upset you or pick a fight. I just thought I would catch up with an old friend," replied Peter Listir. "I am more worried about the lawlessness and criminal gangs that increase their power every day in our area. The weapons left to you may have better uses than tracking the Texans. Let's spend more time together and figure out how we can work more closely."

Mulvaney finally laughed, for the first time that day. Listir was going to recruit him over to the dark side. Everything was upside down.

"You want to know something funny? The Pakistanis and the Indians started full-scale fighting again today. I still get real-time feeds from around the globe on troop movements and battles. What used to be everyone's worst nightmare seems like a sideshow; finally a war between India and Pakistan intense enough that it might turn nuclear. I keep waiting to wake up from all this."

"Vince, we are pretty well screwed. You understand that, right? You've seen the food riots here and across the Northeast. There is no coordination amongst the various authorities that are still trying to function, if you can call them that. In fact, the turf wars continue to escalate. I can go on and on. Let's use those resources you have to do some good locally."

"What do you suggest?" Mulvaney asked, only half interested in the response. His eye ran down the list of threats flagged by Fort Meade's copy of PRISM while Listir talked.

"I think we can use some of that pretty hardware you have to tamp down some problems around here. I have some ideas," said Listir as he lit a cigarette and smiled to himself. *I have some ideas on how you can help me expand my business.* He looked out of the small internal window in the warehouse office at row after row of boxes stuffed with liquor, cigarettes, canned food, and medicine. Chaos creates opportunity. Now, if he could use the NSA's remaining assets to kill off the competition, life might go from good to great.

CHAPTER TEN

Austin, Texas, Republic of Texas

March 13, 2025, 12:13 p.m. Central

Jack pulled up outside the old stone building. He put the Ford Explorer in park and stepped out. His black cowboy boots glinted in the sunlight, the caiman lowers shined to a high gloss. The boots accentuated his height. He stretched; since he fell from a horse during a hunting trip a few months ago, his back had been bothering him. In spite of the tightness in his back, Jack continued his relentless training. Between triathlons and his cycling, he remained in near-peak physical condition, almost at the level he had achieved as a Navy SEAL.

"Hi, Johnny," said Jack to the usher as he flipped him the keys.

"Hi yourself, Jack! Your daddy just went in."

Johnny had served as head usher at the Texas Club all of Jack's thirty-eight years. Both men stopped as a convoy of cement trucks drove by, kicking up dust and drowning out all conversation.

"City sure is changin'. There are more cranes than trees."

Jack could feel Johnny staring closely at him. He tried to look upbeat, but he knew that his whole look had taken on a tinge of sadness.

"You doing OK?" Johnny asked, putting a hand on Jack's arm.

People in the club called Johnny the "club uncle." He knew everything about everyone, never said a word out of school, and offered practical advice. At nearly seventy, Johnny had been at the club longer than most of the members had been alive; he watched them all grow up, and some not.

"I'm OK," Jack said evenly but not convincingly. "Thanks for asking."

Johnny gave him a pat and then sent him on his way, saying, "Git. Don't keep your daddy waiting. Ya know how he gets."

Jack hustled up the old worn stone stairs and pushed through the heavy oak door. Instantly, the air-conditioning hit him like a cool, wet wave. One thing Texans knew how to do exceptionally well was air-conditioning a building. His eyes took a second to adjust from the bright midday sun to the soft glow of the wood-paneled foyer. The place positively screamed Texas, from the cowhide chair coverings to the Western figures and historical paintings lining the wall. Jack had been coming here his whole life, and the place felt comfortable, almost like the home of a relative.

The maître d' greeted Jack like an old friend and led him down the long, wide hall, past a series of frosted glass doors and toward the farthest set of double doors, where an agent stood. Each set of doors concealed a private dining room styled in the form of a library. The club's main dining room was upstairs, and the basement level held a comfortable bar with a beautiful brass railing and several rooms with pool and card tables. The whole place had the faint aroma of cigar smoke, as the Texas Club defiantly ignored antismoking rules and could, since anyone who might enforce the rules was a member.

Jack greeted his father's long-serving primary agent and pushed through the double doors and into the room. He was surprised to see the large, round oak table set for four, as he thought he was meeting only his dad for lunch. His father stood in conversation on the left side of the table with a small academic-looking man.

"Jack, my boy," boomed his father, coming across the Persian carpet to give Jack a full Jackson. With his size, volume, personality, money, and position, Jackson commanded attention.

"Dad," replied Jack as he received a bear hug from his father. Jackson always said, "It will be a cold day in hell for this family when a father can no longer hug his son, no matter the age or setting." Jackson Dodge was smart—some would say ruthless—but he loved his son unabashedly.

"Jack, meet my old friend Les Fowlkes. Les is the archivist of Texas."

Jack shook hands with the smaller man, who absolutely looked like the movie version of a librarian. The man had thinning hair and a small mousy face, made to appear even more pinched with the small round glasses he wore. His jacket was an ill-fitting light blue, and his slacks were a bluish-gray color that almost made him appear to be wearing a mismatched suit. Jack had met numerous academics over the years, and the most brilliant always seemed to have the least interest in their appearance.

"Jack, it's a real pleasure. Your daddy talks so much about you."

The man had a surprisingly confident and deep voice with a thick West Texas accent, and a very firm handshake.

"I am afraid then you have the jump on me, since I thought I was just meeting my dad," said Jack to the librarian, but looking at his father.

Jackson let out a short laugh and clasped his son in the ol' half Jackson.

Jackson Dodge said, "My fault, my fault. But when our fourth arrives, we can all tell each other some tall tales."

Jack started to ask about the fourth diner when the doors to the room opened and two very serious-looking men walked in. Jack could tell that both were packing, a violation of club rules, which required guns to be either left in cars or checked at the coat check in the gun lockers. Neither of these men seemed to care what club rules said about guns as they did a very professional and thorough review of the room. They also did an efficient pat down of each of the three occupants. Jack raised an eyebrow at his father, who smiled sheepishly back.

As the two men backed out of the room, Jack was surprised to see the very familiar first minister of the Republic of Texas come through the door.

Minister Lufkin got a full Jackson and gave the archivist a firm handshake, before turning to Jack.

"Jack, it is nice to see you again. I hope you are doing OK. Sandy and I think about you all the time."

The first minister had an encyclopedic memory for people, and when he spoke to you it was like no one else in the world mattered. Lufkin looked Jack directly in the eyes, and he could see real concern there.

Jack took a deep breath. Anytime someone brought up Marissa in any way, the raw pain would well up inside. He had seen a therapist for a while to talk about Marissa's death but quit when he decided the man did not know what he was talking about. Work and brutal fitness regimens became his therapy. The pain lessened only slightly with the years, but he had learned to keep that hidden.

"Thank you, sir," was all Jack could muster.

The four men took their seats and ordered lunch quickly. Conversation rambled a bit, as the first minister and his minister of external affairs, Jackson Dodge, held forth on the latest gossip running around the capital and the measures being taken to further increase border security. The California refugee problem had been big news in the early days of the Republic, but it appeared the border security was now working, and almost all illegals returned.

"Jack, that was a nice piece of work y'all did last month down in Monterrey," offered the first minister as the plates were cleared.

In late January, Jack's team tracked down the leader of Los Blancos, the largest drug cartel in Mexico, and the group responsible for most of the drug traffic coming over the border.

Jack glanced at the archivist but decided he must have clearance if the first minister felt free to speak so casually in front of him.

"Thank you, sir," offered Jack. "It was nearly a textbook operation. The intel was accurate. We had surprise on our side, and the actual on-the-ground scenario played out as we drilled. I wish they all went that way."

Jack thought back to the operation in Monterrey. Los Blancos controlled the entire section of Monterrey where the compound sat, so the team had relied on drones and a maid they turned with the help of her family members in Texas. The actual snatch and grab of the leader had gone off flawlessly, but there had been some significant fighting on the way out of the compound. At the end of the evening, the group's financial head and security chief were dead, the head in custody. They had also recovered hard drives, enabling the authorities to arrest distributors all over the Republic and seize tens of millions of cash and product.

After coffee was served and the waiter left the room, the first minister stared at Jack across the table. Jack held the minister's gaze and realized Lufkin was making a decision. He waited quietly while the first minister made up his mind.

"Jack, how familiar are you with your early Texas history?" asked the first minister.

"I have the basics down, First Minister," replied Jack. "We learned some of it in grade school. My father also gave me a version of it, but I'm a bit rusty." Jack smiled at his dad.

Jackson Dodge's version of history put Texans at the center of every meaningful invention or event of the last three hundred years. He had once said on a television news program, "If a Texan didn't do it first, it wasn't worth doing."

"OK, then let's have Les tell us a story. The floor is yours."

The archivist nodded and took a quick sip of his iced tea. The other three men settled back in their chairs.

"Thank you, First Minister. Jack, this story takes place in 1850," began Fowlkes. "As you know, Texas was admitted to the United States in 1845, and joined formally in 1846. The addition of Texas had been very complicated, as the Mexicans still claimed it, and the Northern states opposed its admission as a slave state. When Texas joined the US, the state was nearly bankrupt and owed huge debts. These debts became a significant point for negotiation between Texas and the federal government, along with Texas's historic territorial claims to much of the middle and western part of what eventually became the Western US. Complicating all of this were ongoing controversies about the bounds of the territorial expansion of slavery."

As the archivist continued his dive into Texas's history of 170 years before, Jack found himself waiting for the aha moment. It must be coming, because he had never seen his father be so quiet for so long.

The archivist continued with his lesson and finally asked, "Are you familiar with a document known as the Texas Compact?"

Jack thought for a moment. "No. As I said, my history is a little rusty," he replied with a faint smile. He continued to search his mind but could not remember ever hearing of it. He felt like an unprepared student cold-called in class.

"Jack, my boy, no one is familiar with the Texas Compact," said the first minister. "I guess I should say no one alive. Les here discovered a copy about one month ago."

"We were getting ready to host an exhibit of the papers of Sam Houston. During preparations, I found the compact mixed in with a stack of letters and personal papers we only recently discovered," offered the archivist excitedly. "These papers were bound together with a strip of ribbon and did not appear to ever have been opened since they came to the Texas Archives."

"I guess I am a little slow today, but are we all meeting to discuss Sam Houston's hundred-seventy-year-old paperwork?" asked Jack, looking around incredulously.

All three men nodded.

"Yes, because the Texas Compact puts the entire existence of the Republic of Texas in jeopardy," answered Jackson Dodge very softly.

The archivist reached into his breast pocket and took out an oversize photocopy of an ancient-looking document. He handed it across the table to Jack, who read it, looked up, and read it again. He might not remember the compact from history class, but he remembered the men who signed it across the bottom. Almost everyone who took American history in high school knew about the Compromise of 1850, and now here was a document that specifically referenced being an integral part of that agreement. However, the Texas Compact included some secret provisions that had not made it into the regular history curriculum.

Jack understood instantly. The former United States of America was bankrupt and splintered, and the Republic of Texas born of its ashes. Texas walked out of the union and the South, and most of the Mid- and Mountain West had joined it. The new country was rich in agriculture, energy, natural resources, and manufacturing, and best of all, it was financially strong. The Northeastern US descended into near anarchy.

In the west, California had collapsed under its own debt, with a massive earthquake in the Los Angeles Basin in 2022 making the situation much worse. Things in Southern California were so bad that several groups emerged calling for a recombination with Mexico, which rejected any such notion. No one wanted California. The Pacific Northwest joined Western Canada, which in the second financial crisis had split from Eastern Canada.

"I'm sorry, but if you have the compact, and it has never been part of written history, why tell me?" said Jack, looking from face to face.

He watched as the three men exchanged glances and knew he would now find out the true purpose of lunch. His father studied the condensation on the side of his water glass. Jackson Dodge stretched out his thumb and scrubbed one side of the glass clear, then wiped his thumb off on his white linen napkin.

"The copy we have is not the only one. There is another, and we need you to find it," said the first minister of the Republic of Texas so quietly that his voice was barely audible over the hum of the air-conditioning. "You see what's in it. It needs to disappear one way or another. Permanently."

*

Outside Austin, Texas, Republic of Texas

March 13, 2025, 6:47 p.m. Central

Jack sat on a large wood and leather chair on the stone patio of his house, his feet up on a wood and leather footstool. He looked out across the patio—over the infinity pool, where the hillside fell away—and watched the lights of Austin come on in the distance. In the gathering darkness, the numerous cranes disappeared, leaving only their aviation lights blinking, floating in the night sky.

He slowly twirled the tumbler of Glenlivet he had balanced on the arm of the chair. The only sound besides the crickets came from the occasional faint clink of ice against the sides of the glass.

He sensed the visitor before he heard him. Instinctively, his hand moved from his glass to the grip of the Glock in his shoulder holster.

"Don't shoot your daddy," drawled the familiar voice.

Jack immediately relaxed his grip. He stood and turned to face his father, his bare feet feeling the warmth still embedded in the stone from the Texas sun.

"Hi, Dad, you surprised me. Can I get you a scotch?"

Hugs exchanged, Jack walked toward the bar through the french doors.

"Now there is the best thing that anyone has said to me today," called Jackson Dodge. "Don't pollute mine with ice like your sissy drink."

Jack moved to the bar just inside the doors and grabbed another cut crystal glass, then filled it with a large measure of eighteen-year-old Glenlivet. He dropped three cubes in his own glass and freshened it up a bit. Returning to the porch, he found his father occupying his former seat.

"Cheers," said Jack as he handed over the glass.

"Cheers," replied his father before taking a deep pull on the drink. "Now, that is good stuff." The elder Dodge smacked his lips and said, "I love the view from here."

"Dad, a heads-up before lunch would have been nice," Jack said, perched on the footstool, looking at the twinkling city lights. "Also, I hate the fact that we are talking about the Northeast. I have spent the last few years trying to forget everything about all that."

"Jack, you run our intelligence service's operations division, so you go where we need you to go. Also, you understand the need for confidentiality. The first minister wanted to discuss it with you personally and made that very clear to me. Who the hell else other than my son are we going to trust with something this important?"

Jack recognized the tone from his childhood, the same tone his father used when telling him he did not care that he did not want to work in oil fields for the summer at fifteen. *"Jack, I don't give a crap what your friends are doing or not doing. You are a goddamn Dodge, and you will learn the oil business from the bottom up, starting now."*

"I am not fifteen anymore, Dad. I understand why you asked me, but I am telling you, respectfully, that I think other men on my team could do this assignment. Men who would bring less baggage," offered Jack in a calm, measured tone.

"We did not ask you, Jack!" Jackson Dodge was always charming until he was not getting the result he wanted. "The head of the Republic of Texas and your ultimate boss, along with your father, gave you an assignment. A mission which must be successful, or all this"—the minister waved his hand in the direction of Austin—"could be a mirage."

*

Harper Packing Company, Austin, Texas, Republic of Texas

March 14, 2025, 8:16 a.m. Central

Jack Dodge exited the elevator on the sixth floor of the forty-story glass office tower in downtown Austin. The Harper Packing Company occupied floors five through eight of the building, nearly one hundred thousand square feet of space. The reception area immediately faced the elevators and lay shielded from view by two heavy frosted glass doors, etched with the images of longhorns. In reality, both doors were bulletproof and bomb-resistant Starlite plastic.

Jack entered the code on the keypad and then put his eye to the retinal scanner before the doors clicked open. He pushed through and walked into the reception area, which was made to look like it belonged on a ranch. The small room contained a brown distressed-leather sofa and two wing chairs, a Persian rug covering a wide, polished plank floor, and paintings depicting cowboys out on the range rounding up cattle. A large wooden desk sat at the far end, but the receptionist did not arrive until nine o'clock.

Jack entered another set of electronic codes on the keypad next to the one door leading out of the reception area and repeated the retinal scan. There was an audible click, and he pushed open the door that looked like polished wood on the reception side but was in reality bomb-resistant carbon.

Harper Packing Company was a sixty-year-old, very large Austin-based beef packer owned by the Dodge family. The actual cattle company occupied the seventh and eighth floors of the same office tower. Harper also happened to be the cover for the operations wing of the Texas External Security Services. Nothing like a large company with operations across the Republic and in eighteen overseas locations to provide legitimate reasons to move people, money, and equipment in and out of places with reduced suspicion. Hiding in plain sight.

Once through the door, Jack found himself in the familiar rows of cubes and offices that stretched across the sixth floor. He walked down the corridor, headed for the stairwell in the center of the building, which led to the fifth floor. At the bottom of the stairs, he slid his card key through the reader and opened yet another secure door to the floor that housed his office, those of his direct reports, and the communications and analytics nerve center of the field operations.

As a creature of habit, Jack dropped his stuff in his office on one of the visitor chairs and made for the coffee station in the center of the floor. After pouring himself a large cup of black coffee, he walked toward the communications center and cleared through yet another electronic barrier. Inside the doors, he walked up two steps onto the raised floor of the large open-plan room, which positively hummed from all the small fans cooling the servers and other equipment.

"Good morning, Alan," Jack said as he walked up behind a prematurely gray-haired man sitting at a desk facing out across the room.

Alan Herring stared at one of the six oversize computer monitors that lined his desk and delivered feeds from operatives, signals intelligence, and other assorted data sources.

"Jack," said Herring without turning around. "Nothing unusual."

Jack smiled as he stared at the unkempt back of Herring's head. Jack always said Herring was a bit of an acquired taste, a genius with an abrasive personality. He enjoyed dealing with his machines more than people. But as a Kansan, he had answered Jack's call and left the NSA to come to Austin when the former United States of America started to break apart. With the help of many more NSA, DIA, and DISA refugees, Herring built the new Republic of Texas a world-class signals-intelligence platform based off the NSA's architecture.

"Could you believe the way that game ended last night, Alan?"

Jack smiled as Herring turned to stare at him with a look reminiscent of a man who just ate an onion sandwich.

"Do you have a specific purpose in bothering me this morning, or should I stop what I am doing and spend my time entertaining you?" Herring shot back, and then smiled the faintest of smiles. Even Herring had become self-aware that he should try to be less antisocial.

"Alan, that was almost a joke. Good for you. As usual, it's a pleasure to make small talk with you. I could spend all day enjoying your company. However, I do have an actual purpose today." Jack never stopped smiling, and Herring reciprocated by looking annoyed. "Can we go sit in your conference room for a few minutes, please?"

Herring opened his top desk drawer, and both men left their cell phones inside. Herring locked the drawer, stowed the keys in his pocket, and then led off toward a small set of stairs in the corner of the communications center, which led to a SCIF. A SCIF is a sensitive compartmented information facility, which is to say a conference room immune from signals penetration where absolutely secure activity or conversations can occur.

The two men settled into the small conference room, and the door closed behind them. Alan touched a button on the pad lying on the table, and the room's electronic countermeasures fully engaged.

"Alan, this is a project for you only. I do not want anyone else on your team working on it for now." Jack spoke quite seriously, the time for playing around clearly over.

Herring took a pen from the holder in the center of the table and grabbed a pad from beside it. "OK, shoot, Jack."

Jack talked for about ten minutes, first telling Herring the specifics of the Compact, then detailing various pieces of information he required, from database searches to floor plans. As he spoke, Herring continued to write, filling up several single-lined pages of the pad. Jack could read the words upside down written in Herring's careful script—*floor plan, Library of Congress*; *Senator Clay's papers*; *aides to Senator Clay*; *Senator Webster's papers*; *compacts + Texas*—and the list continued.

Finally, Jack stopped and said, "That's all I have for the moment."

Herring continued to write for some time.

"OK, give me until the end of the day," replied Herring.

Typical Herring. He did not challenge the task or ask superfluous questions. If anyone else had put out such a rapid timeline, Jack would have laughed in his face, but not Alan Herring. He benefited from an eidetic memory and incredible skills with computers.

"You want the information on secure electronic tablet or hard copy?" asked Herring.

"Secure tablet, please." Herring often loaded his reports onto tablets that were encrypted and could only be loaded with direct cable interface from the system. Trying to link the tablets to any other machine would cause the devices to erase themselves. Furthermore, the tablets were encrypted with the latest in retinal scanners to ensure not only that the operator was authorized, but also that the ongoing reader was the authorized party.

Jack watched Herring read his notes through one time and then run them through the shredder. The paper dropped out of the bottom and into a burn bag. Herring's memory had a perfect picture of what had been on the pages.

Back in his office, Jack waited for Danny Winters. He heard him before he saw him. Danny's morning routine was to arrive slightly later than the rest of the unit and then greet everyone in his rich baritone as he walked through the office just in case they did not know he was late again.

"Morning, Jack," said Danny as he came through Jack's door.

Coming through the door was the right way to think of Danny Winters entering a room. He was six feet seemingly by six feet; the man's build approximated a brick house.

He threw himself into the chair facing Jack's desk and pushed a paper coffee cup at him. "Double espresso, my brother."

"Thanks," replied Jack, smiling. "And thanks again for being on time. Your leadership by example is just exceptional."

Even with all that had gone on in recent years, Danny Winters made Jack, and frankly everyone around him, smile. Danny was brilliant and irreverent, and unless someone was shooting at him or one of his team members, nearly always relaxed and full of humor.

"Jack, you know that I am just trying to level the playing field, give everybody a head start so that maybe they can keep up with me."

Danny smiled while putting his feet up on Jack's desk, eliciting a frown from the desk's owner. Danny's feet, like the rest of him, were enormous. Jack found himself staring into the waffle soles of Danny's combat boots or, as Danny called them, "his slippers."

Danny stretched back in his chair, ran his hands over his tightly trimmed hair, and proclaimed, "Am I not the most beautiful black man in Texas?"

It took a while, but Jack finally stopped laughing. "I actually have been waiting for you to get in, Danny. We need to go to the closet."

The professional soldier across from him snapped to attention, the boots hitting the floor with an audible thud. The "closet" was a term they used for the SCIF.

Settling back into the SCIF, Jack retold Danny the story of the Texas Compact that he had heard the day before. Danny was uncharacteristically quiet and listened intently to every word. When Jack finished talking, he sat watching Danny, while his friend leaned back, eyes closed and hands together, almost clasped in prayer. The room was deadly quiet, with only the soft hum of the air-handling system. Jack continued to wait, until finally Danny leaned forward.

"I am not sure what to say," said Danny, rarely, if ever, caught speechless.

"I understand your quandary," replied Jack. "There are a lot of moral questions I have been wrestling with all night."

"Hell, Jack, personally I don't care what the damn thing says or does not say, but I doubt the press, our people, or people around the globe are going to see things the same way. There is no question that we have to find this damned thing."

"It's not going to be easy to find a single piece of paper in the chaos up there," offered Jack.

"You know that I just came back from there," Danny said softly. "It's a total mess. Order is nonexistent, food is scarce, disease rampant, and crime is off the charts. Remember that time we had to go to Somalia and deal with those terrorists? It's like Somalia there. Fucking Somalia."

"Danny, you know I have not been up there since…Well, you know." Jack stopped. "But I am well aware from the field reports how bad it is."

"Look, Jack, it's no problem. I can take a team and go."

Danny was always ready, something that drove his wife of ten years, Cynthia, crazy. She rejoiced when Danny joined the clandestine service because she thought his SEAL days of danger and travel were behind him, only to find him volunteering for the most dangerous assignments. Danny thrived on the adrenaline rush and truly believed that a leader's place was only in the front. Cynthia constantly complained to Jack about Danny and asked him to limit Danny's assignments. Danny asked for the opposite.

"Danny, I am in on this one. Appreciate your friendship always, but it's not open to discussion," Jack said matter-of-factly. "Frankly, I sat awake last night and decided that it might actually help me move forward. Anyway, we need to start making a mission plan. Herring is already gathering all the data he can, but let's be clear, we are going into a war zone, searching for a single needle in a stack of needles. This would be a difficult document to find under the best of circumstances, but with the kind of chaos up there, it's impossible."

"That is exactly what I am worried about," said Danny. "When I go up north, I like to go in with an absolutely clear objective, accomplish the op, and get out fast. Searching every bookshelf in Washington is not going to be quick, and slow equals danger."

"Also, this is absolute need-to-know, and besides you, Herring, and me, we are under strict orders that no one else needs to know exactly what the Texas Compact says. Actually, you are not even supposed to know, but I want you to know in case something happens. We need to succeed here."

Danny made a face and said, "Jack, I do not like keeping the team in the dark."

"Noted," replied Jack.

*

Harper Packing Company, Austin, Texas, Republic of Texas

March 14, 2025, 4:36 p.m. Central

"Christ." Jack nearly jumped out of his chair upon seeing Danny Winters standing silently in the corner of his office. "Why the hell do you do that?"

Winters's grin stretched from ear to ear. "It never gets old. You just get lost in that computer screen. I could bring a marching band in here and you wouldn't notice."

"Shut up," said Jack Dodge, smiling. "You are going to give me a heart attack one of these days. I assume you're here because you came up with a plan." Dodge leaned back in his chair and stared at his friend.

"I have the outlines of a plan to go over with you. I think we can do this with a team of four and some local support on the ground. We should go to the closet so I can walk you through it. You can try to poke holes in it, though it's perfect. Who knows? I might pretend to accept some of your suggestions to make you feel better."

Jack smiled because he knew that the plan would be well developed, even if only in rough draft form. Winters was a gifted tactician and a very detail-oriented guy.

Three hours later, Danny leaned back in his chair. The chair creaked in protest against the bulk it was being asked to support.

"I think we have it," Danny announced.

The two men had been going back and forth, challenging each element of the plan. The whiteboard at the end of the SCIF was a mess, with half-erased items and arrows heading in every direction, but they had taken Danny's outline and turned it into a detailed, actionable plan.

It was a relatively simple plan. A four-person team consisting of Dodge, Winters, Justin Manning, a computer and communications specialist, and Britney Marelli, a former CIA agent and now Texas field operative, would infiltrate Washington, supported by one local resource. Using whatever information Alan Herring could source, they would begin the hunt for the Texas Compact, most likely at the Library of Congress, based on early research. The plan was to find the document and any related documents they could and get out quickly. The thing they could not plan for was what would happen if the document could not be found in any of the possible locations Herring might identify.

"I think we should start bringing Britney and Justin up to speed," said Jack. "I also think we should reach out to the quartermaster and get him working on the supplies we will need for this little trip."

"Done," said Danny as he watched Jack scrub down the whiteboard with a special cleaning fluid that eliminated any trace markings. The papers dropped into the shredder in the corner that, unlike a normal shredder, cut them horizontally as well as vertically, leaving only confetti that fell into a burn bag. Content that all traces of their strategy session other than the final plan on Danny's secure tablet were erased, they departed.

Austin, Texas, Republic of Texas

March 16, 2025, 9:50 p.m. Central

The two Dodge men sat in the living room of an apartment one of their companies kept for visiting executives. The building was adjacent to the Four Seasons Hotel in downtown Austin. Though comfortable, the apartment was not opulent. It had simple furnishings, Western Art, and a bit of a contemporary feel.

After an hour, the conversation waned as they waited for the first minister to arrive. He was speaking at a banquet at the Four Seasons Hotel, and their current location offered a minimum of travel time and therefore possible attention. Jack walked his father through the plan twice, and the old man made a couple of worthwhile suggestions, while asking several thoughtful questions that Jack knew would lead to refinements when he could review them with the team. After a while both men just sat in the comfort of each other's company and sipped scotch.

As the grandfather clock in the hallway struck ten, Jack heard a rap on the door. He stood to greet the first minister as he walked down the hall and nodded to the two agents who came in with him.

"Good evening, First Minister," Jack said, reaching out to shake hands.

The elder Dodge gave the first minister a full Jackson.

The Republic's leader asked the agents to wait outside so they could all speak privately, which they did after a quick inspection of the apartment.

"Nice to see you again, especially so quickly, Jack," the first minister started off as he took a chair. "I'm sorry to be late, but my dinner ran over because the damned speaker droned on and on. There was no good way to excuse myself to attend an unscheduled secret meeting."

"Would you like a nightcap, First Minister?" Jack asked, standing next to an open armoire that revealed nearly every spirit anyone could desire.

The first minister looked at the large tumbler in front of Jackson Dodge and requested the same.

Handing over the drink, Jack took his place across from the two men and began his report. The first minister listened without interruption until Jack had concluded fifteen minutes later.

"What are your thoughts, Jackson?" the leader of the Republic of Texas asked.

"I think it's a good plan," offered Jackson Dodge. "Small team, minimal footprint, targeted, based on the best intelligence we can gather. My only worry is that we are looking for a needle in a haystack that has been on fire for three years, and where no one even knew there was a needle in the first place. Finding it is going to be a bit like winning the lottery, twice."

The first minister got up, walked to the windows of the apartment, and stared down at the black space where Lake Austin sat, invisible in the dark night. Neither Dodge did anything to interrupt him while he stood quietly and sipped his scotch.

Without turning, he finally spoke. "Jack, this thing is too important to leave even the slightest possibility of it existing. You need to chase down every lead, and if you cannot find it, you need to destroy whatever you do find that points to it so that there is no chance we leave it to be found by someone else."

Jack thought for a second. "First Minister, I want to be very clear. We will chase down the leads anywhere they send us. Failing to find the documents, you want us to destroy anything else we find that is related, in case we miss something. Also, I assume that I can take it on your authority that we can deal with any party or parties that we need to accomplish the mission."

"That is exactly what I am saying. My office will deliver signed orders in the morning giving you full authority to request any and all cooperation and resources necessary."

CHAPTER ELEVEN

Fort Meade, Maryland, former USA

March 18, 2025, 11:22 a.m. Eastern

Mulvaney sat in his office and looked down at the floor below and saw that a couple of the desks were actually occupied. However, he doubted any work was being done on behalf of his former country. About three months before, Mulvaney had found that one of his computer analysts was running one of the largest human-trafficking rings in the Washington area, using the agency's computers to redirect what little law enforcement and military remained and to help move his cargo. Mulvaney had had the analyst arrested and placed in one of the military prisons that had sprung up, but he heard that the analyst had bought his freedom a few days later with a couple of well-placed bribes. The only laws still enforced were those being written in gold or by a gun.

A slight knock on his door brought Mulvaney out of his daydream, and he looked up to see Stan Reed, a hulking computer analyst, standing in the doorway.

"Boss, you have a minute?" Reed's thin voice was incongruous with his bearlike physique.

"I have nothing but minutes," Mulvaney responded, and Reed ambled over to one of the office's visitor chairs. He lowered his massive bulk into the chair, and then distractedly ran his right hand through the thick, messy mop of black hair that topped his head. He pulled out a few sheets of paper and began speaking.

"I have been trying to track Herring's movements online."

Mulvaney felt himself shift forward in his chair. His entire body leaned and tensed involuntarily. "Go on." He did not want to break Reed's flow.

Reed looked down at the notes in front of him. "About a month ago, one of the computers at Harper accessed our system, but whoever was using it did not properly mask and secure their activities. While they were interrogating our computers, I gained access through their connection and limited access to their overall network." Reed paused and looked up. Receiving a nod of encouragement from Mulvaney, he continued. "Their stuff is good. The encryption is extremely strong, and the design of their systems is simple and elegant. It is clearly the next generation of where we were."

"Alan was always very good. Have you been able to maintain this access?"

Reed cleared his throat. "Kind of. I am in the system, but it is incredibly hard to maneuver, and I can only do limited things."

"What sort of limited things?" asked Mulvaney. Even in the early days of the breakup, when the NSA was still fully staffed and functioning, Herring's systems had been one step ahead. The NSA had been able to read Putin's secure email to his rhythmic gymnastics lover along with his daily briefings, but the Republic of Texas systems had proven nearly unbreakable.

"Well, I can see some of their outbound traffic before it is masked," replied Reed. "That is the thing that has really piqued my attention. For the past few days, they have had a massive amount of traffic interrogating our system, numerous other agencies, libraries, universities, and research institutions looking at historical documents."

"Why didn't you discuss this with me when it first started?" asked Mulvaney, trying hard to sound neutral. He could not get mad at Reed; heck, the guy was not paid anymore, and the fact that he was doing any real work was a surprise. At the same time, habits were hard to break, and Vince Mulvaney wanted to be kept informed of whatever was happening.

Reed hemmed and hawed and finally said, "I did not want to tell you until there was something worth discussing."

Mulvaney nodded and then urged Reed to continue.

"I am not sure what they are doing. They are pulling massive amounts of data related to American history from 1840 to the present. If I did not know better, it would look like they are trying to create a comprehensive catalog of American political history."

"They have never cared much for America or American history, as evidenced by their actions." Mulvaney tapped the desk with a pencil for a considerable while. "Stan, keep on this. My gut tells me there is something important here. And keep it between us."

"Got it," said the analyst as he hefted himself up to leave.

Mulvaney watched him go. He sat for a while in his office thinking but decided he needed to discuss it with someone else, so he picked up the phone. The NSA still had dedicated telephony circuits, so unlike the rest of the area, their lines generally worked. This was in spite of many telephone central offices having been ransacked for copper and electrical equipment, or just fallen into disrepair.

The familiar voice on the other end of the phone answered, and Mulvaney quickly outlined what he had learned so far.

"What do you think it means?" asked Listir. Mulvaney could hear Listir take a drag on a cigarette.

"I am not sure. I was hoping you might have some ideas," replied Mulvaney.

"Could they be looking for something? Something to provide moral or historical justification for some action they want to take?"

Listir closed his eyes and thought. The Texans had been very careful to justify every move that they made with historic documents, geographic features, even Spanish and Native American history. Maybe they had some new piece of the former US they wanted, or some way to further justify their existing claims. Not that they needed to, because possession had proven to be not nine-tenths of the law but simply the law.

"What else is there for them to take?" Mulvaney hated the Republic of Texas. He hated watching it take his life's work and make it meaningless. All he had ever tried to do was secure the United States, and on his watch the United States had ceased to exist. He saw the Republic's existence as a personal failure.

"I will swing by later today and bring you a present. I was able to score some real scotch, not that crap you have," said Listir, smiling as he looked at the rows of shelves stocked with the best of the best. Business was very good, and throwing the NSA guy some liquor to gain access to their systems was well worth it.

Austin, Texas, Republic of Texas

March 18, 2025, 11:45 a.m. Central

Jack blew on his coffee and looked at his team. Justin, Britney, Alan, and Danny were all staring back at him. The team had worked together numerous times before, most recently on an operation in Panama, where they took down a network that was trafficking both people and drugs into the Republic of Texas. They knew each other well, but even more than that trusted each other and their respective skills. After serious reflection, Jack had gone against his orders and decided to tell Britney and Justin; Danny had persuaded him that they needed to know.

"OK, everyone knows why we are here, so why don't we get down to business and start going over what needs to be done?" Jack looked around the table and found Britney shaking her head. "Britney, you want to go a different direction?"

"I want to discuss this a little bit," Britney replied in a strong, confident voice, pushing a strand of her long black hair out of her eyes.

Britney Marelli was thirty-three years old, half-Mexican and half-Italian. Tall, thin, with olive skin and dark eyes. She was beautiful, smart, and tougher than most men. Time and again the opposition had underestimated Britney. Best of all, she was incredibly calm in difficult situations.

Jack inclined his head and Britney continued. "You know I do not mind going into high-risk places. But it seems a bit absurd that we are going into a place as dangerous as Washington, DC, to find an old piece of paper, no matter how morally or politically dangerous it is. Let's be real: it's a hundred seventy years old, and though it makes me sick, it will not change anything." She paused and saw Justin was nodding in agreement. "DC is a mess, and we are going to find some piece of paper in the middle of all that?"

"Britney, I understand your concerns, but the first minister says this is important and one of his primary concerns." Jack paused. "I have violated my direct orders by telling you all what we are seeking, and I know you all understand its importance. All of us will need to wrestle with our consciences and with risking our lives for it. I want you both on this mission, but if you want off, I will respect that decision."

Britney stared at the ceiling for a while and then said, "I don't want out, but I wish we were going into Cuba or somewhere else after some bad guys."

Justin sat with his head bowed, his close-cropped brown hair the only thing visible. Raised in Midland, Texas, Justin had been a standout athlete in both baseball and soccer, with an unbelievable gift for math and science, but it came with a daredevil streak. After Justin was locked up one more time for going 125 miles per hour in a 25 mph zone, his dad walked him down to the recruiting station, and the army had found a way to marry Justin's capabilities with his desired level of excitement. They called it Delta. Within Delta, he had made a name for himself as having a gift with computers, gadgets, anything with an on/off switch.

"Britney raises a good point, Danny. This feels bad. I am not thrilled about what this document says. For the first time I questioned my right to be a Texan. I understand why we need it back. It is potentially explosive, dangerous even, but probably not fatal to the Republic. On the other hand, there are a lot of things I do not mind getting shot at over, but old pieces of paper are way down that list." Justin looked up from the table as he spoke and locked his brown eyes directly at Danny. "But I am good to go."

Danny looked over at Britney.

"I am good, Danny," replied Britney.

Danny nodded at both, and then everyone turned their attention to Alan Herring.

Herring looked around the SCIF and opened the file in front of him. He leafed through a couple of pages, then pulled out a blue-bordered document. "I have been searching every database I can find in order to get some leads. Let me start with what I do know. There were six principal actors in the discussions around Texas's debts, land claims, the expansion of slavery, and all the other issues: Houston, Webster, Douglas, Clay, Seward, and Dickinson. We can expand this group a bit and assume that the president of the United States, secretary of the Treasury, attorney general and the governor of Texas at a minimum would have all been involved in some way." Herring flipped pages and continued. "This constitutes a minimum of ten people who would have had a reason to directly know about the negotiations between Texas and the United States. However, I think the number should reasonably be closer to twenty, because almost every single one of those people had a personal secretary, more like an aide-de-camp, with whom they shared nearly everything. This is what I considered the core group for the analysis we did.

"Given the fact that there is only one copy of the agreement here in the Texas Archives, I feel it is logical that there is only one other copy in existence," Herring continued.

"Why is that a safe assumption, Professor?"

Justin always called Herring "Professor" due to his speaking style and overall bearing. Herring's annoyance at the term was obvious to all.

Herring's face briefly flashed anger before he answered calmly. "There is no definitive answer to your question, Justin. However, based on the factors that we think we know—and I emphasize think—it seems logical. One, the compact was clearly secret and intended to stay that way. Two, I can find no mention of the document in any searchable database, research document, or published materials. Three, there were only two sides to this agreement, Texas and the rest of the United States. Four, we only stumbled upon our copy by mistake. Therefore, my assumption is that Sam Houston received one signed copy, and another signed copy was left on the side of the United States with one of the other parties. If there had been more, I feel like it would have been found by some enterprising researcher."

Herring stared at Justin.

Justin stood up, went to a whiteboard, and wrote down everyone Herring had just mentioned with a "+1" next to each of the ten names. He then turned back to the group.

"Professor, so your number is really not twenty, because we take out Houston and the governor of Texas plus their two aides, so we are really talking about sixteen potential parties, correct?"

Danny smiled. Both Justin Manning and Alan Herring were brilliant, and their discussions almost always improved the team's analysis, but rarely the relations between the two men.

"Justin, can you please drop the professor title?" Herring moaned. He looked at Justin's whiteboard. "Yes, sixteen would seem to be the logical starting universe. But I made some further eliminations. Though probably privy to the discussions, I think it highly unlikely that the president, attorney general, secretary of the treasury, or their folks would keep the document."

"Sorry," Jack interjected. "Not being as fast as Justin, Professor, can you please walk through why you eliminated those six?" Jack gave Herring a winning smile but received an icy glare in return.

"OK, the next person who calls me 'Professor' is going to have the mother of all viruses installed in their home systems," said Herring. He glared at each of the other four, and then he walked over to the whiteboard. "If you look at this list of ten people, I think it is informative that there are only six names on the document, and that they were all sitting US senators. My team and I spent a bunch of time looking at this period of American history, and the Senate was significantly more active than in the modern era in actually driving the legislative agenda. It seems likely to us that this was a deal developed and executed in the Senate.

"What we have been trying to figure out is where the document might have been lodged. For instance, Senator Webster's papers can be found at the Library of Congress, Dartmouth, and the New Hampshire Historical Society, amongst other places. Most of the senators on the list stand amongst the most famous members of that body of all time. Numerous books and monographs have been written about each and every one of these men and the events they helped shape. We made a hypothesis that the more famous the senator, the less likely they were to have held the other copy; therefore, we are not going after Webster as a starting point. A Webster researcher would have found it.

"Our next hypothesis was that the document stayed in DC, more likely than not, as that is the largest pool in which a drop of water might hide, so we are starting with the Library of Congress's collection."

"Do we know what the status of any of these facilities is, either from your research or, Danny, from any of our on-the-ground assets?" asked Justin.

"There has been damage to many of the facilities and their collections," said Herring. "For instance, in New York, we know that the New York Historical Society was burned to the ground, so all of its works are assumed to be lost. The Library of Congress suffered extensive damage to the Madison Building when it was looted and fires were set. The other two buildings seem to be intact, though what looting has taken place we simply cannot gauge. We know that within these facilities there are storage facilities that are designed to securely seal off, so there may be significant amounts of surviving materials."

"All right, Alan, back to your analysis." Jack stood up, went to the board, and circled the five non-Texan senators' names. "So, if we accept this rationale, it still leaves us with nearly ten individuals who might possess the document. How do we narrow it down further? And let's assume that we can narrow it down, how do we figure out where to look if these people's papers are spread amongst so many different locations if we cannot find it in DC? We cannot really spend an extended period of time over the border. Eventually, we will attract attention."

"Those are the two seminal questions, Jack, and I am working on both of them," offered Alan. "We have an operating hypothesis that the individual who had the document in their possession is either obscure enough that their papers do not attract any scholarly interest, or their papers are so voluminous that the single sheet of the Compact could be lost amongst thousands of pages of documents."

"We also have to think about what ends we are willing to go to before we decide that we are on a fool's errand," said Britney. "It has been almost one hundred seventy years. This document could very well have been lost or destroyed anytime over the past two centuries. Also, we are talking about going into territory that is incredibly hostile, where we have limited on-the-ground assets, and where the multiplication of possible targets for each individual is nearly unknowable. Hell, even I know that some of Daniel Webster's papers are in private collectors' hands, or were."

"Good points, Britney," said Jack. "This is not our typical assignment, where we go and neutralize someone who is hostile to the Republic, or recover data or intelligence that we need, but this is very serious." Jack looked at everyone around the table. "We are going to have to narrow the target set as well as we can and then try and execute this mission."

Herring jumped back in. "We are going to continue to analyze these ten individuals through every database we can. Give us a couple of more days."

"I want to be in a position to go over the border in three days," said Jack. "We need to finalize a target list quickly so we can get some accurate intel of the on-the-ground situation. Also, we need to get our local resources ready. Alan, we need you to have narrowed the search list as much as possible by the end of the day tomorrow so that we can finalize our plans. Possible?" inquired Jack, still standing at the whiteboard.

"We'll do our best," said Herring. "As we get closer, I will load four of the mini-tablets with the background data on each individual, the distribution of their papers, and the available schematics on each of these locations. I will also pull in all known threats in each of the areas, and possible open transit routes to each site." Herring got up and exited the SCIF after finishing.

"Britney, let's move on to weapons," said Danny after the door closed behind Herring.

*

Fort Meade, Maryland, former USA

March 18, 2025, 6:46 p.m. Eastern

Mulvaney walked down the rows of empty cubes. The light from the screen in Reed's cube stood out as literally the only bright spot in the entire cube farm.

"You are working late?" Mulvaney said, peering over the wall of the cube.

"Nowhere to go," said Reed. "Wife left me over a year ago and went back to her parents' home in upstate New York," he added.

This type of story had become wildly common as people left spouses and families to go wherever they could that might be safer for them. Nothing like chaos to bring out everyone's survival instincts. They said the Civil War divided brothers; the destruction of the US divided everyone.

"I am sorry," offered Mulvaney quietly.

Reed just shrugged. There was a long, awkward silence before Mulvaney finally broke it.

"Have you found anything else?"

Reed grabbed a notepad off his desk. "I found a little bit more today. There were a couple of moments when I had clear access to their outbound traffic. It all continued to be focused around historical figures and sites." Reed looked up and continued. "They did a huge amount of research on Senate history and the Library of Congress."

Mulvaney leaned against the back wall of the cube and stared at the ceiling. "There is no way that Alan Herring is doing archival research on behalf of the Republic of Texas. This has to be intelligence related. Herring is simply too valuable." He paused for a long period of time. "They are looking for something, but what? Jack Dodge would not waste Herring's time, and there is no way Herring would deign to do it if it wasn't important.

"Reed, continue monitoring their traffic, but meanwhile can you cross-reference everyone and everything they have searched for with Texas-related historical matters and see what you come up with?" Mulvaney's eyes bored into the analyst.

"I will do the best I can," offered Reed, "with what we have."

Mulvaney knew that was not much.

*

Outside Austin, Texas, Republic of Texas

March 18, 2025, 7:00 p.m. Central

Jack arrived home to find his father's government-issue SUV parked in the courtyard and two agents standing by the vehicle.

"Good evening, Tom. Mike," said Jack as he exited his Explorer and walked up the steps of his house. "How long has the ol' man been inside?"

"Hi, Jack," replied the senior agent, Tom Murphy, checking his watch. "He's been waiting about twenty minutes."

"Great. All my scotch is gone," replied Jack, slipping inside as the agents tried to suppress their grins.

"Dad?" Jack called out while standing in the stone foyer.

"Out on the patio and running perilously low on hooch," replied his father's booming voice.

Jack walked into the pantry and grabbed a full bottle of eighteen-year-old Glenfiddich. He picked up a heavy crystal glass from the bar, filled it with ice, and headed out to the patio.

Jackson Dodge sat on one of the chaises and held out his glass for Jack with a big smile on his face. Jack walked over, uncapped the bottle, and poured a healthy measure of scotch. He filled his own glass and sat down on the chaise next to his father.

"You should have let me know you were coming over, and I would've been here to meet you," offered Jack as they sat staring at the lights of Austin.

"Just a spur-of-the-moment thing. I wanted to check in and see how the plan is coming along."

"Dad, how worried are you about this?" said Jack, moving so he was sitting sideways on the chaise and could look directly at his father.

"I do not like it at all," said his father. "The world has fallen apart, and we have built a pocket of stability out of the remnants of a once-great empire. Europe has descended into anarchy, with the exception of Germany and the Nordics, but even the German situation post-EU is difficult. Without booming exports, German unemployment has soared, and the only thing holding back a collapse is their rearmament. Think 1933. You were just there. What did you see?"

Jack had just returned from Germany, where he met with his counterpart on security issues. Though the industrialized world was falling apart, they still had to contend with Muslim extremism, a problem made worse by the complete disarray in France, and the seething eighteenth, nineteenth, and twentieth arrondissements of Paris. Sharia law was the law in those arrondissements and Marseilles, and roving bands were brutally enforcing the measures. Stonings had become common in Paris. The Germans were dealing with their own issues by deporting Turks by the trainload.

"It's literally like an old movie; everywhere you look are blond men in uniforms."

"In Asia, the states are splintering faster than we can figure out what to call 'em, and insurgencies and battles are breaking out all over Southeast Asia. What's interesting is that some of the poorest countries are actually holdin' up the best." Jackson paused and smiled. "Who would've ever thought that Argentina would be one of the more stable countries? But it is. I guess they had the most experience dealing with crises. I can go on and on, but basically the world has fallen apart, while we are rebuilding. We have food, oil, gas, minerals, and a purpose. This document probably would not change anything, but it might diminish our sense of purpose and our moral authority."

The two men sat in silence for a while. Jackson closed his eyes and appeared to be sleeping, but Jack knew he was just thinking. His father often closed his eyes when he wanted to focus.

Finally, Jack broke the silence. "We have a solid final plan, but this is not going to be easy, and success is not a sure thing." Jack then walked his father through the plan in detail, with the old man poking holes in different elements and offering advice. They went over it a couple of times before Jackson stood up to leave.

"I will let Lufkin know these last changes," said Jackson Dodge as he turned to go.

Jack walked him to the door and received a full Jackson from his father.

"Remember, there's one thing more important than finding the compact, and that's you comin' back safely," said Jackson Dodge before he walked out the door to his car.

Jack watched the taillights on the SUV as it wound down the drive. He could not remember a time before when his father had been openly worried, even when he and Lufkin were leading the secession.

CHAPTER TWELVE

Austin-Bergstrom Airport, Texas, Republic of Texas

March 20, 2025, 7:00 a.m. Central

The team stood in the hangar and watched their gear being loaded into the cargo of the Citation X. The tail had the familiar Harper Cattle longhorn symbol emblazoned in red and black across its otherwise gleaming white surface.

The arrival of a Harper Cattle aircraft attracted very little attention in many parts of the world. Today, the team would fly to Richmond, Virginia, where there would be two vehicles waiting for them, provided by the Richmond field office. This would be their jumping-off point for the move over the border.

"Jack, we're ready to go if y'all are," said Captain Michael Ramsey, a pilot Jack had known for years. Ramsey was short, fit, with a buzz cut and simple black glasses. Ramsey knew how to keep his mouth tightly closed. He also willingly flew into some very dangerous places.

"All set, Mike," Jack replied, and the team hustled up the airstairs and into the tight cabin.

The Citation X sat eight passengers but offered a very narrow cabin. The plane's design sacrificed spaciousness for speed.

Captain Ramsey did his required safety briefing and then climbed into the cockpit beside his copilot, Todd Peterson. Peterson looked like Ramsey's twin, only ten years younger.

He turned around from the cockpit's left seat after consulting with Peterson, and said, "We should be there in just under two hours, but there is some fog in the area, so we may have to circle a bit. We'll keep you updated."

Jack nodded, and the team settled into the club chairs and pulled out their tablets, going over the mission plan in detail again. Midway through the flight, the team had already drained the plane's coffeepot.

Almost exactly two hours from takeoff, the Citation X rolled out down a wet runway at Richmond International Airport and turned off the taxiways toward the fixed base operator. Outside the plane's windows, fog hung in the air, and a light rain fell.

The team walked around to the tail, grabbed the duffels containing part of their gear, and headed for fixed base operation building. They walked through the small building and emerged to find a thin black man with a beard, diamond ear stud, and sunglasses in a rain slicker standing next to two older-model Ford Explorers. The Explorers had old DC plates.

The man quickly walked over to Danny and they shook hands. It was clear they had met before.

Danny took a quick look around and, seeing no one else, he said, "Jack, this is Simon Baker."

Jack shook the man's hand and found the grip very solid. Jack had read Simon's field reports and knew Danny highly regarded the man's skills and contacts.

"Why don't you load your gear in the two vehicles and we can get moving?" Simon pointed to the two SUVs. "Jack, you and Danny can ride with me, and Justin and Britney can follow in the other vehicle."

The team loaded the duffels as an airport worker and Mike Ramsey pushed a cart through the sliding glass door with a couple of hard aluminum cases, which they loaded into Justin's vehicle. Justin looked at the two cases and made sure they were secure.

Danny leaned over to Simon. "He is very protective of his babies." In this case, the babies being computer gear, communications equipment, and drones.

When the gear was loaded, Jack got in the front passenger seat next to Simon. Danny sat behind Jack and stretched his legs out across the back seat, leaving wet marks from his boots across the stained cloth seats. Simon checked the other car in his mirror. Seeing that they were ready, he slipped the car into gear and headed for the airport access road.

"We have a safe house in Fredericksburg, really a safe apartment." Simon talked while simultaneously driving the car and monitoring Britney and Justin's vehicle. Traffic was surprisingly heavy. "I am going to take us there, and we can go over the plan. Also, I have the identification cards that will allow us to pass through the checkpoints and make our way into DC. We will spend the night in Fredericksburg and enter the District at dawn. That will give us a full day of daylight to work with."

"We are still going in as an aid team assessing medical needs?" Danny asked.

"Yes," replied Simon. "Recently, a couple of the barely still-functioning hospitals found themselves low on basic medicine, and there were many reported deaths from everyday illnesses. The Republic regularly monitors the situation, because as you know we don't want epidemics slipping over the border. Recently, we shipped in penicillin and other urgently needed basic drugs, but medical care is getting worse every day. Any doctor with a connection to the Republic has relocated; those who have stayed are trapped or true humanitarians. Either way they are overwhelmed, and our aid workers have become regular visitors."

"Can you give us a sitrep on the security situation?" Danny interjected.

"Sure. The on-the-ground situation in DC is dangerous, as you well know. Crime is rampant, and basically gangs are controlling the city block by block. Different block, different gangs. Turf wars are constant. The former federal government still has control of a few facilities, and there are still some employees who are showing up and manning their jobs, trying to figure out what to do. Going into DC is not easy. We can expect some problems. We may need to pay bribes. We also run the risk of being tracked, either by the criminals or remnants of the former federal authorities, some of which are trying to reestablish authority, or just displace the criminals with their own 'gang.' The best course of action is to go in with a specific target in mind, hit it hard, and get out."

"How are our on-the-ground assets?" asked Jack.

"We have multiple safe houses in DC, and we have cultivated a pretty good network of informants," said Simon. "Additionally, we have relationships with some of the larger gangs, which we feed with a supply of black-market goods they can resell in return for information or support."

"What about the situation beyond DC?" Danny asked.

The visibility had worsened, and traffic was moving quite slowly. Simon's hands clearly tightened on the wheel, as evidenced by his whitening knuckles. Very few red taillights could be seen ahead due to the poor visibility.

"About three months ago, you may recall that we had to go up to Wilmington to retrieve a package." Jack saw Simon grip the wheel a little harder as he spoke. "It depends on where you need to go outside the city. Many towns have set up roadblocks and barricades to keep criminals and looters from entering their areas. In certain areas, former military authorities have set themselves up almost as mini-warlords. It's an expensive and difficult proposition to move from one location to another. Things get easier above Philadelphia, where General Rogers has carved out most of New Jersey and parts of Pennsylvania, dipping down into Maryland, into the Mid-Atlantic Military District. Rogers controlled Fort Dix and used his position to prepare for the fall. When the US collapsed, Rogers was ready and has established a military dictatorship that is expanding. Things are increasingly normal in his area of control."

All of a sudden it was like someone turned on the lights. The fog lifted, and traffic picked up.

"You all ever see a movie called *Escape from New York*?" asked Simon.

"Sure, Kurt Russell played Snake Plissken, fighting his way through Manhattan, which had been turned into a prison," answered Danny. "Awesome movie."

"Well, now you know what New York City is like," said Simon, who flipped on the blinker and headed for the off-ramp.

Jack sat quietly for a while, and then said, "But it can be done? You can travel around the Northeast?"

"Sure, Jack," replied Simon. "You give me access to enough Texas money, medicine, and other goods to bribe people, and we can get around. However, it will not be safe; certain parts are very dangerous."

Danny laughed. "Simon, merry Christmas. We have enough

firepower to have a celebration, and bags full of everything we could need to make friends and influence people."

*

The SUVs turned off the road into a modern suburban apartment complex composed of multiple two-story buildings. The buildings were Tudor in style, which explained the sign out front labeling the complex "Manor Village." The faux Tudor building had multiple small balconies, each of which seemed to contain a Weber grill.

Simon followed the street through the complex to the building at the very end of the roadway. They turned into a spot marked with yellow spray paint "Building 7, Unit 2C Only."

Danny looked out the front window and remarked, "This place is the Ritz compared to the safe house in Mexico."

Jack laughed as they all got out of the SUV. The safe house they had used in Mexico was a small adobe hut, with an outhouse and a wide selection of large bugs as fellow occupants. To add to its ambience, it smelled of body odor and general decay.

Without any direction, all five took up stations and examined the surrounding buildings and windows. Seeing no prying eyes, they relaxed a bit.

Simon and Britney completed a quick canvas of the building entrance and hallway and the apartment. The team unloaded the gear and moved it up the stucco-walled stairwell and down the pastel-carpeted hall. Arriving at 2C, Simon opened the door, and they filed into the small, spare living room and stacked the gear against one side of the room.

Britney made a pot of coffee while Simon unpacked a bag of sandwiches he had bought on his way to the airport. Justin broke out a handheld sensor and did a sweep for bugs, declaring the apartment clean. When everyone had a mug of coffee, the five crammed in around the small wooden dining table, and Britney unrolled the now-familiar map of the Library of Congress area of Capitol Hill.

"Working with Herring's analysis, we believe that the information we are looking for is most likely located in the Jefferson Building if it is still there or ever was," Britney began. "Herring has identified three primary and three secondary targets whose documents we are going after."

They went over the plan the entirety of the afternoon.

As the sun began to set, the parking facility outside the building filled with returning office workers. Eventually, the team grilled steaks on the Weber on their small balcony, made a large salad, and enjoyed a few Coors Lights. They went to sleep early; the mission plan called for a long and potentially stressful day to follow.

CHAPTER THIRTEEN

Arlington Memorial Bridge, Virginia, Republic of Texas

March 21, 2025, 5:08 a.m. Eastern

The arc lights illuminated the Republic of Texas side of the bridge, while across the river most was in total darkness. The Lincoln Memorial was faintly visible with the coming of day. They wanted to be early to have as much daylight as possible with which to work.

Simon edged the lead SUV toward the barricade. They all watched the soldiers surround the truck in front of him. One soldier climbed up on the passenger-side running board and examined the driver through the window, while two more opened the cargo hold and another examined the driver's papers. Two gun emplacements backed up the four soldiers around the vehicle, one on either side of the examination area. Farther on, beyond the steel barriers and the tire-shredding barriers, were more gun emplacements facing the bridge and DC.

Danny watched gunboats move lazily on the Potomac, with large searchlights scanning the water. He counted five in total, two toward the 14th Street Bridges and three moving upriver.

"Lots of gunboats," said Danny to no one in particular.

"Yes, the increase in the number of illegals trying to get out of the US territory caused an increase in border security everywhere, but especially here," Simon offered. "After the Republic did the last mass deportation, many of the illegals stayed in the District, trying to figure out how to make it back over the border, but the wall that was built has really made it difficult for them. Funny thing that the wall was built here and not on the Mexican border."

The truck was waved through, barriers were dropped, and it drove onto the bridge. Simon moved his SUV into position and noted that Britney advanced to the ready spot.

"Good morning, sir. Papers please," asked the sergeant, his team in position around the SUV.

Jack turned and looked at the soldier outside his window, a stern-looking young man with the Republic of Texas flag sewn on his left soldier—red, white, and blue vertical lines with a single gold star in the middle.

"Purpose of your transit," continued the sergeant as he thumbed through their paperwork. The paperwork would pass any inspection, since Simon had had it issued directly from the appropriate ministry. The documents were genuine, the information within completely fabricated.

"As our papers state, we are from the Republic Ministry of Health on our way to assess what medical relief needs to be offered. We cannot have an outbreak of disease over there getting out of control. It could end up here."

The soldier nodded in agreement.

"One more thing, Sergeant. That SUV behind us has two more

members of our team."

"All right, Doctor," answered the sergeant. "Your paperwork looks good. You are free to enter, but remember that it is dangerous in there, and it is my duty to inform you that no Republic of Texas forces will be sent into the area under any circumstances, so please use extreme caution. You are on your own once you pass this checkpoint. Good luck."

The sergeant waved them through and turned his attention to Justin and Britney as the barriers slid down. Simon engaged the SUV, and they began driving across the bridge. Jack looked out the window, seeing that the signs hanging on the barbed wire facing DC said, "Halt! Live Fire Area! No crossing without clearance!"

Jack looked ahead to the Lincoln Memorial, no longer gleaming white the way it had been when he lived in DC, now dingy and graying. When Jack left for Texas, it was just after Marissa's death. Things were difficult, and crime was rising, but the United States of America still existed. The view outside Jack's window was of another world. Briefing photos could not do justice to the decay.

As they turned onto Ohio Drive and drove past the Lincoln Memorial, Simon had to maneuver around significant debris in the street. Outside the car, people emerged from the tents and lean-tos erected on the grass around the monument. Jack could see the tent city stretching down what used to be the Mall.

"Justin's close behind us, so we are good. City seems quiet. Barring any surprises, we should be at the safe house near Fifth and A Street Southeast in about thirty minutes," said Simon right before he swerved to avoid an oil drum that sat in the middle of the street.

"They build their fires in the oil drums to not only keep warm but also to cook with as some kind of improvised grill," offered up Simon. "We are going to make a number of moves to ensure that we are not followed. You all might want to keep your weapons ready in case we run into any gang roadblocks. Just a FYI: I have cash and small packages of medicine, primarily antibiotics, that we will use as currency to move through any roadblocks. Generally works."

"Generally," Danny muttered from the back seat. "I prefer always."

Jack smiled to himself and settled in for the ride to the safe house.

*

Washington, DC, former USA

March 21, 2025, 11:20 a.m. Eastern

Jack watched Justin step into the alley and collect the AeroVironment Switchblade C. It had been launched when they left the safe house in Virginia, and Justin had flown it as overwatch during their drive.

Justin brought the micro unmanned air vehicle (MUAV) back into the small fenced enclosure behind the townhouse and swapped in a new set of rechargeable batteries. The MUAV looked ungainly, with its bulbous nose containing a wide array of sensors and video and infrared technology, along with a single missile that could be fired by the operator, basically no more than an airdropped grenade.

The Switchblade C was the latest in soldier-launched unmanned battlefield surveillance vehicles, built on the success of the Raven RQ-11B, used extensively in Afghanistan. Battery replaced, Jack heard the Switchblade's motor flip on and watched as Justin threw it back up into the sky. The small drone quickly soared out of sight.

Justin returned to the house and declared, "Good to go."

He then sat down at a desk, more a card table that had been turned into the team's on-site command and control center.

"All set?" Jack asked Danny, Britney, and Simon, and received thumbs-ups from all three.

Jack touched his holstered Glock and gave his body armor a slight tug back to center. The entire team wore jackets that allowed rapid access to their weapons but did not reveal the outline. Each also was wearing the latest in body armor underneath.

"Justin, you have us clear on comms?"

Jack employed a secure throat mic. Justin would be providing real-time aerial support, as well as any data support they needed.

"I have you clear on comms and good signals on your locators," replied Justin, staring at the screens in front of him.

"Leaving now. Start the clock," replied Jack.

Danny opened the back door of the house, and the four descended a couple of patio stairs and moved through the small, sad-looking dirt area that in better times would have been a yard.

Danny was first to the gate, opened it and looked both ways. After a moment, he signaled the go sign, and they moved down the trash-strewn alley toward Fifth Street.

The plan was simple. They would walk down Fifth to A Street, take A Street to where it ended in the back of the Folger Shakespeare Library, and then maneuver around to Independence Avenue and the Library of Congress's Jefferson Building. Simon had been clear that they should use the main streets as little as possible, because the gangs patrolled the more significant streets, looking for people to shake down and protecting their turf.

The capitol area still had some remnants of security, as units loyal to the former federal government, made up of troops who had no connection to the Republic and no possibility of escape, tried to keep gangs out of the government buildings that the troops were using as their homes. However, these security forces had basically become their own gangs.

There were pockets of the Northeast that were relatively calm—basically areas in proximity to military bases and more rural in nature. The larger cities were all in various degrees of complete anarchy. Only those cities close enough to Republic of Texas or Canadian territory, which could receive regular food and humanitarian aid, maintained some semblance of order.

Near the end of the alley, the men stopped, and Danny communicated using hand signals. Jack moved up on the edge of the left side, Danny on the right, and Britney and Simon covered their six. Danny and Jack each studied Fifth Street carefully, paying special attention to windows, where they still existed, and open spaces in the frames of the houses, as well as parked vehicles. They watched for several minutes and saw a few figures pass on each side of the street, in every case moving as fast as possible.

"Bird sees no threats."

Justin watched their position and the area around it through the MUAV camera and sensors. The street looked relatively clear, so Jack signaled Danny, who immediately moved out with Britney and across the street to the far sidewalk. Jack and Simon took the near sidewalk and followed down the street about five meters behind the lead unit. The five meters plus the staggering of the team across the street had been prediscussed as a way to have a possible semblance of protective cover and limit the success of an ambush.

As they neared A Street, Justin said, "Car approaching. Four men visible, windows down."

About thirty seconds after Justin's notice, they heard the vehicle; it clearly had some kind of amplified exhaust system, along with loud music. Everyone had already sought cover behind various working and burned-out vehicles. The music had a deep bass and a rhythmic thumping. They watched as a group of gangbangers drove by on the cross street with a couple of shotguns clearly visible poking out of the back windows.

Jack heard Simon's voice in his secure radio. "That is a group of foot soldiers in the Lords, a gang that basically controls this area. Every occupied house will have to tithe to the Lords for protection. Generally, the people do not notify the Lords, because they do not want to invite attention from them, but be aware."

All three waited as the music faded out, and Justin finally gave the all clear. They continued down A Street toward the back of the Adams Building of the Library of Congress. Based on the most recently available collection-distribution data, Alan Herring had focused their search on the Jefferson Building and potentially the Adams Building. The question that no one knew the answer to was, What was the condition of the collection? Satellite surveillance showed damage to all three buildings. The Madison Building clearly had suffered a major fire, with part of the roof caved in from the flames. The other two buildings showed missing and boarded-up windows and doors, graffiti, and were devoid of fixtures and other valuables.

Jack had stared at a picture of the Jefferson Building. He remembered visiting the collection with his grandmother on his first trip to Washington, and now was shocked to see the dome missing its copper. The intelligence reports said the copper had been stolen for scrap, but the image was shocking.

They stopped at the corner of A and Third Streets, received an all clear from Justin and took a quick right on Third before turning left on the access alley between the Folger Shakespeare Library and the John Adams Building. Their goal was the Jefferson Building. They would start there. Jack, Britney, and Alan Herring had spent considerable time creating the search grid for the library.

The team came out on Second Street and approached the back

entrance. It had a loading dock, which photographic assessments indicated might offer the easiest point of entry.

"Justin, two unknowns in the parking lot behind target," said Britney.

The team had moved off Second Street and crouched behind a pile of debris that was a former guardhouse. Britney held a Zeiss monocular and studied the back of the building. She passed it to Jack, who studied the two men. They seemed middle-aged and did not look particularly dangerous.

"Switchblade has the unknowns," Justin replied. "Both are in civilian clothes, one smoking a cigarette. Both unknowns are keeping their eyes outward on the street, like they are nervous. They are middle-aged, and actually appear…" Justin paused and brought the MUAV around for another pass. "If I did not know better, I would say they are academics. One is even wearing a sweater vest. Looks like my high school chemistry teacher. Only class I liked."

Britney and Jack exchanged glances and smiles and then continued to scan the area. They had almost blown a mission in Venezuela a few months before when they came upon two road workers eating their lunch outside the drug compound they were raiding. They had judged the men not to be threats, which had proven incorrect. They were still mad at themselves about that slip.

Jack studied the building and then said, "I have multiple outdoor cameras. The one over the door is clearly inop."

Danny and Simon looked at the camera, which hung at an unnatural angle.

"The two high on the corners may or may not work. Of course a lot will depend on the power and whether or not there is still a monitored station. We should treat those cameras as operable as a precaution," Britney offered.

From their various perspectives, the entire team watched the two men return into the building and pull the heavy metal door closed behind them. Danny, Jack, Britney, and Simon waited a solid five minutes but saw no further movement.

Jack outlined a quick plan where he and Britney would move across the back of the building, check the far side, and then converge on the back door from the left. On their way to the door, they would check the loading bay, where the gate seemed to be jammed about eighteen inches from complete closure on the left side, and ensure there were no hidden threats. Danny and Simon would be responsible for watching their six and then approach the back door from the right.

Britney looked at Danny and said, "Do not let anyone sneak up behind us. I do not want people laughing at my funeral because after everything I was killed by a gangbanger."

"I got your back, lady," Danny said, laughing. No one is going to get you from behind."

Jack did a crouched run across the back of the building near the street. Britney followed just behind. Nothing else moved. They proceeded down to the left of the Jefferson Building and checked around its side. Once again the scene appeared clear of people. They continued to watch and then moved along the back toward the loading dock.

The interior of the loading dock area was dark, so Britney lay down against the side of the building and slowly peered under the jammed door. Leaves and debris had blown under it, but the dock was clearly not abandoned. A small truck sat inside the loading bay and appeared to be in reasonable condition. Britney could see no threats from her position, but much of the bay was obscured.

Britney keyed her mic and said, "I'm going under the door for a quick recon. Sixty seconds max on my count."

She knew if she was not out in fifty-seven seconds, Jack would be in like the cavalry.

She slid herself under the door and quickly moved to the front of the truck. She dropped down to her stomach and looked across the floor of the loading dock. She saw a rat skitter across the back end of the bay, but nothing else moved. Britney slowly rose back to a crouch and peered around the right side of the truck. There was a heavy fuel smell, and she counted a number of oil drums lined up, probably containing extra fuel for the truck. She moved quickly around the loading bay but found nothing else of interest. She slid out under the door before fifty seconds had passed and moved toward the back door.

"I was about to go in after you," Jack said.

"Always my knight in shining armor," responded Britney.

"Anything?" Danny asked through the earpiece.

Britney replied, "A rat. I hate rats. Otherwise, all clear."

Danny and Simon moved up quickly and took positions on the opposite side of the door. All four crouched at the back of the library, where a hand-painted sign was plastered to the metal.

"Warning! Intruders will be shot!"

They studied the sign and leaned back against the wall. Danny reached into his backpack and removed a thermal-imaging camera and held it up to the door. The camera showed no heat signatures of any note and nothing moving.

"I think we're better off in the loading bay," said Britney. "It's out of sight of any street traffic or individuals if any happen by. That area is deserted. There is a door that, from its position, leads to the same hall as this exterior door. I think we can safely assume their security system is degraded and potentially inoperable."

Danny nodded, so Britney turned and led them off toward the open bay. Jack and Simon made it under the door right behind Britney. However, Danny, with his barrel chest, had difficulty getting under. Jack and Simon had to pull on the door and raise it a couple of inches for him. They then tried to push it back down a bit, with limited success.

"Where is your friend the rat?" asked Danny, smiling.

"I'm not sure you need anything else to eat after that performance," replied Jack, earning a raised middle finger in response.

The team advanced through the loading bay in a diamond formation, moving alongside the van, up a ramp, and to the back door. This door carried the same warning, so Danny pulled out the imaging camera, but he saw no thermal images of note.

"Clear," said Danny as Jack removed a small pouch, pulled out his lock-pick tools, and went to work on the locks. Each of the three locks fell relatively quickly. There was no light on the HID card keypad, showing that the electronic lock was disengaged.

Jack nodded at Danny, who signaled his readiness. Simon and Britney took up position next to the door. Danny crouched down behind Jack as Jack removed his KA-BAR from its ankle holster and slid the knife into the doorjamb. Holding up three fingers, Jack began the countdown and then pried open the door. Simon grabbed the swinging door and pulled it open wide as Britney trained her AR-15 on the darkened hallway and scanned through her night-vision scope. Nothing moved in the hall and nothing emerged from the door. No sound emanated from inside.

Jack signaled, and Danny ran around him and into the hall. The other three team members moved in behind him, and Jack stopped to resecure the door.

There was a faint glow provided by a fading safety light well down the hall that was clearly on its last bit of battery power.

"This area of town receives intermittent power," offered Simon in a whisper.

Judging from the low light, it had been many hours since the last power had charged the battery.

The four moved up the sloped service hallway, which emptied into another hall running perpendicular. Jack pulled out his tablet and looked at the schematic of the Jefferson Building that Herring had downloaded. They were in the service area. Jack quickly found their location. Herring had marked the route clearly to the northeast stacks in the basement of the main building. These stacks were deemed the highest-priority search area. Herring's research had directed them to focus on Seward's papers, as well as select papers belonging to Dickinson and Clay. They needed to go to the left to find the stairwell, which would take them down to the conservation area and workrooms. Beyond the conservation facilities were the electrical and air-handling equipment rooms and then the stacks.

Jack made a series of hand signals to indicate next movements and then stowed the tablet.

The building was eerily quiet. Herring had put a Global Hawk over the city for the last few days. The sensor-loaded UAV had revealed a few people moving in and out of the building and infrequent signal emissions, primarily cell calls or attempted cell calls. He had been able to pull electrical power usage, which, when compared to precollapse levels, indicated that even when the city's grid had power, the building's systems were functioning at only a small percentage of their previous levels, either due to lack of demand or continued degradation of systems.

Arriving at the stairs, they repeated the process of thermal review prior to moving through the door in a combat formation. The stairwell security lights were completely burned out, the batteries exhausted. With the assistance of their night-vision goggles, they headed down the stairs silently. Britney had her AR-15 at the ready. Each man had their Glock deployed, with laser-aiming assists active. Danny walked down the stairs backward, ensuring no one came up on their six.

Simon signaled the all stop at the bottom of the stairs and deployed the thermal-imaging camera. The camera did not show anything on the other side of the door, but Jack pointed toward the wall. He indicated the floor plan displayed on the tablet, and it showed a large open room adjacent to the stairwell. Simon placed the camera against the wall and held up two fingers. Jack and Danny studied the image, and then Jack pointed to their location on the floor plan again. When they opened the door, the team would be in a hall with the door to the room with the two figures directly to their left. Worst of all, the room was on their way to the stacks.

Jack tried the door but found it locked. He removed his pick and quickly heard a satisfying click. He nodded, and then Britney pushed through the door, staying low and moving quickly left. Simon came through and covered the right, followed by Danny, who moved behind Jack and covered the hall to the stacks. Jack pointed at the room where the two unknowns were, making a kicking motion with his fingers. The team took up position. Simon moved in front, checked the team's readiness, and then kicked the door open.

"Please don't shoot!" yelled an unseen person.

"Show yourselves and put your hands in the air!" Simon commanded as each team member switched on the LED light fixed to the end of their gun and shined it into the dimly lit room.

Two figures emerged from behind some boxes labeled us aid. One was an older man in a threadbare tweed coat. The other wore jeans and a baggy fleece and had his chin pointed down and face hidden behind the brim of baseball cap.

Simon motioned the two forward with his gun. Danny and Jack stayed in the hall watching for any approaching unfriendlies. Simon frisked the older man thoroughly and then moved on to the younger, quickly realizing the second figure was a woman, not a man.

"Clean," Simon said.

Britney kept her weapon trained on both figures.

"Who are you?" Danny asked over his shoulder

"Who are we? Who are you to come into our library with your guns out?" replied the man indignantly. "Please put them away. I don't like guns, especially guns pointed at me."

Jack and Danny exchanged glances. They both liked spunk, and the old man had it.

"We're going to keep our guns out, but we will stop pointing them at you as long as you cooperate. Deal?" Jack replied.

"Cooperate with what? So you can steal whatever is left of the country's treasures? We will not cooperate with thieves!" The old man's face flushed.

"Let's calm down, sir. We're not thieves, and we don't want to steal your treasures. We're just looking for some information and figured the library was the right place to start." Jack tried to take the temperature down. "However, we do know how dangerous the city has become and we need to protect ourselves. Am I to assume that y'all are librarians?"

"I am Dr. Lawrence Chandler, the assistant librarian of Congress, and this is my daughter, Dr. Katrina Chandler, a historian," replied the librarian with a crisp patrician accent. "And who might you be? Because I do not believe you are library patrons doing research."

Jack found himself liking the guy the way a student is drawn to a passionate professor.

"I am Jack, sir. My friends are Danny, Britney, and Simon," Jack replied, walking forward and offering his hand.

Dr. Chandler hesitated and then offered his own.

Jack noted the firm, dry handshake. Dr. Chandler may be an academic, but he was one cool customer.

"How many other people are still working in the library?" asked

Danny.

"We are down to five people," replied Dr. Chandler, "but there really is little left to do. Between the damage from the fire, the thefts, and what we have been able to transfer, all that remains is to try to protect this treasure of a building." Dr. Chandler waved his arms, indicating the building. "I am afraid if you truly are here for research, there is little left. However, we do not have many requests for research help these days, so may I inquire what you are seeking?"

Danny quickly asked, "Where are the other three?"

"They are in our quarters, which used to be the conservation lab. Just down the hall." Dr. Chandler motioned in that direction. "You should know that we keep our shotguns there."

Jack signaled to Simon and Britney, who moved off to secure the other three librarians.

Jack looked up and continued the conversation. "We are interested in Senator Seward's papers."

"Interesting."

The woman had finally spoken, and Jack took a minute to look at her. She had raised her head, and he found himself looking into big gray-green eyes flecked with gold. Her face was absolutely striking.

"Senator Seward? The fact that you called him Senator and not Secretary, which is the period of his life that most historians study, indicates you clearly are not interested in his time in the executive branch."

Jack found himself staring at the woman. She removed her hat and shook out a beautiful head of long sandy-blond hair. Jack tried to refocus himself but felt his cheeks flush.

"Yes, ma'am, we are more interested in Seward's senatorial career," said Jack, staring into her eyes.

"Well, as you must know, Senator Seward spent most of his career fighting against slavery, and his maiden Senate speech, referred to as the Higher Law speech, is considered one of the most influential and important in the history of Senate debate on the issue."

Jack realized she was speaking to her father more than the three of them.

Dr. Chandler studied his daughter intently. "That was a beautiful speech, appealing to the morality of all the members to recognize that there was 'a higher law than the Constitution,' and that slavery must not be extended to the territory acquired in the Mexican-American War," said Dr. Chandler.

Jack and Danny turned and stared at each other for a second with incredulous looks. Normally, people tended not to have academic discussions with heavily armed strangers watching over them.

"I apologize for interrupting the fascinating history lesson. I remember studying that speech in one of my black studies courses." Danny smiled as he spoke. "However, we are on a bit of a tight time schedule, so would you mind showing us to the appropriate stacks and the senator's papers? We have an exam coming up."

Neither Dr. Chandler seemed to share Danny's humor on the topic.

"Unfortunately, it appears you may have a tough time preparing for your exam," said Katrina. "We can show you the stacks but not the senator's papers. We were able to move most of the contents out of the North East Stacks before things deteriorated to the point where transporting documents became impossible."

Simon came over the secure comms. "We have the staff quarters secured, three librarians accounted for, and we are in possession of two double-barreled twelve gauges and a couple of boxes of cartridges."

Jack turned slightly and spoke into his secure throat mic. "Copy that. Keep the three there."

Turning back, he was struck again by the beautiful researcher who had moved closer to him. He caught a faint scent of jasmine. She stared back at him with her beautiful, unblinking eyes. He took a deep breath and looked away before saying, "I'm sorry, ma'am, but where did you happen to take the senator's papers?"

"We took ninety-five percent of the North East Stack materials to the National Archives facilities in College Park, Maryland," said the younger Dr. Chandler. "I know for certain that the Senator's papers were removed, because I removed them myself."

*

Hearthstone Mountain, Maryland, former USA

March 21, 2025, 2:36 p.m. Eastern

Listir stared at the phone on the desk in front of him. He was thinking about his next move. The information Mulvaney had just passed along was startling. However, he needed more before he could fully formulate his plan.

Since the fall of the United States, Peter Listir had become powerful in a way he never was or could have been in his CIA days. His empire continued to expand in the black-market trade in and around Washington, DC. He had begun to run guns and other supplies up to the Mid-Atlantic Military District, in New Jersey. Somehow he knew in his gut there was money or power to be earned in what the Texans were up to. He could not put his finger on it yet, but he knew this was significant.

Mulvaney had his suspicions about his current occupation, but Mulvaney could never conceive that Listir was actually thrilled with the demise of the US. He knew Mulvaney just assumed he wanted, and was working for, a reemergence of organized government. Meanwhile, Listir had focused on enlisting as many former CIA agents in his network as he could. He also cultivated people like Mulvaney in the hope that they would provide him with the means to expand his activities.

Listir had commandeered former secure sites around DC for his business. As his black-market activities expanded and he increased his geographic coverage, he had begun using former military and intelligence sites for storage and distribution. He even had a warehouse facility in northern New Jersey with amazing security that had been a DEA front. He particularly liked the facility at Hearthstone Mountain, a former CIA-controlled communications and operations center. It still bore faded AT&T logos all over its security fences that had been part of its cover since the day it was established. Post-collapse, Listir had occupied the facility. It offered a secure location, good access for running weapons and medicine further into the Northeast, and proximity to DC.

Listir picked up an encrypted satellite phone and listened to the familiar hiss as his call was connected to another facility that Listir and his people utilized.

"Go," came the clipped greeting.

"Get ready to move hot. Still confirming location in DC. Will call with more information when available. I am coming down to join you shortly."

Listir closed the line quickly. It was a habit from the old days as a way to avoid traces, but really did not solve anything, given the capabilities of modern technology. PRISM and systems like it captured everything. He knew PRISM was still pulling information from the ether around the globe for the remnants of the NSA, but the severely depleted former agency did not have much of a staff left to analyze what it captured.

The Texans, on the other hand, had the technology and the resources to analyze everything sucked into their new data center in Omaha at Offutt Air Force Base, as well as the former NSA site in Utah. In a bow to STRATCOM's heritage, the Texans called their system Looking Glass, after the former US Air Force program that kept a command plane airborne at all times in case of nuclear war.

Listir turned toward the workstation in front of him and opened his browser. He quickly typed in the address of a cooking blog. It was time to generate a favor balance with his most important customer. Consulting an app on his cell phone, he opened the recipe for poached halibut and left a comment. He had no doubt that the Texans were monitoring, but he still followed the protocol.

*

Fort Dix, New Jersey, Mid-Atlantic Military District, former USA

March 21, 2025, 3:24 p.m. Eastern

The comment, posted on one of the pages being monitored by a small command post 183 miles away, came up on a large control screen. The few technicians in the "communications center" noted the message, and one of them printed a copy and took it to the officer in charge. They briefly discussed the message, and the officer left the communications center, headed for the duty officer's desk.

The comms tech presented the post to Captain Carpenter, who took one look and decided to report to Lieutenant Colonel Symmonds. Symmonds held responsibility for the network of suppliers that fed the ongoing need for material in the Mid-Atlantic Military District, or MAMD for short. Lieutenant Colonel Symmonds read the message and asked the captain to accompany him to the general's office.

Master Sergeant Baptiste sat in the anteroom. Functioning as the general's de facto chief of staff, the master sergeant screened everyone and everything that reached the general.

Baptiste stood and greeted the two officers with a smart salute.

"Master Sergeant," replied the lieutenant colonel, returning the salute. "I need to see the general."

Symmonds quickly outlined the situation, and Baptiste immediately moved to the general's door and rapped twice on the laminated surface.

The master sergeant disappeared into the office. Less than ten seconds later, the door reopened, and two officers came out clutching their hastily gathered papers, while the master sergeant waved Carpenter and Symmonds into the office.

"Good morning, Lieutenant Colonel, Captain," said General Rogers, returning salutes. "At ease."

"Good morning to you, sir. Thank you for making time." The lieutenant colonel remained standing, as Rogers had not indicated that they should sit. "As you know, we have a supplier in the DC area, a former CIA officer who has built a substantial network and provides us with significant weaponry and medical supplies."

The general nodded.

"This source has not only been a source of material but also of information, due to his group's cross-border activities and his personal contacts within the remnants of the intelligence and security services."

The lieutenant colonel nodded at the captain, who began, "Today we received a message from the man, Peter Listir, which was marked urgent."

Rogers indicated that the captain should continue.

"In the last few hours, he has learned that a MUAV is circling over DC using standard Texan encryption protocols. Additionally, he notes that the Texans have shown a recent and as-yet-unexplained interest in American history, with numerous computer searches regarding US history and research facilities where historical artifacts and documents are kept. Mr. Listir's contacts believe the two are related and that the MUAV may indicate that the Texans have a team on the ground in DC."

The general thought for a minute and said, "If the protocols are standard encryption, can the MUAV feed be tapped?"

Captain Carpenter pondered the question. "The short answer is yes, they can. However, that would be the case if the MUAV was circling our fort and my team could access the signal. In this case, we do not have signals resources down in the DC area, and we would need Listir's contacts to tap the feed and provide us with the data, so probably unlikely. They might be able to decrypt the feed and tell us what they are seeing."

The general said, "Immediately try. Use that phone and call the comms center please, Captain."

The captain made the call and asked the comms staff to respond to Listir immediately via satellite phone.

"Captain Carpenter, as you may know we are in meaningful discussions with the Republic of Texas on creating a closer working relationship," said the general. "If the Republic of Texas is operating north of the border, there may be opportunities for us to be of assistance and thereby gain their favor or some type of advantage in the negotiations for the Mid-Atlantic Military District."

Rogers turned his chair to face Symmonds, who stood at parade rest. "When was the last time you coordinated with your contacts in the Republic's army?"

"I talked to General Severs two days ago, and I am slated to meet with him in a week. He will stop here in the MAMD while he is on his way to Montreal for a coordination session with the Quebec government. You might recall that I suggested you may want to consider dropping by at the end to extend your greetings if we are making progress."

Rogers thought for a minute before responding, "The Texans are not in the practice of putting MUAVs up beyond the borders. The KH-11 satellites they now control do almost all their surveillance, and most of their UAV efforts are on border control. A MUAV is different and makes me think they have serious boots on the ground in the DC area, and serious boots mean serious issues for them and potentially opportunity for us."

"I don't disagree at all," replied Symmonds. "Our own experience suggests they are reluctant to send their own people into the Northeast, or at least not without local assistance. This would appear to be nonstandard."

"I am convinced we need to know what they are doing and find a way to maneuver this to our advantage." Rogers shifted in his chair and continued. "It would be very helpful to the push we are making deeper into Pennsylvania if we could get some more hardware and support from the Texans."

*

Basement of the Library of Congress, Northeast Stacks, Washington, DC, former USA

March 21, 2025, 2:43 p.m. Eastern

Danny and Jack moved into the stacks after instructing Dr. Chandler and his daughter to stay put. They wanted visual confirmation the room was empty, which it was. Floor-to-ceiling rows of empty shelves.

After the fire door closed behind them and they assured themselves they were alone in the large space, Danny stated, "Nice looking lady. Quite smart as well."

"I hadn't noticed," replied Jack, trying to sound even.

"I am just glad to see that that part of you still works." Danny smiled as he spoke.

"Fuck you, Danny." Jack smiled back. "I am not in DC to find a date. I am focused on the mission, and I am already uncomfortable with how long we have been in here, and I fear we have only a few more hours of daylight as it is."

"Well, boss, what's the plan?"

"It's clear we need to go out to Maryland, find the facility, and pull those papers. My guess, though I forgot to ask, is most of the other papers will be in the same place, so we can at least run down some leads if Seward's papers are not the key."

"OK, what do you want to do with the librarians?"

"Nothing *to do*. We leave them here," said Jack. "But we need to get a full rundown from them on the location of the facility, the specifications of the building, security, and the location of what we need."

Danny clicked his mic and walked the rest of the team through the plan, offering up that they would be leaving the library no later than 3:15 p.m. to return to the townhouse for the night. They would all go to Maryland in the morning; travel at night in DC was an unnecessary risk.

The two men walked back to the storage room and found Dr. Chandler and his daughter exactly where they had left them.

"Dr. Chandler," began Jack, "we need to know everything you can tell us about the facility and the location of the papers."

Dr. Chandler removed his glasses and rubbed them with a small cloth before returning them to their perch. "I can tell you everything you need to know, but first I have a question for you."

Danny rolled his eyes and sighed, while Jack replied, "Given the circumstances, Doctor, I would prefer to ask the questions."

"I beg to differ. You have broken into my library, looking for papers you cannot find without our help. I think now is the perfect time to ask my questions," said Dr. Chandler quite firmly.

Danny laughed, until Jack gave him a sharp eye. "Given those circumstances, please go ahead, Doctor," sighed Jack. He had to respect the older man's spunk.

"You are from Texas, correct?" asked Dr. Chandler, eliciting a nod from Jack.

Dr. Chandler looked over at Katrina, and then continued. "Katrina's mother, God rest her soul, was from Oklahoma." Jack looked over at Katrina. Under the Republic of Texas's Constitution, Katrina was entitled to move to the Republic.

"Why are you still here?" Danny asked her.

"There was a lot of work to be done to save what we could of the library's collection, and my father, a native citizen of New Hampshire and a widower, is still here, with no legal right to move south," said Katrina. "I wanted to help him save the library and also will not leave without him."

"Katrina should not be here any longer; none of us should. One of the librarians in the other room is from New Mexico originally. He stayed behind because his love of the library was stronger than his concerns for his own safety. But we have all done all we can." The sadness was clear in Dr. Chandler's voice. "We have a proposal for you. Katrina will escort you to the Maryland facility and help you locate what you need, which would be more challenging without a guide. Afterward, you will take her back to Texas with you. It is simply too dangerous for her here."

Katrina started to protest that that was not what she and her father had agreed, but her father held up a hand.

"However, what you are seeking is clearly important to you. If she helps you find it successfully, you come back and get the rest of us. Do we have a deal?"

Jack glanced at Danny, who nodded almost imperceptibly. Jack stared at the doctor for a long while; the librarian had a much stronger backbone than even Jack had first suspected.

"Deal," said Jack, extending his hand.

*

Hearthstone Mountain, Maryland, former USA

March 21, 2025, 4:35 p.m. Eastern

Listir tried to keep his voice casual; he needed to maintain Mulvaney's confidence. Mulvaney was one of the last true believers, and he was not going to be motivated by anything other than patriotism. Helping the MAMD forces would not appeal to Mulvaney and might even turn him off, but after the call he just received from the MAMD, Listir was highly motivated.

"We lost the feed," Mulvaney was saying. "We were trying to tap into the data stream and thought we had it when the feed went off the air."

"You lost it, or it went off the air?" replied Listir. He took a deep breath. He had an enormous and violent temper, but occasionally he could keep it under check with great effort.

"I don't see a big difference, but we think it went off the air," replied Mulvaney. "There was no signal fade. One minute the MUAV was transmitting, the next it wasn't."

Listir sat drumming his fingers on the desktop, considering his next question. He lit a cigarette and took a few puffs while he tried to sort out his thoughts. "Do you have tapes of the data feed?"

"Not the whole feed. We caught the signal in process and have that piece of the encrypted signal."

"Obviously, you will want to crack that signal," said Listir evenly.

Mulvaney sighed audibly over the phone as his gaze moved from his desk to the rows of empty cubes. At full strength, the staff that used to occupy the floor could have cracked the signal in seconds.

Listir interrupted his thoughts. "My guess is that the feed may tell us what the Texans are up to. It seems out of character for them to be putting heavy resources into DC."

"We are going to work on the feed, and if we find anything of value I will let you know," replied Mulvaney. He spoke with more confidence than he had; it was just him and Reed.

Listir ended the call and placed another. "Stand down for now."

"Copy that," replied the clipped voice of Listir's right-hand man, Brown.

He took his time with the next message. He checked his app, logged into a German opera festival website, and posted a comment.

In New Jersey, a technician printed the message and headed down the hall for Captain Carpenter's office.

CHAPTER FOURTEEN

Fort Meade, Maryland, former USA

March 22, 2025, 4:56 a.m. Eastern

Mulvaney was sound asleep on the couch in his office. He decided to stay at the office reading the threat dashboard from the PRISM data feeds that continued to collect intel. It was significantly more interesting than what was waiting for him at home.

At some point during the evening, Mulvaney accessed the performance metrics for the underlying tracking systems. None of them reported anywhere near the five-nines performance considered the minimum required just a few years earlier. Some were recording below 60 percent availability.

Ever since power plants shut down and the electric grid started to fail due to lack of maintenance, the supply of power alone degraded the agency's capabilities, before accounting for the agency's own decline.

Mulvaney was in the middle of a dream. He felt someone shaking his shoulder but could not quite come awake. Then he got shook again, and he came awake with a start.

"What the hell!"

Reed jumped back.

"Reed? What do you want?"

Reed looked down at the papers in his hand and then back at the sleepy older man. "I think I have something interesting," Reed said, holding out the papers.

Mulvaney looked at the first sheet and saw a grainy image of a man.

"Who is it?" Mulvaney asked, still studying the picture, not able to make it out clearly without his glasses.

"Justin Manning—" stated Reed, but Mulvaney broke in.

"Ex-Delta, currently a key player in Jack Dodge's Republic of Texas intelligence service, or should I say an executive with the Harper Cattle Company?"

"You know him?" Reed asked, shifting his bulk into an uncomfortable government-issue chair.

"Christ, I need coffee," Mulvaney said. He thought back to the evening before. He had had several scotches, and his head felt the effects. "Yes, I have met Justin. Hell of an operative. Guy has a talent for the business and is incredibly facile with electronics," added Mulvaney, remembering an operation they had run back when everything was different. Mulvaney's team had provided intelligence and real-time imaging and signals support. Justin had been the on-the-ground interface with the team, led by Jack Dodge. They had taken out a leader in a Venezuelan cocaine-shipping business and destroyed his warehouse.

He smiled to himself as he remembered the signals traffic they intercepted from Chavez's palace in the aftermath. The diminutive dictator had not been pleased over the loss of his steady 10 percent.

Mulvaney looked at Justin's picture and leaned forward in his chair. "Any idea where this was taken?"

"I was able to pull this picture out of the feed. Most of it was heavily encrypted, but these few seconds had a diminution in the encryption cycle, and I was able to decode this image. I am working on the rest, but honestly I am not optimistic. This picture shows the subject probably at the launch of the MUAV, and my guess is that the power-up process had something to do with the light encryption, maybe a power glitch. As to the place, it is definitely in the District and somewhere around the old Union Station, but other than that, I am just not sure. I tasked a machine to try and verify the coordinates, but due to communications equipment issues it appears we do not have a multipoint hit on the signal, so the area is vague."

They both sat in silence for a little while before Mulvaney spoke. "Justin is a real asset to the Texans. He would not be here alone. Which means there is a team on the ground in our area. The Texans have everything they need and, other than humanitarian aid that looks good to the few functioning countries that care, they have no interest in the failed states. They are here for a reason, and my guess is that it matters. Reed, you are doing great work. Please keep at it."

*

Capitol Hill Area, Washington, DC, former USA

March 22, 2025, 11:13 p.m. Eastern

Jack sat at the battered metal desk in the far corner of an otherwise empty living room. A row of screens was arrayed across the desk, showing the front, back, and both sides of the house. In total, the screens gave him sixteen different images, both visual camera angles and thermal images.

The house itself was nearly bare on the inside other than mattresses in each of the three small bedrooms, some appliances in the kitchen, camp stoves for when the power was out, and the living room desk. Though from the outside the windows looked normal with closed curtains, behind the curtains were bullet-resistant shutters. Simon's people kept the place clean and stocked with MREs, but other than that it was a glorified tent.

Danny walked up and handed Jack a cup of coffee. "No action?" he inquired.

"Nothing, which is good." Jack leaned back in his chair and took a sip of the strong coffee. "I'm going to talk to Herring again in a few minutes. You want to join that conversation?"

"Sure. I hope he has learned some more, because I don't like the idea of running all over this wasteland looking for something that may or may not exist," Danny said while sitting down on the floor behind Jack and studying the monitors. "Especially now we have a civilian in tow."

Jack nodded in agreement. "I get it and don't disagree. We need Katrina, but I agree that the dynamic of having someone from outside the team with no training, and for whom we are responsible, is a meaningful handicap."

The tablet resting on the desk emitted a series of low beeps. Jack picked it up and hit the flashing icon. He waited while the encryption algorithms loaded and synced before Alan Herring appeared on the screen.

"Jack, anything new?"

"No updates," Jack replied. "Everyone is down for the count except for Danny, who is here with me."

"I spent some time over at the Archives tonight. Fowlkes is an interesting individual with a wide range of knowledge and interests…"

"Focus, Alan," said Jack while watching a stray cat move in front of the house. He quickly checked all the other images to ensure no one had caused the cat to move.

"Sorry. We reviewed the diaries of Minister Wharton, who was Texas's minister in DC during the period in question," Alan said, resuming his story. "Minister Wharton mentions Senator Seward a significant number of times and also makes references to Daniel Dickinson. I am working on Dickinson's papers, but our analysis continues to narrow on those two individuals. I have also been working on the particulars of Dickinson's Senate papers, as well as identifying both Seward's and Dickinson's chief assistants during the period in question."

"Alan, I don't think that I ever heard of a Senator Dickinson until this little exercise," said Danny.

"No, you would not have, but he was actually considered by Abraham Lincoln to run on the ticket in the 1864 reelection as Lincoln's vice president," said Herring.

"Seriously?" Danny had stood up and was looking over Jack's shoulder at Herring's image on the tablet. "That would have made him president instead of Johnson when Lincoln was assassinated."

"I am always serious, Danny," said Herring. "Dickinson was a very well-connected New York politician, who had served as a US senator. He was a meaningful player in US politics in that era, but is unknown to us today."

Jack interrupted. "Gentlemen, it's late. Alan, we're pushing off from here tomorrow morning at 0600 and heading for the facility. We've gone over the schematics and identified the access points with the librarian, Dr. Katrina Chandler. She has no idea if there is anyone left at the facility, as they have not been able to get there for some time. We'll take the entire team and be prepared for anything, but I would like you to task a Global Hawk over the place and see if there is any chatter, signals, or anything moving."

"Consider it done," replied Herring. "In the meantime, I'll keep digging."

"Thanks." Jack signed off and turned to Danny. "Go to sleep, Danny. I've got this watch. Simon's going to spell me at one, Justin will take over at three thirty, and we can all wake up at five fifteen for a six-o'clock departure."

*

Bethesda, Maryland, former USA

March 22, 2025, 5:04 a.m. Eastern

Listir woke up instantly at the sound of his phone ringing. He had driven back to Bethesda from Hearthstone Mountain late. He joined up with the crew that Brown had assembled and settled in to wait for a call from Mulvaney.

"Hello?" Spook's voice was a bit groggy.

"I am sorry to wake you," replied Mulvaney. He sounded groggy as well.

"No worries," said Spook, flipping on the overhead lamp before searching for his cigarettes on the side table. "What did you find?"

"We pulled a picture off the UAV feed. The picture was of a former operative who now works for the Texans in intelligence."

"That's very interesting." Listir was standing in the middle of his small quarters, pulling on a pair of jeans. "What do we know about him? Do we know where he is?"

"His name is Justin Manning, and he's an excellent agent. We know he does important work, so he's not here on something small. The where-he-is is harder. We know he is in DC around the Union Station area, but we do not know any more than that."

Listir muttered, "Shit" under his breath. "That's too bad," he said over the phone. He tried to sound neutral. "I am really curious about this. If this guy is the real deal, then whatever they are doing clearly must be important."

"I am having trouble seeing the pattern," said Mulvaney. "Why the sudden interest in American history? Why send highly ranked intelligence resources into DC and put expensive assets like MUAVs in the air? I feel like the solution to the puzzle is there, but I just cannot see it yet."

*

Austin, Texas, Republic of Texas

March 22, 2025, 4:36 a.m. Central

Alan Herring walked back toward his desk to see a small icon flashing in the lower right-hand corner of his screen. He clicked on the icon and pulled out his code card. He entered the onetime code and gained access to the Looking Glass system, the Texans' enhanced version of PRISM, with all the latest features.

An audio file sat waiting in his queue. The file was tagged a few minutes earlier and identified the speakers as Dr. Vincent Mulvaney and Peter Listir. Herring looked at the name identifiers and clicked on Listir, as he was quite familiar with Mulvaney. Listir's full jacket came up on his screen; a quick review got Herring's full attention. Herring flipped back to the Looking Glass file and noted the other tag, "Justin Manning," and quickly opened the file.

The file made Herring sick to his stomach. Before the audio finished playing, Herring dialed Jack Dodge's encrypted phone and drummed a pencil on his desk while waiting for the secure connection to be established.

"We have a problem."

"How big a problem?" answered Jack as he began pacing.

"PRISM found the feed from your bird and saw an image of Justin," Herring replied. He could hear an audible exhale from Jack over the line.

"That's not good." Jack still managed to sound astronaut calm. He had an ability to keep his head when everyone else was losing theirs. "Do they have other details?" Jack wanted to know if their location had been compromised.

"They are aware the image originated in DC, but nothing more specific than the Union Station area."

Herring tapped a few keystrokes to increase Looking Glass's monitoring of Fort Meade.

"We still have meaningful time to spend before we can make our exit." Jack's eyes bore into the back of the safety shutters. "We do not need further security issues."

"On the positive, the system immediately flagged the conversation," said Herring. "I have both speakers under highest-level electronic surveillance right now, and we are running full countermeasures, as well as increasing the electronic security. I apologize, Jack. This is an inexcusable failure. We are all over this, and we will be better."

"Alan, when you say that you are running the full set of countermeasures, that's not enough," said Jack. "This operation is too important. I need you to ensure that they are blind. You understand what I am saying?"

"I understand, Jack," said Herring, snapping his fingers and pointing at members of his team. "I am on it."

"Thanks. Keep me updated."

Jack clicked off and sat in silence for a second. It was time to move it, but this information showed the risks were considerably higher than they had forecasted. Jack briefly thought about what he would do in a normal situation: pull the team until he was sure of security. He shook his head. The first minister had not left that open as an option.

Jack walked back into the kitchen and looked around at the assembled group huddled over their disposable coffee cups.

Britney broke the ice. "What's up, boss?"

Jack quickly explained the issues and what Herring and team would be doing. He then paused while the team absorbed the news.

Katrina was the first to ask a question.

"Sorry, not being one of you, if that is all that they know, then isn't this really much ado about nothing?"

Danny laughed. "I like the Shakespearean reference, given all the library visits. It may or may not be anything. That is the question. Jack, I think we operate under the assumption that this is all they know, but we should assume they will know everything soon. So, speed is all that matters now."

While the team was talking in DC, Herring sat with the four best technicians in Austin.

"Nice bolo, Ian."

Alan stared at the young cryptologist from Santa Fe, who had on a bolo with an enormous turquoise clasp, along with flip-flops on his feet. He got a wide grin back for his compliment, but Herring did not smile. Herring had just meant it as a fact.

"We have multiple issues that must be addressed immediately," Herring continued, all business. "We had a MUAV over DC yesterday, and somehow PRISM not only picked up the signal, but they were able to access portions of the data stream. We need that entire file scrubbed from their system. Second, somehow Fort Meade is seeing our outgoing traffic and following our requests. I think they must have some kind of bot installed on our network. Clearly, they used a zero-day exploit to circumvent our security. Find and kill it.

"When this is over, we will conduct a total review of all of our security, and especially any zero-day-exploit opportunities that still exist in the systems. Third, I want them blind. Shut down their access and crash their systems. Lastly, I want all our communications protocols checked and the encryption enhanced. Someone is still working at Fort Meade, and we need to remember that much of what we have is only one or two generations newer than their systems. Moreover, if a degraded NSA is still able to get the jump on us, then what can some of our more advanced enemies do? We are getting arrogant and sloppy and need to improve. Immediately."

The group broke up, and each person went off to perform their tasks.

Herring's people might be a little different than the rest of the employees of the Harper Cattle Company, but they were serious professionals who were very good at their jobs. As evidenced when twenty-five minutes later a piece of malware dropped into the NSA's network thoroughly corrupted the MUAV feed, destroying all its data and rendering it useless for future analysis. A couple of minutes after that, Fort Meade experienced a full system crash.

*

Bethesda, Maryland, former USA

March 22, 2025, 6:40 a.m. Eastern

Listir sat drinking coffee while studying maps of the District around the Union Station area. He had not been down in the area in a couple of months, but he remembered the "Charlton Heston in *Planet of the Apes* finding the ruins of America" scene from the last time he drove past the Capitol.

The old AAA map was spread out on a white Formica table in the small kitchenette of the warehouse. Listir looked at his calculations again. He had found some information on the internet that provided general details on camera resolution, flight time, effective control distance, and other facts related to hand-launched MUAVs. Unfortunately, he still came up with a very broad search area using Union Station as his center. He eliminated the area northeast of Union Station, as he failed to find any sites he felt would draw the Texans' attention. That left him with two likely search areas. The first stretched from Union Station down toward the White House and included many of the departments of the former federal government. The other stretched from Union Station south-southeast and included Capitol Hill and most of the Smithsonian complex.

Spook felt movement before his man appeared and looked up to see Sam Campbell walk in, rubbing his eyes.

"Hey, boss," said Campbell, walking straight for the coffeepot.

Campbell worked exclusively for Brown, coordinating the other smuggling and enforcement resources Spook had in the Washington area, as well as handling the toughest wetwork assignments. Campbell started working for Brown many years before, when he first joined the clandestine services of the CIA, and Listir had seen him execute any assignment without a single qualm. His actions were flawless, but he possessed no soul or humanity. Perfect qualities for a criminal.

"Morning, Sam," replied Listir, holding out his cup for a refill.

Campbell looked over at the map and raised an eyebrow, and Listir leaned back in the folding chair and replied, "There are Texans somewhere around Union Station. I have been looking for obvious targets based on the search queries the NSA has detected coming out of Austin and the flight time of a handheld MUAV, but the grid is just too large."

While Listir was speaking, Campbell handed back his coffee, grabbed his own cup, and moved over to the table to stare down at the map.

"You said search queries. What were the Texans trying to find?" Campbell said while he pulled out a pack of Winstons from his fleece pocket. He offered one to Listir and then lit both with a Zippo.

"Apparently, they made a number of outbound inquiries related to US history in the mid-1800s."

Listir watched Campbell study the map and smoke his cigarette for several minutes. He did not bother to interrupt, hoping a fresh pair of eyes would see things differently.

Campbell finally plopped down in a battered plastic chair ninety degrees from Spook and said, "Shouldn't we think about it like school? Where would you go in DC to study American history?" Campbell poked his cigarette at the map. "Here, the National Archives. The Constitution. Bill of Rights." He then stabbed again, at the Smithsonian buildings, and then again at the Library of Congress, leaving ash covering the US Capitol.

Listir leaned forward in his chair and realized he had been thinking about locations in the context of actionable intelligence, not in terms of a history project.

"God damn it!" muttered Listir. He looked at his watch. 7:26 a.m. "Fuck! I wasted valuable time. Go wake the team and tell them to triple-time it. I want them fully kitted up five minutes ago."

Listir knocked the folding metal chair to the ground in his hurry and left it lying there. He grabbed the map and his coffee and headed for his quarters to change.

Campbell stared after him for a few seconds, shrugged, and then followed him out to go tell Brown.

Fort Meade, Maryland, former USA

March 22, 2025, 7:10 a.m. Eastern

Stan Reed woke up from a brief catnap. He had slept in a small break room that had cots, cots that used to have fresh sheets. He took a chipped cup from the side of the sink, sniffed it to see if it was clean, and then scooped in instant coffee. Real coffee had disappeared from the NSA around the same time the federal government collapsed. He filled the cup with hot water from a dedicated tap, then left the room and headed for his cube.

He turned on his computer and stirred the coffee while the machine ran through its protocols. By the time all the secure connections were reestablished, he had almost finished the cup. He quickly typed in a few instructions and tried to open the file for the MUAV feed. He knew instantly the file had been corrupted. "Shit," he said quietly. He quickly worked on the file, trying to figure out if it had been an amateur deletion, but no recovery was possible. Someone very good had destroyed the data.

Reed looked up, but the lights were out in Mulvaney's office. He scrolled through his contacts, searching for Mulvaney's. Finding the right contact, he clicked the dial icon, but the call failed. Reed shook his head; the cell phone network had suffered dramatic degradation. He tried again, and this time the call went through. After a few rings, he heard a gravelly voice.

"Hello?"

"It's Reed. Something has happened to the files."

Reed had continued to try and access the location files, search queries, everything he had collected over the last few days while waiting for the call to connect. Reed tried to check the links to the Texans' Looking Glass system, but nothing would open. In fact, he could not access the outside world.

"What's happened?"

Mulvaney sounded angry. Mulvaney was in the food storage area searching through the stockpiled MREs for something worth eating. Reed's message caused him to leave and charge back to his floor.

"I took a quick nap. When I came back to my workstation, I went into the MUAV file. It had clearly been deleted, and not by mistake or by an amateur. The file was scrubbed clean. No record other than the file name exists," Reed said as flatly as he felt. "They are very good. There is not a single trace of them coming or going, but the files are wiped clean. Everything." Reed's fingers were flying over the keyboard, going database by database.

The line was silent for a while, other than periods of static, a common occurrence these days, with the crumbling network.

Mulvaney finally found himself in the cube farm and clicked off. He came up behind Reed, breathing heavily.

"How bad is it?"

"Bad," said Reed. "We are effectively blind. They did a full denial-of-service attack on us and have basically rendered us blind, deaf, and dumb. We are going to have to bring it down and slowly bring it back up. And hope it comes back up."

"Damn it!" Mulvaney yelled across the empty floor. "Fucking Herring!"

Wisconsin Avenue, DC/Maryland border, former USA

March 22, 2025, 7:38 a.m. Eastern

"Good morning," said Listir, looking at the screen as he answered and trying to sound upbeat. "I hope you have some good news for me."

Listir looked out the car window as they passed a line of burned-out stores, long ago looted. The car they were traveling in accentuated every bump, as the extra armor plating weighed it down on the road.

Listir and his team had "liberated" a few former United States Secret Service vehicles heavy on safety and security features but light on comfort. Everything outside the thick glass had a slightly distorted look, but Listir had long ago grown used to the bulletproof view.

"No, I don't," said Mulvaney as he played with a pottery mug his daughter had made in school some thirty years before. "Everything has been wiped off our system overnight. The Texans must have infiltrated the systems, but according to my analyst it was a beautiful job. They have also completely shut us down and put us in a full hard reboot. Not only will that take hours, these days it is unclear what will not come back up because of crap maintenance. We at least have confirmation that whatever they are doing is hyperimportant."

Listir held the phone so tightly his fingers turned white. He sensed this was an opportunity that may never come around again, and it was slipping away. Unlike most people, Listir benefited from the collapse. He had acquired wealth, power over life and death, and status such as he never had as a minor government functionary. He and his crew controlled the smuggling of liquor and medicine in the area in and around the former District of Columbia. They ran girls. They also had profitable side businesses smuggling people out of the North into the South. His arrangements with General Rogers added to his prestige, as he could call on the resources of one of the most powerful military leaders to emerge in the disintegrating North. Other warlords had started employing his services. The only real threat to Spook's business was the expanding power of General Rogers. "Too much order is bad for business," Listir told his crew.

"So, we lost the information?" asked Listir with the little remaining calm he could muster. He wanted to drive to Fort Meade and put a bullet through Mulvaney's head.

He hung up and exploded. "Motherfucker!" he screamed, and the other men in the car winced.

More and more, Listir's temper was manifesting itself in fits of violence. He kicked the seatback in front of him with such force that it propelled the 240-pound Brown forward toward the dashboard. No one spoke while Listir continued to mutter to himself.

Finally he said, "Archives. Get us to the fucking Archives down on the Mall."

CHAPTER FIFTEEN

National Archives facility, College Park, Maryland, former USA

March 22, 2025, 7:14 a.m. Eastern

Two Explorers pulled over to the side of Adelphi Road just at the entrance to the long drive leading to the National Archives facility. The guardhouse looked deserted, but the hydraulic road barrier was engaged and blocked the path forward. On the exit side of the road, tire spikes barred entry.

Simon sat quietly behind the wheel of the lead vehicle while Jack watched the image from the Global Hawk's real-time feed on his iPad. The resolution from the UAV was exceptional, and Jack could see nothing moving or remotely threatening. He zoomed in on a few parked vehicles, but in each case the vehicle appeared abandoned. Jack looked over at Danny, who was in the second Explorer, which had pulled up alongside the first, and gave him the thumbs-up.

Jack turned around to Katrina Chandler, who sat beside Britney in the back seat of the Explorer, and held up the tablet. "Show me where you want to go in again—the closest entry to what we are seeking."

Katrina studied the image for a minute. "It is a different perspective to see it from the air, but I am pretty sure it is the second from the last of the structures, and that door we want," she said, pointing to a rectangular building. "All the buildings are interconnected, and there are levels below ground. We made so many trips back and forth to here before we had basically emptied the Library of the key documents and the roads became too dangerous that it is hard to say exactly where everything is. We had no time to create a clear catalog. However, I am pretty sure this is the right point for documents from the period of interest."

Jack signaled Danny, and both cars continued down Adelphi Road to the second gate, which led to the staff parking lot and a service road that abutted each of the buildings. Here again, the glass from the guardhouse windows lay broken on the ground and the hydraulic gates stood fully engaged. However, unexpectedly the concertina-wire-topped fence was breached, and it appeared from the grass that numerous vehicles had driven through the fence breach around the barriers and back onto the access road.

Jack signaled, and Danny's vehicle took the lead through the breach.

"This is where it begins to get a little dicey," Jack said quietly to Simon.

"Dicey how?" asked Katrina, leaning forward from the back. She seemed more curious than afraid.

Jack turned in his seat and eyed her. She was absolutely beautiful, even with her hair pulled back and body armor around her torso. Jack was surprised at his own reaction.

"Dicey how?" she asked again.

"Whenever we go into an area with a restricted entry and exit point, we decrease our degrees of freedom of movement." Jack returned his gaze to the front windshield, pulling his eyes off Katrina and back to the job at hand, and scanned for threats. "The risk is enhanced by the fact we have extremely limited knowledge of the condition of the building and the area. There are threats that may exist inside the building. So, in our business this is the period of time when risk goes up." He looked back at her. "Our job is pretty simple after the mission is detailed. It becomes all about risk management. Decrease the unknowns, and the likelihood of success goes up, as well as the safety of the team increases."

The two vehicles pulled up outside the building Katrina had indicated. They maneuvered so both were facing back out the way they came but staggered their distance and alignment so they were not in the same line of fire should a threat emerge. The Texans studied the buildings intently, looking for any sign of movement.

A voice came over the secure microphones from Austin. "I have no movement on the grounds and limited heat signature from the building. The heat signatures we have are stationary, so they could be building systems."

After a few minutes of waiting, Jack and Danny exited their respective Explorers and met near the rear bumper of the one in which Jack had been riding.

"Awfully quiet," said Danny. "I expect the guy with the hockey mask to show up at any moment."

"Great. An image from my childhood that still scares the heck out of me," said Jack. "Seriously, the place looks deserted. I think we continue with the plan as detailed. Justin stays out here to guard our six and handle the electronic interfaces with Austin and the team. You and Simon take that door over there. Britney and I take this door here," Jack said, indicating two fire doors on the respective sides of a loading bay. "Assuming the initial penetration is clear, Britney comes back for the librarian and we start our search."

"*Librarian*? I like that. Kind of a hot-for-teacher thing," said Danny with a big grin. "Was that Van Halen?"

Jack returned his smile with a withering look.

Jack gave the go signal, and the others climbed out of their vehicles, did a quick comms and weapons check, and moved toward the building. Jack and Danny found both doors locked, but a scan revealed no heat signatures or obvious threats behind. Unfortunately, the doors had no locks for picking, so they applied a little primer cord and stepped back. Following a small rumble, both doors gave way.

"Look at what you did. Now you people have left these facilities and their documents vulnerable," scolded Katrina when she joined them inside the facility. Her eyes flashed in anger.

Jack stared at her dumbfounded; he had no clue what to say.

Britney jumped in. "We have an acetylene torch in the back of one of the vehicles. We can reseal the doors when we leave."

Katrina seemed a bit mollified, and Jack muttered a thanks to Britney. He actually felt disappointed in himself for having not pleased Katrina. He needed to focus.

The team stood inside a dark hallway with no sign of working light. They all reached into their packs and put on their night-vision goggles. Britney helped Katrina with her set. Danny signaled and took point. Jack took up the rear and walked backward, guarding their six.

They moved down the hall and came to the entrance of the staircase. Based on Katrina's information, the library documents had been moved to subbasements B, C, and D of the building, with the most likely location of the materials they sought on level C.

Danny gave the go sign, and Simon kicked open the door, moving quickly to cover the down staircase, while Britney moved in behind him and covered the stairs leading above. The team stood for several minutes, but no sound emanated.

Jack heard the three clicks through his earpiece, indicating Danny wanted to move out. Jack responded with two clicks, indicating no issues, and the group began to descend. The descent was uneventful, and they soon found themselves outside of the door to subbasement C. Katrina and Britney crouched down against the concrete steps, out of any immediate firing lines. Danny gave the signal, and Simon slowly eased open the door, revealing an empty hallway.

After a quick recon, Danny issued the all clear, and the entire team assembled in the hall. Simon remained at the doorway, watching the stairwell and hall and ensuring early warning of approaching threats. The team continued down the hallway to a set of double doors that Katrina had told them to expect. The area was completely dark, with a strong odor of mold and dust in the air. Clearly, it had been a considerable amount of time since the facility had any power to run the air-handling systems.

The double doors opened with a bit of force to reveal a cavernous room filled with shelving. Katrina directed them toward the far reaches of the room, where file boxes were piled four deep on shelves stretching the width of the space and to the ceiling. The symbol of the Library of Congress was visible on many of the boxes. Britney and Jack removed a couple of tripods from their backpacks and set up some temporary lights, while Katrina examined the boxes. Danny continued a thorough search of the storage facility, ensuring no threats were present.

"It would help a lot if I knew specifically what you were looking for," Katrina said to Jack, staring at him closely.

"We have been over this, Katrina," replied Jack calmly. "We need to find the papers of Senator Seward from around 1850. We are interested in the negotiations leading up to the Compromise of 1850. We believe there are some papers that will be historically significant for future generations of Texans, and we want to get them before they disappear in the chaos."

"So you say," said Katrina, her hands on her hips and her attitude indicating that she suspected there was much more to the story.

Jack broke off eye contact. He did not want to lie to this woman. He decided to retake control of the situation before Katrina could ask another question.

"Let's move quickly. We are three floors underground in a facility about which we know very little and on which we have no current intelligence. We are out of comms with Austin, which means we will not know if unfriendlies approach. So, let's pick up the pace."

Katrina hesitated and then said, "We moved all of this pretty haphazardly," indicating the endless rows of boxes. "Initially, we tried to get all the stuff tightly organized and consistent with its placement in the Library, but as the situation became worse, we just moved the documents here as fast as we could."

Simon said, "Great. Here we stand in a field of haystacks, but we are not sure even in which stack to look." He eyed the endless rows of boxes.

"That is not what I said," Katrina responded sharply. "I said we started out in an orderly fashion and then changed as circumstances warranted. However, in the early days we made an inventory, which we left here," she added as she walked to the end of the shelving and pulled off a clear file folder. "If the materials in question were in the early move, they would have been noted here."

Katrina scanned the list, and the team held their breath.

National Archives, Washington, DC, former USA

March 22, 2025, 9:34 a.m. Eastern

Listir stood in front of the Archives smoking a cigarette. The place was an absolute shambles. They walked every square inch of the facility and found file cabinets and display cases broken, papers lying everywhere, and squatters living throughout the building. If there had been anything in the place of value, it had been burned for heat or simply destroyed.

His satellite phone rang, and he recognized the number. "Good morning," answered Listir.

"This is MAMD Operations. Sitrep, please." The question was more of an order than a request.

"We are literally going facility to facility, trying to locate the opposition or where and why it has been here," offered Listir.

He eyed a vehicle moving slowly down Constitution Avenue toward his location with the windows down. He saw several men crammed inside. He did not like the look of the situation, so he moved the AR-15 he had slung on his back forward, muzzle clearly visible and facing up the street. He watched the car slow to a stop and then execute a 180-degree turn and head away from his position.

He returned his attention to the telephone. "Do you have anything to offer in the way of intel on the current situation?"

He waited, knowing it would take several seconds for his question to transmit through geosynchronous orbit and the response to begin its return journey. In the meantime, he finished his cigarette and debated lighting another off the still-burning embers but decided against it.

"No, we have nothing to add at this time. We are very interested in this and, of course, any information may be worth a substantial bonus."

The call ended, and Listir took a deep breath while dialing the number he knew by heart.

"What have you found?"

Mulvaney sat at a barely lit desk in the analysis center at Fort Meade. He responded, "We are suffering another near-total power failure. The grid is highly unstable today, which will happen with zero maintenance and people stealing backup generator equipment to sell for scrap. We do not have much, because frankly few of our tools are working. We are slowly getting back online, but our friends were clearly pissed. They did meaningful damage. Where are you now?"

"Archives," replied Listir, looking up the street and seeing some of his team coming toward him. "Just leaving the Archives."

Reed sat across the table and held a list that Mulvaney had just finished reviewing. "We thought about your order and think you should try the Library of Congress next. If nothing there, then you should go to the Smithsonian, not the other way around. Beyond that, we have a list of historical associations devoted to certain aspects of American history of the relevant period dotted all around the possible search area. There are small research libraries associated with most of the former departments, and of course the universities."

Listir covered the mouthpiece on the phone with his hand and said, "Library of Congress," then returned to listening as they got into the SUV.

Mulvaney continued to talk about their possible search options. The vehicle moved up Constitution Avenue alongside the tent city that was now the Mall. Listir looked out at the sea of tarps, tents, and scrap-material huts. It looked like an image from an old *National Geographic* of the capital of some West African dump, not the capital city of the world's only superpower. Former superpower, he corrected himself.

Now, the Republic of Texas was the superpower.

"We are making our way to the Library now, but it will take some time to get there," Listir said as he watched his man turn off of Constitution Avenue onto Fifteenth in order to avoid what looked like an improvised roadblock several blocks up.

*

Fort Dix, New Jersey, Mid-Atlantic Military District, former USA

March 22, 2025, 9:34 a.m. Eastern

"General Severs, it's Lieutenant Colonel Symmonds."

Carpenter sat across the desk watching Symmonds.

"Colonel, nice to hear from you. I am looking forward to seeing you next week," Severs replied in his deep Southern drawl.

Severs sat in his own office in the command bunker of the Curtis Lemay Command Center in Omaha, the Republic of Texas's Strategic Command Office. General Severs's office was nine stories underground with a view out over the operations center, bustling with technicians monitoring the forces of the Republic of Texas and the threats they faced.

"Yes, General, I am looking forward to it. However, I have a question to ask in the meantime if I could impose."

Symmonds and Carpenter had thought about the phrasing a lot. Gaining Severs's assent to ask away, Symmonds plunged on.

"We have reason to believe that you have a team, either military or intelligence, on the ground around DC, and we wanted to know if we could help."

There was a pause on the line. Carpenter watched the digital clock on Symmonds's wall as the seconds ticked away.

"I do not believe we have any resources on the ground anywhere outside of our borders other than in the Illinois area, where we have intervened to provide some humanitarian assistance and stop a genocide."

"Well, General Rogers wanted to make sure that, in the spirit of our existing and hopefully expanding cooperation, if there was anything we could do, we do it. We do have some assets and influence in that area, not unlimited but some. We would be happy to help."

Carpenter had watched nine full seconds tick away, which meant the general was either checking something or unsure of how to answer.

Severs finally responded. "Much obliged, Colonel, much obliged. We do not have anything going on in the area right now, but you never know about the future. I will pass along to my colleagues your willingness to help us. See you next week."

The call ended, and Severs consulted the directory database, locating the number for the liaison officer who handled coordination between the various branches of Texas's military and the intelligence services. Texas would not have the coordination problems that had plagued the old US intelligence apparatus.

Less than fifteen minutes later, Jack Dodge's office transferred General Severs to Alan Herring, whom he questioned about the call from New Jersey. Herring listened but, with no clear direction from Jack, did not immediately pass along any knowledge of a mission.

"Mr. Herring, I think you are lying, and I want to speak to Dodge immediately," exclaimed an unhappy General Severs. "Am I understood?"

"Yes, sir," said Herring. "As I told you, Mr. Dodge is currently out of the office, but I will track him down and ask him to call you."

Herring leaned back in his chair. The image from the Global Hawk showing the outside of the Archives facility in Maryland displayed on the monitor. He tightened up the image on the team's vehicles. There was no movement anywhere. Herring looked at another screen and saw he still had no comms with any member other than Justin, which he expected, but he felt an urgent need to talk to Jack or Danny. *How do the MAMD forces know there might be a Texan operation in the DC area?* Somehow, some way, people knew there was a team in Washington, and in Herring's experience once people knew something like that, they would find the trail.

"Justin, you need to get in the building and tell Jack we just had an inquiry from Omaha regarding the presence of a team on the ground," said Herring.

"Copy that," replied Justin. "That's definitely not good."

Herring watched Manning exit the driver side of one of the Explorers and move into the building. Now Herring was their perimeter defense, so he widened the view of the Global Hawk and increased his attention to the monitors.

*

Fort Meade, Maryland, former USA

March 22, 2025, 11:26 a.m. Eastern

Mulvaney stared at his desk. Something nagged at him. He knew a course of action existed, but it seemed to be just outside his grasp. He absently picked up a pencil and started tapping out of nervous habit. The pencil hit the telephone and then it hit him. He jumped up from his desk, slamming the chair into the battered credenza behind the desk, and raced down the stairs to the cube farm. He found Reed sitting at his desk.

"I have an idea," Mulvaney said. "Can you still access all the voice-pattern files?"

"I think so. I also think I see where you are going," Reed said excitedly, turning to the screen in front of him.

He started pounding on the keyboard and opening up his applications. He found the directory he was looking for and had started to enter his passwords when Mulvaney stopped him.

"You will need to use my passwords. If all the files are still accessible, only my security clearance will give us access to the information we want."

Mulvaney leaned over and entered his username, then his codes, and finally another code from a digital card that generated onetime passwords, which he kept in his worn wallet.

Both men leaned forward as the directory opened. It seemed to load properly, which was a surprise. Back in 2014 there had been articles about how Fort Meade had maxed out on power availability and every system was optimized. The agency had built a major site in Utah to provide more capacity and capabilities, but that facility was lost to the Republic.

"Check the archives. There was a mission in 2014 where I know extensive communications files existed and were retained." Mulvaney leaned over Reed's shoulders as he started querying the system. "The mission involved tracking some money movements of al-Qaeda through the Nigerian banking system. We went after a banker in Lagos, but before the team could snatch him—literally just before—he was shot to death getting into his car. We do not know who shot him, but there were some suspicions. The team on the ground was caught in a tight situation. There was an inquiry."

Reed kept moving from directory to directory and finally found subfiles referencing Nigeria, February 2014.

"Let's hope the voices were tagged," he said as he ran the program.

Both men watched the bar on the screen slowly showing files searched. It seemed to move excruciatingly slowly, until finally an electronic ping sounded.

Reed clicked on the presented file and they heard Justin Manning's voice emerge from the speakers on either side of the monitor. For the first time in a long time, Mulvaney and Reed shared a smile and a high five. Reed also noted that there were tags for Jack Dodge as well as one Peter Listir. Mulvaney did not remember that angle. He made a mental note to go back over the complete file later.

"OK, we have a voiceprint. We need to get this signature into PRISM and task what little resources we have left to search for this pattern within…?" Mulvaney stopped and thought about it. The resources they had left to pull communications out of the ether were scarce. If they set too wide a search area, say including Texas, they would not have solid coverage and could miss something as easy to capture as an ordinary cell call. If they focused the resources tightly, they could pick up almost anything, but they ran the risk of missing the target. "Let's say within thirty miles of Fort Meade. If he has left the area, we cannot do anything about it anyway, so we might as well hope for the best."

Reed went to work on setting up the necessary queries and tasking the remaining assets. Reed looked at the directory and it hit him again.

"Boss, look at all the resources that are supposedly available to us."

Mulvaney looked at the screen, which detailed an almost endless array of SIGINT assets and tasking options.

"So few of them still exist or remain in our control," said Reed.

Mulvaney turned away and gazed out across the cube farm. "I don't need to look at the screen. I am surrounded by the detritus of our former capabilities."

He walked away to his office, while Reed finished the commands.

Library of Congress, Washington, DC, former USA

March 22, 2025, 12:18 p.m. Eastern

The SUV pulled up to the back loading dock of the Library of Congress, and the men poured out. Listir came out last. He jumped down onto the pavement, his combat boots making almost no sound.

He took out a cigarette and his satellite phone while taking a look around. He had not been up on Capitol Hill recently, and it had fallen apart. Buildings were pockmarked, and some showed signs of significant fire damage. Windows were broken everywhere he looked. Where there had once been manicured lawns, hedges, and flowers lay piles of garbage.

Listir joined the other men at the back of the SUV. They stood there checking their weapons. One of the men pulled out a lighter, and he leaned in to ignite his cigarette as well. Brown stood puffing, waiting for instructions.

"OK, Greg," said Listir. "I want you to take Dan and Sam and do a quick recon on the building. See if there is anyone here. I am going to make a call. Hood, you stay and guard the vehicle. I don't like the look of this neighborhood…anymore."

Everyone laughed, and the men moved off in standard military formation, sliding under the loading-dock door one at a time.

The call made the familiar hissing sound as it located the satellite, and then he heard ringing.

"Mulvaney."

The connection had more static than normal, which Listir remembered was caused by changes in atmospheric radiation.

"Hey, my friend, anything new to report? We finally made it to the Library."

As usual, Listir tried to sound friendly. There was a pause on the line, and Listir became concerned that Mulvaney might be holding back on him.

Finally Mulvaney answered. "We found some old data that we are using to try and track the guy from the picture."

Listir breathed a sigh of relief. He could tell Mulvaney was still looking at it from a national security perspective. The man was unbelievable; he seemed unable to understand there was no nation left to secure.

"That is promising." Listir ground out his cigarette after only a couple of drags. "Any idea how long it might take?"

"Forever or a few minutes," Mulvaney said. "We need a considerable amount of luck. If anything comes of it, I will let you know."

Listir disconnected. Staying on the line just increased the certainty that the Texans would track the call. He turned and saw Brown motioning to him from the loading dock.

"You will not fucking believe this but we found a few librarians, who have been taking care of the place," Brown said. "Fucking dumbshits! They say no one has been here, but I think they are lying."

Brown led the way into the building and eventually down some stairs to what looked like a bunkroom. Five older men clustered in one corner while two of Listir's men kept AR-15s trained on them.

Listir looked at the librarians and tried his best smile. "Boys, I do not think these gentlemen pose a threat." He smiled again at the librarians, while his team lowered their weapons. "Washington has become very dangerous these days, gentlemen, and maybe we are overly cautious. Apologies if we frightened you. Cigarette?"

Listir held out the pack, but all of the men shook their heads. He took his time lighting his own so he could study the men a bit more. He noticed they all seemed to be glancing in the direction of one man.

"My name is John Phillips," Listir lied smoothly, using his old cover name. It felt good to be back in the field on a mission. "Who might you be?" He stared at the man.

"I am Dr. Lawrence Chandler, assistant librarian of Congress." Dr. Chandler had moved slightly forward of the other men, and though older and bookish, he seemed slightly defiant. "We do not allow smoking in the building."

Listir smiled at him again, letting forth a stream of bluish smoke. "A pleasure, Dr. Chandler." He cocked his head, took another drag on his forbidden cigarette, and said, "Why are you still here? It's not safe in this neighborhood, and you aren't being paid."

Dr. Chandler looked to his right and left and said, "We love the institution and have done our very best to preserve its treasures in the hope that somehow this nightmare ends. In spite of our efforts, as you probably saw we lost one of our buildings to a fire and looting."

Listir inclined his head to the gentlemen. "Impressive commitment. Maybe if everyone had been so committed to doing the right thing we all would not be standing here right now wondering why everything had turned to shit."

Listir's crew laughed, but none of the librarians did.

"What do you want with us?" Dr. Chandler asked.

"Nothing. We mean you no harm. We are just looking for some men."

Listir watched them and saw all the librarians glance quickly at the floor at the mention of men. Bingo. He was on the right track. They had been here.

"The only people here are us," Dr. Chandler said, and waved his arms at the men behind him. The others nodded vigorously.

"Really?" Listir dropped his cigarette on the linoleum floor and ground it out with his boot. He had only smoked a small part to annoy the librarians. "No one else has been here, say, in the last day or so?"

He stared directly at Dr. Chandler, who broke eye contact again.

"Brown."

The command was simple and Listir never raised his voice, but Brown reacted immediately, raising the AR-15 and firing a single shot directly but barely over the head of one of the librarians. The shot sounded like a thunderclap in the tight room, and the smell of cordite filled the air. Dust came flying off the wall from the shattered plaster. The librarians all instinctively crouched down, hands up in the air.

"Shit, boss, I missed. Sorry," said Brown, laughing.

"Let me ask you once again, and please do not lie to me, it insults my intelligence. Has anyone been here in the last couple of days?" Listir asked with no smile, his voice hard.

"Yes," one of the librarians in the back answered, and Listir watched the other men shoot him hard looks.

"Thank you. See, that was not so hard. Can you tell me what they were doing?"

Again no one moved to answer.

"Dr. Chandler, is it? I am going to make this very simple. Either all of you start talking, or I am going to have my friend here kill one of you." Brown raised the gun. "Answer or die—I am sure you smart men can do the math. So, let me ask once again, who came here? What did they want? Where did they go?"

Dr. Chandler stood up, while the other men still crouched on the floor. "Some men came yesterday. They said they were from Texas and were looking for some historic papers. However, we had moved out all the papers, and they left empty-handed."

"See, that wasn't very hard. So, what were they looking for specifically, and where did you move the papers?" Listir asked.

"They did not say specifically what they wanted. However, they were focused on congressional papers from the mid-1800s, but we had moved all of that out of here." Dr. Chandler spoke with no hesitation. "As to the where, we moved the documents many places. In the early days, we actually brought more documents here, foolishly thinking the federal government would survive. Then we started to move things to other institutions, and the Archives facilities. Eventually, it became too dangerous for us to move around the city, but by then we had moved most everything we could anyway."

"Where did you send the men?" Listir asked while removing his pistol.

All the librarians stared at the gun in Listir's hand.

"That is what I am telling you," replied Dr. Chandler. "It became a bit frenzied, and we stopped keeping records. After the vandalism and fire in the other building, we just started moving everything we could wherever we could. They could be at Georgetown, a storage facility we took over at Andrews, or the Archives facilities. We just don't know."

Listir tapped his thigh with his pistol while thinking. Something was bothering him. He turned around, walked out of the room and into the hall and paced a bit. Turning what the librarian had said over and over in his mind.

He walked back in the room and asked, "Why do you keep saying Archives facilities? We went to the Archives. It makes this place look like a palace."

All the librarians froze. Over the years he had interrogated enough people to know when he had found the right thread to unravel. He motioned at Brown, who started to raise his rifle.

"No!" shouted Dr. Chandler. "We are telling you the truth. You went to the National Archives, but the Archives also maintained a large facility just outside the District in Maryland. Much of what we moved we moved there. We told the men about the various facilities, but the Archives facility was the biggest repository. That is all."

Listir stood still, tapping his gun against his thigh again. Brown held his rifle at the ready. After a few minutes, Listir motioned for him to lower it.

"You are going to tell me everything you know about the Archives facility and each of the other facilities. And you are going to tell me quickly and truthfully, because if I find that you held anything back, we are going to come back here and kill each and every one of you."

Listir smiled again, this time for real. Brown started laughing.

*

National Archives facility, College Park, Maryland, former USA

March 22, 2025, 1:23 p.m. Eastern

Jack Dodge felt like he was choking to death from all the dust. The air was filled with it, as well as fibers from the papers, books, journals, and other documents they opened. Without any air-handling systems, the already-bad air became worse. Jack opened his pack and grabbed another water bottle, pulling out one for Katrina as well.

With Katrina's help, the team had been able to find a large quantity of papers belonging to Senator Seward, as well as some other papers belonging to Senators Douglas and Webster, but very little for Dickinson.

"Jack."

Danny stood next to Jack holding a small leather-bound book with a clasp with worn gold letters on the front. Danny handed it to Jack, who took a minute making out the three letters, which were gothic in typeface.

"DSD?" Jack asked.

Danny held out Herring's list with his thumb near one name, Senator Daniel S. Dickinson, who was a United States senator from New York, 1844–1851. Jack knew from Herring's briefing notes that Dickinson was the chairman of the Senate Committee on Finance, in addition to being a staunch antislavery advocate. He played a significant role in the Compromise of 1850 because, though ostensibly about slavery, it basically revolved around economics and the financial structure of the young nation.

Danny glanced at Katrina, who was examining the contents of a box at the end of the stacks.

"Read these few pages," Danny said.

Jack started to read and then looked for the date. "February 22, 1850" was written across the top of the page in very careful cursive writing. Jack went back to reading.

Last night, we endured a long evening in Clay's office in the Capitol. Clay, Douglas, Webster, Seward, and me on one side, Sam Houston on the other. I said next to nothing, content to let Clay and Webster spar with Houston. The entire exercise perturbed Seward mightily. Once again, the argument in question had at its heart slavery. The abomination of slavery will be the death of the Union.

Houston held slavery over us like a sword. The negotiation lasted late into the evening, with Houston playing his few cards like a riverboat gambler. In the end, we achieved agreement. We have enshrined the concord in a secret document. Seward and Houston will each hold the infernal bargain. I fear that in the end this pestilence on our nation's liberty will continue to advance no matter what we do.

Jack flipped forward through the other pages of the diary to where Danny had marked another passage. Jack looked at the date: November 21, 1850.

Seward has just left me. He came to speak with me before my departure. I will miss his comradeship as I leave this body and wished him Godspeed in stopping the spread of slavery. May God bring forth an end to its wickedness. I am exhausted by my efforts and disgusted by my lack of achievements. I will leave it to the Sewards of the world to continue the fight.

Seward made a request that I could not deny but wish to not have thrust upon me. I am removing the Compact to New York. Webster and Clay feel that their general conditions leave them unable to be entrusted with the document. I have agreed to accept this horrible responsibility.

Jack stared hard at Danny, who stared right back. Jack stood up so that they could whisper into each other's ears.

Danny said, "It is pretty obvious that this guy, Dickinson, took the document with him to New York. There is not a lot of stuff here with his name on it. I literally have everything I could find over there in one file folder. I do not like standing around here, three stories underground with no comms, when it seems like the damn thing, if it still exists, is not here."

Jack looked down the stacks to where Katrina and Britney continued to examine boxes. Danny was right; if this was all there was of Dickinson's stuff, then they needed to leave. Jack thought about how to play it.

"Britney, Katrina, Danny found references to what we are looking for, and we at least know the documents are not here," Jack said. "They are further north, so let's get out of here and we can figure out our next course of action."

"Hold on a damn minute," Katrina said with her hands on her hips.

Jack looked back at her and saw from her eyes that she was not going to just fall into line.

"What did you find? And who said you could take these documents out of here? They belong to the Library of Congress! We did not spend all this time saving things so that you could just steal them, which, by the way, you promised my father you would not."

Jack stared at her, dumbfounded.

Danny leaned over and said, "Be cool," while stuffing the file into his pack and moving off toward the stairs with Britney in tow.

"Katrina, I understand your concerns and promise that we will do our best to preserve these documents. However, at this instant my primary focus must be the safety of the members of this team, you, your father, and his colleagues." At the mention of her father, he saw her body language relax, so he decided to stay on that track. "It is not safe for us to remain three stories underground in hostile country one minute longer than required. I also worry that there are forces in this area that would be very hostile to us. I fear our visit to the Library may bring danger to your father. I would like to get the heck out of here, keep my promise to your daddy and his colleagues, and get us all back to Virginia safely. We can discuss this matter further en route, but now we need to go."

Jack held Katrina's eyes. He was being as honest as he could with her, and after one more minute of defiance she moved.

"You are going back for my father?" asked Katrina quietly.

"Yes," replied Jack. "We have come close enough to finding what we need with your help. We owe him that."

"Thank you," she said softly.

They regrouped at the bottom of the stairs, and Simon led the way out. As they ascended, Simon briefed Jack on what he had just learned from Justin regarding the general's call.

The team exited and stood blinking in the strong midday sun. Simon and Danny grabbed the torch and made quick work of at least sealing the door, so that it would remain closed. Katrina sat in the back seat of one of the Explorers, with Justin driving and Jack sitting shotgun. Danny jumped into the other Explorer's passenger seat, with Simon taking the wheel and Britney occupying the rear seat.

Jack looked at his watch, which showed 2:05 p.m. With some luck, they would be in Northern Virginia before sundown.

Justin keyed his mic. "Let's start this rodeo."

Simon, in the lead vehicle, began to move out.

A satellite tasked by Reed, 22,300 miles up, recorded the voice.

*

Fort Meade, Maryland, former USA

March 22, 2025, 2:31 p.m. Eastern

Reed returned to his desk carrying a bowl of noodles. He missed the days of the huge cafeteria with choices. He could kill for a hamburger with all the fixings. He could not remember the last time he had something from a grill. Everything was so expensive on the black market. All Reed could do was trade technology and computer work, which was not very valuable now, for what he needed. Thinking about hamburgers caused a pang of guilt about the last time he had walked out with a couple of routers to trade for food. However, everyone left was doing it; there was just no other way to survive.

Reed sat down and started to slurp his noodles. He entered his codes in between bites and watched as access was granted to his machine. Instantly, he saw the icon flashing. He jumped up and screamed Mulvaney's name.

While Mulvaney came running down from his office, Reed opened the icon and ran through the protocols. Mulvaney joined him in the cube, breathing heavily. They both stared at the screen while the audio clip played "Let's start this rodeo." Reed clicked on the geolocation feature and waited. He realized he was holding his breath. The icon opened and showed a circle about 250 yards in radius in Maryland.

"Where is that?" Mulvaney said, still breathing heavily.

Reed narrowed the search area and watched the map clarify. "College Park, Maryland." He continued to hammer away on the keyboard. "There is a school, a church, an Archives facility. Archives!"

Mulvaney took out his phone and hit a key for a preprogrammed number. He listened as the call failed.

"Shit!"

He tried again; still nothing. Finally, on the third try he got through, but the connection was terrible and he found himself yelling into the phone.

"We got lucky. Archives in College Park, Maryland!" He turned back to Reed. "When was the hit?"

Reed said, "About a half hour ago," which Mulvaney passed down the line.

Listir responded, "We are actually already on our way there. We found some intel at the last place. We have had some difficulties with the routing due to roadblocks but are probably only ten minutes away."

Listir thought about the "difficulties" on the routing. They got caught in some limited traffic and, trying to get around it, almost ended up in a firefight with a gang that controlled an area of Northeast DC, which caused an even longer detour. They should have been there thirty minutes ago. Listir was pissed. The driver, Rick Evans, had already gotten a hell of a chewing out.

National Archives facility, College Park, Maryland, former USA

March 22, 2025, 2:56 p.m. Eastern

Listir's team pulled off Adelphi Road and went through the gate. The place seemed totally deserted. Eventually, they found their way through the fence break and drove to the main doors of the facility. Everything was locked tight. After a quick discussion, they decided to split into two teams. Listir, Evans, and Hood drove up one side of the facility, checking to see if there was anything out of the ordinary or if any of the other doors provided easy access or looked recently used. Brown and Campbell went the other way on foot, doing the same.

They had checked five sets of doors when Listir received a call from Brown. "We found a door that has clearly been broken open. It was resealed, but the job had clearly been performed quickly and recently. There were some tire prints in the dirt and debris outside it. I think we found the door where the Texans went in."

The three men came around the building fast in the SUV and pulled onto the curb. Brown showed them the door and the tire prints.

Listir said, "Evans, you stay with the car. You four come with me."

They tied a chain around the door handle and gave Evans the signal. The heavy car made easy work of pulling the door off its frame.

Campbell led on point, followed by Brown, Hood, and then Listir. Listir was smart enough to never take point in an unknown building. "Let someone else die first" had always been his motto.

They found themselves in a corridor and turned on their flashlights. They were moving down the hall when Brown stopped by a stairwell door.

"That look like multiple boot prints to you?" Dust had accumulated, and boot prints stood out by the opening to the door. Brown got down on his knees and looked at the floor more closely. "The prints go both ways, so whoever it was has come and gone."

"Let's go have a look," Listir said. "Fucking fast! My guess is they are gone."

They moved quickly, ruling out both the A and B levels before arriving at C level. C looked like it had seen plenty of activity, with smudges in the corner of the stairwell where it appeared as if someone had stood guard.

Campbell led the way through the door, and they found themselves in the storage area, with stacks going on into the distance. Moving row by row, they found nothing out of order until the end of the stacks, where multiple boxes sat askew on the shelves. One still rested on the floor at the end of the row.

"God damn it!" yelled Listir. He took the butt of the AR-15 he was carrying and slammed it into a cardboard file box on one of the shelves.

The team froze. An armed and aggravated Listir could be hazardous to the health.

"Don't just stand there. Start checking the fucking boxes and see what's in them!"

Listir marched off to the box on the floor and found it filled with obscure US congressional papers from the early 1850s. The other two men started pulling boxes off the shelf and looking at what they contained.

After about twenty minutes, with the men yelling out the various different contents to each other, Listir called a halt.

"Let's get out of here. We have no idea what they were looking for, but they clearly have found it and left. Let's find them!"

Brown said out loud, "I don't understand what the fuck is so interesting about Congress and the 1850s!"

"Back to the fucking library now!" ordered Listir.

Evans had the heavy SUV in gear and moving before all the doors were closed.

*

Library of Congress, Washington, DC, former USA

March 22, 2025, 4:13 p.m. Eastern

The two Explorers pulled up to the rear of the Library of Congress. They had made exceptional time, guided by Herring using a Global Hawk to steer them around roadblocks, traffic, and numerous areas of possible gang issues. Herring had also used the trip to tell Jack the details of the phone call from General Severs. Jack knew he would have to call him back at some point.

Both Danny and Jack sat quietly studying the street and the back of the building. Something had changed. The security door on the loading bay that had been nearly fully lowered when they last departed had been raised about a meter off the ground.

"You see that?" Jack asked quietly over the radio.

Danny answered with a squawk of the radio; typical mission protocol cautioned against unnecessary chatter. Jack sat a little while longer and, seeing no movement, made a decision.

He got out of the Explorer and moved up alongside the passenger side of Danny's vehicle. The two men stood shielded by the Explorer on one side and the loading-dock door on the other.

"Something happened here," said Jack.

"Clearly, that loading-dock door is significantly higher," responded Danny. "I'm worried about what we might find."

An image of several dead librarians flashed through Jack's mind. He glanced over at Katrina and then averted his eyes.

"OK, here's the plan," said Jack. "You, me, and Britney go in fast and hard. We leave Justin and Simon out here with Katrina, but especially to guard our six. We clearly are not alone, and I fear they could still be here."

Danny nodded, and they explained their plan to the others. At some point during the team discussion, Katrina slipped out of the vehicle and joined the group. She expressed significant worry about the safety of her father and the other librarians, but Jack denied her request to come with the three-person strike force.

Jack, Danny, and Britney moved up on the back of the Library in classic tactical formation, swapping leads and taking cover to ensure they were not exposed for very long. Arriving at the loading dock, Britney and Danny went under simultaneously, and Jack followed right behind. They made their way into the building and headed down the stairs to where they had last seen the librarians.

Using their night-vision goggles, they made their way to the break room that the librarians had used as living quarters. There was a vague smell in the room, and Danny said, "Cordite." Then Jack noticed the mark on the wall and walked over and rubbed the masonry. He pointed at the obvious bullet mark and started to move rapidly down the hall. An image of having to tell Katrina her father was dead flashed through Jack's mind. He shook it off.

The three quickly made a recon of the storage room and other areas off the hall and then approached the stacks. They took up position by the doors, but when Danny kicked it, it did not budge. He turned to Jack, and both men tried together, and still the door barely budged. But they heard the scraping of metal and some footsteps.

"Dr. Chandler?" He heard some whispering. "Dr. Chandler, it's Jack.

We have come to get you out."

"Jack, oh thank God. Is Katrina safe?" The relief in Dr. Chandler's voice was palpable.

"Yes, sir, but we need to move out now!"

Jack heard the librarians talking and the sound of metal scraping as they worked to move away the barriers they had erected. Jack and Danny continued to push on their side, and finally it opened. There was enough space for the men to just squeeze through.

"Jack, some other men came after you left. They threatened to kill us if we did not tell them where you were. They even fired a shot at us," Dr. Chandler explained as the group moved up the stairs.

"We gathered from the mark on the bunk room wall," said Danny.

"I prayed that they did not find you at the Archives," Dr. Chandler said. "I was so worried about Katrina."

"No one found us, but we need to get out of here. When they find nothing at the Archives, they are going to come back here at a gallop," Jack said as they followed Britney out of the building, toward the loading dock door.

"Jack, I am seeing activity from the UAV," said Herring over the secure radio. "There is a black SUV closing on your position at high speed."

"ETA?" asked Jack.

"I estimate less than two minutes."

"OK, y'all heard the man," said Danny quietly over their secure comms so as not to alarm the librarians. "Time to get this show on the road, five minutes ago. Let's move, people!"

Jack turned to the librarians and said, "There is hostile activity in the area. We need you all to move very quickly and follow our instructions exactly."

The librarians looked scared, but all nodded their agreement.

Danny issued orders to the team about taking up defensive positions and weapons readiness while Jack continued to marshal the librarians.

"All right, let's go under the loading-dock door now, and everyone get in the vehicle to which you are directed."

"Maybe sixty seconds, Jack," said Herring.

Jack had everyone under the doors and pushed the librarians toward one Explorer or another. Jack put Dr. Chandler in with Katrina and Britney, along with one more librarian on top of the gear in the rear cargo area. He took the passenger seat next to Justin. Three more librarians got in the back seat of Danny and Simon's SUV.

The vehicles started to move before everyone was properly situated. They could see the SUV closing on their position, interfering with their exit.

Danny's voice came over the secure comms. "Jack, I'm gonna light them up with a few armor-piercing rounds."

"Copy that," said Jack, but his assent was pointless, as Danny was already leaning out the window firing controlled bursts into the SUV's windshield. Jack watched the rounds impact on the glass and then said into his radio, "Bullet resistant." He watched a couple of more rounds impact and added, "It's clearly degraded with time. Concentrate your fire on the driver's side and we'll add our own fire."

While Jack quietly talked over secure comms with Danny, Britney switched clips on an AR-15 to armor-piercing rounds, lowered her window and matched Danny's fire on the same area of the SUV facing them fifteen meters away.

In Listir's SUV, panic had taken over. Everyone yelled at once, and Listir could not establish any control. The windshield splintered; the bullet-resistant glass required constant maintenance and without it degraded.

Evans had stopped the vehicle when the first rounds started

impacting the windshield and sat frozen in his seat.

"Move! Move! Move!" screamed Brown.

Evans started to turn the wheel and then slumped forward.

"Fuck!" said Listir, reaching forward and pulling the small man off the steering wheel. He looked at where Evans' face should have been, but there was nothing left. Blood spurted across the dashboard and onto Brown. The SUV was moving. With Evans dead and the vehicle still in gear, they drifted uncontrollably toward the grass.

The occupants of the Explorers continued to rain fire down on Listir's crew, and the engine began to smoke. Listir watched as the two Ford Explorers started to move toward them.

"Somebody fucking fire at those assholes!"

As they sped by, gaining speed, Jack locked eyes with Peter Listir. The windshield was shattered, and though it partially obscured the inside of the SUV, there was no mistaking the man.

"God damn, Listir!" said Jack over the secure comms.

Britney and Danny continued to fire on the vehicle, but their changing angles made it more difficult to penetrate the defenses.

The Texans accelerated and raced away from the Library of Congress.

Meanwhile, Listir's vehicle hit a tree and stopped. Listir jumped out and pulled Evans from the driver's seat, throwing his body to the ground. He got in to the driver's seat and threw the car in reverse to follow the Texans.

"What about Evans?" asked Brown.

"He's dead. Fuck him," replied Listir, putting the SUV in drive and turning in the direction the Texans had fled several minutes before. The engine had clearly taken several rounds and seized.

The two Explorers raced away from the Library. Jack took a card from his operational folder and dialed the printed number as they headed down Independence Avenue toward the bridge. After the secure link had been established, Jack ran through the security codes with the major on the other end of the phone and told him they expected to reach the bridge in twenty minutes. The major promised to alert border patrol, and the call was terminated.

"Simon has been hit in the bicep," Danny said calmly. "He is still able to drive, and we have decided that it's more important to keep the speed up than change drivers given that the wound is not life threatening. The bullet appears to have gone straight through with no other damage, but there is a fair bit of blood and he is in pain."

Jack looked at the GPS. "Copy that. We have less than three blocks to the bridge. Do not stop under any circumstances!"

"The SUV attempted to follow, but based on the smoke coming from the engine, they are no longer an active threat," Herring added.

Dr. Chandler was telling Katrina about the librarians' horrifying encounter with John Phillips.

"Dr. Chandler, can you describe John Phillips?" Jack asked.

He wrote down every detail Dr. Chandler and the two other librarians could remember about the man called Phillips, Brown, and the other men in the room. Jack listened and knew exactly who John Phillips was. The last time he had come into contact with the man, in Nigeria, he had vowed to kill him. It confirmed what he thought he had seen less than eight meters away a few minutes ago.

At just about six o'clock, the two Explorers pulled onto the Memorial Bridge and made their way to the barriers. In spite of the late-afternoon sun, the floodlights were already on, and the entire company had their heavy and light weapons at the ready.

Jack stepped out of the vehicle and walked to the barrier, where a lieutenant met him. Jack verified his codes, and then a platoon was dispatched to examine the vehicles and their passengers. Finally, the two vehicles were waved forward and directed via a labyrinth of steel barriers to a holding area, where Jack held a discussion with the company's captain and went through the approvals again.

The captain made a call and cleared the two vehicles to enter the Republic of Texas. They stopped at the border clinic and waited while Simon's arm was treated.

Before they drove off to Virginia, Jack told Danny and Justin who he suspected had been after him.

Justin spoke through clenched teeth, "Now I'm sorry we didn't stop so that we could have killed that lyin' piece of shit. Would have liked to skin him like a rattlesnake and wear him as boots."

CHAPTER SIXTEEN

Bethesda, Maryland, former USA

March 22, 2025, 6:31 p.m. Eastern

After a wait for another vehicle to come pick him up, Listir returned to the warehouse. Other men were loading and unloading liquor, cigarettes, food, gas, weapons, anything anyone needed and they could sell. Listir said nothing as he made his way through the warehouse to his office, where he kicked out the bookkeeper so he could use the phone with privacy.

He poured himself a large vodka and drained it in one gulp. He filled his glass again and picked up his phone. His first call was to Mulvaney. He lit a cigarette while he waited for the call to connect and then relayed what they had found during the day at both the library and at the Archives. He left out the firefight with the Texans.

"Amazing. It's really amazing that those librarians would be so devoted to their duty," Mulvaney replied, the awe clear in his voice.

"I'm not sure that's the important part, but whatever," Listir replied, trying to hide his annoyance. "What we do know is that they were looking for something to do with Congress from around 1850. Unfortunately, they may have found it. I have to think that the librarians knew more about what they were looking for, or at least led them to the right place. They knew what was in those boxes."

"They sound like true patriots," said Mulvaney. "They probably held back because they were unsure of your motives. You should go back and talk to them."

"Great idea," offered Listir. *I would of course go back, you fucker, and talk to them with a gun to their heads. Unfortunately, they are now in the Republic of Texas, and one of my guys is dead.*

After terminating the call, Listir dialed another number, at Fort Dix. He waited for that call to connect, and then walked the duty officer who answered through the events of the day. The officer transferred the call to Lieutenant Colonel Symmonds.

"You said that they were clearly Texans?" Symmonds asked.

"Affirmative," Listir replied, lighting yet another cigarette. "We verified both a photograph from the MUAV and a voiceprint. Ex-Delta, current Texas intelligence officer." His hand shook slightly, not from fear but anger. Listir held back the fact that he thought he saw Jack Dodge as the cars passed his position. He was not sure why he chose to hold back, but he did.

"Interesting. I personally spoke to the Texans earlier, but they indicated that no operation was underway and therefore no assistance was required," Symmonds replied. "I am surprised. Either the military was not aware of the mission or they chose to hide it from us."

Listir replied, "We need to find out what the fuck they were doing and how we can use it to our advantage."

He waited while the phone line hissed and popped. He was about to ask Symmonds if he was still there.

"Mr. Listir, may I remind you that though we have business arrangements, we may have greater concerns than how this impacts you, and our goals may diverge? Stand down on this matter barring further direction from us," Lieutenant Colonel Symmonds ordered, and then disconnected the line.

"Fuck you, asshole," Listir said into a dead phone line as he ground out his cigarette.

He sat for a minute, rage building inside him. He picked up a heavy metal paperweight from his desk and threw it as hard as he could at one of the fiberboard walls. The paperweight broke through the thin board, leaving a nasty gash in the wall.

After a minute, he lit another cigarette and poured himself another large vodka and sat brooding. This was a big-money opportunity. Whatever it was, it was clearly important, and the Texans were the biggest game left on the planet. It was slipping through his fingers. Jack Dodge was slipping through his fingers.

*

Outside Richmond, Virginia, Republic of Texas

March 22, 2025, 9:14 p.m. Eastern

The drive from Washington had been uneventful. Simon slept in the passenger seat most of the way, the painkillers doing their job. Traffic remained relatively light until the convoy reached the outskirts to Richmond.

They arrived in Richmond and deposited the librarians at the immigration intake center. Herring had already electronically filed all the necessary approvals on behalf of the Harper Cattle Company so there would be no problems for all six of the librarians. Jack provided Dr. Chandler and Katrina with his contact information and told Katrina he hoped he would hear from her. He was not sure he would, but for the first time since Marissa's death, he found himself hoping a woman would call.

The team retired to a safe house in Richmond that Simon maintained for informants and select inductees from the North. It was a huge step up from the house on Capitol Hill, with a kitchen well stocked with fresh food. Danny got to work cooking. He was by far the best cook in the group, and soon the house filled with the smell.

Jack grabbed a beer, sat down with his secure phone, and called his father with an update. He dialed his father's office and was put through to the ranch. He waited for his father's aide to establish the secure line and find his father.

Jackson Dodge's voice boomed over the line. "Thank God, Jack. Where the hell are you? You OK?"

He'd never known his father to be openly worried about him.

"I am fine, Dad. Just had a long day. By the way, Washington is like the face of the moon. You would not recognize it, nor would you want to."

Jack told his father the events of the preceding days, minute by minute.

"I'm surely sorry about your fella, but glad that it's not serious," said his father. "Where to next, son? Your mission either has to end with the goddamn document in hand, or confirmation that it's lost."

"Yes." Jack knew what his father was saying. "We're working that out."

"Are y'all gonna take the librarian along? Y'all should." Jackson always cut to the heart of the question.

"I hadn't thought about that. She's a civilian with absolutely no training. We just had a professional shot, so this is clearly dangerous. Plus, in order to increase her usefulness, I'd have to tell her more about the document. Also, I don't want to put her in danger."

His father was silent for a minute, then responded, "I take it we have a pretty and smart young gal. You always did like the smart ones. Pretty was just fine for me, just fine. Take the filly. You need someone who knows history and has experience with research, and that's not any of you."

Next Jack called Herring and walked him through the entirety of the events and data he thought they would need for the next phase. Herring had a number of helpful ideas and promised to get his team on it overnight. They agreed they would convene for a conference call first thing in the morning with both teams.

The call ended and Jack walked out to join the team. The air smelled absolutely fantastic, with a strong aroma of garlic, pesto, and bacon. Jack realized how hungry he was.

The team was at the table. Jack sat down at the one open place, and Justin passed him a heaping bowl of penne al dente with a garlic pesto sauce filled with big chunks of crisp country bacon. Britney poured Jack a glass of red wine while he dug in. The team ate in silence, and everyone had at least two heaping bowls of the delicious pasta, followed by a spinach and avocado salad. Simon ate voraciously.

"Danny, you've outdone yourself yet again," Jack offered, leaning back in his chair. "Of course I was so hungry I would have eaten roadkill."

That comment earned him a piece of garlic bread to the face.

"I would like to propose a toast to Simon," said Danny, raising his glass. "Simon, we admire your courage under fire and truly taking one for the team."

Simon smiled and raised his bottle of painkillers in the air to clink with everyone else's wineglass.

"OK, now that everyone is finally fed, let's go over next steps."

Jack became serious. He walked the team through the contents of the diary while they passed the book around the table. Jack explained that Herring and his team were researching the next likely search locations and encouraged the team to get a good night's sleep. He expected more long days to come.

Jack took dish duty, but Danny helped so that they could talk.

"My daddy thinks we should bring Katrina with us," Jack said. "He thinks we could use her help."

"I agree, and so would you, instantly, if her name was Tom and you didn't fancy her," said Danny.

Jack washed a salad bowl in silence but knew Danny was right.

"You're both right, we should bring her. On the other hand, I think we should be mindful of the fact that we don't know where the trail is going to lead us next, and we clearly have a posse looking for us," Jack said as he dried the bowl with a towel. "It could be very dangerous for her. We were lucky today that Simon only had one hell of a flesh wound."

*

Outside Richmond, Virginia, and Austin, Texas, Republic of Texas

March 23, 2025, 7:00 a.m. Eastern

Most of the team sat huddled around a Polycom speakerphone perched in the middle of a table. Jack and Danny stood dripping with sweat from the five-mile run they had just completed. They both held large bottles of water and took sips while they waited for Herring's people to ensure not only that the call was encrypted but also that no attempts at intrusion were detected. Neither man seemed particularly winded.

"All clear, Jack. Where do you want to start?"

Herring sounded a little tinny, but Jack knew that could be the result of the encryption software.

"I've brought the team up to speed here on what has transpired. Obviously, I have not read them in on the specifics of the document, just the period and participants," offered Herring.

"What have you discovered about Senator Dickinson?" Danny asked.

"Well, he almost was the seventeenth president of the United States," Tom Rome, one of Herring's guys, answered.

"Interesting," said Jack. Sweat streamed down his face.

"Daniel Dickinson, a former United States senator from the state of New York, was seriously considered for Lincoln's running mate in 1864, but in the end Lincoln selected Andrew Johnson," continued Rome. "However, Lincoln did appoint Dickinson the United States attorney general for the Southern District of New York, a big job even in those days. Dickinson died in 1866, so in any event he would not have been president for very long. Here is a part you may not know. He died in New York City but was buried in Binghamton, NY. Last note: the Binghamton State University Library is the home, or at least was before they went offline with the power loss, to many of Dickinson's papers. We're trying to do a search off some cached databases but can already tell they're incomplete."

"Binghamton. That's up by Canada, right?" Justin asked.

"No, that is Burlington, in Vermont. Binghamton is near the former Pennsylvania-New York border, out near the geographic middle of both states. The area recently fell under the Mid-Atlantic Military District's control. It appears a bit of order may have been restored."

"That's General Rogers's bunch," said Jack, turning to Danny.

"Danny, you dealt with him and his people on that extraction, correct?"

"Yes," said Danny. "Not a bad bunch of people. Very by-the-book military. They have good control over a big portion of New Jersey, some of Pennsylvania and Maryland, as well as parts of Delaware. They are running a pure military dictatorship under martial law. When they take over a region, they tend to establish order very quickly, but with absolute military rule."

"Well, after what we just saw in Washington, that may be the only way," said Britney, sipping a double espresso.

Jack finished his water and jumped in to focus the discussion. "OK, let's stay away from the quicksand of how to reestablish control over the Screwed-Up States of America and stay on topic. We need a new plan, which clearly involves a visit to Binghamton. That means General Rogers. After yesterday's too-close encounter, I don't think we should try to go into an area under martial law unannounced."

"Jack, if you need General Rogers's help, you're going to get to speak with General Severs," Herring added.

The team smiled at Jack. Britney laughed and tried to hide it with her espresso cup and ended up spilling a little.

"That's going to be fun," said Danny. "Can I listen in?"

Danny received a single finger in response.

*

*Republic of Texas immigration intake center,
Richmond, Virginia, Republic of Texas*

March 23, 2025, 11:00 a.m. Eastern

Danny parked the Explorer in the official lot to which they had been directed after flashing Republic of Texas credentials identifying them as supervisors with the Texas Rangers, which functioned as the umbrella for all of Texas's domestic and foreign security operations, along with regular law enforcement.

Jack and Danny went into the facility, which was a converted DoubleTree hotel. Next to the Doubletree sat a large field of Quonset huts on what had probably been an airport parking lot. Tall fences with concertina wire sealed off the whole complex, and the hotel was separated from the Quonset huts by another double fence topped with razor wire.

Inside the sliding glass door, the marble floor was still there, but the rest of the hotel lobby had been replaced with a bulletproof guard booth staffed by three serious-looking guards, who did not respond to Danny's attempts at small talk or humor.

Jack asked for the director of the facility and they were directed to wait in molded plastic chairs in the marble lobby. Eventually, a secretary came through the door and escorted them through security screening and into a cube farm that occupied the former center of the lobby, with makeshift offices around the edges.

"Mr. Winters and Mr. Dodge."

A thin, gray man stood in front of them offering a soft, wet handshake. He wore a gray suit that matched his face and a black tie. Jack thought he looked like an undertaker.

"I am Mark Delaney, the assistant director of the Richmond Immigration Center. How can I help our friends at the Rangers?"

"Pleased to meet you, Mr. Delaney," said Danny with a wide grin. "Last night, we brought in some academics that the Republic expedited for entry. It turns out we need to speak with them and may need to borrow one for an ongoing assignment."

"Oh dear, that is a bit irregular. The people you are discussing are here, but we have not yet finished processing them." Mr. Delaney seemed genuinely disturbed. "As I am sure you understand, we have very rigid policies regarding immigration and processing due to the border security issues. Protocols must be followed, or we might be overrun."

"Mr. Delaney, as I am sure you can understand, we're here on official Republic law enforcement business," Danny said. "We sincerely respect the hard and important work you folks are doing, and we would not ask to break protocol unless it was of vital national security. We really need to move forward forthwith."

Jack smiled. Whenever Danny slipped in a "forthwith," it meant he was about to go full Navy Seal on someone.

"Maybe I should ask you gentlemen to get a warrant so that we can document the process fully," Mr. Delaney said with a bit of a sniff. "I would not want to be responsible for a break in protocol without proper legal procedures in place."

Jack could tell Danny wanted to punch him in the face.

"A break in process can lead to questions later, you can of course understand."

"Mr. Delaney, I understand your concerns. May I borrow your phone please?" Jack asked, trying to remain calm with the functionary. Why was it that bureaucrats in whatever form of government lost their capacity for initiative and had judgment like the weasel? Delaney was a typical government weasel.

"Certainly."

Mr. Delaney sat at his desk and turned the phone around.

Jack took out his smartphone and looked up a number. He dialed it on the desk phone, waited while it rang, and then told the assistant who it was.

"Tucker, been a long time," Jack said. He listened for a minute and then said, "Listen, I promise to call when I am back home and we can go shoot some birds, but right now I need a little help. We're up in Richmond sitting in the office of Assistant Director Mark Delaney of the Richmond Immigration Center. We're just asking Mr. Delaney to help us with a matter, and obviously we are asking him to break protocol. Unfortunately, time is short, so I need an official override, old buddy."

Jack listened for a minute, said effusive thanks, and handed the receiver to Assistant Director Delaney, who stood up while listening to the voice on the phone.

Three minutes later, Jack and Danny found themselves on the sixth floor of the former DoubleTree, knocking on the door of Room 615. Katrina Chandler opened the door and smiled broadly. She invited them in, and they entered the room to find all the librarians sitting there.

"It is nice to see you both again," she said, and Jack found that he hoped she actually meant it.

"We're sorry to interrupt, but can Danny and I speak with you and your father alone for a few minutes?" Jack asked.

The other librarians exited the room but thanked the two men for their deliverance yet again on their way out.

Jack explained that they had not found all they needed and that they must search further.

Katrina looked at her father and then back at the Texans. "This document is really quite important to you. Are you ready to tell me exactly what you are trying to find?"

Jack averted his eyes for a second and then looked at Danny. Danny and Jack had been through so much over the years that they often knew what the other was thinking.

Danny nodded, and Jack began, "Yes, it is important…" He told them most of the story of what they had learned about the compact and why they had been sent to retrieve it. Something made him trust her.

Dr. Chandler looked again at his daughter and then asked if they could have a minute alone to discuss the issue.

As Jack and Danny walked to the hallway to wait, Jack turned around and said, "I think that y'all should carefully consider that what we're asking is dangerous. You saw that firsthand yesterday. We were lucky. It could have been much worse. Though we will do our best to keep Katrina out of harm's way, you know better than we do how destabilized things are in the North, Dr. Chandler."

With that, Jack and Danny went out into the hall to wait.

After what seemed like an excruciatingly long period of time but in reality was about five minutes, Katrina came out into the hall. She had traded her khaki pants and white blouse for jeans, running shoes, and a pullover. All looked brand-new and had probably been provided by the immigration staff. She had a small backpack containing her new immigration-issued possessions, like a toothbrush and temporary ID. Jack looked at her with her hair pulled back into a ponytail and not a bit of makeup and thought she looked stunning.

"Let's go," she said, and started off down the hall.

Jack and Danny fell in after her but stopped when Dr. Chandler called after them.

He said with true seriousness, "You gentlemen will bring her back safely."

Jack replied, "Yes, sir."

It felt like an order, and he would do his best to obey.

Outside Richmond, Virginia, Republic of Texas

March 23, 202, 1:00 p.m. Eastern

Jack Dodge picked up the phone and called General Severs in Omaha. He anticipated that this phone call would not be as smooth as their first and only conversation about a year earlier.

After being placed on hold, Dodge heard General Severs's voice and realized he had underestimated the level of unhappiness.

"General Severs, I wanted to follow up on your conversation with Alan Herring. I apologize for not being readily available yesterday."

"Let me guess. You all had a large operation going on north of the border and decided to keep me in the dark. You have now impacted my credibility with the MAMD, and yours with me, Mr. Dodge." Severs delivered the full spit and vinegar of a one-star.

Jack took a deep breath and went forward with the script he had developed in advance of the call.

"Not exactly, sir. We had a very minor intelligence-gathering operation going on just north of the border on behalf of the Ministry of External Affairs. The operation was neither in nor around MAMD territory and had nothing to do with them or their interests. However, that operation did result in us locating some information required by the ministry, and they're requesting that we actually expand that operation. If you would like, I can have Minister Dodge's chief of staff telephone you to corroborate this conversation."

"No, Mr. Dodge, I do not need your father's office to call me," replied General Severs, his voice ice cold. There was a long pause before the general began again in a slightly less hostile tone. "You and I can handle this matter between us. What do you need?"

"We need to put some people on the ground in Binghamton, New York, and believe the assistance of the Mid-Atlantic Military District could be quite valuable."

"Let's cut through the bullshit." The general was all business, and Jack found he was pressing the phone a bit more tightly to his ear. "We are in a delicate dance with the general. We do not want to get too deeply in bed with him, but we do want to keep him strong enough that he can keep restoring some semblance of order, which alleviates pressure on our borders. Hell, look at goddamn Illinois. We are stretching our resources keeping that flood of people on their side of the borders while simultaneously preventing them from annihilating each other. Asking for a favor when the general is begging for additional support is going to cost us."

"I understand, General, and let me absolutely assure you that I would not be asking if it was not of the utmost importance," Jack said, and then took some time to walk him through exactly what they wanted.

The general agreed to make the call and finished with "No more bullshit, Mr. Dodge. You keep me in the loop, or our relationship and the ability of the armed forces to cooperate with your service in the future will be seriously impacted. You understand me?"

Severs did not wait for the affirmative response from Jack, who realized by the dial tone that it was a promise, not a question.

Fort Dix, New Jersey, Mid-Atlantic Military District, former USA

March 23, 2025, 1:18 p.m. Eastern

"Captain Carpenter, Lieutenant Colonel Symmonds," announced Master Sergeant Baptiste, who then stepped aside so that they could enter. The master sergeant closed the door firmly behind him and resumed his post in the anteroom.

"At ease," said General Rogers, sitting behind his desk. "What's on your mind?" He gestured toward the chairs.

They sat in the simple wooden chairs facing the general's desk, a physical reminder that briefings should be short and to the point.

"I just received a call from General Severs," Symmonds said. The general moved forward in his seat, and Carpenter could see Symmonds had his full attention. "The general called to clarify yesterday's conversation. The Texans did have what was described as a small team doing some historical document preservation work in Washington."

The general did not interrupt; his style was always to wait for the initial briefing to finish and then usually ask very pointed questions. "The general said that the effort was deemed so insignificant that it took his people some time to discover that it was underway as a result of his inquiry following our call. However, whatever they were doing in DC has led them to require our assistance. Apparently, they are on some kind of historical-record and document-recovery mission. They are worried about the destruction of Texas-related historical documents. We are going to receive a request shortly regarding a certain specific location they would like to visit in our territory, as well as support needs."

Symmonds took a quick glance at his notes but had nothing more to add.

"Do we have any better idea of specifically what they are seeking?" the general interrogated them.

"As you know, the DC smuggler believes they are focused on the period in and around 1850." Symmonds glanced back at his notes. "This is a period just after Texas became a state and the Mexican-American War, and marked by a series of contentious land and state-expansion disputes regarding slavery."

"Do we honestly believe the Texans are critically interested in their history?" The general stood up and started walking around the room. "Or do we think there is some other intelligence angle that interests them? Maybe our battle plans for the coming push west."

"Honestly, sir, we have no idea, but that is unlikely, based on the Washington angle," said Captain Carpenter. "We have techs looking at the period of history to see if there is something that sticks out, and we will of course analyze any requests they make of us in the context of our own defense. However, finding additional documents from that period would be consistent with the other steps they have taken to substantiate the legality of their country."

"Obviously, it is good for us that the Texans need our help, and we should use it to our advantage to expand their support for us," said the general, standing at parade rest, back to his officers while he watched a helicopter take off. "Lieutenant Colonel Symmonds, I believe Captain Carpenter should be our direct liaison with the Texans. Wherever they go, she goes. She stays close to them. She has the relevant intelligence insights to analyze the situation as it evolves, and to keep us informed, as there may be more here that further advantages us."

Symmonds looked at Carpenter. "Excellent idea, sir."

Carpenter tried not to smile.

"Dismissed," said the general, retaking his seat behind his desk and refocusing on his paperwork before the other two officers departed.

*

Outside Richmond, Virginia, Republic of Texas

March 23, 2025, 2:00 p.m. Eastern

"We have the number for the liaison officer with whom we will be dealing in MAMD territory," Jack said. "General Severs's office called to provide the information. I am going to get in touch shortly, but if they are able to accommodate we should go early tomorrow."

"Jack, I think you personally need to keep a low profile. This is going to be a tough balancing act," Danny replied. "I think we should go in with Britney, Katrina, and Justin as researchers. Britney can function as team leader and interface with the MAMD people. The rest of us are purely security personnel. We stay in the background. No need to let them know this is important enough to have the head of Texas's intelligence leading the mission."

"In that case, we need to lose the jet. It's a dead giveaway that this is not a research project," Jack said. "We can requisition a plane from immigration, something that is more likely to be seen in and around this area. Official markings."

"I feel like this is one of those Russian nesting dolls," said Danny. "We have been to the Library of Congress, nothing. The Archives, very little. Now Binghamton, and then what? Doll after doll, and nothing but more dolls, and not even of the blow-up variety."

"Ever the optimist," replied Jack.

Fort Meade, Maryland, former USA

March 23, 2025, 6:30 p.m. Eastern

Listir pulled the other desk chair into range and put his feet up, then took another pull on the scotch he had poured into a chipped coffee mug.

"I thought we were going to catch them yesterday," he said. "You and your guy did a helluva job chasing down the leads."

"It still does not make any sense to me," said Mulvaney, very pleased to be drinking the eighteen-year-old Johnnie Walker that Spook had brought. "The Texans want nothing to do with us, they have made that clear. They have moved on happily as if the United States never existed, so why would they suddenly have such a big interest in American history? Does that seem like the type of mission to which you task some of your best intelligence assets? I just cannot figure out what anyone would care about enough, a hundred and seventy years later, to send a team into a war zone."

Both men drank in silence. Listir reached for the bottle and poured them another measure of scotch. He settled back in his chair and stared out over the cube farm.

"You know I keep in contact with some people up in what they are now calling the Mid-Atlantic Military District," Listir said.

Mulvaney raised an eyebrow and replied, "I would guess that a man who always seems to be able to get his hands on the best scotch, gasoline, and any number of other things keeps in contact with lots of different characters."

Listir smiled and tipped his glass at Mulvaney. "Only out of love of country." He received a tight smile in return and continued. "Well, I got a call from a contact I cultivate with a few gifts up in New Jersey a little while ago. It seems they received a request from the Texans to facilitate a visit by some researchers to the Pennsylvania-New York border tomorrow. It has got to be related to yesterday. There is no way the Texans have multiple teams on something like this."

Mulvaney leaned forward in his chair and set his drink down. "At least that gives us something more to go on. Let me go see my guy and get him to try and work on narrowing the search."

He left Listir leaning back in his chair and went down into the cube farm.

Listir tried to look relaxed, but his mind whirled. He had heard from a junior officer in the comms center that the Texans were going to the western area of the MAMD. He called and offered Symmonds his assistance coordinating with the Texans but was firmly rebuffed. The lieutenant colonel made it clear that he only wanted to know if Listir's contact at the NSA learned anything else; otherwise, the MAMD did not require any other assistance on this matter.

Listir did not want to get crossways with the MAMD; it would be very bad for business. However, he sensed there was opportunity for him in whatever it was the Texans were seeking if he could get it first, or even just learn about it. He knew from his CIA days that knowledge was power, which is why he held back the name of the man he had seen in the SUV.

He had decided he would head up to New Jersey tomorrow, as his people were making a large delivery of ammunition, big enough that his presence would not be out of the ordinary. He needed to know what was happening at MAMD headquarters. The trip, though long, was getting easier as the MAMD took more and more control. He and his team would leave early and head northwest through Maryland and into central Pennsylvania and then begin the long trip back to New Jersey. Unfortunately, they could not go the more direct way up through Baltimore and Philadelphia; he did not feel like dying tomorrow.

Mulvaney reappeared, looking a bit excited. "Reed is going to work on trying to create search algorithms focused on Texas history from the time it was first a republic in 1836, up through statehood until the Civil War. He is poring over databases, at least whatever he can find that still exists online and/or in cached form here, as well as Texas sites, of which there are many. He is going to cross-reference that with materials that might have been in the Library of Congress and then try and relate that to people and events in Pennsylvania and New York State. Maybe if we are lucky something will come out of that which will help us figure out what is so important to them."

"Your guy, Reed, seems pretty good," said Spook.

"He's my guy!" said Mulvaney with a bit of an edge. "Stay away from him! Got it!"

"Whoa, fella," said Listir, holding up his hands. "We are on the same side. Just to prove it, I am going to let you in on a little secret. I am going up to New Jersey tomorrow on a regular visit, but I want to be nearby just in case I can learn some more about what is going on."

Mulvaney relaxed a bit. "Sorry, Reed is about the only guy around here besides me that still gives a damn."

*

Hearthstone Mountain, Maryland, former USA

March 24, 2025, 4:30 a.m. Eastern

Listir stood outside smoking. The air held a chill. He zipped up his fleece and shoved his free hand deep inside his pocket. He had a hangover. After leaving the NSA, he had driven back to the Mountain and knocked back a couple more than he needed. The scotch combined with the early morning caused his head to ache.

"We're all set, boss," said Brown. "We have two extra tires, repair kits, enough gas to get there and back, though I'm sure we can fuel at Fort Dix. The cargo truck is fully loaded and ready to go as well."

"OK, let's roll out," said Listir, flicking his cigarette butt away.

*

*Richmond International Airport,
Richmond, Virginia, Republic of Texas*

March 24, 2025, 6:25 a.m. Eastern

The team sat in a conference room off to one side of the hangar. The room was bare-bones, with imitation wood paneling and a large sliding glass door that allowed easy access as well as a view of the hangar and the tarmac beyond.

A coffeepot nearly drained of its contents burbled on a hot plate on a metal side table. All six team members were arrayed around the table ready to go, but the pilots had decided, based on satellite imagery, to delay departure until 7 a.m. due to the potential for low clouds and fog in the Binghamton area. Given that there was no functioning air traffic control system in the North, nor any on-the-ground airport personnel to consult on local field weather, caution was warranted.

Based on the plan the team had devised, Jack, Danny, and Simon were dressed in the current version of border security uniforms. Each man wore combat boots, thick khaki trousers, button-downs, and vests. They were all armed with 9mm Glocks with extended clips in holsters, as well as AR-15s. Meanwhile, Britney, Katrina, and Justin tried to approximate a version of academic wear: running shoes, jeans, polos, and fleeces. Each carried a backpack that contained notebooks, pencils, academic research books on the origins of the Civil War, and, in the case of Justin and Britney, an inner pocket with a Glock and extra clips. Their two regular pilots would also be wearing side arms, and the plane contained an ammunition locker with another AR-15, a couple of shotguns, and extra ammunition.

Danny helpfully pointed out, "Hey, you know the last time some boys from Texas went north into Pennsylvania, it was Gettysburg, and they got their ass kicked at Little Round Top."

Everyone got a chuckle out of that, while Britney responded that this time it would be fine because they were taking women along.

"It's critical that we all play our roles well," said Jack. "As you know, we had some limited personal dealings with the Mid-Atlantic forces on a recent extraction. They are organized, efficient, and professional. However, they are also involved in an active series of battles to both restore order in areas they control as well as expand their territory. Given that the leadership is all ex–US Army and that most had combat experience in either Iraq or Afghanistan, they are battle hardened. They will be studying us closely. They will be friendly but are not our friends. They will certainly be trying to figure out if there is a means to use our visit to their advantage. Britney?"

Britney flipped a tablet around and placed it at her end of the table in the middle so all could see the screen.

"As you can see, the campus is located to the south of the town and accessible from the main highway. We have almost no current intelligence about this area, which on the flip side would indicate it might be fairly stable. We understand that limited power services have been restored following the Mid-Atlantic takeover, and satellite imagery does reveal some regular road traffic.

"We are going to be picked up by Captain Carpenter and a security force from the Mid-Atlantic," Britney continued while she punched up some new information on the tablet. "I spoke with her both last evening and again this morning to advise of the delay via satellite phone. She has indicated that the Mid-Atlantic considers this area to be only fairly secure. The Mid-Atlantic is trying to push deeper into the Marcellus Shale area, which is controlled by multiple other military forces, criminal gangs, and other elements. These groups fight back through ambushes and forays into Mid-Atlantic-controlled territory. She advised me that we should use full security precautions. Simon, try not to get shot again."

Simon gave Britney a clear view of his middle finger, while everyone else laughed.

Britney pointed at the screen. "That is the Bartle Library on the Binghamton campus. Based on what Herring's people could surmise, we will be focusing our efforts on the fourth floor, where Dickinson's papers appear to be housed. Or, at least, the last time there was a usable database they were there. Questions or comments?"

Jack took over. "We're going to move directly from the plane to the library, find what we can, and get the heck back on the plane. At all times, everyone should be aware there is danger from the forces opposed to the Mid-Atlantic. Also, we should not be confused about the popularity of forces from the Republic of Texas to both the Mid-Atlantic soldiers and the general population. Good?"

Everyone nodded.

The team started to relax. Chairs scraped as people got up to get more coffee when Katrina said, "What if the papers are not there?"

"Excuse me?" said Danny.

"What if when we complete the search of the library, we do not find Dickinson's papers, or at least not the ones we are looking for? You have given that some thought, right?"

Jack and Danny stared at each other, and then Jack found himself locking eyes with Katrina. He lost his train of thought for a minute before Danny said, "Jack." Jack looked at Danny, refocused and spoke.

"That is a possibility. As you all know from the discussion last night, Dickinson spent a considerable amount of time in New York City and actually died there. We are hopeful that the documents we are looking for are in Binghamton, or evidence of their destruction is there. Failing that, there is a chance that some of us may have to go to New York, and Herring and his people are actually researching everything they can find about Dickinson and his New York activities, places, et cetera. I also have one member of the staff working on a rough plan for how we might get in and out of New York, which is no joke."

Jack looked up to see Mike Ramsey walking across the hangar. Jack waved, and the pilot gave the thumbs-up. The team got up, grabbed their gear, and followed him out to the King Air 350, which already had its right propeller turning.

CHAPTER SEVENTEEN

Binghamton, New York, former USA

March 24, 2025, 9:42 a.m. Eastern Time

The flight across Virginia into Maryland and Pennsylvania was smooth, and visibility was good. The team took note of the fact that fields that five years ago would have looked ready for plowing in many cases were overgrown or untended.

As they approached Binghamton, the pilot asked Britney to please check with her contact and ensure the runway was clear of debris, and to try to ascertain wind speed as well as direction. Britney got through to Captain Carpenter on the satellite phone and verified that the runway, though relatively rough due to lack of maintenance, was clear, and winds were nonexistent.

As they came nearer, ground fog appeared in the valleys. The immediate area around Binghamton was only hazy, and as the plane slowed and descended for landing, the team could clearly make out burned-out buildings, abandoned cars, and a general sense of decay.

Danny said, "Remember, folks, this is a relatively good area compared to the cities."

They touched down with a firm bump, and the pilots brought the plane to a halt using as little runway as possible in order to avoid any extended jarring over unmaintained tarmac. They turned onto a taxiway and made quickly for a soldier who was signaling, standing in front of three Humvees. The pilots taxied to where the soldier indicated and then shut down.

Britney said, "Showtime."

Danny was first off the plane, followed by Jack and Simon. They took up stations around the airstairs and surveyed the situation. Danny slapped a hand on the fuselage, and Justin, Britney, and Katrina descended. The three "security" men positioned themselves to the right, left, and just in front of the three researchers.

A woman in combat fatigues emerged from between the Humvees and walked up to the group.

"Welcome. I'm Captain Carpenter from the Mid-Atlantic Military District."

Britney walked forward and shook hands with Captain Carpenter. "I am Britney Marelli. This is Dr. Katrina Chandler and Justin Manning."

Britney waved at the three heavily armed men. "These three gentlemen are our security personnel, Jack, Danny and Simon. Of course, we also have two pilots, but they will remain with the aircraft."

Captain Carpenter eyed the three hard-looking men with serious weapons accompanying the research team and gave them a nod.

She said, "Two of my men will remain with your pilots to ensure their safety and the safety of the plane. I assume the pilots are armed."

It was not really a question, but Britney nodded in the affirmative.

"Instead of standing here in the open, why don't we move out to the university? You three can ride with me in the center Humvee, and your security people can jump in the one on the right."

Jack cleared his throat and said, "Dr. Marelli, I'm sorry, but protocol requires that one of us be with you at all times."

Britney looked at the captain and shrugged. "They have all these rules. Not a world we academics tend to live in, but they call the shots."

"OK. Why don't one of you come with us? And Britney, you send one of your colleagues in the other vehicle with the other two gentlemen."

Sorted out, everyone piled into the Humvees, and they immediately got under way toward Binghamton. Jack noted that the gate in the airport fence was lying on the ground, and numerous abandoned and ransacked vehicles were visible behind the hangars. The road out of the airport was little better, with vehicles pushed off to the side and significant potholes every twenty feet or so.

"Can you tell me any more about what you are looking for?"

Captain Carpenter was seated next to Britney in the middle seat, and Jack found himself with Katrina in the third row. The space was tighter, and he was wedged up against Katrina, a condition that was exacerbated each time they hit a pothole. He could feel the warmth of her arm against his and it was distracting. He was hundreds of miles into unfriendly territory and thinking like a teenage boy. He had to remind himself to focus.

Jack concentrated on the conversation in front of him and heard Britney saying, "We are working hard to document all of Texas's history from the time of independence from Mexico up until the American Civil War. The Texas Archives are obviously the preeminent source for materials about the First Republic, but we have found that our forefathers were deficient in maintaining historical documents from before and into the period of US statehood. We would like to gather all the important materials we can about events like the Mexican-American

War, the Compromise of 1850, and the run-up to the Civil War. We hope we can rectify the deficiencies in our records before the remaining documents are potentially…" She struggled for an inoffensive word, but the Captain jumped in.

"Compromised?"

Britney continued. "Yes, compromised is an elegant way to describe it. Thank you for your diplomacy."

The Humvees made good time in spite of obstacles on the road. Eventually, they turned off the highway and found themselves on surface streets. Jack could see what the captain had identified as Binghamton University in the distance. The area surrounding the university showed signs of neglect and disrepair, with shops with boarded-over windows. However, he could see that this was different than DC. There were people on the sidewalks, going in and out of stores. A pickup truck stood near an intersection with a selection of produce in the rear, and several people clustered around it.

"What are the people using for money?" Katrina asked as they rolled past a small group clustered around the back of a farm truck.

"In some cases, it is barter. Some have access to Texas dollars. Others trade work. It is basically whatever the seller is willing to accept," said Captain Carpenter. "In most of our district, we have been rolling out a currency of our own. Mid-Atlantic pounds, we call them. We pay for things that we buy with them. We accept them in payment, and they are starting to take hold."

"How long have you all had control over this area?" asked Jack, already knowing that the Mid-Atlantic forces moved in during the early fall to what had basically been a lawless region, each town responsible for its own security.

"We gained control here in September and extended about sixty miles to the west before the winter caused us to suspend forward advancement. We now have firm control of the area from the Atlantic Ocean to mid-Pennsylvania, just below the city of Newark, to the Philadelphia-Camden area in the south. We do have some parts of Delaware and Maryland under our control. Though the line was pushed well beyond here, we are still firming up our control of this region." She indicated the heavily wooded hills. "This is tough country, and we need another season of good weather to root out all the problems."

"What about the cities?" asked Katrina. "Any plans to reestablish control over the bigger cities?"

The captain glanced back at the questioner. "It is not worth it from our perspective. The cities are lost. Crime has become the rule of the day, and we do not have the resources to deal with all the people."

Katrina started to respond, but the vehicle came to a halt.

"This is it, ma'am," said the young corporal driving the Humvee.

"Copy that. Signal the other Humvee, and let's set up a defensive perimeter."

The two men in the front seat jumped out, carbines at the ready. They were joined by the second team from the other Humvee. Within a minute, Jack, Danny, and Simon joined them, and the seven men fanned out to check around the entrance to Bartle Library. Danny and Simon entered the building through poorly boarded-up doors and made a quick recon of the first floor. Other than books, paper, debris, and furniture lying everywhere, the place appeared deserted.

Captain Carpenter got out and joined the seven men.

The corporal from the lead Humvee spoke.

"Ma'am, a quick recon shows no threats. I would suggest that we leave two men here, one over there." He pointed to a clump of dying bushes about twenty meters to the east of their position, near a stone embankment. "Another over there." He indicated a point about an equal distance to the west where a concrete pedestal stood, probably the base for a statue that had been hauled away and likely melted for scrap.

The captain concurred, and two men were dispatched. The three researchers joined the soldiers and Texas security forces and walked into the building in the middle of a diamond formation of security.

Once inside, Katrina let out a low whistle. The library was trashed. Documents lay all over the first floor, like someone had come through and just run by the shelves, throwing everything on the floor. Jack and Danny looked at each other and Jack knew they were thinking the same thing. *If the document is here, we could walk on it and never see it.*

"Do you have a specific search area in which you want to start?" Captain Carpenter asked.

"Let's go to the fourth floor," replied Britney. "That is where we think documents from the relevant period left to the university by politicians, soldiers, and government bodies were, according to the last available cache of the website."

As the group stated to move up the stairs, there was a loud bang from above, and everyone froze. Two Mid-Atlantic soldiers were in the lead, and Captain Carpenter immediately signaled for them to move forward and check out the noise.

There were slit windows in the walls that provided light in the otherwise darkened staircase. Jack and Danny moved forward of the rest of the group into the spaces vacated by the two soldiers. Simon and Captain Carpenter took up position at the rear, guarding their six.

After a couple of minutes, one of the soldiers reappeared.

"There is a dog up here," the soldier said. "We are not sure how it got in, but it looks to have mange and be in an awful way."

"Shoot it," replied the captain.

Katrina looked shocked but held her tongue.

The soldier moved off, and a couple of seconds later they heard the snap of a shot.

"Clear," came the call down the stairs.

The group began to move up the black rubber-coated stairs. The soldiers stayed out in front, and in a couple of minutes everyone was standing on the fourth floor. The dead dog lay in the corner of the stairwell. Katrina held a hand to her face as she stared at it.

Captain Carpenter sent the two soldiers off to do a sweep of the floor headed one way; Danny and Simon went the other. Jack guarded the stairs, and Captain Carpenter kept her eyes trained for threats coming from where the men were sweeping the floor.

Jack was impressed. The captain was an organized soldier and displayed excellent field tactics.

"Afghanistan or Iraq, Captain?" asked Jack over his soldier.

"Both," she replied.

"Me too," offered up Jack.

The four men returned from their floor checks, and one of the soldiers spoke.

"The floor appears clear, though based on the garbage, people have been here and potentially might even be residing here. A couple of the conference rooms look like makeshift sleeping quarters. There are three additional stairwells, two internal and one fire escape."

"Copy that," Carpenter said, and pointed at the two soldiers. "One of you guards this stairwell, the other guards the fire escape. No one comes in or even near this floor. Shout a warning. If they keep coming, fire a warning shot, and then you are authorized to use all necessary force."

Carpenter turned to Jack and said, "I need two of your men to guard the other two stairwells, and then I suggest when the entrances are secure that you make another recon before we take the researchers onto the floor."

Jack nodded and moved out, as did Danny, Simon, and one of the soldiers. The men did a sweep of the floor, and each time they hit a stairwell someone peeled off for guard duty, first Simon, then an MAMD soldier, then Danny.

"All clear, ma'am," said Jack as they regrouped.

"OK, let's move out," said the captain. "You take point," she ordered Jack.

The group moved out behind Jack through the stacks toward the northwest corner. The fourth floor was in considerably better condition than the ground floor, with most materials still on the shelves, but there was a sour smell in the air and plenty of debris on the floor indicating human activity.

Britney signaled when they were in the right place, and the three researchers fanned out.

Britney said, "Captain, given that the stairs are secure and you are stationed out near the walkway, could I borrow Jack to help us sort materials?"

The captain indicated her satisfaction. "That would be fine."

The team quickly set to work, methodically going shelf by shelf, examining each set of documents. Jack initially focused his efforts on the documents and materials strewn across the floor. He moved slowly down the aisle on his knees, casting aside land records from the Binghamton area, pamphlets on abolitionist meetings, and even some accounts of the Mexican-American War written by a reporter for a local paper. The rest of the team worked methodically, having broken the collection into three sections.

After about an hour's search, Britney called a quick break, and the four assembled in the middle of the stacks. Jack saw Captain Carpenter move down the aisle, still facing outward but clearly positioning herself to hear the conversation.

"There is a tremendous amount of varied material here," Britney said. "I just am not finding any systematic organization that would allow me to jump more efficiently to"—she paused and glanced down the aisle—"to topics that relate specifically to Texas."

"Actually, there is some order. It just took me some time to understand the collection methodology," said Katrina. She had everyone's attention. "The materials are assembled in groupings of interest. The reason they seem haphazard is because they are larger categories. It dawned on me when I found a section containing census records, tax records, birth and death records, and muster records for the Civil War that section organization related to demographic evolution."

Katrina walked over to another area on the stacks. "Here, look at this," she continued. "In this area, there are agricultural production records covering most of the nineteenth century, records related to rail, mining, forestry, and then a section of building permits. This section clearly relates to the economic evolution of the region. What we need to do is to take the sections and do quick samples to categorize each area. When we have the categories, then we can more thoroughly search that section."

After about another hour of searching, Britney shouted, "Politics!" The other three immediately moved over to join her. "Look at this, I have voter records. Election results. Town hall records. Court records. Here are some papers from a judge, including his case notes."

The section was particularly dense. All four levels of the shelves were crammed full of small plastic holders, each packed with numerous documents.

"OK, take a shelf and start searching," said Britney.

Jack took the top shelf and began taking down the plastic holders. Each box basically seemed to deal with a person, event, or office. He found himself looking through a box containing the court records dealing with a long-ago sensational murder trial. He quickly finished with that box and moved on to the next. Here Jack found the personal and professional papers of a long-serving mayor of Ithaca.

He glanced at his watch; it was nearly one o'clock. At some point, they would face the decision about how long to continue the search. Should they leave and return? Stay working as late as necessary, including flying out at night, or stay at the airport overnight and return for a second day?

"I have something." Katrina held up a file. "Here are the calendars of a specific United States attorney."

All four smiled. Everyone grabbed a folio box from that area and started going file by file. Jack and Justin came up empty-handed, but Britney found three boxes containing personal correspondence covering a large period of the former senator's life.

Jack decided to offer up a security consideration and focus the conversation. "Instead of trying to go through all these letters here, what if we set these boxes aside? Triage everything else, and then we can remove these records in their entirety, if that is OK with the captain, and read them at our leisure, instead of trying to study the documents here, given the security risks not only to our team but also to the captain's personnel. We can return to Captain Carpenter any of the nongermane information."

Captain Carpenter said, "Actually, that would work well from my perspective. I would like to head back toward central command while there is still plenty of daylight left. If we can wrap up here and get you all back on your plane by fifteen hundred, we can make it back to Fort Dix near sunset."

Britney nodded at Jack and took back over command. "OK, Jack. I believe your security plan is wise. You have a duffel in your backpack?"

Jack nodded.

"Good. Why don't you pack up everything on these two shelves, plus those three folios? Katrina and I will quickly triage the remaining areas to make sure we are not leaving behind any other materials related to the history of Texas."

Jack got to work, while the two women went to the remaining floor-to-ceiling stack. Jack finished and joined them. After a search of the remaining shelves, three more plastic folios of materials were added to the large nylon duffel. These documents related to the Civil War and the politics of the region.

The duffel was stuffed to the breaking point. The zipper would not seal. Jack bent down to lift it and realized just how heavy it was. He got it up and stretched the shoulder strap crossways across his body. He held his gun but sincerely hoped they would not see any action while he had a baby elephant strapped to his back.

"OK, let's move out," Jack said. "Captain, can you take point, since I am clearly less than nimble?"

"Copy that," the captain said, and moved out.

They quickly gathered up the other members of their group and headed back down the stairs, with the Mid-Atlantic soldiers leading the way. They reached the front doors and exited from the gloomy library in to the bright sunshine.

Jack pulled on a pair of wraparound sunglasses, as did most of the other soldiers. He found himself staring at the light reflecting off of Katrina Chandler's hair. Since Marissa's death, he had not paid attention to a single woman, and not for their lack of trying. Now, he could not stop looking at Katrina.

"Let's not stand in the open." The captain broke Jack's daydream.

Everyone got back into the vehicles in the same configuration as the trip to the library, and they immediately headed back toward the airport. The streets showed even more signs of life than earlier. There were a couple of trucks making deliveries in town. A few Mid-Atlantic soldiers were visible on the streets. Several cars moved around. Unlike in DC, the people in Binghamton did not seem particularly fearful of being out in the open, though they did look at the passing Humvees with a bit of wariness.

"Captain, how long will it take you to return this area to something more closely resembling normal?" Jack asked, watching a little girl and her mother walk hand in hand down a sidewalk under the watchful eye of a soldier in full combat dress.

"It will take some time. To date, we have reestablished order and basically eliminated most fighting near here. Crime, which you could basically call armed gangs stealing from and harassing the population, is almost eliminated. We have a very simple approach to crime, which tends to aid in its reduction. We shoot the offenders on capture. Based on our plans, we should have complete control of this area within the next month, and that means zero crime. At the same time, we are bringing back up some essential services, such as power and water. Some of that work is already completed. The final piece of the puzzle, which takes more time, is developing a functioning economy. It's not an easy task to reboot an area, but the general has developed a pretty strong team and plan, which we have now executed multiple times as we add territory."

"I'm sure it's not easy to bring back an area," said Jack. "I hope you have great success. It seems like y'all have a good handle on it."

The captain appeared pleased with Jack's praise. He knew that the Mid-Atlantic Military District wanted to expand its relationship with the Republic of Texas. Clearly the captain wanted to show that they would be responsive and meaningful potential allies, and wanted the Texans to think of them as a responsible governing authority.

The captain reoriented herself and spoke into a radio, alerting the airport personnel that they were approaching. She listened and frowned slightly. She gave a few instructions and then signed off.

"The team reports that they saw a couple of men at the tree line on the opposite side of the field about an hour ago," the captain said in her best command voice. "The men were studying them with binoculars and had rifles. Due to the lack of extra personnel, my soldiers stayed with the pilots and kept the plane secure, but we have to assume that the men are nearby. Based on that, I have told my men to get your pilots in the plane and engines turning. When we get there, I would like you all to get on board and out of here as fast as possible." She paused, looked at the far side of the field, and then said, "Your pilots have been instructed to wait for us to drive over by the tree line. We will set up a perimeter between the runway and the tree line."

"Copy that, Captain," said Jack.

He then spoke into his own secure radio and gave Danny a heads-up on the plan.

Britney resumed her role of operation commander and said, "Captain, we would like to thank you for your assistance. We apologize for any inconvenience our visit caused and sincerely appreciate all of your team's efforts."

Jack continued to speak to Danny in low tones as they approached the airport. Finally, he spoke to Britney.

"Dr. Marelli, when we pull up, let Danny and the guys get out and take a defensive posture. When the team is set, you two can exit the vehicle and head for the aircraft at full speed. I will load the bag. Danny spoke with the pilots. We will be moving as soon as the Humvees get to the trees."

Both Humvees swept onto the tarmac and rolled up to the plane, which had both engines turning. The two soldiers were stationed at either end of a Humvee, which was now parked between the plane and the tree line, about 120 meters away. The two Humvees in which they were riding accelerated across the tarmac and stopped dangerously close to the aircraft. Danny, Justin, and Simon were out of their Humvee before it even fully stopped moving, weapons at the ready, facing outward.

Jack ran the bag over to the plane and then returned. He took a quick look around and said, "Go!"

Britney and Katrina jumped from the vehicle and ran the three meters to the air stair, then disappeared into the plane. The Humvees were already moving again across the runway and toward the tree line before Justin and Simon raced up the stairs. Jack clambered in as the plane started rolling. Jack had trouble sealing the hatch as they bounced over the tarmac.

The plane accelerated down the taxiway at well above normal speed, and Jack began to wonder if the pilots just planned on taking off from the taxiway. However, the plane slowed, quickly executed a rapid turn onto the runway, and then swept down the runway at maximum thrust. Jack heard "V1…V2 rotate" from the cockpit, and the King Air leapt into the air with the wheels coming up instantaneously. However, the climb was very shallow.

Ramsey came over the loudspeaker. "Simple physics, folks. We can either use thrust to climb or go fast. We chose fast. Enjoy the view while we put some serious distance between ourselves and the airfield before we climb."

Jack stared out the window as they went by a farm with a few cows grazing in a field. The cows stared at the plane, and Jack felt sure they were on eye level. He found himself hoping there were no transmission lines left in the area.

Back at the airfield, Captain Carpenter and her team stood looking at the King Air disappear, and then got back in their Humvees. The convoy headed for New Jersey. She took out her satellite phone and hit the preprogrammed number. While she waited for the connection to be made, she went over her short brief one more time in her head.

"Yes?" The voice on the other end of the phone belonged to Lieutenant Colonel Symmonds.

"Team departed with a large package. Will brief in person, but little luck in discovering if there was anything beyond research project. Returning to base," said the captain, ever mindful that someone in Austin would be listening, and possibly a faction or two in Western Pennsylvania trying to do the same.

"Copy that," said the lieutenant colonel. "Report in person the minute you arrive."

Meanwhile, Danny and Jack had their heads stuck in the cockpit quizzing the pilots on the men that had been seen around the airport. The pilots did not have good descriptions, but from what they reported the men sounded more like survivalists than Listir's team.

*

Richmond International Airport, Richmond, Virginia, Republic of Texas

March 23, 2025, 4:13 p.m. Eastern

The King Air touched down and rolled to a stop before turning off the tarmac and heading for the secure hangar. When the left engine stopped rotating, Jack dropped the airstairs, and the team began exiting. Jack thanked the pilots for an exceptional piece of flying and then followed the team toward the conference room where they had begun the day.

Jack was the last to enter, and he dropped the heavy duffel on the floor. Simon closed the sliding door behind him. Justin removed a small jamming device from his pack and placed it on the table, immediately rendering any electronic monitoring impossible.

Jack pointed to the duffel and said, "OK, everyone should grab a heap of documents and start reading. I'm going to step out for one second and see if we can get some pizzas delivered, because I am starving. I cannot eat another MRE, if it can be avoided. Everybody good with anchovy?"

"No!" came the collective response.

Katrina said, "Please do try to be careful with these documents. Many of them are nearly one hundred seventy years old, if not older. I am going to use this laptop and create an index." She cleaned off part of the side table where the coffeepot sat. "Let's pile the documents that are not related to our efforts over here for return to the Mid-Atlantic authorities."

Danny openly smiled at Jack as he said, "Sure, that's a good plan. Let's all be careful."

CHAPTER EIGHTEEN

Captain Carpenter's Humvee pulled up in front of the command post, and she exited the vehicle. It departed while she was still walking up the path to the front door of the redbrick facility. She returned the salute of MPs inside the lobby and then swiped her pass and entered through the electronic gate. She walked down the hall toward a bullet-resistant door marked "Intelligence," swiped her card again, and heard the click of the locks disengaging.

Behind the door were rows of cubes. Off to her left was a door behind which stood the Electronic Operations Department. At the end of the room were a series of small private offices, one of which was hers, but she did not go there. She walked to the office in the corner and knocked firmly twice.

"Come," said a clear voice, and she opened it and passed into the spartan office.

"Good evening, Captain Carpenter. Nice to see you back in one piece." Lieutenant Colonel Symmonds looked up from the papers in his hand.

"Good evening, sir," said Carpenter.

Symmonds waved at a metal chair, and the captain took a seat.

"So, tell me all about the Texans," offered Symmonds as he refilled his coffee mug from a thermos and offered the captain a cup.

"Thank you, sir, it has been a long day." The captain took a sip and then started in on a full but concise rendition of the day.

She reached the end of the story, and Symmonds said, "So, we do not have a good idea what they were looking for."

"No, sir, and not for lack of trying." The captain paused. "It was odd. They were clearly focused on documents from before and around the Civil War, but they did not indicate anything in particular. They also were very interested in Senator Dickinson from New York, about whom I know nothing but will find out. I almost got the impression that some of the team members only had a general idea of the full scope of the project. However..."

"However what, Captain?" Symmonds shifted forward in his chair.

Carpenter took another sip of her coffee. "At one point, one of the Texans yelled 'Politics,' and literally the entire team shifted into high gear. Meanwhile, they had earlier found some muster records and related documents from the Civil War and had almost no interest."

Symmonds leaned back in his chair. "Politics?" He stared at the ceiling. "Let's have one of the techs search the political history of the period as well as the senator and see what he comes up with that would be of interest to our friends. Something was important enough for the Texans to send a team up here and request our assistance in the middle of negotiations. Not the normal time you want to be building up a favor deficit."

"Copy that, sir," replied the captain as she stood, knowing she had been dismissed. "One more thing, sir. We have the photos of the team. Do you want to get in touch with Listir and get them run through the databases at the NSA?"

"Interesting that you mention Mr. Listir, Captain," said the lieutenant colonel. "He arrived here just a few minutes before you did. I understand that he and his people are over at the mess having something to eat."

"I'm sorry, sir, but did I miss something?" asked the captain. "I did not know he was coming. I actually thought we would keep him out of this matter going forward."

"You are correct. No one knew he was coming, Captain," replied Symmonds. "As I understand it, Mr. Listir accompanied a delivery his people were making. He told our people that it was a routine check on his part, on conditions on the route, given the size of the shipment. However, we do not remember any routine visits in the past. I think that we all have to assume that Mr. Listir's appearance is directly related to what is going on with the Texans." The lieutenant colonel was not a fan of Mr. Listir and had never made any attempt to hide it. Time and again Symmonds publicly stated that though the MAMD needed to deal with the black market to support its activities, it did not mean that he approved of the black marketers. "Let's run the photographs here with databases we have, but given their limited nature, I think that unfortunately you may need to ask Mr. Listir to contact his friend at the NSA. However, you should carefully limit your discussions with Mr. Listir. He may supply us, but he is not on our side, or frankly anyone's but his own."

Fort Meade, Maryland, former USA

March 23, 2025, 9:23 p.m. Eastern

Mulvaney sat at his desk, mainly for lack of anything else to do. The Texans had successfully cut off all his inroads into systems in Austin and deleted the information obtained earlier. He and Reed were running out of ideas. Mulvaney decided not to go home; no point going home to an empty house. He had poured his second scotch of the evening when the phone rang.

"Mulvaney," he said, and quickly heard Spook at his most upbeat.

"Hey, buddy, have I got something good for you," said Listir. "Just tell me the most secure way possible to get you some photos."

Mulvaney read off a secure email—well, semi-secure at least.

"Wait until you see who is in the pictures!" Listir hung up.

Mulvaney logged in to the system and went through a series of drop-down menus to find the secure email account he provided to Listir. He opened the folder and waited. He knew it would take several minutes for the filters to clear the traffic, but finally a message appeared. Mulvaney analyzed the routing and realized it had come directly from Fort Dix. He made a note to ask Listir more about his relationship with the Mid-Atlantic forces. He opened the folder and found himself standing at attention, never realizing he had stood up.

"Reed!" he screamed at the top of his lungs. "Reed!" He went to the door and yelled again, "Reed!" He finally saw the big man get up from his cube. A couple of other heads lifted up in the cube farm. "Come up here now!"

Reed came trotting.

"What is it?" The big man sucked in oxygen walking into Mulvaney's office.

"Look at this." Mulvaney was pointing at his computer, and Reed slid around behind the desk to take a look.

"That's that guy Justin from the MUAV, but that is no MUAV behind him," said Reed. Mulvaney started moving the cursor to show the next picture, and the next. "Who are the other people?" asked the analyst.

"Reed, see this guy?" Mulvaney pointed at a tall, good-looking thirtysomething man.

Reed shook his head.

"That's one Jack Dodge, head of Texas's intelligence operations," said Mulvaney. "This guy is Danny Winters, Dodge's number two and alter ego. The Latin-looking lady is Britney Marelli, an operative. This is a veritable who's who of Texas's field force. This last woman and man I don't know, but we can run them and see if we hit anything."

"Where were the pictures taken?" Reed had taken over cursor control and was going slowly back through the pictures, one by one. "And who took them?" Reed started tapping away on the keyboard.

"All good questions. Let's get the answers!"

Mulvaney grabbed his phone and dialed the number for Listir's phone. He got through on the fourth try, but the connection was excellent.

Listir said, "I knew you would like that photo album. What did you find about the others?"

"Not so fast, Listir," said Mulvaney. "I have a few questions for you, such as where did you get these pictures?"

There was a long silence on the phone, and Mulvaney heard the telltale static of a satellite call before Listir responded, "I was given them by a business associate."

"Cut the crap, Listir!" said Mulvaney with a bit of anger. "We may be on our ass, but we still can do the basics around here. The email came from a masked server at Fort Dix, so from the MAMD directly. You are going to answer my questions to my complete satisfaction, or you can go fuck yourself."

Reed looked surprised to hear his boss so angry.

Listir stood staring at a place on the ground, trying to control his temper. Who the fuck did Mulvaney think he was? Now was not the time for him to start acting all need-to-know, especially not while the MAMD people sat waiting for results and Jack Dodge was so close. Listir walked a very fine line here, trying to enhance his position with the MAMD while potentially playing his own game with respect to the Texans.

He lit a cigarette while weighing how to deal with Mulvaney. The truth was pretty simple. Bottom line, Listir still needed him.

"What do you want to know?"

"What is your relationship with the Mid-Atlantic Military District? Because it is clearly more than a simple trading relationship," said Mulvaney.

His voice still carried a fair bit of anger. Listir was amazed at the man's backbone.

"They are the emerging power to the north of DC, and in my line of work I need to deal with them," said Listir.

"Can we stop the charades? I am not completely incompetent. I know some about your line of work—let's call it profiteering. Specifically, what are your and their interests here?"

Listir recognized he was on thin ice. Patriotism motivated Mulvaney; Listir's blind love of money and power would not translate or influence him.

"Look, Mulvaney, I want what you want, a return of order, and I do what I can to help that as best as I can. But I also realize that it's slipping away. I also believe in helping some of the forces around us, who may not be perfect but at least try to bring order and peace to parts of the country. I hope that long-term a return of order and some sense of normalcy may enable us to pick up the pieces. In the meantime, I also am trying to make a bit of a better life for myself in this mess."

Another long pause, and then Mulvaney asked, "Why are you at Fort Dix now?"

Mulvaney took a drink of scotch. He pushed the bottle and a cup to Reed, who waved him off.

Finally, Listir answered. "I came up here to discuss yesterday's events with some of the Mid-Atlantic people I deal with. I thought it was significant that an operative of the prominence of the one you cited was on the ground in DC, and I wanted to see what the people knew here about why the Texans, who have spent so much time and money sealing the borders, are now so interested in our ancient history."

Now it was Mulvaney's time to weigh what he had heard. "Where were the pictures taken? By whom? What was the context?"

"The pictures were taken earlier today. They have not told me where. I am trying to find out. The MAMD people do not tell me everything. I did learn that the Texans called requesting a favor, wanting to drop some researchers in and search for historical documents." Listir paused and lit yet another cigarette before continuing. "The Mid-Atlantic people sent out some forces to provide direction and security, and the Texans flew in on the plane you see in the background. What airport I just do not know. They apparently spent about six hours on the ground, most of which was used to go through some archives, and then left. I have answered your questions. Tell me what you know."

Reed had continued hammering away on Mulvaney's keyboard. The photos were JPEGs, and Reed ran a few protocols on the embedded data. He opened another window and pointed at a flashing dot on a map.

"By the way, the geolocators on the photos tell us that these pictures were taken earlier today just outside Binghamton, New York. This was no cutesy research trip," said Mulvaney. "You have the pictures in front of you?" He gained a positive response from Listir. "You know full well that Jack Dodge is not in the field for a normal everyday research project."

Listir stared into the face of the man who had vowed to kill him. He could still hear Dodge's voice from that night. He also still felt bitterness at being dragged through all the inquiries. Dodge fucked up his career and his life. An image of Dodge in a Ford Explorer speeding off on a DC street flashed through his mind.

"The rest are Danny Winters, Justin Manning, and Britney Marelli." Mulvaney stopped speaking and looked up at the sound of tapping, and Reed handed him a slip of paper. "Sorry, the other man we are still searching for, but the woman is Dr. Katrina Chandler, a specialist in American history. Used to teach at Yale, according to a cached version of their site." Mulvaney remembered Manning well.

"Sorry, did you say Chandler?" asked Spook, and Mulvaney confirmed that he had.

Listir stood thinking. Something was nagging him. Finally, it hit him.

"Yesterday! Yesterday, in DC, we met a Dr. Chandler, who was some kind of librarian at the Library of Congress. She has got to be related, which means whatever they were after at the library led them to travel today to the Pennsylvania-New York border, near where significant fighting recently occurred. Not a normal spot for academic research."

The line crackled as neither man spoke for several minutes. Mulvaney focused on trying to think of what could be historically important enough for the Texans to send a team to investigate. Listir only thought of the potential value of whatever they sought, either in real or extortion value.

Mulvaney finally said, "You need to get me any information you can on where they went exactly, and about their search. Maybe we can gain enough information to narrow down the options and make an educated guess. Trust me, Jack Dodge is not checking out books from the library." He ended the call.

Mulvaney looked at Reed. "I know this is going to be a stretch given the overall environment, but we need to figure out what might be in the Binghamton area that would be of interest to the Republic of Texas. Any ideas?"

Listir slipped the satphone back in his pocket, stubbed out the butt of his cigarette, and turned to return to the building. However, before he could make the door, a voice called out to him, "Police that butt, mister."

Listir turned and found a large man with captain's bars staring at him. He decided to pick up the butt and throw it in the receptacle, when he really wanted to kick the arrogant prick in the balls. He fucking hated the military.

*

Fort Dix, New Jersey, Mid-Atlantic Military District, former USA

March 23, 2025, 11:11 p.m. Eastern

Captain Carpenter sat at her desk. Her head throbbed. She'd downed a handful of aspirin about thirty minutes earlier, but they seemed to have no impact on her headache. She was rubbing her temples when the MP said, "Ma'am? I have a Mr. Listir to see you."

"Bring him in, Corporal," she replied. She sighed, knowing that a meeting with Listir would worsen her headache.

Listir came in, shook her hand, and took a seat. He removed a pack of cigarettes from his breast pocket.

"This is a no-smoking building, Mr. Listir," she said.

He slowly returned them and leaned forward. His movements all reminded her of a snake.

"You would think with all that has happened the last few years, everyone would take up smoking again," said Listir. "Anyway, I have news related to your trip to Binghamton."

He checked the captain's reaction and was satisfied with the result. He downloaded the captain on everything he learned from Mulvaney, and five minutes later he and Carpenter were seated in Lieutenant Colonel Symmonds's office, repeating the story again.

The lieutenant colonel listened quietly to the story and then asked Listir to excuse them and wait outside the office so he could discuss the information with Captain Carpenter.

Listir stood but stopped himself by the door. "Colonel Symmonds, one thing to remember is that the more I know, the more I can use my network to help. My NSA contact still has serious resources at his disposal. It may give you leverage in whatever you are trying to do with them."

"Who said we wanted to do anything with the Texans?" asked Lieutenant Colonel Symmonds a little too sharply.

You just did, thought Listir. "No one, but it makes logical sense for the Mid-Atlantic to seek out some kind of beneficial arrangement with them. The Texans are the big dog on the block, and if you are going to expand your territory, they are the obvious choice as an ally," said Listir before he departed, pissed at being excluded.

After the door closed, Symmonds leaned forward in his chair and spoke in a near whisper. "Mr. Listir is correct. The math is simple. The

Texans would not have sent in serious people to find a few historical documents." He paused. "On the other hand, I do not trust Mr. Listir. The man is a thief and liar who will tell anyone anything, appear to be a friend but stab you in the back just for sport. He is only on our side because we are getting stronger and we pay in Texan currency. We need to be very guarded with our information and use him instead of him using us."

"Understood, sir," replied Carpenter. "One thing you should know is that this man"—she pointed at the photo on the desk of Jack Dodge— "played the role of a security officer. In fact, the way they had this set up, these two women led." She pointed at the photo again. "Given that it now seems they discovered this woman yesterday in DC, I would conclude they are moving fast and fluidly, trying hard to find something very specific quickly. We may want to discuss this information with the general, since ensuring that the Texans know that we know we helped Jack Dodge, son of one of their most important leaders, should be worth something."

Symmonds nodded his agreement and told her to come with him to the general's quarters. As they left the office, they asked Mr. Listir to wait in the conference room and then told the MPs to keep a tight watch on him. Captain Carpenter moved at a near jog to stay with the lieutenant colonel as he raced down the hall for his jeep.

A cold front was moving in, bringing a bit of the winter's chill back to the area. Typical March in the Northeast: spring and winter fighting it out. She jumped in the passenger seat, and the lieutenant colonel threw the jeep in gear and headed across the base to the general's quarters. She enjoyed the ten-minute drive and the chance to close her eyes and feel the cool air.

The lieutenant colonel knocked twice on the wooden door and waited. Carpenter heard footsteps, and then the door swung open to reveal a sergeant.

"Good evening, Lieutenant Colonel, Captain. May I help you?"

"Sergeant, could you please tell the general that we are here to see him on a time-sensitive matter?" offered Symmonds.

"Of course," replied the sergeant. "If you would be so kind as to wait here, I will go speak with the general."

The door closed and then reopened forty-five seconds later with the sergeant asking the two officers to follow him. The lieutenant colonel knew the way to the general's study very well, but still he and the captain followed behind the sergeant, who knocked twice on the study door and then opened it to allow them in.

General Rogers wore an old sweatshirt emblazoned with air force and sat behind a desk covered with a stack of papers and a PC.

"Good evening. It must be quite urgent for you to be out so late, especially because I suspect that the captain had a very long day out in Pennsylvania."

The general flipped his reading glasses up on top of his head and eyed the two officers. The only light in the utilitarian room came from a single desk lamp and the bluish-white glow of the PC screen.

Glancing to her left and seeing the lieutenant colonel nodding at her, Captain Carpenter concisely reported everything that had transpired during the day. She then added the more recent details on the identities of the Texas operatives, and the complication of Mr. Listir.

When she finished, the general leaned back in his chair and interlocked his hands behind his head.

"The question is, How do we use this information to our advantage?" asked General Rogers.

Captain Carpenter could not tell if he posed the question to them or just to the ether.

"Captain, you understand that this information is highly confidential, and you are not to discuss it with anyone outside this room?" the general asked.

"Yes, sir," the captain replied, secretly quite pleased to be included.

"This clearly gives you a bit of a bargaining chip in next week's discussion, Colonel," said the general. "Nothing like pointing out to the Severs how pleased we were that we could help the great Jackson Dodge's son with his endeavors. I think it was clear from your conversation the other day that the general had no knowledge of the DC portion of the mission. Logic dictates that the Republic's armed forces would not be requesting favors from us when we are so close to a deal, and we are the supplicants."

The general paused for a minute and then continued. "I want to go over the lists again in the morning and adjust our requests. They clearly want more order on this side of the border. We also have reached the point where they need our cooperation, and we should assume there will be more in the future." The general looked at the lieutenant colonel. "I think we may also be thinking a bit more expansively. Please report to my office at 0800 so we can go over the weapon requirements. Please also alert the economic team to present themselves at 0815. I want to know what expertise and aid might be helpful to expediting the return to a fully functioning economy in our territory."

"Copy that," said Symmonds.

Outside the general's house, Symmonds stopped the captain before they could get in their jeep and said, "You are doing great work. It is unfortunate that we did not know who they were sending before they came, because we could have made our help conditional. But still, your efforts have been valuable."

She realized her headache disappeared somewhere during the meeting.

Richmond International Airport, Richmond, Virginia, Republic of Texas

March 23, 2025, 11:38 p.m. Eastern

The room smelled of old pizza and coffee. After reading for hours, they still had not found anything of real use. A few of the papers belonged to Daniel Dickinson—a couple of speeches, handwritten notes on cases, a few letters—but still nothing pertaining to the compact.

Jack finally stood up and announced he needed to take a walk outside.

"You mind if I join you?" Katrina asked. "I could use some fresh air."

Jack could feel Danny's gaze bore into the back of his neck and knew that if he turned he would see his friend smiling at him. He felt himself start to blush. What the hell was happening?

"Sure. Come along. Company would be nice." Jack tried to sound casual. "Anyone else want to come?" Jack threw the question out, but all demurred.

Jack pulled open the sliding glass door, and he and Katrina walked out into the hangar. The air had turned noticeably colder, and Katrina pulled on a jacket she had been carrying over one arm. They walked through the main doors of the hangar, Jack nodded at the guard stationed there, and they moved slowly down the darkened tarmac. The runway lights were a line of blue, yellow, red, and white stretching into the distance. Even with the lights, a few stars were visible.

"What do you do when you are not doing things like this?" Katrina asked as they walked.

"Honestly, not much," Jack said after a pause.

"You must have some hobbies?" she continued as they passed a line of Cessna 180s.

"Well, like all Texans I hunt and fish. I play a lot of tennis and train for triathlons, something I enjoy. But setting up a new country from scratch has proved time consuming." Jack paused. "Actually, until you asked that question, I never really thought about how much time has passed."

"Passed since what?" Katrina asked.

Jack stopped and kicked at the tarmac a bit with the toe of his boot. He could feel her standing quite close to him, and he realized he enjoyed her company. He almost never talked about Marissa, and when he did it was usually a clipped response to a question designed to stop any further inquiries along the same line.

He looked at Katrina. "I was engaged to a wonderful woman named Marissa, who I loved very much. She was murdered, and I basically stopped living then."

Jack went on and told her the entire story of trying to convince Marissa to move out of New York as the troubles began, her commitment to the students, and her murder. He talked about his devastation at her death, moving back to Texas, and losing himself in his intelligence activities as a way to never have to think about living without her. Katrina never once interrupted, just listened, and for the first time he told someone else about every feeling he had experienced.

They had resumed walking, and when Jack stopped talking they moved on in silence. As they turned at the end of the tarmac, he broke the silence.

"I have never talked so much about myself in my entire life. I apologize," he said, the hangar lights visible far in the distance. At some point during the walk, Katrina had taken his arm, and he found himself enjoying the closeness. "You need to tell me something about yourself."

"I grew up in Washington, obviously, since my father has worked at the Library of Congress almost my entire life. I was always closer to my father than my mother, and somehow his academic side stuck with me. I went to Virginia for college, where I studied history and played soccer. One thing led to another, and I found myself at Yale with a PhD in American history and an academic career. I have never been engaged or anything like that. Maybe I just never found the time or the right person."

She had just started to talk about her personal interests when Justin ran up.

Nearly out of breath, Justin said, "You need to come back now. We found a letter that we are almost sure refers to the compact." He took a deep breath. "You are not going to like what it says."

Jack and Katrina took off at a jog with Justin, winded, following behind.

Danny sat with a faded letter in front of him and the rest of the group huddling over his shoulder when Jack and Katrina came through the glass door.

"What did you find, Danny?" said Jack, moving behind his left shoulder, while the rest of the group made room for Katrina on the right side. Danny began to read:

May 13, 1865

My Darling Lydia

I met with Mr. John Hay tonight. You will remember Mr. Hay as President Lincoln's trusted personal secretary and the man who came to speak with me on the President's behalf about my willingness to stand as Vice President in 1864. So much has transpired since those days that remain so close to now on the calendar.

Mr. Hay is soon to be on his way to Paris, France, to join the American Legation. President Lincoln held Mr. Hay in much esteem for his intelligence, honor, and ability to maintain confidence. I have felt the burden these many years of the document entrusted to me by my fellow senators, and its contents burn at my conscience. Keeping this Compact has been a sacred trust, but I feel that I am not up to the task any longer; my energies lie fully with my role as United States Attorney. Today I decided that if President Lincoln felt content to share his home and confidences with Mr. Hay, then so should I. We sat together this evening for considerable hours, and I shared the sordid story of the Compact. He listened attentively and seemingly without judgment. He never once tried to interrupt my narrative but only asked how he could be of service. His service became the guardianship of this abominable document, a bargain written in the blood of an infernal institution against man and God.

Mr. Hay just departed with a solemn promise to keep the Compact safe, secure and forever private, save if events conspire to require it breach the light of day. I pray it remains private in perpetuity because I relish not to be revealed as party to this bargain of blood. I am free of the burden of protecting this secret and pray it haunt my dreams no more, though I know it will when I seek to enter the eternal kingdom. I pray that the Good Lord allow Mr. Hay to be free of turmoil from the bargains of man's poor decisions, and I for one am blessed to have him take this yoke off me.

Forever yours,

Daniel

Jack reread the letter and then turned to the group.

"So, we now have a new player, Mr. John Hay, whose name I vaguely remember."

"You remember his name because you spent a lot of time in the Hay-Adams Hotel bar in Washington back in the day," said Danny. "If I remember correctly, it was Grey Goose martinis dirty in those days." He smiled broadly. "Instead of booze, what you should remember him for is being Lincoln's personal secretary during the Civil War, later secretary of state and ambassador to the UK, and having his name on over fifty treaties, including the one that gave us the right to build and operate the Panama Canal."

Jack smiled. "No, I'm sure it was the treaties that jogged my memory, not a comfortable leather chair in a cozy bar with a good martini. By the way, Danny, can you print me a copy of the Wikipedia page you used so I can memorize it too?"

Everyone had a good laugh.

"Mr. Hay's papers all went to Brown University to the John Hay Library," said Katrina. The whole team turned and stared at her. "I should know, since I spent an enormous amount of time in that library researching a monograph I wrote on Hay's Open Door policy for China. I could make the drive from New Haven to Providence in just about two hours."

"Hay made everyone in China keep their door open?" Justin asked, completely deadpan.

"No, smartass, in 1899 Hay wrote an influential note to the European powers insisting on forcing an open trading regime with the last Chinese empire," said Katrina, before sticking out her tongue in jest at Danny, who had continued laughing at Justin's joke.

Suddenly, Katrina's expression turned more serious. "I think that the Hay Library burned down. Yes, I am almost sure I heard that from one of the other librarians. Do you all remember the category-four hurricane that slammed into Long Island and then on into New England in 2020 that caused so many deaths?" There were nods all around. "Providence got the worst of it. The storm surge caused flooding in the downtown and significant electrical problems. The surge even destroyed several large fuel-storage tanks, which caused massive fires and created an environmental disaster. Due to the high winds, the fires whipped across the city, and I am almost certain the library burned to the ground."

"You are correct," a voice boomed from the Polycom in the middle of the table, startling both Katrina and Jack, who did not know it was on. Herring continued. "There are some cached tweets about the fire at the library saying that there was nothing left. The building burned to the ground, in spite of the torrential rains. The larger Rockefeller Library, right next to it, also caught fire. Because of the storm, the flooding, and fires burning at the time in downtown Providence, coupled with the fact that the city had cut back substantially on services due to budget constraints, there was no one to fight the fires at the libraries. Everything in both buildings was consumed."

The team stood around until finally Britney said, "Well, I guess that's that. Time to pack up and go home to Austin."

Slowly the members of the team started to stand up.

Jack felt like the air had left the room. What had seemed like a terrible assignment had turned into a bit of a quest. He realized there was one added dimension: as long as the quest lasted, so did time with Katrina.

Jack said, "Justin, why don't you alert the pilots that we'll head for the corral first thing in the morning? Let's pack up and head on back to the safe house. I will take Katrina back to her father and then meet y'all there. Good work, everyone."

Jack nodded at Katrina, and they walked out to one of the waiting Explorers. Jack turned on the ignition and started to drive.

He drove in silence for a little bit before he said, "I hope that I will have a chance to see you in Austin, or wherever else you all decide to settle."

Leaning against the door with her body slightly turned toward Jack, Katrina said, "I hope you mean that, because you will likely have plenty of opportunities to see me. We were told at the intake center the other evening that they would like us to go to Austin. Apparently, the expanding Texas Archives and museum facilities need trained researchers. I will probably see if I can get a position teaching at the university."

Jack glanced quickly at her and smiled; he even realized he was a little relieved. "You will like Austin, and I would enjoy the opportunity to show you around."

He guided the SUV up to the gates of the center and passed through the security to the front of the building. He stopped the vehicle right in front and put the car in park.

Both sat in silence for a minute, until Jack said, remembering, "Hey, you have no way to contact me."

He started hunting for a pen and paper, but Katrina laughed.

"You forgot that you gave me everything the other night." She held up a slip of paper, and Jack realized he was blushing.

Katrina reached for the car door and then turned and kissed Jack hard on the lips. He felt her warm lips and kissed her back just as deeply. Finally, she pulled away.

"I will see you in Austin, sailor," she said before jumping out of the SUV and hustling inside the building.

Jack watched her disappear, still feeling the pressure of her kiss on his lips. He felt very alive.

He had put the car in gear and started to drive when his phone rang. "Jack, go secure."

Herring was on the line, so Jack pulled over, launched the encryption app, and waited for the call to register securely.

"What's up, Alan?" Jack said.

"The Hay Library burned down, but there is a bit of a wrinkle." Jack heard himself groan, but Alan continued. "John Hay was not only a renowned statesman, but he was also one of the first inductees into the

American Academy of Arts and Letters."

"I am not following you, Alan," said Jack. He absently drummed his fingers on the dashboard, magnifying the sound on the line.

"Give me one minute, Jack," said Alan, his voice a little testy with lack of sleep. "The American Academy of Arts and Letters has three large buildings in New York City, on West One Fifty-Fifth Street. Before the Hay Library burned down, the Academy prepared to launch a meaningful exhibit and research project around John Hay's career."

"Do we know exactly what was sent to the American Academy?" Jack had stopped tapping and was leaning forward in his car seat, gripping the steering wheel. He could hear Herring tapping on a keyboard.

"Some preliminary press releases and mentions of the upcoming exhibit discuss a broad survey of Hay's entire career, but so far we have located no specific inventory. I think we should assume that the document was transferred, since we have no way of knowing what was shipped to the Academy or destroyed in the fire. Schrodinger's cat, Jack."

Jack sat in the car in silence, watching the intermittent headlights of cars go by.

"Jack, you still with me?" Herring asked.

Jack replied, "Yes. I remember. Schrodinger's cat states that a cat in the box could be either dead or alive, so further experiments are necessary to prove which. Give me a minute." Jack started drumming his fingers again while his mind ran scenarios. "Alan, what kind of shape do we think the Academy of—what was it again?—is in?"

"Academy of Arts and Letters. Imaging of that part of New York shows buildings in and around Audubon Terrace to appear intact, but the plaza area is filled with debris. That area is controlled by a gang, the Latin Kings, that actually keeps pretty good order. I would assume that is relative to whatever shape the rest of the city is in. The Kings are very hostile to outsiders."

"What is Audubon Terrace?" asked Jack.

He heard more typing and then Herring said, "Audubon Terrace is a complex of eight early-twentieth-century beaux arts buildings located on the west side of Broadway between West One Fifty-Fifth and One Fifty-Sixth Streets in Upper Manhattan. Three of them are occupied by the Academy, but there is also a church and the Hispanic Society. The eight buildings are arranged around an open plaza. The entrance to the plaza is from Broadway, and the Academy's buildings are at the far end."

Jack noticed that the lights of the buildings were taking on a glow, which meant fog was rolling in. Each of the lights appeared softer, more diffuse. Jack stared out the windshield until finally Herring broke the silence.

"Jack, what do you want to do?"

"It's not what I want to do, it's what we are going to have to do," said Jack. "We need to start working on a plan…"

*

Richmond International Airport, Virginia, Republic of Texas

March 24, 2025, 8:00 a.m. Eastern

Jack positioned himself in front of the secure laptop and waited for the connection to be made. Eventually, the frame cleared and he found himself looking at a blank conference room, the seal of the Republic of Texas Air Force on the wall. After a few minutes a trim man in uniform filed into the frame and took a seat at the end of the table, placing a large coffee mug with the emblem of the Republic's Missile Command on it in the center of the desk.

"Good morning, General. Thank you for making time for this videoconference on such short notice," said Jack.

"Morning, Mr. Dodge," replied the general, clearly not concerned with whether Jack's morning was good or not. The general then proceeded to sit back in his chair and cross his arms.

Jack took a deep breath and counted to five in his mind. The general was obviously still angry, and Jack had his father's favorite line running through his head: "Don't poke the bear." Though at the end of the day the general would have to play ball, Jack preferred the catch-the-fly-with-honey route.

"General, first of all I would like to apologize for requesting your assistance earlier but yet keeping you in the dark," said Jack. He watched the general, who did not shift one inch but just continued to stare right back at Jack through the monitor. Jack regretted the picture was in HD. "This is a very compartmentalized operation, and in our best judgment we believed that the one in-and-out to the MAMD-controlled area would suffice. It was our intention to not add any further to the complexity of your ongoing discussions."

"For fuck's sake, is that what you call this…*complexity*?" blurted the general. "I call it a shit show! We were trying to arrange very light cooperation with General Rogers. Now we are the supplicants. Do you know how many different ways you have fucked up the balance of power in this relationship? Congratulations, Mr. Dodge, you are officially the ringmaster of a goat rodeo."

Jack drew in a breath and said as calmly as possible, "Not fully, sir. Why don't you enlighten me as to the problems in the relationship?"

"We are trying to help them bring some order to the Mid-Atlantic, maybe even to the Northeast, but in the lowest-impact way possible. We want to take some pressure off the border and halt the flood of refugees. The general and his people can help with that. We certainly wanted to do that without filling out the general's complete wish list. We were basically done at a level equivalent to buying the island of Manhattan from the Indians for beads, and now you are going to reopen the whole negotiation!" The general ended his screed by poking his index finger in the air to highlight each of the last few words.

Jack sat calmly in his chair and waited for the general to blow himself out. "General, you may not believe me, but we did not know the full extent of your discussions, nor did we have a good idea of the difficulties we would have in our mission. This truly is an unfortunate situation. I assure you that I have only the highest admiration for the work y'all do. Everyone to whom my organization reports, all the way up the chain of command, feels the same. We all sincerely appreciate you using your good offices to assist the mission."

Jack remained calm but made the point that he was head of the Republic's espionage agency and that he was plugged into the power structure of Austin. Jack had spent his entire career being his own man and hated pulling rank, but he also hated wasting time on bullshit.

The two men stared at each other over the videoconference for several minutes.

Finally, the general made an audible sigh and said, "What do you need?"

When it was over, Danny, who stood just off camera, said, "Wow! I haven't seen a staring contest like that since second grade. I think it was a tie."

Jack could barely smile.

Fort Dix, New Jersey, Mid-Atlantic Military District, former USA

March 24, 2025, 9:16 a.m. Eastern

Captain Carpenter jumped to her feet and snapped off a salute as Lieutenant Colonel Symmonds walked into her office.

"At ease, soldier," offered Symmonds, dropping into one of the two uncomfortable metal chairs facing her desk. "You are not going to believe this, but the Texans need our help again." He watched the grin spread across the captain's face. "And it gets better."

Captain Carpenter smiled, sat back in her chair, and felt her day brighten dramatically. "Please, tell me."

The lieutenant colonel put his feet up on her desk, pulled out a cigar, and began chewing on it. "The Texans want to visit New York City, and they need a guided tour."

Carpenter stopped smiling. New York City was outside MAMD control and very dangerous. They had a small base to help with trade and smuggling supplies, but other than that, it was considered well beyond the front lines.

"Your new friends would like to come visit us tomorrow." The lieutenant colonel paused for effect and then added, "The Texans have also now acknowledged that Jack Dodge will personally lead the group."

"What do we get, and what do you want me to do?" asked Captain Carpenter.

"Captain, you are going to be a general someday because you are exactly on point," replied Symmonds. "We are getting the motorized field artillery that the Texans had declined to provide. We are also getting significantly more body armor, guns, and ammunition, as well as help with repairing and upgrading the oil and gas operations in the Marcellus Shale once we have secured the field. We also get economic advisers and more medical aid." The lieutenant colonel shifted his cigar and then continued. "As to what you need to do, everything in your power to assist them, and also to find out what the fuck they are looking for!"

He stood up to go but stopped when the captain said, "One more thing, sir." He inclined his head, and Captain Carpenter continued. "What do we do about Mr. Listir and his merry band, who are hanging around the base?"

"Let's see if we can't move Mr. Listir on," said the lieutenant colonel. "I think we don't need to waste any more of his valuable time on this matter."

He started for the door and then stopped again. "Take every precaution to do it without letting on that we will have any more dealings with the Texans."

*

Richmond International Airport, Virginia, Republic of Texas

March 24, 2025, 10:02 a.m. Eastern

The team sat around a secure laptop staring at Herring in Austin. Jack finished relaying the details of both his initial conversation with the general in Omaha and the general's subsequent callback after speaking with his counterpart at the Mid-Atlantic Military District.

"Crap!" said Britney. "You realize how unpopular we will be with our now-former friends in the military for the foreseeable future?"

The rest of the team shared the same expression of disbelief. Most of the missions run by the Company relied on some component of support from the military. Unhappy and therefore less-than-fulsome support could be the difference between life and death.

"As the guy who just took a trip to the woodshed, I'm well aware of how unhappy our friends are," said Jack. "Trust me, my backside has marks from the general's belt, but it is what it is right now. We need to focus on the mission at hand and get this resolved. As to our friends in Omaha, I'll go there as soon as we are done and kiss their brass asses."

"I would like to be there to see that," said Britney, smiling, a smile that quickly disappeared when Jack informed her that he appreciated her offer and would enjoy her company in Omaha. Then he opened the invitation up to the entire group. Since no one else wanted to go to Omaha, the room grew quiet and the team stared at the coffee mugs in front of them.

"OK, let's focus on the mission."

Jack restarted the conversation and tried to sound more upbeat than he felt. The truth was, the general's unhappiness had increased along with the inflation rate in the price of cooperation with the military in New Jersey. Jack had also received a call from his boss, the minister of the interior, who had received his own angry call from the head of the armed forces. It had been a tough morning, and the workday in Austin had just begun.

"I've started to sketch out a rough idea of a plan, but we'll need to go through it step by step," said Jack. "Alan, do you want to give us a briefing on the Academy facility and a sitrep on the area around it?"

"Jack, before we get to that, can I suggest that we pull Katrina back in?" said Simon. Jack looked at him quizzically, so Simon continued. "She knows more about Hay, his career, and archive organization than any of us. Hell, she proved that last night. She had actually been to Providence and reviewed his papers when the rest of us did not even know he existed."

"She's also a civilian, and we are not talking about a walk in the park here," interjected Britney. "We're talking about New York City, or basically Mad Max's world. We got lucky in DC, and this is ten times worse."

"I think I get that better than anyone," said Simon. "On the other hand, this is an important mission. Any edge is useful."

Danny offered his agreement, as did Herring and Manning.

Jack sat back in his chair for a minute and stared at the ceiling. He did not want to agree with Simon on an emotional level, but he knew he was right. They could use the help. None of them were academic researchers, and anything that enhanced their speed improved the mission's security and potential for success.

"I agree," he said simply. "Let me call her at the intake center and ask her to join us. Simon, can we get one of your guys to go over and pick her up and bring her over here? I am sure she will say yes."

Simon pulled out his cell phone and stepped from the room.

Logistics set and everyone back at the table, Herring began the briefing. Twenty minutes later, Katrina Chandler came into the room, and Jack felt his heart skip a beat. She looked absolutely stunning in a simple black pantsuit, cream-colored silk shirt, and black high-heeled shoes. She gave him a smile, and he realized he was grinning like a schoolboy again. He looked away and found Danny serving up a big wink. Jack returned the wink with a scowl. He needed to focus.

They brought Katrina up to speed and continued the briefing. Three hours later they had a plan, an equipment list, and a mission timetable. The Harper Cattle jet was dispatched back to Austin to retrieve the needed equipment, and the meeting broke up.

Jack and Danny stayed behind to speak with Alan.

"Alan, Jamie Florez handles all contacts with Latin gangs both in the Republic and in Mexico, correct?" asked Danny.

"Yup, Jamie's on point with the gangs. He has excellent relationships with Latin Kings across the Republic, and they are a solid source of information," offered Alan. "The Latin Kings started in Chicago but eventually spread all over the US, making huge profits off the illicit drug trade. They are very interconnected and well organized."

"We need Jamie to work with the Latin Kings," said Jack. "We're not going to be able to do this smoothly without help and coverage from the Kings. Walking into a gang-controlled area without their consent and support could put us in the middle of a firefight with an enemy on their home turf. We need the Kings with us from when we arrive until we leave the city."

"The real question is, Do the Latin Kings in, say, Dallas, Atlanta, Miami, or any of our other cities still have the interconnections with the New York Kings, and what will we need to do to buy their help?" asked Danny.

"Let me get together with Jamie and come back to you," said Herring.

*

Richmond International Airport, Richmond, Virginia, Republic of Texas

March 24, 2025, 1:45 p.m. Eastern

Jack felt his cell phone vibrate and excused himself from the group. Standing at the edge of the hangar, he waited for the security protocols to run on his phone and then heard Alan's voice.

"Jack, I am here with Jamie."

"Hey, Jamie, thanks for getting involved so quickly," said Jack. "I'm sure Alan explained that we need to take a trail ride and would like to buy some travel insurance and tour guides."

"Copy that, Jack," said Jamie. "However, Alan just gave me a crazy timetable. Can you not put off your ride for a few days? Making this happen tomorrow may or may not be difficult. I just don't know what our travel agent's contacts are like with that particular property."

"Unfortunately, no. We only have a couple of vacation days left, so we want to be there tomorrow."

Jack heard Jamie exhale over the phone and then say, "OK, listen. The best travel agents in Dallas have cousins where you want to go. I'll work on arranging a visit, but let me be clear that with this type of timing it is going to cost a lot extra."

"Copy that, Jamie."

"Jack," said Jamie. "One more thing. I'm going to want to come up and join you with one of our travel agents so that we are sure the trip goes off without a hitch and no one at the destination tries to change terms."

Jack stared out at the runway as a Southwest Airlines jet rolled out for a landing. The team would be a little large. The law of large numbers dictated that the more people, the more opportunities for someone to take a bullet, but Jamie was right.

"Jamie, go book the trip and then go get your guy and get to Love Field. Ramsey is on the way to Austin to pick up some extra luggage for our trip. He can then head for Big D. They'll pick up you and your travel agent."

"Copy that, Jack."

The line cut, and Jack continued to stare at the runway. He hated the idea of going back to New York. To him it was a city of death. He could still smell the heavy chemical smell of the emergency room as he held Marissa's dead body. He stared at the runway but could not clear his mind. He saw the tiles on the wall, felt the cold chill of the room, and then saw her still-beautiful, lifeless face. He worked hard to suppress the pain of her loss, but there would be no way to do that now. Not with everything being about planning a mission to New York.

The thrust reversers on a landing plane jolted him back to reality, and he watched another Southwest plane roll out. He took a deep breath and turned to head back into the hangar office. A narrow timetable, a team that would include a couple of civilians—not good.

*

Fort Dix, New Jersey, Mid-Atlantic Military District, former USA

March 27, 2025, 2:10 p.m. Eastern

Listir stood leaning against a lamppost, smoking a cigarette. The base was buzzing with a high level of activity as the colonel continued to prepare for the coming offensive. Trucks moved by headed toward the front gate, loaded with all sorts of equipment, from the mundane to the murderous, the beginning and end of the convoy anchored by heavily armed Humvees.

Listir smiled and pulled deeply on his cigarette. He was making an absolute fortune helping the MAMD outfit for the battle. The general was proving to be a very good customer, paying promptly in mainly bartered goods, which Listir could sell at even higher prices, or in Republic of Texas currency. He took another pull on his cigarette and thought about the flip side of the general's success: too much law and order would be bad for business. He made a mental note to provide some goodies, maybe a few RPGs in the next ammo shipment to the former Pennsylvania and West Virginia national guardsmen who were holding out in the shale region. Longer battle for the Mid-Atlantic Army, more money for him.

Captain Carpenter crossed the road in his direction. He continued to smoke and pretended to not notice her, instead watching a platoon run by.

"Mr. Listir," said the captain.

"Captain, what a pleasure," said Listir, stubbing out the cigarette under his boot.

The captain stared at the cigarette butt and finally said, "Mr. Listir, you need to police that cigarette."

Listir nodded and slowly reached down to pick up the cigarette.

"Mr. Listir, is there anything else that you can learn in Washington about what the team from Texas was trying to find?" Her orders were to convince him to return to Washington under the guise of trying to further ingratiate himself to the MAMD. Symmonds had decided that ordering him off the base would only heighten his interest.

Listir slowly rolled a Zippo around in his hand while holding eye contact with the captain. She held his gaze and stood her ground, prepared to wait.

"Given that the librarians disappeared, I am not sure what else could be learned," replied Listir. "I fucked up. I should have shot one of the librarians and then taken another with us. I could have scared the shit out of the one we took and maybe I would have learned something. Without someone who they talked to, I'm just not sure where else to look. Given the disorganized state of the library and the Archives, there is no way we can figure out what is missing. You have any ideas from Binghamton?" He stopped and tapped a fresh cigarette out of his pack.

Captain Carpenter shifted on her feet, crossed her arms, and replied, "No, we gained no clues. What about your friend at the NSA? Any chance you could work him some more and get his people to break back into the Texas systems?"

Listir lit another cigarette and said through a cloud of smoke, "I can work him and get him to continue to try. Given the decay in his systems and personnel, coupled with the fact that the Texans just caught him in their network and are now on guard, I would not be optimistic." He puffed away on his cigarette and then refocused directly on the captain. "Why is it so important?"

He noticed the captain look away before answering. Listir liked playing poker, and so he always studied people for tells. He had once survived a narcotrafficker's attempt to kill him by reading the man's face as he sat across the table. As the night progressed, the drug dealer had developed an eye twitch; when his mouth started to twitch, Listir fell to the floor just in time to avoid an ice pick. He shot the assassin as the man was still trying to dig it out of the table and then killed the dealer. He pocketed both of the men's cell phones for intelligence purposes, took over ten thousand dollars in cash off the dead dealer, and then calmly walked out of the bar. People in Cali bars at that time tended to not butt into what was not their business. He turned over the cell phones to the agency but kept the cash.

The captain was clearly hiding something.

"As you know, we are making a big move," began the captain. "With this move, we will secure our energy supply and spread MAMD control out to the former border with Ohio and into parts of what was New York. Add this to our existing holdings in Pennsylvania, New Jersey, and Maryland, and we become a reasonable nation. The Texans will be forced to deal with us, and therefore we need to know what they are up to. There will be trade pacts and defense arrangements to be negotiated, so anything we can learn will help. As they say, information is power."

Listir stood eyeing the captain. What she said made sense, but he knew it was only the garnish; no meat for him. He watched the smoke trail up from the cigarette in his hand.

"Interesting," he said, not really meaning it. "Let me get on the phone to my guy at the NSA and see if we can learn anything. I will talk with my boys and come up with a plan for where we might look if we headed back to DC."

"We all appreciate your help," said the captain. "Come check in with me after you have your conversations and before you leave, please. I am going to head over to the mess and then back to my office."

*

Richmond International Airport, Richmond, Virginia, Republic of Texas

March 27, 2025, 6:03 p.m. Eastern

Danny stood at the whiteboard going through the plan one more time with the entire team. The Citation X was forty-three minutes out, carrying their gear, Jamie, and one Jesus Madoro, a very senior member of the Latin Kings.

Danny asked again, "Anyone see anything that they want to change? Any fences that need mending?"

Britney spoke up. "I just think it needs to be said one more time: Katrina is our weak point. She has no combat training. Even this guy Jesus, given his profession, has probably been through tough situations. No offense intended." She held up her hands in mock surrender.

"None taken," said Katrina.

"She has no weapons training and has never been in a combat or special operations setting and therefore will require one of us to watch over her at all times," Britney added. "It's tough enough to be responsible for yourself and the six of your partner let alone watch the six of someone who can't watch yours."

Jack jumped in. "Britney, we got it. You're correct. Katrina is the weak link, and it is a risk. But on the other hand, none of us is skilled in how to find the document in question or knows as much, so she comes." Jack looked at her and then added, "She'll be my responsibility."

Danny frowned at Jack, and Jack knew he would get an earful about making emotional, macho decisions to try and impress the girl versus taking care of business. However, he also knew Danny would say all that in private.

"OK." Danny butted back into the conversation. "We are a go on the mission plan. Let's lock it down. Britney, you are responsible for the weapons check. Justin, figure out what you think we'll need in terms of technology. Simon, why don't you work with Herring's guys? We'll want an armed UAV on overwatch. Katrina, you can hijack this computer and search for whatever you can find on the Academy, Hay, and anything else that you think might be helpful. Also, Alan's boys can help you.

"Jack, since you have been outed by the military, you should call Captain Carpenter and arrange the details on the MAMD side. When Jamie and Jesus get here, we can finalize the details with the Kings and figure out our exact schedule. Let's remember that we'll be going in with the assistance of MAMD personnel. They will try to be helpful but are not really on our team. Add to that the Kings, who are playing solely for their own benefit. This one has some hair on it."

The meeting broke up, and everyone set about executing the appointed tasks. Danny followed Jack out of the hangar conference room toward the tarmac.

"I know what you are going to say," said Jack. "Hell, we've been married for so long, I always know what you're going to say."

"Great," Danny replied. "That saves me the trouble of reminding you that God gave man two heads but not enough blood for both of them at the same time."

"Apparently, you still felt the need to tell me," said Jack. "Anyway, I'm not thinking with my thing."

Danny looked skeptically at Jack, who looked back at the office.

"We need her skills on this mission. If she were a man, we would not be having this conversation." Jack paused and looked out across the airfield. "Damn, Danny, I like her. It has been a long time since I have had any feelings toward any woman. She is smart, funny, and pretty."

Danny softened. "Jack, I'm actually happy to see you like this. It has been too long. You had it all locked down so tight that you have been going through the motions of living. It's nice to see you relax and smile." He paused and moved directly in front of Jack. "On the other hand, we're in the middle of a fucking mission, and people who think with their hearts and not their cold, analytical brains tend to make mistakes and get themselves or others killed. I don't want you to die, and even more, I don't want to die."

"You think I do not know that?" said Jack with a tinge of anger in his voice. Danny was right: distractions equaled danger.

"I know you know that," said Danny evenly, trying to reduce the tension. "However, I don't like that macho bullshit of *I will be responsible for Katrina*. I am happy you like her, but I want you to lock it back down for the next few days. You are the leader, and we're all dependent on you, not just her."

Jack folded his arms and nodded. He was pissed, but mainly at himself.

CHAPTER NINETEEN

Mulvaney stared at the phone on his desk. Listir was not telling him the whole story. However, he needed to decide what he wanted to do. Listir was playing his own game, and Mulvaney had to figure out if he wanted to keep going along even though he did not know what side he was helping. He had foregone lucrative job offers from technology companies as the country fell apart, offers in the new Republic of Texas, because he thought helping the USA was more important. Thinking of those offers made him think of an encryption company in Austin that wanted him to come help with their penetration-testing products just before the breakup. He would have been safe right now in the Republic of Texas. Not very patriotic, but practical.

He reached into his drawer, pulled out the good scotch Listir had given him, and poured a couple of fingers into a mug. He slipped the bottle back in the drawer and took a long swallow. The scotch was smooth. Maybe there were no sides for him anymore. No, that was not right.

He set the mug down, got up, and headed for Reed's cube. He found the big man seated, staring at his screen, which had multiple windows open.

"Anything?" inquired Mulvaney.

Reed started and spun in his chair. "Sorry, I did not hear you come in." He composed himself and pointed at the windows. "I tried to get back into the Texans' systems, with no luck. They have locked it down tight. I then defaulted to just monitoring the traffic. The only thing I could find was a bunch of secure traffic between Austin and Richmond, none of which I could penetrate."

Mulvaney sighed. "So, we have nothing?"

Reed pointed at another screen. "Maybe not. Look here."

Mulvaney leaned in and studied the code. "What you are looking at is the ATC information for a plane that left Austin for Dallas and then flew on to Richmond. Earlier the plane had flown from Richmond to Austin. It belongs to the Harper Cattle Company."

Mulvaney leaned against the cube wall. Mulvaney knew the Harper Cattle Company was one of the largest meat-packers in the Republic of Texas, and also the owner of one of the world's largest ranches. A ranch that belonged to the Dodge family, and a ranch on which the family had found its first oil nearly one hundred years earlier. It was also the company that the Republic used as a beard for its espionage activities.

"That is something. That means someone important is still in Richmond."

"I thought about it similarly. Either someone important is in Richmond or coming to Richmond, but they also could be coming to take someone or many someones back to Austin. However, it is the fact that it went from Richmond to Austin, stopped in Dallas, and is now coming back that has me thinking someone is coming to Richmond."

"Good work, Stan." Mulvaney turned to leave and then spun back around. "Stan, you said there was a lot of comms traffic between Austin and Richmond." Reed nodded. "Now we have a plane inbound to Richmond, probably carrying additional people or equipment. So, can you figure out where the traffic in Richmond is coming from, because maybe not everything there is as secure as Austin's systems?"

Reed immediately turned back to his screen. "Let me look at the source of the traffic. I'll try and catch any voiceprints on the known team members. Who knows? Maybe we'll get lucky."

Reed's reference to voiceprints reminded Mulvaney that he meant to check those Nigerian mission files. He walked back to his office and accessed his computer. It took him some time to find the correct data. He remembered the mission in general, but due to other pressing issues with the Utah site launch at the time, he had not been day to day. The mission, designed as a snatch and grab, went wrong when the al-Qaeda paymaster took a bullet to the head while a team closed in to capture him. Everyone wanted the banker, to pump him for information, and after months of tracking him his death was a blow. The team barely made it out due to a firefight, first with the banker's bodyguards, and then with Nigerian forces. While he searched, Mulvaney tried to remember the details of the subsequent controversy, but it remained just outside his ability to recall.

He found the relevant postaction reports and voice logs from the secure comms traffic during the mission. He opened up a file and got surprise number one. The mission team included Jack Dodge, Danny Winters, and Justin Manning on the ground in Lagos. Intelligence liaison for the mission was one Peter Listir. He read the five-page mission outline and after-action reports quickly.

Leading a team of local contractors, Manning closed in to grab the banker as he came out of a restaurant in Lagos with two bodyguards and one more driving a Mercedes. As the Mercedes approached the door, the banker walked out. Manning and team converged from all sides, weapons drawn. Before they could grab the banker, a 7.62mm shell penetrated the man's skull, killing him instantly. A second, unnecessary shot passed through the man's throat before his body collapsed.

Manning and team were exposed. The bodyguards started shooting. Manning's team killed all three of the bodyguards during their escape but also lost one of their own local contractors. They then fought their way to safety in a high-speed car chase with members of the Nigerian armed forces on their tail. Dodge and Winters came to the team's rescue and ended up exchanging fire with Nigerian forces. The report made note of the significant effort that had been expended tracking this banker, who they felt could unravel all of al-Qaeda's African financial network. The desire was to grab and interrogate, not kill. The report did not explain the need for an inquiry.

Mulvaney clicked on the voice file and listened to the entire tape. He ran over the part around the takedown over and over again. Just before moving in for the grab, the team lost contact with John Phillips, their CIA contact on the ground. Mr. Phillips led the team responsible for identifying the banker and tracking his movements. Mulvaney listened closely as he heard Manning, Winters, and Dodge all trying to reach Phillips in order to get an up-to-date situation report on whether any intelligence changes had occurred. At one point, Dodge suggested they scrub the mission, that something felt wrong. Manning, on scene, declined.

After the shots were fired that killed the banker and Manning's team started to flee, the team continued to call for CIA support and intel, but none came. Finally, toward the very end, Mulvaney heard Jack Dodge clearly state that he was going to "hunt you down, Phillips, and kill you personally." He listened to that clip multiple times, the anger palpable.

Moving on to the inquiry files, Mulvaney found his access denied. He stared at the screen; his clearance should be more than adequate for these files. He opened a drawer and pulled out a small leather book. He looked down the list and found the codes for the deputy director of Cyber Command. One of the benefits of being the only guy left to turn out the lights was he ended up with access codes enabling him to see things beyond his level.

The inquiry file was voluminous, with multiple subfiles and exhibits. He selected the inquiry resolution file and began reading. He flipped from the resolution to exhibits, photographs, and bank statements. When he was done, he sat in his chair, stunned. In spite of the inquiry deciding there was insufficient evidence to bring charges, the circumstantial evidence was damning. Listir in a car in Gambia with a leader of al-Qaeda in the Islamic Maghreb. A known al-Qaeda sharpshooter from Somalia in the Lagos airport two days before. Two wire transfers to a Liechtenstein-numbered account, one for two hundred thousand dollars two days before the shooting, and one for three hundred thousand dollars the day after. A photograph from outside the same bank in Vaduz in 2014 showing one Peter Listir exiting the building. The inquiry suspected Listir sold the mission out to al-Qaeda, but he denied it and, not for lack of trying, the account could not be officially linked to him. Listir's file received a letter of caution, effectively ending the man's CIA career, but, from the evidence, significantly less than it appeared he deserved. Listir eventually had to resign in disgrace.

Fort Dix, New Jersey, Mid-Atlantic Military District, former USA

March 27, 2025, 7:18 p.m. Eastern

Listir stood with his team outside one of the supply staging areas. They reviewed, with one of the supply sergeants, the list of "new required materials" that the MAMD wanted to source. It was a high-value order due to the large amount of medical supplies on the list.

Listir took his vibrating satellite phone out of his pocket and recognized Mulvaney's number. He walked away from Brown midsentence without so much as a word.

"Mulvaney, how goes the war?" He knew he had pushed his contact about as far as he could, and the relationship was a bit tense. He shook out a cigarette and prepared to light it.

"It's time we talked," said Mulvaney. He had poured himself another finger of the scotch.

Listir lit his cigarette and kept his voice neutral. "We've been talking a lot. I enjoy our little talks, don't you?"

Mulvaney stared at the picture of his daughter on his desk and took a deep breath. "Peter, I am not an idiot. I realized long ago that you had connections with the black market, but over the last few days it has become more than obvious that the extent of those connections and your activities were deeper and darker than I ever considered. However, those pale in comparison to the issues around Nigeria. So, let's cut the crap."

"Old news, even if it ever was news." Listir lit his cigarette and waited. If Mulvaney wanted to play in the real world, Listir was happy to play there too.

"We have found more and think that we can find additional information, but it's going to cost you," said Mulvaney.

Listir replied evenly, "It all depends on what you have got." He blew out a stream of smoke. Even the little patriot was willing to sell out. Nothing like a collapsing country to bring out the worst in everyone.

"You've had a free ride for years because I thought we were both still motivated by the same things. However, it's now clear to me, looking back, that you never cared about the country or anyone but yourself," said Mulvaney loudly. "A couple of bottles of scotch is like beads for the Indians. I know this information is important to you and whatever game you are playing this time."

Listir stubbed out his cigarette and lit another one. He was getting bored with the little NSA prick. He thought about how much fun it would be to have Brown put a Glock against his head and then see how tough he would be.

"Vince, I am busy and bored by this. What do you have, and what do you want? Stop jerking my chain, because it's pissing me off, and that's not good for you!"

Mulvaney reflexively sat back in his chair. Listir's voice, both cold and cruelly dispassionate, made him realize he was on dangerous ground. "We know where the people from yesterday are, and we can find out what they are going to do next." Mulvaney oversold, but he had taken a strong line of attack and realized he needed to keep going. "What I want is papers and transport over the border, and fifty thousand dollars in Republic of Texas money."

Listir laughed into the phone. "I can get you out and get you papers, but why should I?" he said, weighing the offer in his head. Although it was reasonable, he could not hit the bid; he needed to toy with the asshole. Who the hell did Mulvaney suddenly think he was? "Why should I give you any of my hard-earned money? All you have done for me is get me a few names of some guys who are no longer here!"

"What if I can tell you where they are going next?" said Mulvaney. Listir stayed quiet. "Are you still there?"

"Yeah, I'm here," Listir said slowly. "If you tell me where they are going next, and that information is accurate, I will get you transport, papers, and half the money."

He killed the line.

Mulvaney stared at the receiver in his hand, which he realized was shaking. He poured another finger of scotch and took it down in a swift shot. He looked up to see Reed standing in the doorway.

Reed handed over a sheet of paper. Mulvaney looked at it and realized it was an enormous number of IP addresses.

"What do you have?" asked Mulvaney.

Reed settled his girth into one of the chairs and motioned toward the bottle. Mulvaney poured him a couple of fingers and handed over a glass.

"You were right," said Reed after a quick sip. "Richmond's not nearly as secure as Austin. I learned a number of things. First of all, at 0900 tomorrow, a Republic of Texas plane is going to lift off from Richmond for Fort Dix, where one Captain Carpenter and a few of her people are going to meet it and a team of Texans." Reed took another sip of his drink and continued. "The MAMD captain is already working on how they are going to get the Texans to the unnamed place they want to go, and I am pretty sure I know where that is."

Mulvaney leaned forward in his chair. "How do you know all this?"

Reed smiled and leaned back in his chair. "I will tell you, but on one condition."

Mulvaney sighed audibly.

"I want out. I want the exact same deal. I also think that you shouldn't tell anyone any of this until we're out. I have done a lot of checking, and your friend is the head of the black market in this region."

Mulvaney sat up straight in his chair.

"Vince, we're a fucking product to him and have reached our sell-by date."

Mulvaney's mouth fell open. He realized Reed had been eavesdropping on his phone. He stared at the tech and it dawned on him that he was absolutely right.

After some discussion, Mulvaney reached for the phone again. The line connected, and the former NSA officer gripped the receiver tightly. "The deal changed…"

*

Fort Dix, New Jersey, Mid-Atlantic Military District, former USA

March 27, 2025, 8:42 p.m. Eastern

Listir stormed across the blacktop, headed for the logistics center of the base. He was ready to kill someone. Mulvaney had exactly what he needed to know and would not tell him until he got that little prick and his fat friend out of the North.

The logistics center stood out, awash in arc lights as trucks continued to back up to the loading bays and small forklifts rolled pallets of material into their open ends. Listir found the SUV and cargo truck parked at the far end of the building, just on the edge of the light pool, and moved off to find his team. He found two of his men leaning against one of the vehicles, smoking. They pointed toward a door in the side of the distribution center, and Listir stomped off in that direction.

The door opened onto a small corridor with various offices off of it. He eventually came to a break room, where he found Brown playing cards with some of the supply personnel. He jerked his thumb at Brown, and the two men retreated back outside.

Standing away from the logistics building in the grass at the edge of the pavement, Listir lit a cigarette and said, "That little prick at the NSA claims he has very important information for us on the Texans and what they are doing with the MAMD. He says the interaction is ongoing. However, he won't give it to us until he is out of the North and standing on Virginia soil with papers and some Republic of Texas currency. He wants the same fucking deal for that fat fuck who works for him."

Brown looked as pissed as his boss. "You want me to drive back there and gut him like a fish?"

Listir held up his hands, clamping his lips down on the end of his cigarette. "Unfortunately, as much as I would like to see him floating in the Potomac, we don't have that luxury. We need to send in our resident garden gnome, Griffin, to get him to our forger for papers and take him out to Virginia. We need to do it by eight in the morning, because Mulvaney said we'll want to know what he knows by then."

"Are you fuckin' kiddin' me?" hissed Brown, staring at his watch through a stream of smoke emanating from a cigarette clamped in his lips. "That's not a lot of time to get papers done and get them out."

"He's standing by at the NSA. Just get that little bastard over there to pick him up and have him take the fifty thousand with him," replied Listir. "Tell Griffin to keep him until he tells us what he knows. If we do not like it, we can drag him back over the border and kill him, but otherwise we let him go."

"Why not just kill them and leave their bodies in the Virginia woods?" said Brown, stubbing out his cigarette.

Listir stood quietly for a minute. "No, we don't need any issues with our friends in Virginia," he replied slowly. "We have too much business going on across the border and can't afford to blow up our routes, as much as I would like to put a bullet in that little prick's head. Tell Griffin to get this done on schedule, or I'll personally put the bullet I want to put into Mulvaney into the gnome's oversized head."

*

Richmond International Airport, Richmond, Virginia, Republic of Texas

March 28, 2025, 6:56 a.m. Eastern

Jack had been awake for nearly two hours. Their gear was arrayed across the hangar floor behind the closed sliding doors. They had organized the necessary equipment into distinct groupings by type. It had taken until late into the evening to get everything ready and the plan as defined as it could be given the limited on-the-ground intelligence. Now he and Danny covered everything one more time. Danny was dressed in gray sweatpants and sweatshirt borrowed from the air force personnel, and Jack had found a pair of jeans that fit and a similar sweatshirt. Both men carried cups of coffee that had long ago gone cold as they moved from station to station.

They were at the comms equipment station and had just finished testing the secure radios and satellite phones. In spite of being charged all night, one of the radios showed a low battery warning, and Jack hunted through the battery spares for the replacement.

"We have four extra radios," said Danny. "Let's leave that one behind since we cannot be sure it's the battery and not some issue with the radio."

Jack looked at him and then threw the radio into a gang box they had commandeered to hold the extra equipment.

He stood up and stretched his back. "I think we're good," he said, looking around. "Weapons are all good. Plenty of ammo. Everyone has a full kit, flotation unit, and body armor." Jack gestured at the dark-gray suits the team would wear for the mission. Black could stand out at night; dark gray disappeared. "Communications equipment now all checks, as does night vision. I think we're good to go. We should have each person load their duffel with another watching to cross-check and then get the bags on the plane. We can get the hell out of here and grab some chow."

"Copy that," said Danny. "I heard chow, and that's all I was waiting to hear." He looked around the hangar one more time and added, "Plus I am sick and tired of sitting around here."

*

Outside Alexandria, Virginia, Republic of Texas

March 28, 2025, 7:37 a.m. Eastern

Patrick Griffin sat in the front seat of a beat-up Chevy Tahoe. In the back seat sat Mulvaney and Reed. The two men had duct tape around their wrists and ankles like shackles. Griffin tapped numbers into a satellite phone while puffing away on a cigarette.

"Could you please open a window?" said Reed from the back seat, his eyes watering from the smoke.

Griffin turned and looked at him and then flicked the butt in the analyst's direction, watching him squirm to try and avoid the burning ember. Griffin laughed, and both of his prisoners physically recoiled.

For the hundredth time since the sun rose, Mulvaney stared at the woods around them and thought about the remoteness of this site.

Griffin spoke into the phone. "I got them with me. Ready?"

He put the phone on the console between the front seats and turned on the speakerphone feature.

Listir's voice came through, sounding a bit metallic. "OK, talk."

Mulvaney looked at Reed, and the heavyset analyst began, "There's a team of people from that other place." The Texans possessed the capability to pull every conversation out of the ether, and it was general knowledge that calls between the Republic's territory and the former US would get a lot of attention. "They're currently sitting in Richmond, but they're about to travel." He looked at the dashboard clock, which read 7:41 a.m. "They will leave in about an hour and fifteen minutes for a place called Dix."

Listir looked across the picnic table at which he was seated with Brown outside the logistics facility and signaled his man to come sit beside him. Brown moved quickly around the table and leaned in to hear the call as well.

"Keep going."

"They've been talking to a Carpenter," continued Reed.

Listir looked quickly around. Fucking Captain Carpenter was continuing to play ball with the Texans and she did not want him to know.

"There were several calls last night, and it all concerned getting them into the city."

Listir was stumped for a minute. "What city?" Why would they need Carpenter's help to get back into the District?

"New York," replied Reed.

"Holy shit!" said Brown, earning a stern look from Listir.

"Why?" said Listir, trying to keep his voice calm.

"No idea," said Mulvaney. "The only other traffic we could see out of the facility was some internet searches related to John Milton Hay and exhibits at the American Academy of Arts and Letters."

"Let me guess," said Listir, fishing out his cigarettes. "The Academy is in the city in question."

"Yes, it is," said Reed.

Griffin smiled as the heavyset man tried to wipe the sweat from his face with his bound hands. The little man had dead blue eyes and unnaturally white, almost albino skin and hair. Griffin was clearly mentally simple and, coupled with his odd appearance, routinely inspired fear.

"It's located at One Hundred Fifty-Fifth and Broadway."

"Anything else?" Listir asked, but he received a firm assurance from both men that they had told him everything.

"You want me to deal with them?" asked Griffin, and for the first time, Mulvaney realized that the man held a gun in his little pink hand. They were screwed. He was going to die in the Republic of Texas at the hand of some dwarfish psychopath. Reed started hyperventilating next to him, and Mulvaney was only vaguely aware that he was whispering to the big man to stop it or he would have a heart attack. They all waited for the response.

"No, a deal is a deal. You owe me your life, Vince," said Listir, and the line went dead.

Griffin pulled open the back door of the Chevy and yanked Mulvaney out by his arm, throwing the older man to the wet grass with a thud. He motioned for Reed to slide across and then pulled him out as well. While the two men tried to get to their knees, Griffin reached across the front seat, took a heavy envelope off the passenger seat, and flung it directly into Mulvaney's face.

"Your papers and things," said Griffin as he turned to get in the Chevy.

"Aren't you going to cut these restraints off?" whined Reed.

Griffin turned and smiled, then reached inside his belt and pulled out his gun. He raised the weapon and leveled it at Reed's head. Mulvaney could not believe that this sociopath was going to actually kill the analyst, but he could see the man's finger tighten on the trigger. The report sounded tremendously loud given the close range, and Mulvaney looked over, expecting to see Reed bleeding from a wound. But instead, he realized, Griffin had shot wide.

"Oops," said Griffin as he holstered his weapon. Then the criminal began to laugh again. "He pissed himself."

Mulvaney looked over at the spreading stain on the front of the analyst's pants and at the tears streaming down Reed's face.

Griffin climbed into the vehicle and drove away.

Mulvaney watched the taillights disappear up the road into the trees, leaving them with only the sound of the birds disturbed by the shot trying to settle back down in the branches.

"We have to get these restraints off, Stan, before that little sicko decides to come back," said Mulvaney. "Look for anything you can use to cut them, like a rock, a broken bottle, anything."

*

Harper Cattle Data Center, Round Rock, Texas, Republic of Texas

March 28, 2025, 8:17 a.m. Central

Just off I-35 stood an office park filled with distribution centers. In the back of the complex stood yet another of the white rectangular buildings with no windows that dominated the utilitarian park. A small car park in the front was filled with about fifty nondescript cars and had a small sign that read, "Harper Cattle Company Data Processing and Receivables Collection."

The sign clearly described the exact activities performed on the ground floor of the facility. However, a side door in the building led to an elevator that traveled four floors underground to another data center, where the clandestine services of the Republic of Texas housed part of Looking Glass, their updated version of the NSA's old PRISM system. The other portions of the system resided in the Utah center.

A technician looked at his screen and saw that one of the conversations in his queue was flashing red. He clicked on the call and read the flag "Herring – Urgent," then picked up the phone and called Dr. Herring's secure cell as directed. The technician waited while the encryption cycle completed and then told Herring about the tagged file.

*

Harper Packing Company, Austin, Texas, Republic of Texas

March 28, 2025, 8:36 a.m. Central

Herring completed listening to the call again and then tried Jack's cell. Nothing. He looked at the time, realized the team was still in the air, and called Jack's satphone. He got through, but the connection was terrible. He found himself screaming into the receiver for Jack to call him when the team landed.

*

Fort Dix, New Jersey, Mid-Atlantic Military District, former USA

March 28, 2025, 9:14 a.m. Eastern

Listir walked into the base's headquarters and asked for Captain Carpenter. The soldier at the desk called the captain's office, and five minutes later she appeared.

"Mr. Listir," said the captain in a very businesslike manner. "I would have thought you would have headed back to Maryland by now."

Listir repressed a smile. "I just wanted to come say goodbye before we left. My friend has come up with a couple of leads that we're going to follow." *You goddamn bet your ass he has*, thought Listir, *and it cost me.* He tried to stay focused, but his mind kept wandering to a nice fishing boat in the Caribbean and an unlimited pile of Republic of Texas money. *Maybe it is time to cash out of the game.*

"That's good news," said the captain, who looked a bit relieved. "We will be very interested in whatever you learn. Please keep us informed."

The two shook hands, and Listir walked out to his waiting SUV, and the convoy headed off toward the main gate.

"Listir finally departed. Returning to DC to check some leads. Not a moment too soon, since our new friends will be arriving in less than a half hour," said Captain Carpenter over the phone to Lieutenant Colonel Symmonds.

While the captain finished her call, Listir's two-vehicle convoy turned out of the base's main gate and drove down the road adjacent to the base. They drove about a mile and half and pulled over to the side. A C-130 passed over on final approach, bucking slightly in the March breeze. After about thirty-five minutes, a private jet flew by, wheels descending, a stylized longhorn clearly visible on the tail.

"That fucker Mulvaney knew his shit," said Brown from the front seat as both vehicles moved out.

Listir smiled to himself. After so many years, he finally had the jump on Jack Dodge.

Now we will see who "personally" kills who, thought Lister.

CHAPTER TWENTY

Fort Dix, New Jersey, Mid-Atlantic Military District, former USA

March 28, 2025, 10:02 a.m. Eastern

The plane came to a halt outside one of the many hangars, and the air stair lowered. Jack's satellite phone began to vibrate, so he stayed in his seat and took the call while the others deplaned. A van had pulled up, and Jack could see Captain Carpenter greeting the team members.

"Hi, Alan," said Jack. "I'm not even off the plane yet. What's up?"

"Maybe you should stay on the plane," said Herring.

Jack looked out the window at the group unloading the duffels full of equipment. His stomach tightened.

"Looking Glass found something. Seems that our old friend Mulvaney has been moonlighting with a two-bit smuggler, former CIA guy named Listir. Rings a lot of bells. None of them good."

Jack's mind flashed. He could see the rain coming down. Justin screaming over the radio for support, and gunfire filling the air. The mission failed, and Listir was the cause; he betrayed them for money. A picture of Listir's face frozen in anger inside the SUV with the shattered windshield completed the image.

"Listir is very interested in your activities and has some tie with the MAMD, but may be acting alone."

"Crap!" said Jack quietly. "How bad?"

"He knows where you are right now and where you want to go."

Jack stared out the window at Katrina. She had no weapons training and frankly no business being here. He needed to talk to Danny.

"Play the clip," commanded Jack.

Herring played it for him several times.

"It appears Mr. Listir may be freelancing," Jack said.

"Could be right. It doesn't sound like he is on the same page as the MAMD."

"Did you tag Listir's phone?"

"Yes, we've got it, and I have it on priority traffic. I also had him geolocated not far from your current position and moving north, though he went dark. He clearly pulled the battery to stop any signals. However, his compatriots are not so smart, and I have their phones tagged now, so I am tracking. FYI, I also have your new friend Captain Carpenter's phone marked as a result of your visit the other day. If he makes contact with her, we'll have it. Jack, Listir is a very bad guy—you know that better than most. You should seriously rethink what we're planning."

Jack hung up, put the phone in his pocket, took a deep breath, and came down the plane steps. He needed to speak to Danny.

"Nice to see you again, Captain Carpenter," said Jack, extending a hand and a smile.

"Nice to see you as well, Mr. Dodge," replied the captain with a grin. "I'm assuming we can all be who we actually are this time."

"Sorry about that," Jack said, and gave her his best smile. "I see you've met the new members of our team. Is there somewhere we can go and discuss the logistics of the mission?"

"Absolutely. I've commandeered the conference room in my offices for you, and we can go there," offered the captain as she waved the Texas team into a large Ford Econoline van. "However, Mr. Dodge, the general would like to personally welcome you to the Mid-Atlantic Military District if you can spare the time."

Jack knew from her tone that he would make all the time in the world for the general.

She motioned toward a jeep parked near the van.

"Sure, it'd be my pleasure, ma'am," said Jack. "If it's OK, I'd like to have Danny join us."

The captain nodded her assent.

Five minutes later, the three of them stood in front of Master Sergeant Stanley Baptiste.

"Good morning, Master Sergeant. We are here to see the general on his orders," said the captain, returning his salute.

On the way, Jack whispered to Danny that they needed to talk alone after the meeting.

The master sergeant turned on his heels, knocked twice, and entered the office behind him. He returned nearly instantly and invited the three inside.

Captain Carpenter walked through the door first, followed by Jack and Danny. She stood at attention while the general signed something before looking up and returning her salute. He next saluted both Jack and Danny.

"It's my pleasure to welcome you gentlemen and your team to the Mid-Atlantic Military District," said the general, rising from his chair, his voice deep and strong.

Jack studied him. Though he was not a large man, he was clearly in top physical condition and exuded an aura of authority.

"Thank you, sir," said Jack. "I'm Jack Dodge, and this is my partner, Danny Winters. May I offer the thanks of the Republic of Texas for your assistance in this matter."

The general studied Jack for a second and then said, "I met your father once."

Jack smiled. Almost everyone he met had an I-met-Jackson-Dodge story.

"Well, I shouldn't really say *met* in the classic sense. I was testifying to a Senate committee on something or other, and your father was giving me a good once-over. The funny thing was that he was doing it in such a down-home style, with a bunch of jokes mixed in, that I barely realized I was being burned at the stake. Please give him my best."

"I certainly will, sir," said Jack. "Thank you for those kind remarks."

The general came around the desk and leaned back against it, with his hands on the edge. "What is the matter at hand, as you so eloquently described it?" said the general, looking Jack directly in the eye.

"We are tasked with locating certain irreplaceable historical documents related to the history of Texas," said Jack, holding the general's stare. He worked hard to ensure that neither his expression nor eyes betrayed any hint of deception. "I would like to be more specific, sir, but I am not at liberty to go into detail. Suffice it to say, as a new nation, we are very interested in preserving our history for future generations. Preserving history is of special interest to my daddy." Jack added the last line in order to explain his presence.

"Well, I think that is obvious," said the general, returning to a standing position. "Captain Carpenter is a very able officer. She has my full confidence, and we will do everything in our power to assist you in this matter. I would note that you are going into dangerous country that the MAMD has consciously decided against adding to our growing territory. The amount of resources required to secure the New York metropolitan area are just not worth whatever benefits could be realized."

"Understood, sir," said Jack. "Our goal is to get in and out quickly. Hopefully, the resources we have brought with us and their contacts in New York will enable us to do so in a safe manner."

The general saluted. "Good luck. Dismissed."

All three returned the salute and walked out of his office.

Once in the corridor, Danny said, "Amazing how all that SEAL shit comes back instantaneously when confronted by a no-nonsense soldier."

Jack nodded and smiled.

As Captain Carpenter turned a corner in the hall, Danny grabbed Jack's sleeve and whispered, "Good thinking on the *my daddy asked me to find this shit* point."

Jack just shook his head and smiled again, but before they rounded the corner, he whispered, "We really need to talk."

*

Middlesex County, New Jersey, former USA

March 28, 2025, 1:00 p.m. Eastern

The going was slow. The roads continued to degrade the closer they came to the New York City metropolitan area. Abandoned cars and trucks and debris littered the path. Listir looked at his watch, a gold Rolex Oyster he had "liberated from its original owner" a few years ago, and could not believe they had already driven for three hours and still had not arrived at Union Beach, New Jersey.

"Hey, boss, can you believe they call this piece-of-shit road the Garden State Parkway?" said Brown, pointing out the window at yet another burned-out building.

The first thirty miles of the trip had been through a relatively normal landscape. However, about fifteen miles earlier they passed a large sign warning that they were leaving the area of active MAMD control, and two miles later, after passing the last checkpoint, they entered an area that had descended into hell. Burned-out buildings, roads in serious disrepair, debris everywhere, and general decay.

"Keep alert. I don't want any problems," said Listir. "You need to watch out for obstructions on the road and roadblocks. We are seriously behind enemy lines, and even when we link up with our contacts we need to stay very sharp."

Listir stared out the window at a completely charred store that had at one time clearly been a Target. He had not been up in this part of New Jersey in nearly five years, and the scene of desolation was worse than any movie depicting Armageddon. Suddenly, it hit him: Homs. The area looked like Homs when he had been there during the Syrian civil war.

*

Fort Dix, New Jersey, Mid-Atlantic Military District, former USA

March 28, 2025, 1:23 p.m. Eastern

Jack stood up. His back ached from hours hunched over maps, going over the insertion with the team and Captain Carpenter's people. He had walked Danny through his conversation with Herring, and the two agreed that they should revisit it after the planning session. Jack moved to the far side of the conference room and stared at an oil painting. It depicted an American soldier straining forward in battle.

"The Ultimate Weapon," said Captain Carpenter, who had quietly materialized beside him. "It's the symbol of Fort Dix, and this painting is of the huge bronze statue outside. The inscription says, "This monument is dedicated to the only indispensable instrument of war, The American Soldier—the ultimate weapon. If they are not there, you don't own it.""

Jack stood silently studying the picture. He had once been that American soldier, going into very dark places for his country.

"A fitting tribute," said Jack. "It's a real shame that the honor and sacrifice of all the soldiers were not enough to keep the country from falling apart."

"Hey, Jack," called Danny, breaking the flood of memories of missions past running through his mind. "We are ninety mikes from helo time. Can I have a word? The rest are going to pack up and head to the mess for some chow."

Jack and Danny talked in a small office that had been set aside for the team's use during their visit. Danny held up a finger to his lips while he deployed one of Justin's jamming devices. Once the device's lights indicated full functionality, they could speak.

"Jack, I talked to Herring again. He got a hit on Listir's phone. The man's moving up the Garden State Parkway toward the New York City area. He's moving at less than twenty miles per hour, which would suggest conditions are as bad as expected on the ground."

"Has he been in contact with anyone here?" asked Jack, looking through the small glass rectangle in the door at Captain Carpenter, who stood outside waiting for them.

"No. He had some calls with what we guess are part of his gang, or whatever you want to call it, in DC about various smuggling activities, and with someone in Northern Virginia. He also had a call with what we suspect is a gang up in northern New Jersey, but nothing with anyone here."

Jack sat down in one of the stiff metal chairs, closed his eyes, and thought for a minute.

"What are you thinking?" asked Danny.

"I'm thinking we have ourselves a smuggler who does business with the MAMD but now is out of the loop and acting independently," said Jack. "We should expect the MAMD probably has to deal with him and his kind on a regular basis to get what they need to run their territory. I'm trying to set aside the fact that we happen to know this particular varmint from our former lives." Jack opened his eyes and looked at Danny. "I think we should speak to Captain Carpenter about him and the fact that he is in the area. If we sense anything off with her, deception of any kind, we abort. If she appears on the up and up, then we figure out what to do with Mr. Listir. Maybe we finally get to honor the promise I made in Nigeria."

Danny remarked, "You're putting a lot of eggs in her basket. We significantly increase the risks by telling her what we know if you have judged her incorrectly."

"I don't see another option right now, do you?" Jack looked at Danny, but the latter eventually just shook his head.

Jack leaned out of the office and asked the captain if she could spare them a minute.

She joined, quickly looked at the device on the desk, and smiled. "I guess you guys can never be too careful."

Jack detailed the situation, and she stared at him, dumbfounded.

"Mr. Listir's a supplier to the MAMD. He and his type are not our first choice of allies, but the circumstances warrant strange partners," she offered. "He has a contact with the former NSA and originally alerted us to the fact that there was a team from Texas in DC. However, as the situation has evolved from us trying to figure out what you were doing to our working with you, we tried to disassociate him from this matter. I honestly thought that we had done so, and that he had left here for DC."

Jack paused and then asked, "Would he know where your New York base is?"

The captain thought for a minute. "I am not sure what, if any, contact he has with the New York area, but I suppose so. It's not hidden, though as you have seen from the maps, it's quite geographically separate and defensible."

"I would think it will be difficult for Mr. Listir to follow us into this area of the city of New York without your resources and the assistance of the Latin Kings," offered Danny, "so let's assume our biggest point of vulnerability is at arrival and departure from the base."

The three of them spoke for considerable time and came up with a plan to ensure the team's security on Shooters Island, and to potentially deal with Mr. Listir, should he materialize.

They called Herring, briefed him on the plan. Part of that plan involved Herring increasing surveillance on Mr. Listir.

A General Atomics MQ-1 armed with two AGM-114 Hellfire missiles launched from Quantico and made its way at three hundred miles per hour to take up station over Listir's coordinates.

Once they had done all they could think of, Danny remarked, "We have thirteen mikes left to grab some chow. You in?"

Jack laughed. "Of course I'm in. It will certainly be the last meal of today that doesn't come in an aluminum pouch."

CHAPTER TWENTY-ONE

Perth Amboy, New Jersey, former USA

March 28, 2025, 3:12 p.m. Eastern

They pulled up to a street with a hanging street sign reading "Distribution Boulevard." Warehouses lined both sides of a road that bore little resemblance to the mental picture of a boulevard. The SUV maneuvered cautiously down the street and turned left into the lot of a large warehouse. The facility was in better condition than the rest and surrounded by a fence topped with concertina wire.

The vehicle pulled up to a gate, and the driver lowered his window and pushed the button on a call box that also had a keypad. They all sat and listened as the call box dialed a number and an extremely tired voice answered in Spanish, "Who are you?"

The driver looked at Listir, who said, "Tell him friends from DC."

The driver repeated the message and, after answering a few questions regarding the composition of the group and their firepower, received some instructions.

"You are to pull up to the rear of the building. Fourth loading bay. Mr. Listir should exit the vehicle alone and come in the door next to the bay."

The driver started to protest, but Listir told him to agree.

The gate slid down, and they made their way slowly around the building. On the backside, the lot was full of vehicles of nearly every type. Panel trucks, Humvees, jeeps, SUVs, and muscle cars. The driver drove the lead car to the fourth loading dock and stopped as instructed.

Brown said, "I don't like it. You shouldn't go in there alone."

Listir checked his 9mm and returned it to his waistband, pulled his jacket down over it, and lit a cigarette. He took a long drag and then said, "I appreciate the concern, but I have done business with Ulysses and his crew for a long time. It's been a profitable business relationship, and he has no reason to want it to end. He's also not a fool, so he's going to be careful. Give me ten minutes. If I'm not out to invite you in, then you may want to come get me or, if you are really smart, leave."

With that, Listir got out of the car, slammed the door, and took a few steps until he was standing by the front right tire. He kept the hood between himself and the building while he checked things again. Other than leaves and debris being blown around by the wind, nothing much moved. Listir looked down the rows of parked cars and saw a skinny feral cat skitter underneath a pickup truck. He looked at the door and the camera that sat inside a metal cage watching him. He took one last pull on his cigarette and tossed it to the side and then headed for the structure.

Just before he reached the door, it opened and revealed a darkened space. Listir walked on in, and the door swung closed behind him. Bright lights flashed on, and Listir stood there blinking. His eyes finally adjusted, and he found himself looking at a semicircle of eight very large men of obvious Puerto Rican descent, each with a 9mm stuffed in his waistband and dark sunglasses shielding his eyes. In the middle stood a short, bald, almost Middle Eastern–looking man in an untucked work shirt, blue jeans, and heavy work boots, with no sunglasses covering his face.

"*Buenos días, amigo,*" Ulysses said, smiling broadly, but his dark eyes revealing no mirth.

"*Buenos días,* yourself," replied Listir evenly. "I like your new backup singers. How's the album coming?"

Ulysses roared with laughter, while his crew stood there staring at Listir. "You are fucking funny, Listir. You get funnier every time I see you. Come on, let's have a drink and talk about how much whatever you wan' is goin' fuckin' cost you!" Ulysses pointed up the steps into the bowels of the warehouse.

"Absolutely, you bastard. I will drink whatever awful liquor you island people drink, but first let me bring my guys in before time expires and they follow my instructions to blow your warehouse up," said Listir with a completely straight face, eliciting another roar of laughter from Ulysses. His entire crew joined in this time.

Listir turned, and one of the Puerto Ricans came forward and opened the door for him. He stepped outside into the dull gray light and signaled his team to come on in.

"Brown, leave someone out there with the vehicle. Stay alert."

He moved back through the door and up the stairs to where Ulysses was standing. They walked down a concrete corridor lit by fluorescent strip lights until they came to room that was obviously Ulysses' office. It was filled with an odd mixture of antiques, as well as velvet and modern pieces of furniture that looked as if they came from various hotel lobbies.

Ulysses walked into the room, flung open a cabinet, and pulled out a bottle of dark rum. He poured two large glasses and threw in a couple of ice cubes.

Turning toward Listir, who sat in an oversize velvet chair with gold-leaf arms, he extended one of the glasses and said, "OK, tell me whatcha wan."

Listir took the glass, drank some of the rum, and lit another cigarette. He then started providing detail on exactly what he needed. Ulysses sat calmly, taking in every word, refilling his glass during the story.

"Holy fuck! You crazy, spy!" said Ulysses when Listir finished. "Fuckin' insane. You and I do bidness together, good bidness, but whatcha askin' iss not bidness! Iss a fuckin' death wish!"

Listir sat calmly. He watched the little fireplug of a Puerto Rican as he stormed around the room, detailing all the things that could go wrong.

"Ulysses, my friend, we have lots of planning to do for this mission so that it is successful, so if you are through with detailing all your worries, can we please move on?"

"Fuck you, Listir," spat Ulysses. "You show up at my place wit no warnin' and ask for my help with this bullshit! I yell for as long as I wan'!" He took another drink and sat watching the dark liquor run down the side of the glass. "This's gonna cos' you a fuckin' fortune, man. Also, no way any of my people go wichu. None. We not crazy."

"Fine, let's get down to business," said Listir. He reached inside the pocket of his jacket and pulled out a list and threw it on the coffee table on which he rested his feet. "I think you will find the list there more than ample compensation for what I propose."

Ulysses approached the table and grabbed the paper. He unfolded it and read the list. He read it again and then threw himself into one of the oversize chairs, continuing to look at the paper. "How I know that you not gonna cheat me?"

"I will have a truck on its way from a warehouse we keep near the

MAMD headquarters tonight with the medical items listed there. You better send some of your men down to meet it at the end of MAMD territory and escort it up here, because that is valuable cargo. You will have to trust me for the rest, but given the value of the medical supplies and medicines that you will get tonight, I think it is worth waiting." Listir finished and lit up another cigarette, letting out a small cough. Maybe he needed to quit.

"I should ax for more," said Ulysses quietly.

"You should, but you won't get it. What I propose is more than fair," said Listir calmly, almost bored. "We are running out of time, so can we please stop fucking around?"

"OK, deal!" said Ulysses. He stopped and stared hard at Listir. "If you fuck me on this, I will kill you all. Just bidness."

Listir held the Puerto Rican's eyes until Ulysses looked away. *No, my little Puerto Rican friend, if anyone is going to do the killing, it will be me,* thought Listir.

CHAPTER TWENTY-TWO

*Fort Dix, New Jersey, Mid-Atlantic Military District, former USA/
Shooters Island (Mid-Atlantic Military District Outpost),
New York, former USA*

March 28, 2025, 3:01 p.m. Eastern

The three Black Hawks all lifted off right on time and headed north in a triangle formation. Jack, Danny, Katrina, Captain Carpenter, Simon, and Lieutenant Wallace of Carpenter's command sat in the lead bird. On their right side and 150 meters back flew a Black Hawk filled with more of Carpenter's people. On the left side and the same distance behind flew the remainder of the Texas team, including their new friend, Jesus Madoro, from the Dallas chapter of the Almighty Latin Kings and Queen Nation.

Jack looked over at Captain Carpenter, dressed in full gray combat dress with a small patch with the MAMD symbol where a United States flag should have been. The Texans all wore similar uniforms, but on their left shoulders was the flag of the Republic of Texas. Same ride, same look, only the flags were now different, which changed everything.

Jack did a quick check of the equipment in his pack. Water. Additional flash bangs and grenades. Multiple spare clips for his automatic weapon and his sidearm. MREs. Satellite phone. Night-vision goggles. He checked his body armor. His automatic weapon was cleaned and ready. He had a condom secured over the muzzle, same as with his sidearm. He would remove it when needed but could just as easily fire through it, something Danny always found hysterical. "Oh, my condom broke" was Danny's regular joke, less funny fifty times ago.

"Twenty mikes," said the pilot over the headset.

Jack took a minute to stare out the windows of the helicopter. Very little moved on the ground below. Jack knew they had left, or nearly left, MAMD territory. The economy in and around New York City and northern New Jersey had totally collapsed. Anyone who could get out to anywhere else had left. Disease and famine had killed off scores of people, especially the elderly. Gangs controlled the area the way feudal lords controlled small parcels of land, and fought endless battles with their neighbors. Welcome to the Wild East. There was no law other than the law of the gang that happened to be in control. Large parts of the formerly densely populated area were now ghost towns.

Jack looked over at Danny, who had his head tilted back and appeared to be sound asleep. He caught Katrina's eye and jerked a thumb at him. She looked at the giant of a man for a minute and then smiled. It never ceased to amaze Jack, but Danny could literally sleep anytime, anywhere, but especially in helicopters on their way into missions. "It lulls me to sleep," Danny always would say. "All that shaking. It's like I am back in my mamma's arms." Jack smiled to himself, knowing that Danny's mother was a petite woman who worked as a pediatric oncologist, not a woman with a lot of time to rock a baby who weighed as much as a bowling ball.

Jack went over the mission plan in his head. It was sound, but there were so many variables, Listir among them. They were relying on a street gang to help with their infiltration, protection, and successful extraction from truly hostile territory. They could not assess the condition of the Academy, nor whether or not they would be able to find what they were looking for in the facility. Simon had raised a good point before they left the planning room: "If we cannot find the documents in question quickly, why not just light the whole place on fire? Destroying is the same as finding, right?" Katrina looked positively stricken.

Jack turned this question over in his mind but knew that it would be impossible for them to guarantee nothing survived. Additionally, he did not like the idea of lighting a fire in the middle of a densely populated area that had absolutely no ability to fight one. He had finally answered, "We're going to maximize our time on the ground by heading out at sunset, 7:11 p.m., and returning no later than sunrise, 6:05 a.m., but much earlier if possible. Including travel time, we'll have a maximum of nearly nine hours on site, so we're going to find the documents, or ascertain that they're not there. Fire is not an acceptable option."

"Five mikes," said the pilot.

Jack felt his heartbeat rise a little bit. Even though they were landing at a MAMD-controlled facility, ironically called Fort Apache, there were still risks. Not to mention that he was now close to where his heart had died several years ago. He felt someone staring at him and looked up to find Katrina's eyes on him. He gave her a smile and quickly realized he was happy to be looking at her. *Danny is fucking right: lock it down, Jack.*

The helicopters, which were already traveling low and fast, dropped down over the water. Jack looked out the front window to see a flat island directly ahead. He knew from the briefing that it was called Shooters Island, and that at the far northern end stood a small MAMD base with a dock and a couple of former US Coast Guard craft.

"There used to be a shipyard on this island a little over a hundred years ago," said Captain Carpenter over the headset. "The most famous boat they built was *Meteor III*, a yacht for Kaiser Wilhelm II."

Jack nodded and watched as Danny came instantly awake. Danny could always sense the start of a mission.

"One mike," said the pilot.

"Katrina," started Jack. "Remember what we discussed. We're going to set down fast, and before we do the doors will open. As soon as the wheels hit the tarmac, we're all going to pile out. Stay low and follow my lead. Danny will be right behind you. Head for the Quonset hut at the western edge of the landing pad. Move fast and remember to stay low."

"Copy that," said Katrina with a smile, pretending to play the part of a soldier.

Everyone smiled back. Danny gave her a thumbs-up. She had a sense of humor. She dressed like a soldier in body armor but lacked an assault weapon and tactical combat package.

The Black Hawks spaced out, and Jack's bird came down first, low to the pad and right next to the Quonset hut. Lieutenant Wallace threw open the door to the chopper, and everyone piled out and hustled toward the building. Wallace led and had not even made it the ten meters to the hut before their Black Hawk took off and the second came in. The choppers would drop their passengers and then come back in and park for the night.

Inside the hut, Captain Carpenter made introductions, and then they sat down to listen to Lieutenant Albers, the officer in charge of Fort Apache. The hut was large, drafty, and filled with folding chairs, tables, and the usual array of maps, communications gear, and desktops.

Jack looked around and flashed back to another hut in Afghanistan, where they had sat down to mission plan an assault on a Taliban leadership post during his time in the SEALs.

Everyone grabbed a folding chair, while the lieutenant stood in front of a bulletin board with an aerial photo of Shooters Island.

"Fort Apache is roughly forty-three acres," the lieutenant began. "We patrol the entire island on a regular basis but maintain a full security perimeter only around this twelve-acre area at the northern end of the island." He pointed to a black semicircle hand-drawn on the map.

"How do you have it secured?" Danny asked. He sat in a chair toward the back of the hut and tilted it up, with the front legs off the floor.

"We have a coiled razor wire perimeter about twelve feet wide and roughly the same high. It even stretches about fifty yards into the water. Inside the land part of the wire, we keep an electric fence that is solar and wind powered, with supplemental battery power. The current can fluctuate, but it should be strong enough to kill most of the time." The lieutenant turned back to the map and pulled out a pen. "We have the men on patrol at all times here, here, and here." He marked the map with small circles. "We chose the perimeter location in order to take advantage of a small ridgeline, which puts the fence down below where our men patrol. We keep an elevated position with no natural obstructions on line of sight. We burn out the land with flamethrowers for fifty yards either side of the fence on a regular basis."

Jack looked back and saw Danny nodding.

"Nice planning, Lieutenant," said Danny. "One more question: What do you consider the biggest threat you are guarding against here?"

The lieutenant looked at Captain Carpenter, who nodded almost imperceptibly, cleared his throat, and said, "Gangs." He turned to the one member of the team who stood out. Jesus Madoro sprawled in his folding chair like it was a La-Z-Boy, the cross tattooed on the right side of his neck clearly visible to all as his head tilted to one side. He wore a bright bandana tied around his head.

After a bit of a discussion, Danny persuaded Madoro to dump his baggy jeans, wifebeater, and plaid shirt, and put on the gray combat fatigues and body armor, but somehow even that looked rumpled. Madoro just rolled a toothpick around in his mouth and eyed the lieutenant.

"In spite of how bad this area is, there's still an incredible amount of trade going on in looted goods, medicine, drugs, women, you name it. Our location allows us to monitor what is moving around the harbor, as well as potential threats to our borders. For the gangs, this position would be prime real estate if you wanted to hijack another group's shipments. Additionally, they would love to have access to our boats and fuel. In the early days, the post used to take a lot of hits, but a few hundred casualties later and people generally do not bother us. However, we like to have the choppers follow combat procedures. We don't need people getting a good look at our activities, or firing off an opportunistic round."

"Lieutenant," Captain Carpenter interjected. She leaned forward in her chair and said, "You were part of the discussion earlier today via phone. Why don't you walk us through the insertion plan one more time in detail?"

The lieutenant flipped over the board while she was talking, showing a laminated map of New York Harbor and the former city with excellent detail. "As we discussed, the plan is relatively simple." The lieutenant pulled out a grease pencil. "We are going to leave here a few minutes after sunset on a forty-seven-foot former coast guard motor lifeboat. We will go up this channel, called the Kill Van Kull, until we hit the mouth of the Hudson River. After that, it's a straight shot up the Hudson, with about a three-knot current at that time. Assuming we are still looking at an insertion at about this point"—the lieutenant drew a circle on the map on the Upper West Side of Manhattan—"we calculate about forty minutes travel time."

"Jesus," Danny said, "you about ready to make another call?"

Jack watched as Florez leaned over and whispered back and forth with Jesus in Spanish. Jesus nodded a few times and took a satellite phone from Florez and stood up.

Everyone sat and waited while one of the most senior members of the Latin Kings in all of the Republic of Texas called the head of the Latin Kings in New York. Jesus leaned against a metal rack stacked with plastic storage containers and whispered into his phone. Jack counted the minutes, and finally Jesus hung up and came back to sit in his folding chair, somehow immediately resettling into a reclined position.

Jesus Madoro whispered a bit with Florez, who stood up and walked to the map. "All set," he said, hitting the map with his finger. "We take the boat up to this point, which will be about One Fifty-Fifth Street. Jesus will make another call, and they will show us their exact location with"—Florez paused, and Jesus held up four fingers—"four flashes of their headlights. We are to answer with three flashes of our searchlight and then go in by Zodiacs."

Florez returned to his seat.

"While you are onshore, we will stay in the vicinity in the river, but we will move around a bit just so that we do not draw too much unwanted attention to us or your insertion point," said the lieutenant. "We want you to return to the boat no later than 5:40 a.m., so we will plan to use the same four lights on three lights back to launch the Zodiacs to retrieve you. If you need us sooner, we will monitor your comms, and the captain can raise us on a backup radio as well." The lieutenant paused and then looked at Captain Carpenter. "Captain, I believe that concludes my briefing, and we have a little more than an hour before we need to move out."

"Thank you, Lieutenant," replied the captain.

Port Elizabeth, New Jersey, former USA

March 28, 2025, 7:01 p.m. Eastern

Listir stood outside the warehouse smoking in the fading March light. The discussions with Ulysses had been a bit rougher and longer than he expected. The Puerto Ricans wanted to keep their distance from the MAMD forces, and even though all they would be doing was inserting Listir's team, they were concerned. He heard the door open behind him and glanced over his shoulder to see Brown approaching.

Brown took out a cigarette and bent his head to accept a light from Listir's Zippo. He took a couple of drags, while Listir waited.

Finally, Brown said, "You know those guys are going to scatter to the wind if any shit goes down at all."

Listir inclined his head and kept smoking.

"What do we really think we're doing up here, chasing after some heavily armed Texans and MAMD forces? Hell, the MAMD is good business for us."

Listir stood thinking for a minute. He watched a cat, maybe the same cat from earlier, snake in and out of the long dried grasses along the fence line.

"Whatever they're doing, it has a lot of importance," he said. "The Texans do not send serious people like fucking Jack Dodge to ground zero without something of huge value being at stake. Yes, the MAMD is important. Running arms, medicine, and everything else up to New Jersey dwarfs all the petty shit we do in DC. But whatever these guys are doing is worth much more. This may be a once-in-a-life payday. If we can take it from the Texans or even learn enough about what it is to blackmail them, we can all retire in style."

Brown looked down at the ground. "It may be worth a lot, but is it worth risking our business, or potentially getting killed?" He looked up at Listir and continued. "You know I'd never disagree with you in front of the others, but what Ulysses said about leaving this shit alone is pretty good advice. We could get our asses handed to us. I also think if we fuck this up the Texans will never let us retire."

Listir was no longer listening. All he could hear was the voice of Jack Dodge coming in over his radio, vowing to kill him, after he had abandoned his assignment in Nigeria. He was sure Dodge and team would be captured and killed, and instead they had somehow survived.

Listir made it through the subsequent inquiry, but only barely, his career at the CIA effectively derailed. They all suspected he had taken dirty money; they just could not prove it. He knew how to hide his deceit. He hated Dodge.

You should have died or been thrown in a prison in Nigeria. No matter. Now you are going to die here.

He looked back at the cat, eyes gleaming in the deepening darkness, and then headed for the warehouse.

CHAPTER TWENTY-THREE

Shooters Island (Mid-Atlantic Military District Outpost),
New York, former USA

March 28, 2025, 7:38 p.m. Eastern

The entire deck vibrated from the engine as the boat edged away from the dock and started up the Kill Van Kull. The sun had set, and a low layer of cloud had come over the area, making the night very dark. The boat crew all wore night-vision goggles, and the Texans did their best to stay out of their way as they moved around the decks.

Jack felt the boat move hard right, and the engine kicked up a bit as the captain expedited the turn.

"Debris in the water," said the closest crew member. "The water here is full of crap that has come loose, been thrown in the water, or floated here. It's an obstacle course."

The guy had been spot-on, as during the duration of the voyage Jack lost count of the number of power surges to starboard or port to avoid floating debris.

He grabbed a thermos and poured two paper cups of coffee from the small kitchen and moved up on deck, handing one to Katrina, who stood by the back railing.

She thanked him and then pointed into the darkness. "What's missing?" she asked.

Jack stared into the dark, trying to figure out what he should see. "The Statue of Liberty."

All that was left was the stone pedestal. Jack remembered a book he had read as a child about the French supplying the statue as a gift, and the US having to run a nationwide fund-raising drive to build the base.

"I guess I have not thought about it, but what happened?" he asked.

Katrina stared hard at the base. "It was so sad. The statue needed some repairs after one of the storms, but there was nobody left to take care of it. I heard about the torch falling off and then looting for the copper..." Her voice trailed off.

Jack stood next to her as the island slipped by, and then he turned to look at the Battery Park area of Lower Manhattan. The buildings stood out in the dark sky against the gray background of the clouds. No artificial lights showed anywhere. As the boat moved into the Hudson, he could see fires in oil drums here and there, but still no lights. He felt a chill run down his spine. He had not been to Manhattan since he came for Marissa and ended up taking her body home to Texas. The city looked truly ominous without lights or cars rushing up and down the West Side Highway. It looked dead.

"How many people still live here?" asked Katrina, staring at the *Intrepid* as they continued up the river. The aircraft carrier turned museum had slipped her mooring lines, probably during a storm, and lay on her side, half in the water and half on what had been the West Side Highway.

"We do not know for sure," came the voice of Captain Carpenter from behind them. "Between people fleeing, the fighting that took place here, famine, and disease, the population collapsed. However, we see a lot of smuggling activity and trade in looted property, so it is certainly still well populated. We estimate maybe eight hundred thousand left in Manhattan."

Jack heard Danny whistle and turned around from the railing. Danny pointed at his watch, and Jack nodded.

"Captain," Jack said. "Do you want to come with me, and let's go back over the Latin Kings' part one more time with Jesus and Jamie?"

Jack turned and walked across the deck to the small cabin. As he passed the boat crew, he got the update: "Twelve mikes, sir."

They sat in the subdued glow of the red-lit cabin, Jesus sprawled on a bench in the corner smoking a cigarette, with Jamie sitting next to him. Jack was not a fan of smoke, especially in the confined space of the gently rocking boat cabin. In spite of the "No Smoking" sign on the wall, there was no point in needling Jesus. He was unlikely to stop. They needed him, and he knew it. He could smoke all he wanted.

Danny stood in the center of the room and began, "In about ten minutes we're going to hold position in the river directly off West One Fifty-Fifth Street. Jesus will call his contacts on the satellite phone. At that point, we should see four flashes from car headlights, and the boat will answer with three flashes from its searchlight. When the light signals are confirmed, we set off in the Zodiacs."

Jack cast a hard stare at Jesus. "Are we sure you have worked out all the arrangements with your contacts? I do not want any renegotiations, nor do I want any complications."

Jamie leaned over and spoke with Jesus, who nodded and looked back at Jack. "*No problema.*" The two men continued to stare at each other until Jack gave a small nod to Danny.

Danny picked back up. "Based on what we have been told, there will be five vehicles waiting for us. A lead and chase car, a pickup, and two SUVs. I'm going in the back of the pickup with Simon and Lieutenant Wallace." Both men nodded. "We're going to take the HK416s with us." Danny indicated the two handheld heavy machine guns. "The remainder of the team will split between the two SUVs, Captain Carpenter in the lead vehicle, Jack in the second SUV. Once again, we should consider this a combat mission that may go to hell at any moment. Let's hope not, but everyone needs to be ready. One reminder: Herring and his team will be on comms the entire mission and have a Reaper in the air over our position on the off chance that we need to bring in some heavy firepower. He has the other vehicle orbiting our friends."

Jack watched Florez lean over to Jesus and reiterate the point that a missile-enabled drone circled on station over their position. Jack watched Jesus cast an eye at the porthole. *Good, he got the point.*

The boat throttled back. They all felt the decrease in speed before the engine noise died down.

"We're on station, Captain," shouted the helmsman.

"Showtime," said Florez as he handed Jesus a satellite phone.

Jesus spoke quietly into the phone, though Jack could not have heard him over the whine of the winches lowering the two Zodiacs into the water anyway. The team made its way to the deck and looked over the port side railing as the boat held position in the river. Four flashes were clearly visible from the shore.

"Please give me three flashes in response," said Captain Carpenter.

The powerful searchlight on top of the cabin flashed three times.

With no orders required, the ten team members split in two and went over opposite sides into their preassigned Zodiacs. Jack sat on one of the ribs and helped Katrina in next to him. He checked the Glock on his hip and verified the security of the condom protecting his AR-15 from the spray. He tightened his grip on his weapon. The chop in the river was much more apparent in the Zodiac than in the larger boat.

The 250-horsepower motor wound up, lines jettisoned, and the raft surged off through the water. Katrina grabbed Jack's arm as the boat bounced. He wanted to look in her direction, but he focused his mind on the mission. As the boat moved closer to shore, he could see the outlines of the vehicles emerging on the shoreline of the river. He smiled at the absurdity of the situation. He was on a raft on the freezing Hudson River in the dark of night speeding toward a rendezvous with a street gang best known for drugs and prostitution so that he could find a highly damaging document from nearly 170 years earlier. Momentarily, he forgot the fact that he was near where Marissa died, and a smile crossed his lips. *FUBAR!*

They were about ten meters off the shoreline, and Jack could make out at least ten men arrayed in various states of staged relaxation against the vehicles. Jack saw that each man was holding either a shotgun or a MAC-10.

Jack leaned forward to Simon and Britney, who occupied the rib in front of him. "Our friends are well armed," Jack shouted over the wind and boat motor.

"Copy that," came the response.

The Zodiacs maneuvered up toward the rocks along the edge of the bank, and four of the gang members moved forward. Jack's raft held back and allowed Danny's—containing Captain Carpenter, Florez, Jesus Madoro, and Lieutenant Wallace—to head for shore. Jack watched as ropes were thrown and the raft pulled fast against the rocks. Then another heavy rope with knots was tossed to the passengers, who scrambled one at a time out of the Zodiac and onto the bank. When the first Zodiac was emptied, the helmsman maneuvered it out into the river, and Jack's boat repeated the process.

As the team stood on the bank in a tight circle, eight of the ten removed the protective latex from their guns. Katrina and Jesus were the only unarmed team members. Arrayed across from them stood the members of the Latin Kings. Jack now upped his count to at least sixteen well-armed men. Florez nudged Jesus, who walked forward toward a heavyset man leaning against the hood of a Ford Expedition. The man pushed off the hood and met Jesus halfway. They hugged and stood talking. The large man signaled a couple of other men, who came over to greet their brother from Dallas. After a while, Jesus turned and called Florez to join the group.

Jack watched as Florez carried a duffel over to Fat Boss, which is what Jack decided to call him. Fat Boss took the duffel over to the hood of his Expedition and opened it. Though Jack could not see the contents from where he was, he knew what was inside. The second third of the payment. Totaling one million in Republic of Texas dollars and another 250 one-ounce Republic of Texas gold coins; this, along with the medicine and other goods, constituted payment for the Latin Kings' help. One-third had been delivered earlier in the day by drone, and the remainder would be airdropped the following day after successful completion of the mission and the safe extraction of the team. The same amount of money was being paid to the Dallas branch of the Latin Kings as well.

Fat Boss returned to where Jesus stood, and more hugging ensued.

Danny leaned over toward Jack. "If you give me a bag full of money, I'll give you a hug."

Jack smiled and replied, "I would give it to you if you promised not to hug me."

Florez walked back to the small group and said, "They're ready to move out. However, you need to know one thing. It seems that all is not completely calm. The Kings have been having some recent issues with some of the other gangs in the area. Just this morning the Kings shot up a Crips location about ten blocks from where we're going."

"Terrific," said Lieutenant Wallace. "We're going to drive into the middle of a gang war."

"Lieutenant," Captain Carpenter said sharply, "I'm sure we all appreciate your field assessment. Mr. Florez, we get that it is dangerous, but standing around in the open is not increasing our security. I suggest we move out, and if we encounter hostile fire, we rely on the fact that we are heavily armed and well trained."

"I agree, Captain. Let's move out," said Danny. "However, I remind everyone that Fallujah was basically a gang war, and having spent a tour there I can assure you that gang wars may be the worst kind of war. Let's be extra vigilant."

Everyone turned and started moving toward the vehicles. Two souped-up Chevrolets waited, with significant amounts of chrome and rear wings, along with two SUVs, also covered with chrome and spinners, and a jacked-up pickup truck.

Jack shuddered looking up from the riverbank at the hulking black towers of Presbyterian Hospital, their dark shape outlined by the light of the rising moon filtering through the clouds. He flashed back to a day years earlier when he had sprinted out of a car and into the hospital, only to find his worst fears confirmed. He could still smell the pine-scented cleaning solution that seemed to hang everywhere in the hospital.

"Jack," said Danny.

Jack realized he was standing alone about five meters from the vehicles and that Danny was calling to him from his seat in the bed of the pickup. He waved a hand and moved toward the SUV.

Jack heaved himself into a bucket seat in the middle of the SUV and found himself sitting next to Fat Boss. He looked at the bench seat behind him to see Katrina sitting between Jamie and Jesus. Simon occupied the front passenger seat. Fat Boss smiled at Jack, revealing a row of gold-capped teeth.

"We appreciate your help," Jack said, offering a hand.

Fat Boss leaned over and grabbed Jack's hand with what could only be described as a sweaty paw.

"You pay, we help you anytime," said Fat Boss. Then he added something in Spanish, which caused Jesus to laugh.

Florez leaned forward and said, "Luis would be happy to also show us the public library for free given what we are paying to see the Academy."

Jack turned back to Fat Boss, aka Luis, and said, "*Gracias.*"

Fat Boss laughed again, and the convoy started to move out.

The roar from the vehicles was deafening. All of the cars had their tailpipes fitted with noise enhancements, so the sound was nearly unbearable. Jack noticed a purple glow coming from underneath his vehicle; the SUV had accent lights, as did all the vehicles. *So much for moving around stealthily.* Meanwhile, the radios in each car that allowed the vehicles to communicate were set at maximum volume and filled with near-constant chatter.

Jack spoke into his secure mic. "Danny, you hear me?"

"Five by five, boss. By the way, how is it inside that nice SUV? Because it's cold as a witch's tit in a brass bra here in the back of this pickup. You should be here. In fact, why don't you pull over so we can switch?"

"You are so good at what you do that I could never replace you," said Jack. "Seriously, stay alert. I feel like we are in a Mardi Gras parade. So much for sound and light discipline."

The vehicles turned up the hill on 155th Street and then made an almost immediate turn onto Broadway, stopping directly between 155th and 156th Streets.

Fat Boss jerked a thumb at his window. "*Aquí!*"

Jack looked out the window and could see the outline of the buildings that together formed Audubon Terrace.

Danny's voice came over the secure radio. "Quiet. Nothing moving. It's go time."

Florez leaned forward and started speaking with Fat Boss, who nodded and spoke in rapid Spanish to the driver, who immediately broadcast the orders over the radio. Doors started opening up and down the convoy.

Latin Kings, Texans, and MAMD personnel all spilled out onto the street. Jack looked at Katrina as they got out of the SUV and reminded her to stay right beside him at all times.

Danny came jogging up to Florez and started issuing orders.

"Florez, tell our friends that we want the street blocked off at One Fifty-Fifth and One Fifty-Sixth Streets. I don't want anything moving down Broadway without the Kings having stopped and checked it. You and Jesus stay here along with Lieutenant Wallace to guard our six and make sure our friends remain alert and in position. The rest of us are going to head for the Academy."

Florez quickly discussed the arrangements with Luis and Jesus. Luis gestured toward the streets and started yelling at his men.

"Luis agrees with your suggestion, but he is going to put both the pickup and an SUV to the south and the other three vehicles to the north," said Florez. "He said that if we get any pressure from the other gangs, it would most likely come from the One Fifty-Fifth side. He is also going to send some men around to the other side of Audubon Terrace so no one comes in through the backside into the complex."

"Alan, you read us clearly?" said Danny.

"Five by five," said Herring from Austin. "We also have a very clear picture from the drone, though you all look a little green. Boat ride must have left you seasick."

Jack smiled at Herring's poor attempt at humor, referring to the night-vision image.

Jack said, "Alan, you have the other targets?"

"Affirmative," replied Herring. "Signal remains strong in Elizabethport, New Jersey, getting close to the island. I have a Predator over their location and infrared."

Jack nodded at Captain Carpenter, who pulled out her MAMD radio and made contact with her people on Shooters Island. After detailing the movements of the black marketers, she gave the command to run the agreed plan. She nodded back at Jack and stowed her radio.

"Let's move out," said Jack.

The team moved off of Broadway and through the entrance to Audubon Terrace. The three buildings of the Academy stood at the very end. Built on the site of a former farm, Audubon Terrace had been developed in the early 1900s into a cultural center. The Academy of Arts and Letters eventually came to occupy three buildings, the last one acquired from the Numismatic Society and linked by a glass atrium to the existing facilities, just as the first global financial crisis hit its stride.

The team moved in full combat formation, sticking close to the buildings on both sides of the plaza and leapfrogging each other as they made their way toward the main building. Jack kept Katrina tucked in behind him, and the two of them followed Danny and Simon on the north side of the terrace. Captain Carpenter and the rest of the team moved up the south side.

The entire plaza was littered with debris. Broken furniture, equipment, and garbage lay strewn everywhere. Broken glass crunched underfoot with nearly every step. The Hispanic Society library building was scarred with heavy black streaks on its stone exterior, especially around where windows once stood. The building sat in the middle of the north side of the terrace, directly opposite the main Hispanic Society building. It had reportedly burned when squatters, using an oil drum to keep warm during the winter by burning the books in the library, lost control of the fire.

Danny held up his fist and everyone crouched down. Jack pulled Katrina lower and closer behind him.

"Movement north side, five meters in front," said Britney quietly.

Jack stared through his night-vision goggles but did not see any movement. He flipped up the goggles and switched to the scope on his rifle. He extended his AR-15 and slowly swept back and forth from the team on the opposite side of the plaza to the end of the terrace.

"Contact," he said. He saw the figure huddled low against the side of the Church of Our Lady of Esperanza. "Five meters forward of our position, against the base of the church by the corner in the wall."

Danny signaled west and pointed Jack east. Jack swung his rifle toward the way they had come and slowly scanned the area for any threats or movement. Danny ran forward in a crouch, followed by Simon. Jack took a quick glance and saw both men standing over the contact, weapons ready.

"Contact is a homeless person," came Danny's voice over the radio. "No weapons present. Give us a minute to ask a few questions."

Jack felt himself relax a bit. He continued to guard the group's six, but at least it appeared that there was no immediate threat.

"Subject says that a couple of hundred people live in this complex, occupying the buildings in the terrace, including the Academy of Arts and Letters," said Simon.

Someone muttered "Shit" over the radio.

"Subject says that the groups are not, repeat not, well armed and basically stay here because there is a bit of safety in the plaza setting."

"Why is subject outside?" asked Captain Carpenter. "A lookout or decoy?"

"Subject is high as a kite and says he came outside to shoot up so he did not have to share with the others in the church," came back as the response.

"Is subject a threat?" asked Jack.

"Only to himself."

"Copy that," said Justin. "Let's move out."

The two teams began to move forward. Jack walked backward, keeping his eyes open for threats from behind. He took a hard look at the homeless man as they passed to verify for himself that he posed no threat.

The two teams converged at the southwestern corner of the terrace, in front of the original Academy building.

"The doors are missing," said Katrina. That earned her a quizzical glance from a couple of members of the team. "The doors were beautiful bronze works of art. They were sculpture."

"They were probably melted for the metal value," replied Captain Carpenter.

"It's so sad, it's all just so sad," said Katrina. She turned around. "I remember a warm spring evening only a few years ago on this same plaza. I stood right over there with a glass of champagne, celebrating the opening of an exhibit on Spanish colonial influence in Florida at the Hispanic Society. It seems like a lifetime ago."

"Katrina," said Jack quietly.

She looked in his direction, nodded, and joined the rest of the group.

Danny began his checks. "Florez?"

"Relatively quiet here. There was a drive-by a couple of blocks away by what our friends said was a Crip car, but it never came close and has not reappeared. Otherwise, no movement."

"Copy that. If the car reappears, I want to know immediately," replied Danny. "Alan?"

"I have no movement on Audubon Terrace, any of the roofs, or within a surrounding block," said Herring. "We saw the car that Jamie discussed and tracked it, but it moved outside of our monitoring area."

"Copy that," said Danny. "Jamie, send Lieutenant Wallace up to join us here. We are going in. I have point. Justin will back me up. We will do a quick sweep."

With that, Danny signaled Justin, and the two men disappeared into the building. Jack kept a defensive posture, scanning the terrace, while Captain Carpenter and Britney trained their weapons on the open front of the Academy, making sure no one other than Danny and Justin came out. Simon moved down the terrace about fifteen meters to give a wider perimeter of protection. Lieutenant Wallace joined Simon in rear guard.

Time seemed to crawl, but Jack resisted the urge to make radio contact. Danny would call if he needed help or had anything to report; otherwise, no need to distract him. He was clearly busy. Jack looked at the glowing dial of his watch and noted that a total of eight minutes had passed.

"Coming out," came over the radio, and within a couple of seconds Justin emerged, followed by Danny.

They rejoined the group, but no one relaxed their defensive posture. Both men took long drinks out of their CamelBaks.

Finally, Danny spoke. "The place is a mess. There are people inside, squatters like our friend back there. Drug paraphernalia everywhere. The people did not bother us, and in fact seemed more than a little afraid of us. There are at least a few in every room."

Justin picked up. "The smell in there is unbelievable. I'm just warning you all that you are going to gag, no way around it. People have been living, cooking, leaving their trash, and using the place as an outhouse for a long time. Think about the worst pigsty. We found open fires in various rooms, making the air quite smoky, though at least with all the missing windows there is some ventilation."

"What are they burning?" asked Katrina, who then answered her own question. "Oh, my God, they're burning all the historical documents and books." She looked down.

"Yes," said Danny. "We made a pretty good scan of the administration building. Shelves are emptied, display cases broken and empty. The file cabinets emptied, and most anything made of paper or wood burned. The administration building is nearly cleaned out. There is nothing of note left."

"OK," said Jack. "Let's move out and do a full sweep of the two remaining buildings. Danny, how do you want to handle it? All sweep together or split?"

Danny said, "I think the threat from within is low, so let's split for time efficiency. I will take Britney and Captain Carpenter and sweep the auditorium building and basement, but I do not expect to find much. I think that you, Simon, Wallace, and Katrina should focus on the annex building. It was the most recently acquired space and would be more likely to have something of value than the auditorium building, so Katrina should go there. Justin can guard the terrace and enjoy the fresh air."

Jack looked at his watch. It was 10:07 p.m. "I mark 10:07 p.m.," said Jack, and the rest of the team looked at their watches and marked the time. "Let's try and get this done by midnight. I think the less time we spend around the Crips the better."

CHAPTER TWENTY-FOUR

Elizabethport, New Jersey, former USA

March 28, 2025, 10:46 p.m. Eastern

Listir stood on the dock. Missing and rotted boards made footing treacherous. The speedboat rocked gently, the lines creaking as the vessel strained against the ropes. Listir lit a cigarette and went over the plan again in his mind. Ulysses could be right. He was out over his skis and should walk away. However, he couldn't. Jack Dodge was so close, and so was whatever would bring him to New York.

"*Vámanos!*" called Ulysses.

Listir nodded and signaled his men, and they all marched down to the boat.

Ulysses knelt down beside the craft after Listir dropped onto the deck. "OK, my friend. My men take you to the southern side of Shooters Island. They come back at sunup tomorrow. We take you and get you. That's all. In morning they wait ten minutes, you not come, they leave.

Your fight is not ours."

Listir nodded. The boat started and lines were cast off. The chill off the water made the night seem even colder than it was. The boat slowly moved out into the channel but kept its speed down.

Brown pointed to the front of the boat, where one of Ulysses' men stood with a gaff, ready to push any debris out of the way. It moved slowly down the Elizabeth River. The captain used night-vision goggles, and the moon provided a bit of light on the waterway.

"Eyes out, boys," said Brown.

Everyone had weapons ready and kept their eyes trained on the riverbanks.

The boat began a wide arc and turned into the Elizabethport Reach. Listir felt the motor increase its vibrations before the speed actually increased. The chop on the water increased as the reach widened the nearer they came to Newark Bay.

After about twenty minutes, the captain pointed dead ahead toward a low shape on the water. Listir looked at the emerging mound on the horizon and guessed he was looking at Shooters Island.

*

Harper Packing Company, Austin, Texas, Republic of Texas

March 28, 2025, 10:08 p.m. Central

Herring grabbed his tablet and opened the notepad application. He picked up the phone on his desk and dialed a satellite phone 1,738 miles away. It was answered on the first ring.

"Albers," said Lieutenant Albers, head of the MAMD forces on Shooters Island.

"Lieutenant Albers, this is Herring. We have package en route to you via water, ETA roughly five minutes to far-southern end of your position."

"Copy that, sir."

Albers cut the line and commanded his men to execute their assignments per Captain Carpenter's orders.

CHAPTER TWENTY-FIVE

Audubon Terrace, New York City, New York, former USA

March 28, 2025, 11:14 p.m. Eastern

Winters's team joined Jack Dodge's in the annex facility.

"The auditorium building was completely empty," said Danny. "Seriously, empty. It was like someone went through and literally stripped out everything down to the studs."

Jack said, "We worked from top to bottom in this building as well. There's a bit more here, but still the upper floors are nearly bare. We found a couple of volumes of historic papers, some partially burned, but not what we want. All that's left is to sweep the basement, and then we can declare this a dead end."

Katrina sat against the wall taking a couple of sips out of her CamelBak. Captain Carpenter took out some energy bars and offered one to Katrina, who waved it off.

"Thanks, but the smell in here is making me nauseous," said Katrina.

The captain smiled, ripped open the bar, and took a big bite.

"Let's move," said Jack. "Simon, I don't like going underground, so why don't you and Lieutenant Wallace stay here and watch our six? Alan, we're headed underground, unsure about comms, so current sitrep?"

"Still very little movement," said Alan. "A few more vehicles moving around, but nothing within a couple of blocks of your position. The Latin Kings remain in position and Florez reports all quiet. On the other situation, the package arrived, and Lieutenant Albers will take delivery."

Jack exchanged looks with Captain Carpenter and then said, "Copy that. Now, let's hope it all goes according to our plan."

"Terrace clear and quiet," said Simon, who moved outside for a quick look.

Jack nodded at Danny, who headed down the stairs. Britney followed him, then Justin, Jack, and Katrina settled in, with Captain Carpenter bringing up the rear. The stench in the stairwell was nearly unbearable, and the floor slippery underfoot.

Danny reached the bottom of the stairs and held up a fist. Britney took up position against the cinder-block wall. Danny tapped her on the shoulder. He held up his hand and indicated that when the door opened she should go through to the left; he would head right. He then counted down from three with his fingers and kicked the center bar, forcing the door open. Britney went through low to the left, and he rolled through right.

The call came out: "Clear."

Jack crouched on one knee, scanning the room, weapon at his side but ready to fire. They were in a large storage area. It looked like a bomb had gone off. Crating strewn around. Papers spread everywhere. What shelving remained sat nearly empty.

"Movement left, movement right," said Britney.

Jack glanced behind him and saw Katrina in the doorway. "Get back behind the wall," he hissed, and did not turn back until she was gone from view.

"Jack, we are going to take the flanks. You and Carpenter take the middle," said Danny.

"Copy that," said Jack, and they quickly began to move forward down the rows of metal shelving.

In many places the shelving was missing. They reached the end and found three people crouched against the wall. Jack moved left and Carpenter right, and they quickly verified that there were no others hidden nearby.

"We're cool, man," said one of the figures. "We've nothing to steal."

Jack said, "I'm not here to steal anything. Stay cool and we're good. No interest in what y'all are doing." Jack glanced around again, but still no Britney or Danny. He turned his attention back to the figures. "Is this all there is down here?"

Jack noticed one of them glance at the man on the left side, who answered, "Yeah, this is it."

Jack did not believe him.

"You hungry?" Jack asked, and got an affirmative from the guy. He reached behind his back and pulled off his pack. "I have some food, which I'm happy to give you, but I need something in return."

Jack turned on the light on his gun and illuminated the people. He watched as the three figures shifted a little away from him. They were clearly afraid, afraid of what he might want in return.

"We got nothing, I told you," said the man.

Jack pulled out one of the MREs and tossed it to the smallest figure, who looked to be a younger woman. She clutched her prize, and the other two figures stared at her jealously.

"Tell me what else is down here and you can each have one. That's all I need," said Jack.

The man spoke again. "There are three more rooms, or at least we think there are three more rooms."

"What do you mean?"

The man shrugged and then said, "There's a mechanical room over there." He pointed to one side of the basement. "Most of the equipment was stolen long ago. Over there is a locker room area. Nothing left there either. There's another door, which probably leads to another room in the middle, but it's busted. Nobody can get it open."

"How long have you been living here?" said Jack while flipping the other two MREs to the people.

The man stared at his silver foil–covered delicacy before answering, "What's the date?"

Jack paused and then said, "March 28, 2025."

"About a year and a half," said the man after a pause.

Jack heard a noise and saw Danny coming up from one side of the room. A few minutes later Britney joined him.

Danny said, "There's some kind of room. I think it was a staff locker room or break room. Nothing there."

Jack nodded and said, "My new friends here say there's also a mechanical room, but almost everything has been stripped."

Britney said, "I can confirm that. Stripped completely clean, and luckily nothing works, because electrical wires are hanging free and gas lines broken open. If any power ever comes back on in this area, that is an explosion waiting to happen!"

"But most interesting, this gentleman here tells me that there is a door that cannot be opened, at least not in the year and a half they have been here," said Jack.

"Why not?" said Danny.

"The door is some kind of special thing, and it's completely busted shut," said the man between bites. His two companions were completely absorbed in their MREs. "We tried everything to get that door open. Who knows what's in there?"

Danny looked at Jack, who looked back at the squatter.

"I think we may have a key that will work, but y'all should probably move to the far side of the room," said Jack.

"Whatever's in that room belongs to us!" exclaimed the man.

"Sure, big fella. You can have the room after we've had a chance to go through it," said Jack, both hands up. "We only need to find something we lost. That's all."

The homeless man glared at Jack defiantly for a few seconds and then led the other two off away from the door, to where he had been directed.

The metal security door used two substantial locks—one at the top and one at the bottom—both severely damaged from attempts to breach it. The handle was broken off and nowhere to be seen. It had sustained heavy scarring around the edges from crowbars and other implements. There were no hinges on the side facing them, so clearly the door opened in.

"Going to be a bit of a bang," said Danny, smiling. Holding his flashlight, he was analyzing every inch of the door. "How much C-4 do you want to use? I would recommend a bunch, because this is one serious door."

Jack laughed, and Britney whipped a pack off her back, and they began putting the strips of C4 on the edges of the door. After they got the explosives where they wanted them, Danny put in the radio-controlled detonators, and the three of them retreated back to the stairwell. Jack checked to make sure all the squatters had moved away from the area.

"What did you find?" asked Katrina, still where she had been told to wait behind the cinder-block wall in the stairwell.

"We found a bunch of empty space and one locked door," said Danny. "I suggest that we all take cover while I unlock it."

Carpenter smiled, but Katrina looked confused. Jack pulled her deeper into the stairwell, and Danny counted down.

The bang was deafening in the enclosed space of the basement. "I think you used too big a key," said Britney.

The entire group got up and moved toward the far side of the basement. The smoke and dust stirred up by the explosion filled the air, obscuring the visibility.

About three-quarters of the way to the far wall, Jack passed a piece of bent, still-smoking metal that looked vaguely like the former door.

"I think your door is here," said Jack.

Danny laughed and kept moving.

The wall where the door used to stand now had a gaping hole in it. Captain Carpenter shined a light into the room and caught a couple of bronze sculptures in the beam. Dust and smoke hung thick in the air, stopping anyone from seeing more than a few feet.

Danny and Jack went into the room. It was a storage room, maybe eight meters by eight meters but filled floor to ceiling with shelves stuffed with boxes, crates, and a couple of statues.

Jack looked at Danny. "If it's still in existence, it's here."

Danny called out, "Captain Carpenter, can you watch our six? This room's still intact, and we need Britney and the good doctor in order to move through this efficiently. Simon, why don't you go watch the stairwell and keep an eye on the three people outside?"

The four team members assigned to the room immediately fanned out and started reading the labels on the storage boxes and crates.

CHAPTER TWENTY-SIX

Shooters Island (Mid-Atlantic Military District Outpost),
New York, former USA

March 29, 2025, 2:13 a.m. Eastern

Listir could see Brown about twenty meters ahead and to the right. The rest of his five-man team spread out over the barren landscape of Shooters Island. The island had been nearly denuded of standing trees, but whoever cut them down just left them where they fell. They were making terrible time over the branches, downed trees, and bushes.

Listir came up on Brown, who crouched behind a large tree trunk and knelt down beside him. The wind blew so hard, Listir leaned in to hear.

"This open strip of ground is the end of the line," said Brown. "See that rise?"

Listir stared through his night-vision goggles at the upward-sloping ground. He caught a quick flash of the moonlight on razor wire.

The rest of the men converged on their position. Listir and Brown studied the wire. Ulysses warned them about the electric fence and wire. He said that it was suicide to assault Shooters Island. His men had tried a while ago.

One of the men removed a cigarette, and Listir held out his Glock.

"Fucking light that thing and I will shoot you in the head myself!"

The man returned the cigarette slowly to the pack.

"How many times do I have to tell you people to practice light discipline? This is not fucking DC!"

The voice in his head blared at Listir. This was not a CIA operation. He was effectively going into a war zone with a bunch of two-bit punks. He could still rethink this entire thing, take to ground, and wait for the boat.

CHAPTER TWENTY-SEVEN

Audubon Terrace, New York City, New York, former USA

March 29, 2025, 2:58 a.m. Eastern

Jack looked at his watch again. Time slipped away, but there were just too many damn boxes and crates to go through. He had wanted to be out of here nearly three hours ago.

Danny came over to Jack and pointed at his watch.

Jack nodded and said, "I know." Time equaled risk.

Jack heard Justin over the radio. "Danny, Jack, where are you?"

"Storage room at the back of the basement," answered Danny.

"ETA?" said Justin.

"Unclear. There is a lot of material down here, and it's slow going," said Danny. "Anyway, we still have time before we need to be back on the boat."

"We have a bit of a developing situation out here," came back Justin, who sounded a little too calm.

Jack and Danny stared at each other intently and then looked at the boxes strewn around. Ten boxes marked "Hay Papers" still needed investigation.

"What's the situation?" asked Jack.

"A couple of close-in probes by the Crips. One vehicle fired a few errant shots at the Latin Kings. The Kings called in a few more crews, but Herring is tracking a couple of unknown and potentially hostile vehicles moving around the area. We need to move out before we are caught in the middle of a gang war."

Danny looked at Jack and said, "When I was a kid, my mother was always worried I would get mixed up with a gang. Maybe she was right all along."

Jack gave a small smile at Danny's attempt at humor under stress.

"Justin, keep us up to speed. We need a bit more time," Danny replied. He then looked at the boxes, and at Britney and Katrina.

"OK, people, you heard the man: we're running low on time," said Jack. "Let's make this very simple. We are going to put aside one box, and let's triage these boxes. We can either find something, discard stuff as not what we are looking for, or throw stuff in the box for later, but we are only taking one box."

Everyone grabbed a box and started examining the materials as fast as they possibly could. Jack sat down on the floor next to a box and tore through it. Almost every document dealt with Hay's involvement in maintaining the Open Door policy with China or with the Hay-Bunau-Varilla Treaty with newly independent Panama, leading to the creation of the Panama Canal. Nothing in the box related to the Texas Compact. He moved on to the next box and slowed down, finding numerous papers related to Abraham Lincoln and the end of slavery.

Jack looked up and saw the other three working quickly through their boxes.

"Anything?" asked Jack.

Danny shook his head, as did Britney and Katrina.

They moved quickly and methodically. Materials flew into the discard pile, and some papers and files into the box for later review. Eventually, each person got down to a last box. Jack focused on the last box in front of him and kept thumbing through the materials. He flipped by bundles of letters tied with ribbon, checking the dates, but none matched the period in question. He came to a large leather-bound diary, the book sealed by a locked leather clasp, but he found no key on it or in the box. Jack pulled out the knife from his belt and slit the leather open. The book was clearly a diary, with letters, scraps of paper, and keepsakes stuck throughout.

"Danny," said Jack barely above a whisper.

Danny turned and looked at the large paper unfolded on Jack's lap. He stopped what he was doing and came over. Jack rested the diary on his thigh, but he had pulled out and unfolded a very large piece of parchment. Sam Houston's sprawling signature was clearly visible across the bottom of the document, as were the other five senators' signatures.

Katrina and Britney joined the two men, and all four stared at the document.

"Danny, the situation is deteriorating out here. Done or not, we need to move," Justin came over the radio, the tension clearly etched in his voice.

"Copy that. We are good to go," said Danny.

Jack folded the document up and placed it in a zippered pocket inside his fatigues.

"Jack, there are only about eight or nine inches of documents left in that box," continued Danny. "I think you should take the rest just to make sure that there is nothing else in there, no commentary or anything."

Jack nodded and stuffed the rest of the documents in his backpack. Danny took the papers that had been thrown in the box to be reviewed later and stuffed them in his pack, removing the MREs to make room. Jack grabbed the MREs so he could toss them to the squatters on their way out of the basement.

The four of them moved quickly out of the storage room and back across the main basement toward the stairs, picking up Simon and Captain Carpenter on the way.

As he passed the squatters, Jack shouted, "Room's all yours, but it's mainly a lot of paper." He tossed them the MREs.

The team charged up the stairs and out onto the terrace. The night smelled absolutely fresh after the fetid air of the Academy. Justin and Lieutenant Wallace fell in, and the group started to move down the south side of the plaza toward Broadway.

"Florez, Herring, sitrep," ordered Danny.

"Intermittent fire from vehicles," said Florez. "One of the Kings took a round through the shoulder, and one of the Crips' cars was disabled and all inside eliminated. However, the Crips continue to make approaches, and we need to vacate this stationary position soon."

"I have three inbound vehicles about four blocks away, moving quickly," said Herring. "These cars have been repeat visitors to your location and are flagged as bad guys."

The team moved down the side of the terrace at an expedited rate. Jack kept ensuring Katrina remained fast on his six. They were maybe five to ten meters from the end of the terrace.

"Vehicles increasing speed," said Herring. "Two blocks from your position and closing."

"Alan, light up the lead vehicle!" said Jack. "I repeat, light it up!"

"Copy that," said Herring.

A few seconds later, the team heard the distinctive incoming sound of a missile, followed by a loud boom and a flash of light. Anyone who spent time in Iraq or Afghanistan knew that sound.

"Target destroyed. Other two targets halted," said Herring.

The team came out of the terrace and onto Broadway to find Florez, Madoro, and the Latin Kings crouched behind vehicles.

"Florez, let's move out now," shouted Jack, sprinting for the closer SUV. He had Katrina by the arm and literally pulled her along.

Florez started shouting orders in Spanish to the Latin Kings, which were soon repeated by Fat Boss, and everyone scrambled into vehicles. Katrina, Britney, and Simon piled into one of the SUVs with Jack and Fat Boss. Lieutenant Wallace jumped into the front passenger seat and lowered his window, sticking his weapon out of it. Jack and Simon lowered their windows too, ready to fire.

"Katrina, get down on the floor," commanded Jack. He looked back and saw her hesitate, so he used his best command voice and said, "Do it!" He was not going to lose another woman to New York. "Wallace, you keep your focus forward on the chance that the Crips flanked us!"

The Kings, for all their relaxed posing, moved rapidly and had the convoy ready to roll. They lurched forward and raced down Broadway toward 155th Street. Jack listened in to Captain Carpenter ordering the Zodiacs back to the pickup point.

Herring broke in. "The two stopped vehicles are moving again toward you. Two more vehicles have moved up to join them. Speed fast and accelerating."

"How far?" said Jack. The response did not make him happy; they were less than two blocks away and closing fast. "Alan, you have missiles left?"

"Affirmative. One," said Herring.

"OK, light up the lead vehicle on my mark," said Jack. He stared out the front windshield as they approached the riverbank. Assuming they would continue coming, he calculated the point of attack that would buy them the most time to board the Zodiacs by blocking the road. He heard automatic weapon fire and realized it came from the Crips. "Now!"

The speeding cars came closer. A round shattered the back window of the SUV, and glass flew all over the interior. Katrina screamed in surprise as glass covered her. Rounds continued to fly by, their high-pitched whine sounding in the air.

"Where the fuck is my missiles?" Jack yelled at Herring.

Wallace let out a small yelp in the front seat. About three seconds later, Jack's question was answered when the missile found its mark. A second later, a second explosion lit up the night sky. Jack did not know what had caused the second explosion. Maybe one of the other cars ran into the first.

"Lead and chase vehicle both destroyed. Second vehicle in convoy ran directly into first vehicle and has caught fire. Third vehicle stopped," said Herring. "I guess the balance of power between the Latin Kings and the Crips just changed."

"Thank you, Alan! Nice shooting!" said Danny, beating Jack to the response.

The convoy sped to the riverbank and skidded to a stop. Jack saw that the Zodiacs were just off the bank of the river.

Jack realized Lieutenant Wallace was moaning slightly. "Wallace, what's wrong?"

"I think I'm hit, left shoulder. Hurts like hell," replied the lieutenant.

Jack leaned forward and examined the wound. He reached into his pack and removed a pressure dressing and pressed it against the lieutenant's shoulder. He grabbed a band from his pack and fixed the dressing in place.

"Wallace, the dressing will hold until we get to the boat," said Jack.

"You're going to be fine. It's going to hurt a lot, but we have to go."

Jack jumped out of the car, and he and Simon took defensive positions facing back toward the burning Crips car.

Jack called out, "Britney, get Katrina on the first boat with you, Justin, Simon, and Lieutenant Wallace. Captain Carpenter and I will follow with Danny, Florez, and Jesus. Go!"

Jack cast one glance over his shoulder to confirm that everyone followed orders. Simon had Wallace under the right shoulder and was helping him to the boat.

Fat Boss stood in the open near the bank of the river. Jack shook his head. They had fired two missiles, one of the Latin Kings had been shot, multiple Crips clearly died, Wallace had a slug in his shoulder, and the head of the Latin Kings looked so relaxed Jack thought he might fall asleep where he stood. Fat Boss was one calm cowboy.

Jack heard the first Zodiac rev its motor and head out into the river. The second Zodiac came in, and Danny and Captain Carpenter jumped on. Jack walked over to the head of the Kings, clasped his hand, and said, "*Gracias.*"

"*De nada,*" answered Fat Boss, who was now truly the King of New York, with dead Crips everywhere.

Jack jumped into the Zodiac, and instantly the boat headed out into the much choppier Hudson River. Only when the boat made it away from shore did he realize how exhausted he was. He also felt a burning sensation in his right arm and looked down to find a large piece of metal from the car sticking out of his uniform at his bicep.

CHAPTER TWENTY-EIGHT

Shooters Island (Mid-Atlantic Military District Outpost),
New York, former USA

March 29, 2025, 4:23 a.m. Eastern

Listir crouched near the fence. There was absolutely no cover in this area. They cut a small hole in the wire after hooking up some jumper cables across the electrified wire to keep the circuit closed. Ready to move through the wire, Listir realized this was the last moment that they could walk away.

He knelt in the open. Logic said to flee. They were outnumbered, with absolutely no support, and facing an enemy significantly better armed and trained. However, he just could not give up. He could still feel the shiver that went down his spine when Jack Dodge promised to kill him. He needed to slay the dragon. There would never be another chance.

"Move out!" Listir hissed above the rising wind.

Brown pulled apart the wire and went through the fence first, and then the others followed. Listir came last and took a quick look back.

Jack sat on a molded bench in the cabin of the boat with Danny, Captain Carpenter, and Katrina. They had treated the lieutenant's shoulder more thoroughly. He would be fine; it did not appear that the bullet had nicked an artery or other major organ, but he would need surgery on his clavicle.

Now it was Jack's turn. They cut the sleeve off Jack's uniform to expose the arm. Danny held a flashlight in his mouth while he examined the shard in Jack's shoulder. Katrina and Captain Carpenter pulled various items from the first aid kit. The triangle-shaped piece of metal measured roughly four centimeters at its widest point.

"I cannot tell how far it is in there, but it appears very deep," said Danny.

"Well, it's not supposed to be in there and it's a little uncomfortable, so can you stop wiggling it and just pull it?" said Jack through gritted teeth.

Katrina laid out saline, antiseptic ointment, gauze, and bandages. Danny reached down and yanked the metal out as the boat rocked a little. The shard gave way, but not without enlarging the cut slightly. Jack involuntarily screamed "SHIT!" and bit down on the sleeve of his free arm's fatigues. Captain Carpenter grabbed the bottle of saline and thoroughly washed the wound, then covered it in antiseptic and wrapped Jack's bicep in a field dressing. Jack thanked her through still-gritted teeth.

Danny handed him the piece of metal and said, "There you go, you big baby. You can add it to your collection. Sorry I don't have a lollipop."

Danny gave Jack a smile, but Jack could tell he was concerned.

After Jack was taped up, they started going through the contents of his backpack. The documents were amazing: diary entries that discussed conversations with Abraham Lincoln, notes about battles in the Civil War, and personal remembrances. They went page by page, but nothing referenced the Texas Compact.

"We can toss all of this," said Danny.

"No!" said Katrina. "Are you kidding me? All of this"—she waved her hand at the documents—"is important historical information, and just because it does not relate to your specific concerns does not mean it should be tossed into the Hudson River."

Jack looked at her as she glared at Danny, her cheeks flushed and fire in her eyes. She looked beautiful.

Danny held up his hands. "OK, sorry. You keep it and do with it whatever you want."

Katrina stared at him for a minute longer and then realized he was not mocking her.

The boat moved into the Kill Van Kull and the captain said, "Five mikes."

Captain Carpenter picked up the cabin radio and alerted Lieutenant Albers that the time had come to execute the rest of the mission plan.

Jack took a quick look around the cabin and realized his tired team was not focused and ready.

"People, we're not done yet. Look alive!" commanded Jack.

He watched as the team checked their weapons, night-vision goggles secured, and prepared for landing.

Listir heard the boat. His team crawled to near the end of the helipad. The throb of the boat motor carried over the water. He heard the sound of his men's weapons being clicked into place. They were spread out on the ground with interlocking fields of fire.

He ran through the math again and again in his head and kept coming to the same conclusion. Because of the advantage of surprise, he and his men could get off two shots each before anyone could respond.

If accurate, those two shots should dramatically change the numbers and leave him and his men in an excellent position vis-à-vis the few remaining troops in the Quonset hut and from the boat.

The boat's motor dropped to an even deeper pitch as it slowed. Even with the night-vision goggles, he could not yet make out the darkened boat against the pitch-black sky. He could hear no sound other than the throb of the boat. A light flashed in the distance as the door to the Quonset hut opened and closed. Listir tracked the figure as he marched around the far side of the building.

In a few minutes, whatever had brought Jack Dodge to New York would be his, as would Dodge. It had been worth the risk.

The MAMD soldier opened the door on the side of the hut and five Alsatians shook as they got up. He shooed them out into the night air. For a couple of seconds the dogs seemed to circle next to the hut, and then they began to run. The soldier had not even closed the door when the dogs began to bark. Listir heard the sound.

"Motherfucker!" exclaimed Brown.

He jumped up and turned to run. Listir swore under his breath. You could count on Brown to be the first to run, the first to blame someone else, the first to sell out his mother.

"Find the dogs! Everyone pick out a target!"

Listir knew the element of surprise was gone, the focus gone in an instant from taking down Jack Dodge to survival.

Listir looked around him and realized his entire squad was up and running for the hole in the fence. The dogs barked incessantly, the sound coming ever closer. So close and yet so completely defeated. He found a dog in his scope and got off a shot. Before he could get off another round, the snap of a gunshot came from right next to him. Soldiers rose to their knees in full sniper camouflage and started methodically picking off his team. He was totally fucked.

"Jack, we have multiple figures south of the helipad," said Herring. "It appears they are fleeing, and the MAMD soldiers and the dogs have them well in hand.

"Helmsman!" yelled Jack. "Do not land. Hold off in the channel." They would not land until the situation was under control.

"Alan, keep telling me what you see," said Danny.

"I have five figures on infrared. Three inert," said Herring. "One appears to have been taken down by the dogs, two by rifle fire. Two are through the fence and moving, but the dogs and troops are in pursuit."

Captain Carpenter got back on her MAMD radio. Jack heard her clearly.

"This is Captain Carpenter. If at all possible, let the dogs take them down."

The dog's jaw bit down on Listir's leg with such power, he screamed involuntarily. There was absolutely nothing he could do. He had dropped his weapon when hit and slipped down the hill. He heard the soldiers coming, clearly firing as they moved. The dog continued to bite his flesh, each shake of the dog's head causing him to scream anew.

Two lights lit him up, but the dog was not called off.

The boat continued to stand off in the channel. The chop had increased considerably due to a strong wind from the north, which was also lowering the temperature. March in the Northeast could feel more like winter than spring.

"Four are confirmed dead," said Captain Carpenter. "The dogs have the last intruder. He apparently killed one of the dogs with a well-placed shot, but the others are getting their revenge. They have him secure, and we are going to dock."

Jack walked up to the deck from the cabin and found Danny standing there. The boat swung in to the dock and the lines secured. Danny and Jack hit the dock running before the gangplank was even in place, jumping over the gunwale. They charged across the helicopter pad and down the grass toward the pinpricks of light held by the soldiers.

"Release!" said one of the men as Jack and Danny joined the circle surrounding the figure on the ground. Jack took a LED flashlight from his belt and illuminated the bloody figure on the ground.

"Listir. A promise is a promise," said Jack. He swiftly removed his Glock and fired two shots, eliminating the last threat to the team.

Danny looked up at the sky, which had just a hint of light in the east, and said, "I think the world just got a little bit better."

"All clear," said Lieutenant Albers over the radio.

"Confirmed. All clear on my screens," said Herring.

CHAPTER TWENTY-NINE

Austin, Texas, Republic of Texas

March 31, 2025, 4:50 p.m. Central

The heat rising from the road obscured the blacktop. The temperature hovered over ninety degrees in the late afternoon, and a strong wind blew. Towering thunderheads stood on the horizon, promising storms later and hopefully a break in the early heat wave. Pure Texas in early spring.

Jack pulled up to the gatehouse and showed his credentials to the guard. He was directed toward a visitor parking lot and told to leave his vehicle and return to the gatehouse. He did as requested and walked back across the blacktop. He could feel the heat through the soles of his boots. He walked up to the door and waited to be buzzed in. Walking into the gatehouse, he shivered; the air-conditioning roared at its maximum level. Texans loved air-conditioning.

He looked around and smiled at the Texas Rangers who manned

the building. Four Rangers stood around the body scanner and X-ray machine, and two more sat in a booth with blast-proof glass. Jack removed his sunglasses, straightened his tie, and approached the screening area.

"You carrying, son?" asked one of the Rangers.

The man was tall, made more so by the large white cowboy hat on his head. Even though probably fifty-five or sixty years old, he stood ramrod straight and eyed Jack with clear, dead eyes.

"Yes, sir," said Jack.

He opened his blue blazer and removed his Glock from his shoulder holster with two fingers. He handed it to the Ranger and received a small plastic disc with the number 20185 on it.

"Please state your business, sir," said another Ranger, holding a tablet.

Jack handed over his credentials once again and explained that he had come for a 5:30 p.m. appointment with the first minister. The Ranger checked his credentials, reviewed the information on his tablet, and spoke to someone on his radio. Apparently, all was in order, since he waved Jack through the scanner. Jack placed the manila envelope on the X-ray conveyor and walked through the body scanner. This was followed by a wanding and pat down.

Cleared, Jack was directed out of the guardhouse and up the long, sloping drive of the newly constructed first minister's residence. He followed the drive nearly three-quarters of the way to the house and then took a path to one of the wings. The house was very similar to the Texas governor's residence: white with columns and large porches. The most prominent difference came from the addition of two wings off the central building, containing numerous offices for the minister's staff.

As Jack approached the double doors, one of them swung out to reveal a young, eager-looking man.

"Mr. Dodge," said the fresh-faced kid. "I am Brian Dinsdale, one of the first minister's aides. Would you mind coming with me, sir?"

Jack followed Dinsdale down the wide, exceedingly quiet hallway. Jack had not been in this part of the building in a long time; he usually went directly to the Operations Center beneath the central part of the house. The walls were painted a very pale blue, and a large Western landscape hung every few feet. The cream carpet was impossibly plush. They passed a number of closed doors along the hall, and other than Dinsdale pointing out various "features," Jack heard no sounds but the air-conditioning.

Dinsdale finally stopped near the end of the hall and opened a heavy wooden door, stepping back so Jack could enter. Jack looked in the room and smiled as he saw his father sitting at the small mahogany conference table.

"Hello, Dad," said Jack.

He walked in and received a very strong full Jackson. Jack winced when the hug crushed his wounded arm.

"Jack, thank God you are back in one piece," said Jackson Dodge. "I understand you had a hell of a trip. Even had to use a few missiles."

"How did you hear that?" asked Jack, staring intently at his father's face and wondering who on his team leaked the information.

"I have my sources," Jackson said, and then pointed at a sideboard covered with a full bar setup. "Join me. It's past five here."

Jack walked over to the bar, grabbed a heavy crystal tumbler, and dropped in a couple of cubes. He added a good measure of single malt. He had picked up the drink when he heard the door open behind him.

"Pour me one of those, Jack, my boy, if you would," said the first minister of Texas as he came in the room in his shirtsleeves, tie undone. "I've had a hell of a day."

Jack poured the first minister a drink and then joined the two men at the table.

"So, Jack, you found the other copy. God damnit but you are good at your job! Let me hear the whole story, if you would." The first minister took a sip of his drink and waited.

"Yes, sir," said Jack, proceeding to tell the highlights of their search.

As he finished, he opened the envelope and handed over the folded document. Jack watched as the First Minister unfolded the document and Jackson Dodge went and stood behind Texas's head of state. Both men read the document, and spent some time looking at the signatures. Jack listened as the leader of the Republic of Texas read aloud.

"Resolved, the Great State of Texas hereby acknowledges and affirms that should the time ever come to pass when said state is no longer a part of the United States of America, a portion of any and all debts, liabilities, or similar such obligations of the nation as a whole shall be duly apportioned and attached to said state. The portion apportioned to the Great State of Texas shall be equal to their pro rata portion of all such debts, liabilities, or similar such obligations that then apply or attach to the Federal Government of the United States of America and national obligations of that august body. The apportionment of claims shall be based on the Great State of Texas's total lands as a percentage of the United States of America's land, such percentages calculated based on the lands that existed on December 31st in the Year of Our Lord 1849."

In spite of the deep lines where the parchment had been folded, the signatures of all the senators were as legible as if the document had just been signed.

Time seemed to stop as Jack and the First Minister both studied the document.

"The other Texas Compact! Amazing the damage that this one little piece of paper could have done. To think it was just sitting in a locked storeroom," said the First Minister. "I have a mind to burn it, but I am going to give it to the archivist to file in secret with our copy. Maybe someday we can figure out how to handle its existence."

"First Minister, may I ask a question?" asked Jack, who, receiving a nod of encouragement, plunged on. "This document is very clear. We based everything we have done on our legal right to secede. This document makes it clear that if Texas were ever to leave the United States we would have to take our share of the debt, a share based on our amount of the land in 1849. Texas clearly agreed to a deal that would have left us with about $9 trillion dollars of debt and God knows how much in the way of other liabilities. Faced with that reality, secession would have been nearly unthinkable, and all of this would have never happened. What do we do now?"

Jackson Dodge took a drink, cleared his throat, and said, "First Minister, let me take this, please. Jack, on one level you are right. If we had known about this deal from the start, then our legal and moral position would have been highly questionable, probably illegitimate. However, we acted in good faith and in accordance with the legal framework that we all believed existed. Hell, no one argued that we had a deal that forbid all this. Based on what has happened over the last few years, it's impossible to put the genie back in the bottle. What is, is."

Jack started to object, but Jackson Dodge held up his hand and continued. "Exposing the existence of the Texas Compact and the fact that Sam Houston negotiated away our right to secede without taking our share of the financial obligations of the United States would serve no good purpose. We cannot put the US back together, and we certainly are not going to hand trillions of dollars over to the Chinese government and various other parties with an 'Oops, we made a mistake' message. What's done is done." The stern Jackson Dodge replaced the good ol' boy.

Jack said, "I figured you would say that, and on certain levels it makes sense. However, it's just hard to go north, look at the wreckage, and not think that somehow we share responsibility for all that suffering."

"Jack, eventually we will fix it," said the first minister. "We did not cause it, but maybe our politicians over the years were part of the problem. Texas will continue to expand, and as our prosperity increases I am sure we will eventually annex much of the remainder of the former US. However, expansion will be on our own terms, and so the result will be different than the train wreck of the last sixty years." With that, he drained the rest of his scotch, stood, and held out his hand. "In the meantime, you and your team have my profound thanks."

Jack shook the proffered hand and thanked the first minister for his continued confidence. Then he and his dad sat alone.

Jackson Dodge looked at his son. "You aren't going to go all bleeding heart on me, are you?"

"Of course not," replied Jack, meeting his father's gaze and holding it.

"You want to join me at the club, maybe eat some big steaks or a lobster?" said Jackson, breaking the silence, standing and straightening his coat.

"I can't. I have a date," said Jack as calmly as he could. He enjoyed watching his father's head swing around so fast that he feared the great man would have whiplash.

"Did you say 'date'?" Jackson Dodge managed to get one eyebrow up and a wry smile on his face all in less than a second. "Maybe there is still hope for me to be a grandfather."

The two men walked down the hall.

"It's a date, Dad. I'm not engaged or anything. Put your horse back in the barn," protested Jack.

"Who's my future daughter-in-law?" asked Jackson, earning a

pursed look from Jack.

"My *date* is the researcher who helped us out on the mission. Her name is Katrina."

Jackson Dodge smiled at his son and threw a large arm over his shoulder, earning an "Ouch" from Jack as they walked out the double doors and into the late Texas afternoon.

"I need grandchildren," said Jackson.

ABOUT THE AUTHOR

Chip Schorr has been a senior partner in the private equity industry for over two decades. He has completed transactions totaling over $100 billion in aggregate value. Additionally, Mr. Schorr has been a featured speaker on financial services matters in forums in the US, Europe and Asia. He lives with his family in New York City.

To find out more about Chip and his books, please visit:

chipschorrbooks.com